KV-371-591

FINDING INNOCENCE

BOOK ONE

Karen Keith

COPYRIGHT

Finding Innocence © Karen Keith 2020 All rights reserved. No part of this book may be used or reproduced in any manner whatsoever without written permission except in the case of brief quotations embodied in critical articles or reviews. www.karenkeith.co Cover art and design © Karen Keith. The characters and events portrayed in this book are fictitious. Any similarity to real persons, living or dead, businesses, or locales is coincidental and is not intended by the author.

DEDICATION

I dedicate this book to Elizabeth Tenhouten.
You got me here from start to finish! Luv you!

PROLOGUE

Sitting up in my cot, I pull my knees to my chest and peer at the bunk bed three feet across from me. My eyes are bleary, and I do my best to blink away the last remnants of the dream. It's been the same one, on repeat for weeks now. *Weeks!* What the hell is in Green Mont, California, anyway? I've never been there, let alone heard of it. And yet, there it is, every night, literally written on a sign in big bold letters.

As the bunk bed before me comes into focus, I note Vic's foot draped over the top. And Shells' form under the ratty blanket on the bottom bunk. My two best and only friends are taking up the prime real estate in our walk-in closet of a room. As Vic lets out another monster snore, I search around me until my eyes light up on an ankle sock. I wad it up into a tight, little ball and sneak up the ladder to the top bunk. Vic's mouth is wide open. I pause considering the choking hazard. She lets out another earth-shaking snore, and I stuff it in her mouth.

Forcing myself to contain my laughter, I stealthily shoot back to my bed and pull my blanket over me, turning to face the wall just as the guttural sounds of snorting confusion followed by shouting, wake the rest of the community home.

Good. Let those nasty shit heads wake up.

"What the hell? HEY! Oh my god!"

Shells' annoyed, sleepy voice joins in the yelling. "Ugh! Shut *up*, Vic!"

"I could have died! I'm going to kill you!"

"What the hell are you — ouch! Wait! Stop! *Stop*!"

The sound of pillows smashing, squealing, and laughter ensued, and I burst from my cocoon with a war cry and my own pillow. "Gotcha, birthday girl!"

"Alex! You're *so* dead!" Vic sounds totally serious, but her smile belies her threat as she turns on me. We're both crouched with our pillows raised in a manic, gleeful standoff. She's coming at me when Shells ambushes her from the side, and we tackle her to my cot. "Wait! Stop! That's *so* not fair! I demand —" She's laughing so hard as Shells pulls her arms up and I raise my pillow in threat, that she's barely able to get the rest of it out, "—a re-match!"

"Sorry not sorry!" I smack her with the pillow one last time for good measure.

Our door bursts open, and Ruby stomps in. Her yellow matted hair a greasy mess. Tasha is right behind her. And unlike Ruby who is sputtering, she's so pissed, Tasha is silent. Ruby has beat the shit out of me before, but Tasha is who I worry about. When I'm not dreaming of Green Mont, I'm having nightmares of Tasha.

Ruby is eighteen in one more month. But she sounds like a sixty-year-old who's been smoking from the day she left the womb. "I told you whores to shut the fuck up in the mornings! I gotta get my beauty rest!"

We're all standing now, pillows all but forgotten. I've palmed the knife from my mattress and a quick glance tells me Shells has hers too. *Good girl.*

Vic's snicker sounds from just behind me, and barely loud enough to hear she mutters, "Rest is not doing shit for that."

I smirk and look back at Ruby's mottled angry face. "A bit early for the bloodshed, don't you think?"

Tasha finally speaks up. "Sweet child, there's always time for that."

I try not to let her get into my head and keep the smirk plastered on my face, but she totally creeps me out. "We're really sorry we messed up your beauty rest. I know how important beauty is to you."

The much louder snort that comes from behind me pushes Ruby over the edge. "You think this is funny? I'm going to fuck you up! You won't even be able to say *beauty* when I'm done with you!"

"Ruby!" The cold voice from the door freezes us all.

Miss Brown remains in the doorway with the room already too packed. Ruby and Tasha swing around to face her. I see a glint of metal as Tasha tries to dump her weapon in our room. This is going to hurt later. Guaranteed. But I'm not going to let her get either of my girls into trouble with a half-assed frame job. "Careful, Tasha. Wouldn't want to drop that."

"Drop what?" Miss Brown's eyes land on Tasha but I speak up before she can respond. "The cards behind her. It's Vic's seventeenth birthday today. Shells and I made them for her." That distracts Miss Brown long enough that Tasha is able to pocket her weapon, the one she will probably cut me with later.

Miss Brown sniffs. "That's *right*. Well, we're out of ice cream, so your privileges for the day will have to be postponed." By postponed, she means never. The state allows an allowance to the home with suggestions like ice cream on birthdays and such, but we never see any of that. And everyone here knows better than to ask.

"Ruby." Miss Brown's voice might be sharper than my knife. "Don't think because you have one month left here, you can get away with murder. I won't have the other girls here threatened. ...You're out."

Shock fills the room. None of us wants to be here, but the alternative is so much worse. For once, Ruby actually sounds human. "But my cousin won't be in town to pick me up for another three weeks! *Please*, Miss Brown, you can't do this!"

Don't get me wrong. I hate Ruby. I truly do. But I wouldn't wish the streets of Hammond, Louisiana, on my worst enemy.

"Miss Brown ..." I try not to shrink as her shrewd gaze falls on me. "The girls and I ... I mean Shells and I, we were singing to Vic ... for her birthday... and we got carried away, and it was loud and ... disrespectful to the rest of the house. Ruby was concerned for the other girls' rest. She wasn't actually going to hurt me. We just threaten each other sometimes. It's kind of our thing. But it doesn't mean anything. Right, Ruby?"

"*Yeah*, Miss Brown, it doesn't mean shit. We're cool. See?" Ruby takes a few steps back and puts her arm around my shoulder. My eyes burn as her body odor threatens to make me hurl.

Miss Brown sighs. She was working here long before any of us came into the picture, and I suspect she will remain here long after. No doubt she sees right through our ploy. She mutters something under her breath and shakes her head, looking tired. "See that you are ... cool, or you're out Ruby. ...And no more chances. Happy birthday, Victoria. Make sure the other girls let you use the bathroom first today." She leaves just as quickly as she came but leaves the door open in typical fashion.

I shove away from Ruby and hold myself back from checking to see if my skin smells where Ruby touched me. Vic flanks my side and addresses Ruby. "Looks like you owe Alex now."

"The *fuck* I do. *Please*. I won't beat yo ass today. There. We're even. By the way, the shower's *mine*. I'm going to be there awhile. Catch my drift?" The way she licks her yellow teeth makes me feel ill all over again. As soon as they're out, I shut the door behind them. I would lock it if the doors here had any locks. "My wish for your birthday was that Ruby didn't stink up your special day. Dreams really do come true."

We laugh off the tension and the girls don't give me any trouble for helping Ruby. As much as some of us don't get along here, there is a code we all live by. We don't let anyone get kicked out if we can help it. And we don't snitch. Everything else is fair game. "So, Grandma, are you going to bust a hip if we go dancing tonight, or you think you can keep up?"

Vic rolls her eyes at me. "Look who's talking! You're almost seventeen too!"

I moan and flop back on my cot, tucking the knife away. "Ugh! Don't remind me!" None of us knows what we are going to do when we age out of here. We each have a bit of money squirreled away, but it's not enough to start a life on. And if we had any family that could help us, we wouldn't be here in the first place.

Shells and Vic sit back next to me, and I reach over for the cards, handing them to Vic. "Happy birthday."

"Thanks." Vic's voice is gruff as she takes them and begins unfolding. We can't afford anything that's not stolen, so we have gotten really good at making cards. The paper trembles slightly as she reads my message to her. This is the one time of year I open my heart to her and write to her how much I love her.

I have never seen Vic cry, and we have been through some serious shit together. This is as emotional as I ever see her. And that's about the same for Shells and me too. Emotions are weaknesses here. And none of us can afford to be weak in a place like this. I rest my head on her bony shoulder and take in her familiar scent of lemon and vanilla as she continues reading.

CHAPTER 1

I'm not crazy. *I'm not crazy, I'm safe. I am not crazy.*

The words chant through my mind like a mantra as another layer of dripping stress breaks out over my body. My rigid arms ache from gripping the steering wheel, but instead of loosening, my sweat-slicked hands squeeze tighter. I lean close to my cracked window, hoping for some relief, but all I get is more hot air stinging my nostrils. I breathe it out in a burst through parched lips and break my internal chant long enough to note the next mile marker. And it's better than a breath of fresh air. It's my freedom that I'm after … and I'm getting closer.

My newly purchased, Jurassic Chevy, Marty, began complaining three long states ago, but now it's full-on with the dramatics—the coughing, wheezing, rattling of a metal body pushed past its limits. The radio is static, and the AC, all bark and no bite, but it's not the glaring sun that has me sweating this way— It's the crippling fear that we're not going to make it.

But somehow—through pleading, cursing, and charming—Marty has gotten us to the exit I had placed high atop a pedestal I had no real hope of ever reaching. Against all odds, the sign "Green Mont" looms before us like a prophesy come to life, straight from my dreams. It magnifies under my focus, only to speed past as Marty and I finally exit the highway.

As if he knows the heroic race to Green Mont, California is ending, Marty lets out a last jagged battle cry and dies on me. I do my best to navigate him off the road. And as we drift to the shoulder, I silently thank Vic and Shells once more for pooling their meager savings to help me get this far. With a sense of unreality, I exhale and wrench my heavy door open. The loud whine of creaking metal has several birds abandoning a nearby tree. Hopping out into the midday sun and squinting at my surroundings, I am suddenly galvanized by the incredible awareness that I have made it so much farther than I ever expected. I reach back in for my duffle bag and water bottle, I kick the door shut behind me, pull down my cap, and salute Marty, before picking a direction to walk.

As I try to work out the stiffness and vicious kinks of my journey, I more hobble than walk the first block. Stopping under a patch of shade and stretching, I pull out my phone and deflate a bit. Five percent. *Crap.* Calling the first auto shop I find; I explain where Marty is and agree on a price to have him taken care of. Getting another beater would probably be cheaper. But that wouldn't be any way to repay my unlikely hero. Besides, I'm already attached to the rusty beast.

Feeling the wind rustle through my hair, I turn toward it, and with the resolve of no better option, I start walking north. Most people would call me crazy for following my dreams to a town I have never been to before. But I have had intuitive dreams since I was a kid. And I learned the hard way that burying my head in the sand and ignoring them comes with too high a price. And in this case, I didn't have much of a choice anyway. I had to leave. And if I didn't want to be found, what better place than the secret and random town banging around in my head for the last several months?

As I amble past the quaint and cheerful shops and into the suburbs, I don't take particular note of my surroundings until the perfectly manicured lawns and greyscale homes become sporadic. Velvety, short trimmed grass gives way to more trees and wildflowers. A sense of history and warmth permeates from these houses and the yards that hold them, and I slow down.

Hoping my luck will miraculously stretch into prolonged battery life, I check my phone. *Nope.* It's as dead as dear Marty. I stop and look around as if that will somehow orient me as to where the hell I am. But then chills run down my spine, and my back gets tight at the reality of stopping. I automatically move forward and with a souring mood and start looking for "RENT" signs.

Despite my strange and persistent dreams, I'm not a superstitious person. I'm not prone to flights of fancy. I don't believe in magic, and fairytales just annoy me. And yet... I feel deep down, that I am exactly where I am meant to be. Besides, trusting in an idea as fantastical as fate and that somehow everything is going to sort itself out, is far more appealing than imagining myself on a park bench for the night.

Quickening my strides with purpose, I move further into suburbia and closer to the normal, boring life that I am desperate to fit myself into. Growing agitated at the miserable lack of rentals, I tell myself once again: *This is where I am meant to be*, and I try to put some gusto into the thought as I will away the dawning awareness of being completely lost without a solid plan or even my phone to fall back on.

Passing another house, I have graduated into cheering myself on by running bumper sticker slogans through my head: *You can do it! You have got this!* I let out a frustrated sigh and mentally roll my eyes as I pass another house. Even thinking it, I sound idiotic. *God, I can't wait for this to be over.* I'm so tired I could just drop right into the pristine yard next to me and pass out.

I haven't had a full night's rest in days, and e*verything* hurts. The hopelessness and exhaustion I have been fighting since I began this journey finally gets the better of me and with no grace at all, I plop down on the edge of a stranger's yard. Stopping is reckless and I know it, but for the moment, I let my self-pity weigh me down.

With a ferocious yawn, I lean on my side and rest my head heavily onto my hand. My elbow sinks into cool, moist earth and God, this feels better than a feather mattress. Risking just a second to close my eyes, I listen to the sounds of birds and kids playing somewhere in the distance. I need to calm my knotted stomach and put all my anxiety back in the Pandoras Box it belongs in. I know I can't go any farther if I let fear take over now.

Breathing slowly, I repeat my mission: *Get to California. Go to Green Mont. Find a month-to-month. Get a cash job. Lay low ... and then what?*

The pesky question I have been dodging stubbornly rears its ugly head. I try to shove the negative thought away. But it's harder this time. And all of it gets more jumbled and confused the longer I try to not think about it.

∞

Something cold and wet is hitting my face, and I become aware that my whole body is shivering. Coming awake all at once, I realize it's raining and it's dark out. A gust of wind slams into me, and I sit up, hunkering down into my damp shirt. *Shit, shit shiiiit!* I cannot believe my stupidity! With rising panic, I stand up and desperately look around. Shaking off the last vestiges of sleep, I yank my sunglasses off my face and wipe wet strands of hair away.

With the shades off, I readjust to the light and note, with a small measure of relief, that it's not as dark as I thought. That's something at least. Mentally kicking myself, I think I *would* have been better off on that park bench. Ugh! I *cannot believe this!* —or the fact that I actually *did* pass out. And in the open no less! So now I know three days of no sleep is my limit, and I can be better prepared next time. But what good is finding a silver lining when you're stuck out in the cold and going to freeze to death? My teeth are chattering, and I bite my tongue as I involuntarily jump at a loud crack of thunder. This just keeps getting better.

Of all the stupid, moronic, self–sabotaging ...

Lightning spears across the sky and I am momentarily stunned out of my shame spiral. And that's when I see it.

There! Just across the street is a sign—a *literal sign*—that reads: Libertine Library.

The library is housed in a Victorian mansion with grand white towers and gracefully sloping roofs, framed by ornate trellises and made complete with a double widows peak. Give this place a coat of black paint and it's your quintessential Dracula's mansion. I cross the street. The idea of vampires and ghosts doesn't scare me. The reality of predators in the night does. Without thinking about it, I reach for my phone to check the time and huff when I remember it's dead. Looking at the lowering sun, I know it can't be later than six in the evening. Libraries are public institutions, and it's Monday, so I might be in luck.

Hesitating at the edge of the yard, I consider how strange the location of this library is. I'm miles from town in the middle of suburbia. I haven't spent a lot of time living in cute little neighborhoods, or in libraries for that matter, but even so, I always believed that what libraries still remain in the world, belong in cities and towns. Not *here*.

Movement at the large bay window on the ground floor catches my eye. Moving closer, I see what looks to be a very big, very ugly dog. Stepping onto the walkway and leaning in, I note that its ears are perked, and it must be looking at me too. I wonder what I look like out here, all wet and bedraggled. Another freezing wall of wind slams into me, and my mind is made up. I cross the yard in six bounding leaps and bang on one of the gigantic double doors, belatedly noticing the knocker. *Whoops... come on, come on!*

Bouncing up and down to keep my circulation going and a bit of heat running through my body, I reach up and try again to smooth my hair before realizing I left my hat behind where I had fallen asleep. *Damn.* I don't want to be turned away because I look deranged. The curtain of rain obscures the other side of the street, and I give up on the hat and look around. I take in the romantic wraparound porch with two big, old rustic chandeliers at either side and a large wooden bench swing as the prominent features. If the sun were out, this would be a postcard— though the place could definitely use a bit of work.

Just then the doorknob jingles and I turn. Through the stained glass of the door, I see a hulking figure. I take a cautious step back as the pair of doors open. There before me, stands a mountain of a man. Suddenly I'm blinded by more hair and made even colder with another gust of wind. I fight to remove it from my eyes while taking another step back, and I start to stumble.

Before I can fall, two massive hands take hold my shoulders and steady me. I am surprised by the rush of security I feel at their warmth, just before they let me go. And I'm finally able to scrape away the hair.

"Careful there," the man says to me.

I want to look at him as his deep rumbling voice reaches me. But I am too busy noticing the monster of a dog that now sits at his side. It's even more ugly in person! This is the biggest, and truly, most hideous dog I have ever seen in my life! It looks like a demon fell for a wolf and this ... *creature* is the result.

Okay, so maybe this wasn't my best idea. Maybe I made a snap decision that was worse than my choice not to stay the hell awake today! Because these two clearly do not belong in a library, let alone this neighborhood.

"Oh, I'm sorry. I think I must have the wrong place. I saw the sign—" I point lamely in its general vicinity, ""—and I thought that this was a library." My laugh sounds hollow even to my own ears. I take another step back, not faltering this time. "I'm sorry for disturbing you. I really didn't mean to waste your time."

The man crosses huge tattooed arms in front of him, the Dorse (dog/ horse) or whatever you would call that *thing*, never leaving his side. They both regard me, and there's something in that stare that has me halting in my tracks. When you come from the streets like I do, learning to read people is survival, and these two are not sizing me up like I'm prey. They are asking themselves if I'm the kind of punk kid that scams and loots.

Un-offended, I relax a little— that is until the massive Dorse closes the space between us and sniffs me. I don't dare move as I imagine the gruesome death that might come from upsetting him. Its snout is reaching all the way up to my neck! Instead he just snorts, spraying me with disgustingness, and then licks me to seal the deal. Sitting back, he starts wagging his tail like I have passed his test, giving me what I swear is a grin. And It's the kind of grin that's contagious, like genuine belly laughter, and I can't help but thaw out a little and smile back.

Thunder, much closer this time, breaks the moment, and the man's face cracks into a lop-sided grin of his own.

"Hell of a day for a walk," he says, and just like that, he turns around and heads inside, leaving the door open for me to follow—or stand outside in the freezing cold. The Dorse makes a whining sound and nudges my chest, instead of my hand, like a normal dog.

Reminding myself it's *me* that came to *them*, I step inside and pull the door shut behind me. Blessed warmth envelopes me, and I am so relieved that I close my eyes for a second. My eyes adjust to the soft yellow lighting, and I shrug off my soaked hoodie, looking around. I'm noting all potential exits, threats, and weapons when I notice I'm alone with the smiling Dorse. He's just sitting there. thumping his tail and looking at me. Relaxing a smidge, I allow myself to really *see* where I am. The entrance room I'm in branches out into the rest of the house from all sides but the entrance where I came from. And just from this view, I know I've never been inside a place this nice.

The mansion is clearly old, but it's well taken care of. All around me is gleaming wood, glowing crystal lights, and stained glass. The double doors to my left and right are as big as the massive entrance doors. And they are a work of art! Deep colored glass fused to depict a wind-swept maiden on each door, reaching for the golden floral door-knobs that stand out in beautiful, twisting relief. Each of the four maidens seems to represent an element that makes them even cooler.

But what takes my breath away is through the open doors on my right. Beyond them, looms a massive room holding shelf after shelf of books. I don't know what I was expecting, but as I step into the doorway, I look past the shadow of an intricate winding staircase at the back leading to the second level of books that circle the whole room. Above, is a high vaulted ceiling dripping with two giant chandeliers. It's hard to see in the darkened room, but I can just make out an incredible mural of stars on the ceiling, forming complex geometric shapes.

"Surprising, isn't it?"

I whirl around on a sharp intake of breath.

"Sorry," he says, pushing an old fashioned tea trolley. "I thought you could use something warm."

The delicate tea service looks ridiculous next to his massive tatted form. But then, the distracting smell of cocoa reaches me as he pours us each a steaming mug. I wait for him to sip his own before trying mine.

"That's insane!" I exclaim.

"Right? They don't make chocolate like that in the U.S." Resuming his scrutiny of me he says, "You don't look like you're from around here."

"Well, you don't look like a librarian."

He barks out a laugh and turns to put down his mug and rustle through a closet by the door. Turning back to me, he hands me a heavy shearling coat that's almost bigger than my body.

"The fire is still going in the living room if you want to take a seat and dry out some." He looks around the large foyer, like he is searching for something, then looks back at me uncertainly. "This place belonged to my Granddad. He passed and now it's on me to figure out what the hell to do with it. You're welcome to stay until the storm passes or someone picks you up." He walks through the doorway facing the library and I follow behind, listening to the gravelly timbre of his voice.

Walking into the living room, I am struck anew by how amazing this place is. It feels like going back in time. I can't help but be enchanted by the grand piano in the nook of windows and the adjoining wall literally covered in" –Are those all cuckoo clocks?"

"Yeah. Grandad liked collecting them. He has them all set to go off at the same time and it's so fucking loud you can hear it from the third floor." He must have noticed his language because he turns a bright shade of pink and mumbles, "Sorry."

I don't want to let my guard down any more than I already have, but that is getting harder as the big guy goes from pink to red. "You have three *floors*?"

"Four floors. Five if you count the towers."

Huffing, I say without thinking "It looks so much *smaller* from the outside!" Immediately catching my insult, I trail off and sheepishly glance at him.

"It's okay, I thought the same thing. The book wing takes up the whole right side of the house and goes up almost three stories high. When you go in there, it makes the place feel more like a castle than a mansion." He leans back on his heels and scratches the back of his head. For an older dude, he's handsome. Not my type at all, but some of the girls from my group home would have majorly crushed on a big 30 something, macho man.

"I'm Dill, but my friends call me Pickle," he says with a totally straight face and puts out his hand.

I am slow to reach out and shake it, even while I try not to laugh. Not wanting to be rude, I settle on smiling. "I'm Alexa, but my friends call me Alex." I can't help myself. "Do your friends really call you Pickle?"

"Sure do." With that, he turns to his side and shows me the inside of his arm. It displays an amazing assortment of tats that trickle together into an intricate sleeve of a vicious looking dragon with its jaws wrapped around a ...smiling pickle with Potato Head eyes.

The laugh that escapes me is so sudden and loud, my eyes pop wide, and I try to cover my mouth before anything else impolite comes out. But the more I look at his arm, the harder I laugh. swiping at my tears, I force my face away from the stupid surprise pickle face and try to re-cover. "I am so sorry, I wasn't expecting that."

"Nah, that's exactly the kind of strong reaction a good piece of art should elicit. I love my little pickle." At that, we both start laughing. "I didn't mean it like that," he says turning a deeper shade of red.

Smiling at him, I look over to the Dorse, who is wagging his tail so hard the whole floor vibrates. "And who is this?"

"That's Ugly." Again with the straight face.

"What?"

"You can't tell me you didn't think it." The dog gives one deep bark at hearing his name and turns a tight circle before landing on his front paws and sticking his rear in the air. "*He* seems to like it." Dill gestures to Ugly with a smirk. "My Granddad never mentioned having a dog and the mutt didn't have a tag. So, until I can root out some paperwork on him that's the nickname that stuck."

Dill sits back on a leather studded chair, and I take the moment to drop my duffle in front of the fire and root through it. Finding my charger, I look for the nearest outlet and see Dill point to one by a fragile-looking table. I scoot my damp bag a little closer to the fire before sorting out my phone.

Hefting the big coat with me, I take a seat on the far side of the green velvet sofa. Arranging myself with the coat, I notice my coco before me, refilled now and steaming. I take in the rest of the room filled with multiple rugs, and an eclectic mix of antiques that don't match but fit together, nonetheless. Aside from the piano, my favorite part of the room is the huge fireplace before us. It's almost as tall as I am with wicked little gargoyles and unknown creatures framing its mouth.

Ugly miraculously fits himself between the sofa and coffee table and lies down at my feet, resting his heavy head on my knees. His bushy eyebrows go up and down as he lets out a contented sigh and gazes up at me. Okay, maybe he's a little cute. Like in a so-ugly-it's-cute kind of way.

I'm smiling again. And at that moment I realize how utterly safe and warm I feel. And how it's the first time I can remember laughing in so long.

All at once, I am swallowed up by sadness. Maybe it's knowing this is just a moment of security that can't last, or simply being shown kindness after so much solitary struggle. Whatever it is, I have to swallow hard to keep back the unexpected tears.

Hoping Dill hasn't noticed my lapse in mood, I look up and see him eyeing my duffle. Then his eyes meet mine, and I feel like he can see right through me and my secrets.

Before I can get too uncomfortable, he shouts "Alexa! Play 'Here Comes the Sun' by The Beatles!"

Smiling tightly at the stupid joke I have heard a million times, I roll my eyes at him. "See? This is why I go by Alex ... *Pickle*." I enunciate his name with a bit of drama and his lop-sided grin makes a comeback.

Somehow I know, with everything I am, that Dill is a good man. And I have the beginnings of an idea in my head, but I have to work fast. The hustler in me, the part of me that needs to survive, gets hit with a little spike of adrenalin, and everything becomes super focused. Trying not to get too hopeful, I form my next words carefully and strive to sound casual. "Do you really have so many things to sort through, that you can't find out the dog's real name?"

Dill is back to scratching his neck. "Yeah, it's a real mess. The old man has a study and it's a lifetime's worth of paperwork. Not to mention the rest of this damned mansion... and some of those books. Hell, most of them are probably collectibles they're so old. The amazing thing is, he seems to have records for all of it, but there is just so damn much of it, I don't know where to start. Shit, I don't know if I'm coming, going, staying, or what this place is to me yet. I have been here for a month and have hardly scratched the surface. And suddenly I have a dog to look after? I didn't want it at first you know." He rubs his knees with his hands. "The house or the dog. But Ugly grew on me and then the house– it just has a pull to it, and I feel like I need to sort it. If nothing else, for my grandad."

He's looking into the fire now and seems a little sad and lost. Wanting to distract him, I ask, "Have you ever had a dog before?"

Chuckling, Dill says, "No."

"What were you doing before this place fell into your lap?"

He looks at me then and, with the wisp of a smile, responds softly, "Just traveling around here and there on my Harley. I have a band and we book a decent amount. I also do bodywork on bikes for my friends. I paint a little, and that comes in handy with the body work" He rubs his chin where the beginnings of a beard are forming.

I speak my next words carefully before he has a chance to change the subject. "It seems to me you could use a little bit of help around here." I go silent after letting that not-so-subtle seed drop.

His eyes do that crinkling thing they did the first time he assessed me. I have the feeling that Dill is much smarter than he lets on.

With an internal sigh, I mentally throw up my hands and dive. "I don't know if I'm coming or going either, but I could use a job. I'm a hard worker, and I have a knack for organizing. And—" I look down at Ugly, "—the dog likes me. I could help you with him too."

Dill leans forward resting his elbows on his knees. He's silent for a little too long but the interest I'm reading from his posture has me feeling dangerously optimistic. "Are you running from anything?"

"No," I lie.

"Are you in trouble of any kind?"

"No," I lie again.

"Have you ever stolen anything or had trouble with the cops?"

"No." This lie has my face heating, and I hope he doesn't notice.

"Are you over eighteen?"

"Yep, I just turned twenty-one," I say, feeling a little better. I'm used to this lie.

There's a long pause, that I don't interrupt, while he's considering. Even though I'm trying not to feel too hopeful, my traitorous heart thumps in my chest. And excitement seeps into my muscles, making me want to get up and move.

Please Just one win. Please ...

"Okay. Propose something."

"What?"

"Tell me what you're offering and what you expect in return."

"Oh! Right!" Optimism rushes through my body, and I can't help smiling when I tell him, "I can be like a general caretaker to this place," I gesture wildly at everything around me. "And the dog, if needed." I look down at Ugly when I say that, but when I feel Dill's eyes on me, I look back up and give him my most winning smile. "I can cook, clean, organize, and help you figure out what to do with it all. And in return, you provide all living expenses like food and rent. Plus ..." I pause, thinking as quickly as I can, "you give me twenty percent of everything I help you sell as extra incentive to move it all. Or a little salary. Also, this place is bigger than you need. I can take a room here to save on the living expenses part. And if it's not working out, you know, like I wash your whites with your reds and ruin all your clothes–or all the cuckoo clocks going off drives me mad—we can end the agreement at any time."

When I finish, my face is flushed and my heart is pounding. I have to put my cocoa down so he won't notice it trembling in my hands. Just the idea of finding a place to stay the night would be an incredible relief. But a *job*? Somewhere to lay low while I figure out my next move? It would be the equivalent of winning the lottery.

"You can cook?" he sounds dubious.

Stalling, I say, "Why? Do I not look like someone who cooks?"

He just stares at me and doesn't respond.

"I can cook simple things really good. Like mac 'n' cheese, steak and eggs, French toast. Mostly breakfast foods. But who doesn't love break-fast?" I have to stop myself from rambling, and I hold my breath while I wait for his response.

The leather of his chair creaks as he leans back and folds his hands over his flat stomach. "Ever had a dog?"

"Yep." I almost say two, but I'm lying so much I'm going to have trouble keeping it all straight in my head as it is. So I leave out the de-tails.

"Do you have any references?"

My heart deflates a bit, and I have to tell him the truth on this one. Shaking my head, I look down at Ugly.

He leans back and sighs and I try to look calm under his shrewd gaze. With nothing but the clicking of cuckoo clocks and the crackling of fire in the background, it seems an eternity before he finally says, "You can have a room on this floor, rent-free, as that's where the lion's share of work is. I'm up on the third. I'll pay to cover your food, but no additional salary. And you can have ten percent of what I give you the 'okay' on selling. Plus, you'll get two days off just like any respectable job. If you break anything, it comes out of your earnings. If you steal anything, it goes without saying, you're fired." He's quiet and waits for my response.

No. Flipping. WAY! I quickly replay what he just said to be sure I'm hearing him right. When he doesn't change his mind, I have to fight the need to do a victory dance. Instead, I settle on doing cartwheels in my head and tell myself I can wig out later. On the outside, my face is still trained to stay calm. So as not to seem too eager, I counter, "Fifteen percent of whatever I sell, and you have a deal."

CHAPTER 2

My new room is at least three times bigger than the shoebox I shared with Vic and Shells. I move to its center and turn a slow circle. I cannot *believe* that this is where I have landed. Of all the scenarios I imagined, it never looked anything like these high ceilings with crown molding, that crystal chandelier, or the carved marble fireplace I am currently gaping at. And the cozy set of high-backed chairs before it are nicer than anything I have ever sat on. And just forget about the huge bed behind me with four pillows! I swing the rest of the way around to be sure. *Yep. Four!*

There's a writing desk in the corner and next to it is an alcove of windows with a bench seat bigger than my cot was. I'm completely mystified, and I'm still trying to wrap my mind around this place being my *home*. Even if just for a short while. I want to pinch myself but I'm too practical for that. This is *real*. I'm *really* living here. And this is *really* my room.

With a burst of laughter, I jump into my winning dance. It's rare that it happens, so when it does, I give it my all. My natural calico red mane tumbles free of my bun as I twist, jump, and whirl around my new room. The weight of it following my movements and fanning around me as I go. I don't know how crazy I look, and I don't care. I'm living in the joy of this moment because I don't know when or if the next one will come.

Breathless, I fall back into the four-poster princess bed and close my eyes, letting out a contented sigh. I have a roof over my head. And thinking of Dill, I realize that he's maybe the first adult in my life to show me any real trust or kindness. I promise myself that I'm not going to make him regret hiring me. ...I'm going to be worthy of his show of faith, and this place.

With a moan, I realize there is no way I'm ever going to sleep through all of this excitement.

$$\infty$$

My eyes slit open, and I blink against the bright light as I stretch and feel my bones crack. Yawning, I scoot up to a sitting position and try opening my eyes again. *Wow. This room.*

Reaching for my phone I glance at the screen. Six thirty-two a.m. Moving till my feet hit the floor, I notice how loose my limbs feel and the headache I was sporting for the last week is gone. *I feel good.* And the thought is a revelation.

I switch off the lights I had forgotten and move to the windows. Pushing the curtains aside, I gasp. There's a garden straight out of a fairytale in front of me! Flowers and plants of all kinds are sectioned off by a stone walkway lined in old lamp posts. Vines climb over trellises and spill over with yet more flowers. Everything is organized, but it feels a little wild. And *holy bejeezus, I can hear the faint sound of water! OMG, if there is a pool out there, I will literally die!*

Grinning from ear to ear, I step away from the windows and move back towards the four-poster bed where I left my duffle. I almost feel guilty looking at all that fluffy real estate and knowing it's just for me. Thinking of Vic and Shells, I *do* feel guilty. I wouldn't have made it here without them, and I miss them with a depth I haven't allowed myself to wallow in.

I wish I could share this with you guys so badly!

Shells would've loved this! And Vic would've had the whole place cased and her pockets lined in the first five minutes. Nostalgia washes over me in a bittersweet rush. Letting out a sigh, I smile to myself. I have to find a safe way to reach them and let them know I'm okay.

Dressing quickly, I make a mental checklist of what I want to get done. I don't know when Dill gets up, but I'm hoping to beat him to the kitchen and surprise him with breakfast. Opening my door, I stumble over something large and crash to the floor. *Ouch!* I'm not fully up before the culprit is licking my face.

"Gross! Get off of me, you disgusting beast!" Ugly lets out a deep woof, and pounces over me. His butt's back in the air and his tail is moving fast enough that he might just helicopter himself away. But the monster just goes back in for another smooch. "Don't you dare! I will find your every toy and destroy them!"

I'm laughing now as I struggle to push him off of me. "*You're so big!* Aaaagh! Stop!" It's so gross, but I can't stop laughing. Finally managing to push him away with my feet using all the strength I have in my legs, I quickly stand up, and before he can knock me over, and in as firm a voice as I can muster I say, "Sit down!"

It's like a different personality takes over Ugly, and before I have even finished the command, he's sitting with his ears cocked, waiting for my next one.

"What the..."

He cocks his head as if he didn't quite catch that and is trying to decipher my meaning. It's a totally endearing gesture. "You're smarter than you look, huh?"

Wanting to know what else he can do, I say "Shake hands." He lifts his paw, and I take it, oddly proud.

"Lay down!" He does.

"Play dead!"

When he rolls on his back and lets his tongue flop out, I nearly bust a gut with laughter. Excited now, I tell him to roll over. He does, but in the process, he knocks into a hallway table and a priceless-looking vase topples over. I reach for it as fast as I can and manage to stop it from shattering on the table, but I fumble and down it goes. The whole horrific incident seems to happen in slow motion. And I know before it breaks that my job here is already over. With my heart in my chest, I futilely try to save it.

What happens next has my breath catching. Ugly tries to snatch it between his massive jaws. It slips out of them, but he has slowed the fall enough that I can catch it just before it hits the floor.

"Good boy!" I croon at my new best friend.

Clutching the vase with trembling hands, I carefully replace the ancient-looking thing on the table then look back at Ugly. "Are you clever, or what?!" I scratch behind his ears and love the happy, snorting noise he makes at my praise.

He follows me to the kitchen, and I am gratified to see that Dill hasn't been here yet. I rummage around until I have everything I need, and then start putting my breakfast skills to work. On goes the coffee. Then bacon. And in a separate skillet, I start frying the eggs. Just as I'm sticking bread into a toaster, Dill walks in. I try to read his face while I go about my business. But he gives nothing away. He absently rubs Ugly's head and takes the black coffee I offer. I have left enough room for a little milk if he wants it. But he just sips it and closes his eyes in enjoyment.

"Ahhh, you found the fancy stuff," he mumbles approvingly while snatching a strip of bacon off the cooling plate.

"No Folgers for *my* boss. Are those beans really from Australia?"

Dill smirks at that. "Yeah, the old man has spices and condiments from all over. That and coffee beans were his guilty pleasure when traveling for rare books. That cocoa I made last night is from India."

"Your Grandad sounds like a cool guy."

"He was. Taught me most everything I know and he raised *me*. So he's damn near a saint."

I want to ask him more about it, but something in his eyes stops me. Moving the plates to the little table by the windows, we go about setting it together in silence. He doesn't say anything again until we start eating.

"Good." He simply says around a mouth full of food. The simple praise has me glowing and I take my first bite.

I can't stop the delighted "Mmmmm" that rolls out of me. My eyes are still closed as I shovel another fork full in. It's been too long since I've had a decent meal and it's like my taste buds are absorbing every salty, greasy bite. Dill is looking at me funny, but before he can comment on my total pig out, Ugly's head bangs the underside of the table and makes everything atop it jump and clang as it falls back into place.

Ugly has gone for the bacon I was *trying* to sneak him and is snorting loudly as he gobbles it up. *I guess I'm not the biggest pig in the room after all.* Ugly might be smart. But he's *definitely* not stealthy. I look up at Dill hoping he's not mad, and see that instead, he's trying to hide a smile.

"Damn bull in a china shop. It's amazing Grandad put a dog like him in a house like this."

"I think he got him to guard it."

"We talkin' about the same dog? He can't be trusted to find his own damn tail. ...He's BFFs with the cat next door... And he has an awkward as hell make-out session with the mailman every day. I don't know...— maybe the old coot got him on one of his trips, because he sure as shit doesn't understand English. He's got less going on upstairs than a one-story house."

Giggling, I decide not to mention Ugly's training because listening to Dill rant about him is way more fun. And Dill probably already knows but just likes teasing him. Getting up to clear the table I ask, "Do you have time to give me a tour? I plan to start organizing in your Grandad's study, but it will be good to see what I'm working with."

Surprise flickers across Dill's face. It's just there for a second, but I catch it before he gives me a nod and small smile. I guess neither of us really knows what to expect out of this, but I'm more determined than ever to prove myself. In a short amount of time, Dill has given me more to be grateful for than I have had in longer than I can remember, and I'm eager to even the odds.

∞

Manor La Book, as I have dubbed it, is far bigger on the inside than it looks from the outside. Getting its square footage from height rather than its girth. I don't know much about architecture, but I'm marveling at the incredible conservation of historical details. Mosaic, wooden floors and busy foliage wallpaper make up the lion's share of each hallway. The other portion being a dizzying array of lights. Not one the same as the next. I stop at a particularly detailed sconce of two dancing women woven around each other and holding aloft a light in each hand. "Whoah …"

I feel a little like Belle, in the Beast's enchanted castle. At that moment, Ugly sneezes and sprays me with snot. *And there is the Beast!*

"Eeew! Turn your head away when you sneeze! Gross!" I wipe away the wetness I feel on my cheek and glare at him. He has the decency to look guilty, and I can't help but chuckle. Still wiping my face, I look up at Dill, who's clearly amused. I try—and fail—to glare at him too.

We make our way to the third floor where Dill is staying, and I'm surprised to find the ambiance here is different than the rest of the house. Moroccan styled star lights gleam from the hallway ceiling, rather than the crystal chandeliers on the previous floors. The floor is black and white tile instead of wood. And murals with scenes of an exotic land, boasting elephant carriages, lions, and palm trees cover the walls. Instead of sconces, perforated copper lanterns line the hallway.

I'm eyeing the armoire in the room Dill is showing me now. I'm pretty sure it was used in the movie *The Lion, the Witch, and the Wardrobe*. Just as with the rest of the house, an eclectic mix of antiques furnish the room. But instead of the heavy-looking curtains on the other floors, the rooms here are airier with long ivory curtains that glitter with little mirrors sewn into them. This place is like being in a movie. And I'm convinced there has to be a secret room or passage somewhere. I file the thought away, under "things to do on my day off".

Dill shows me his room next, and we move through this part a little quicker than the rest. Clearly, Dill is uncomfortable sharing his personal space, but I can see why he chose this room. His balcony is the biggest in the house and overlooks the front. He's set up a hammock outside and the empty beer bottle and half-read book tells me he spends more time outside.

His room is by far the most sparse, utilitarian looking space in the manner I have seen at this point. And I find it funny that he's sleeping on an air mattress in front of a grand fireplace when almost every other room in the house has a real bed. Sensing his discomfort, I don't mention it, but my curiosity gets the better of me at the darker outlines in the wood that almost look like shadows. "Did you move out the furniture that used to be in here?"

"Yeah, I did. I don't need that froufrou stuff in my room. Queen Ann something or other, blah, blah." I laugh at his eye roll as he goes on. "I'm like the dog. Not a graceful bone in this body. There's no way any of it would have lasted longer than a week in my care." His expression has me smiling, though he just revealed a personal but important bit of information.

He doesn't think he's good enough to have this place or anything in it, which explains his hesitancy to figure out what to do with all of it. I can relate to that, which is probably why I can see him so clearly at this moment. The unexpected parallel between us surprises me and has me feeling a new sense of kinship.

The fourth floor has fewer rooms and lots more space and light. I wouldn't have thought it possible, but it has even more character. The sharp, sloping ceilings and large, wooden beams give off a vibe that's different from anywhere else in the house, and the windows and nooks here are more sporadic in size and shape.

"What was this floor used for?"

"I didn't have the pleasure of knowing my grandmother. But when she was around, she liked to paint. This floor was her art and dance studio." He points to a wall of mirrors. "Granddad mentioned something about it years back. After she passed, he never used this floor again, but you can still see splatters of her paint in places. I'm told I get my skills from her."

This is the most Dill has ever shared and I want to keep him talking. " Did she fix up old Harley's too?"

He laughs at that and shakes his head. "No, not that I'm aware of, but word has it she was quite the rebel. She questioned *everything*. Loved debate, smoking cigars, drinking gin, and she got a job *before* the war, not during, and not after like the rest of the pack. So who knows. Maybe she did paint up some bikes. I wish I had gotten the chance to meet her. Grandad loved her. She was the last thing he talked about before he died."

"You were there with him?" I feel bad when Dill's smile evaporates.

"No. I was out of town on a gig. His nurse told me."

I don't know what to say. "Sorry" never feels like enough in the face of true loss, but I say it anyway, "I'm sorry, Dill."

He looks at me. "I believe you are. But don't be. He had a great life. And his last words were 'I can't wait to see her'."

For some reason I can't explain, that chokes me up. I turn to a window and get myself under control. I never cry, and it's not like I don't know tragedy, but there's something about that kind of love ... The closest I have ever been to it is hearing this story.

Squeezing my eyes shut, I surreptitiously wipe them and feel Ugly almost knock me over as he nudges me. Smiling down at him, I turn back to Dill. "I guess you don't know how old he is?"

"He looks old enough to be one of these antiques Grandad loves. But don't be fooled. Underneath all that silver scruff is an energetic bastard. If I don't exercise him every day, he becomes completely unhinged. The shit."

Ugly sneezes—away from me this time.

"I'll add that to my everyday list then. Taking him for walks at least. It will be a chance to get to know this neighborhood better."

"You have a list?

"Yeah, how else do you expect me to organize if I'm not organized?" I make a face at him, and he chuckles. I'm glad to see him smiling again.

"The towers are on each side. They are both pretty much the same so I'll just show you one for now. I have to get going after this, but you can check out the other whenever you want. And sorry we didn't make it to the library. This is the first time I have been through all the rooms since moving in, and I forgot how much there is. Who needs this many damn rooms?"

On this floor, the hallway forms a "T". At each end of the smaller hall is a door. The one we are standing in front of is nothing special in form, but the beautiful oil painting over it has my eyes bugging out. "What in the world?"

It's a realistic version of the library and salon doors. A windswept maiden reaches toward the door handle. Only instead of representing an element, she seems to represent the night. It reminds me of the Medieval paintings I saw with my class at a museum. "Yep, that's Grandma's work there. She painted it and the door at the other end too."

"It's amazing! Do you paint like this?" Dill just smiles and turns a little red. "*Seriously!?* I want to see your stuff!"

"Then go to one of my gigs and check out the parking lot. I'll bet I have touched at least *half* the bikes there."

"You're a pretty cool g—" Whatever I was saying drifts off as we enter the tower. It's round and smaller than the other rooms, but it has the most incredible wood mosaic floor. The wood spirals out from the center in an intricate patchwork of tones that gleam against the sunlight. Across from us is an oddly shaped fireplace that emulates the shape of the tall and arching stained glass windows.

But what has my mind completely blown is the stained-glass ceiling! The whole room is illuminated by it in a dazzling display of jewel tones. A smaller version of the downstairs library's spiral stairs leads to a balcony. As I make my way up, I discover it's a walkway that circles the room and encases the stained glass. It's a viewing tower that offers a view of the outside from all sides. But then I look down through the stained-glass and make out the bedroom below.

From up here, I can clearly see how the glass artfully emulates the swirling pattern of the wood floor below. Only the cooler tones to the glass and added stars make it look more like a swirling night sky with constellations. At its very center where the swirl tightens into a point, is a two-tiered chandelier with matching star crystals.

"*No way!*" Looking up, I see a steeply pointed, mirrored ceiling cut into eight facets, emulating a giant mirror star. I laugh in wonder. The mirrors refract the light from the windows and reflect the stained-glass constellation. It's absolutely amazing. A chain comes right from its center and goes down through the stained-glass to hold the chandelier above the bedroom. And just ahead of me is a telescope that doesn't look a day under one-hundred years old.

"What *is* this place?"

"I saved the best for last. This is the south viewing tower. The north is pretty incredible as well." Dill says from behind me, still at the stairs. I turn around and look at him, speechless. He chuckles. "I'm not sure why I don't come up here more. Hell, I guess I never feel dressed enough." He scratches the back of his neck, in what I am fast becoming aware, is another Dill-ism.

"You can stick around here if you want. I have to run, but if you can take the monster out for a stroll, that would be appreciated. You'll get a kick out of it, *I'm sure*."

I'm too busy looking out of the windows at the incredible view to ask him what he means. "You can see all the way to town from here!"

"Isn't that something? No one can legally build this high anymore. So, for as long as she stands her view will remain unobstructed. She may not be the biggest house in this neighborhood, but she's the tallest. Ugly's leash is by the door and there's yogurt in the fridge. Oh, and don't steal anything while I'm gone."

"Too late," I shout at his retreating back.

"You're fired," he says in a droll tone.

"Be back in time for dinner! I'm making mac 'n' cheese. *Not* from India!" I get out just before he disappears from view, chuckling.

CHAPTER 3

Dill is right. Walking Ugly *is* entertaining. But it's not him providing the entertainment. It's one of the first warm days of May, and everyone that's home from work seems to be out—gardening, walking, washing their car. It's a suburban dream made complete with matching landscaping and outfits.

This is the nicest part of the neighborhood as far as I have seen. The cars, the mansions, and even the gates are fancy. But the way neighbors feign disinterest, then stare at you the moment they think you're not looking, is anything but. It has me wanting to taunt them—badly, but Ugly is on his best behavior, so I am determined to be on mine.

He walks beside me leaving his leash between us remarkably loose. Not pulling too tight by moving ahead or lagging behind. His gate is long and far more graceful than I expected. His head is high and his ears are perked. He looks every bit the proud, purebred canine. *Yeah, and I'm the heiress of Doritos.*

An older, smartly dressed guy doing the whole not jogging, just walking fast thing, moves towards us on the sidewalk. I shift to the side as I have for everyone else when I notice that instead of feigning disinterest, he's ogling me at a level eight point five on my perv-dar.

I'm seventeen, dude! Gross much?

Just as I decide to shame him loud enough for the neighbors to hear, Ugly shouts at him instead! I don't speak dog, but I'm pretty sure that bark decodes to, *Back the fuck off!* And apparently, he gets the memo because he stumbles back then falls into the wet grass, soiling his perfect white shorts.

As we pass him, I smile, and Ugly stares—hard—like he's daring him to say something. My day just keeps getting better and better. I give my real smile to Ugly, imagining the treat I'm going to make him when we get back, so when the leash suddenly gets tight, I'm not expecting it and almost lose my grip.

"Heel!"

He instantly halts, and I am totally delighted. I have never had a pet before, but he makes me think I have been missing out more than I realized... He looks back at me, big golden eyes pleading as he lets out a pathetic little whistle whine. My interest is piqued at his mood change.

"What is it, boy? What do you want?"

Again with the whining. This time a bit more insistent.

"I'm still in charge. But lead on." I don't know how much he understands, but he takes the lead without pulling too hard. I'm pretty curious now that he has us going left, away from the street we were going down. "Where are you taking us?"

One block later the answer becomes clear as he walks me to the most trim-looking park I have ever seen. We pass the playground full of squeals and laughter, and he pays no mind to the beautiful pond with two fat swans. His focus is solely on the patch of land behind it, sectioned off by a fence and a sign featuring a dog outline in three sizes.

The whining is back and he's tugging a little harder. I have to jog to keep up but he's been so good that I don't mind. As we draw closer my enthusiasm about seeing him play is diminished as I notice the rest of the dog owners sectioned off in cliques.

You would think people with dogs and kids in a park on a sunny day would look more friendly. But to me, they look like hungry piranhas teaming up and waiting for the latest piece of gossip. Something about their entire vibe reminds me of the adults I've rubbed shoulders with all my life. The well-attired hopefuls that came to my foster homes, looking for a dream. The ones that thought I was never cute enough, sweet enough, young enough, or whatever enough to earn the right to join in their ranks. After years of rejection, I eventually gave up and decided it was them who weren't good enough for me.

As I catch their attention, I have a moment of panic. I don't have to hear what they're saying to know what they mean. *Who is that? What is she doing here? What is she wearing? Oh dear, oh dear, ...yada, yada.*

I don't belong here, and we all know it. *La-freaking-da*!

Straightening my shoulders, I walk Ugly into the leash-free zone and shut the gate behind us with an audible click. I'm not dimming his day for anyone.

With a devilish smile and no idea what's going to happen, I let Ugly off his leash. I don't think they were expecting it to go down quite like that because audible gasps sound as people instantly react. A man in pink yells out, "Sammy? Sammy, come! Come on, Sammy!" And another much older woman simply gets up to leave, a poodle under each arm. *Seriously? If their feet are too good for dirt, why come to a dog park?*

Looking closer at the angry disrupted flock, I see the telling signs of socialites, divas, and gossips. *This must be the Who's Who in the neighborhood. That's why the old lady comes. No wonder she carries her dogs more like a Prada bag than a pet. They're accessories! ...Well? What better way to make an entrance and introduce ourselves?*

I can't help the laugh that escapes me at the shrieks of the startled owners, as Ugly takes off across the dog park. He beelines straight for the largest assembly of dogs. If you could call *those* dogs. *Poodles, Pomeranians, and Pugs, oh my! Ha!* Some of these breeds I can't recognize, but all of them freeze when they see Ugly rocketing towards them. He doesn't slow down as he nears and lets out a *woof* as they freeze.

At that moment, I see he was doing his own spin on the fast walking, not jogging thing we saw earlier. Because if I thought he was fast before, he is lightning now as he picks up more and more speed the closer he gets to his target. Mother of crap! I'm starting to doubt my bright idea to let the lion play with the canaries when, impossibly, Ugly picks up even more speed and cuts right through the fluffy brigade.

Excited barks and yips greet him and follow him as he runs circles around them. Little butts go in the air and tails do that helicopter thing I'm starting to recognize as a universal "I'm game" signal. They are loving this! Ugly does his thunderous pounce move at the only other large dog I see in there —a full-grown Great Dane with a beautiful spotted coat like a Dalmatian's.

The Dane, a full head shorter than Ugly, gives a wide, toothy grin and pounces back. And just like that, they are off! The other dogs go wild as they give chase to the two. It's as if he's set off the primal urge of their beings, and they shed their genteel training and breeding to go into full-on beast mode. They run as fast as their little feet can carry them—tongues out, tails waving, and literal shit-eating grins on their faces. I didn't know a dog could run that fast, but Ugly outpaces even the Dane by a mile before he circles back.

Most of the furballs have fallen well behind now, unable to keep up or unwilling to go on when their owners are all yelling at them to come back. But some of them, the wild ones, the fighters, and the proud ones, keep up the chase! And just when I think they might catch up to Ugly and the Dane who is now rolling around, making mud, they are off again.

Those dogs are having a party, and I wish I was there because they are not playing around. They're going hard. Dirt flying, grass chunks spraying–snot, drool, mud—and it's on! The owners that couldn't reign their dogs in are now out in the field trying to catch up. They finally get within a few yards, and seeing them, Ugly does his signature crouch and lets out another earth-shaking *woof*! The owners freeze just like the fluffy brigade had. One of them actually put his hands up! And I lose it, laughing so hard my eyes are watering.

And off the dogs go again—running, jumping, chasing. Something about it causes my heart to race. This magnificent, clever, wild beast is a leader. And right now, he is teaching these stuffy dogs about freedom and the power of being an *animal*. To me he's never looked more glorious or beautiful than he does right now.

"Excuse me? *Excuse* me!" A voice pulls me from the moment.

Turning to the silver fox in pink, I wipe my eyes and cough down the rest of my laughter. Before I can say anything, he asks, "Do you have registration for that... That... Exotic animal!?"

I look at him dumbly.

"...Because he does *not* belong here! Large dogs are not allowed in with the small dogs."

"Sorry, I'm a little lost. Is it that he's exotic? Or large?" I look around me and find the sign that has both small dogs and large dogs pictured, I pointedly stare at it. "I don't think his size or breed is the issue here."

"That is the largest Irish Wolfhound I have ever seen! He was not bred in the States, I'm certain of it! And *believe me,* I would know. That breed is made to kill! He's dangerous! Just look at the size of him! One wrong step and he could crush poor Sammy!" His voice goes up to a hysterical pitch on Sammy's name. My eyes follow his finger to a French Bulldog covered in mud, looking as happy as a clam. "I live here, and it's understood between all of us that we do not mix types. " He looks at me as he says this, rather than the dogs. Enunciating the final words as his eyes rake over me.

Angry embarrassment flushes my face as I look from him to the neighbors behind him, who are clearly eavesdropping. "Oh, okay," I say innocently. "I didn't know that. It's so nice of you to tell me the way things are. Otherwise, I might've gone on thinking, it's a beautiful day in the park where everyone is welcome! I had no idea that this park is so special and this—" I gesture to the leash-free zone, "—was so exclusive! Is there a member's fee I wasn't aware of? A club I have to join to be here?"

As the now red-faced man opens his mouth to reply, I put up my hand. "No need. I don't think I'll like this club. It smells. ...Like shit. And there are too many basic bitches." I give him the same once-over he gave me, and eye everyone else as he takes an audible breath. "Don't worry. He will leave. ...Just as soon as you *make* him."

I smile sweetly with that and move past the man and through the loitering throng to recline on the nearest bench. And like I have all the time in the world, I lean my head back to catch some sunrays and close my eyes. Ignoring the death glares and the pandemonium as everyone retreats to get their dogs. Even though I *really* want to see it, I'm too proud to show them I care, so I keep my face serene and my body relaxed.

"Hi." A tiny voice sounds at my side.

I crack open an eyelid and look down. There's a little girl beside me that wasn't there before. She has long, wavy brown hair and big, brown, guileless eyes with freckles to match. Cute kid. She's looking up at me waiting for my response. When I don't offer her one, instead of taking the hint, she smiles, revealing a missing front tooth.

"I'm Maddie and that's my dog." I think she's pointing to the Dane.

"The spotted guy is yours?" Remembering myself, I immediately ask "Where is your mom?" I am happy enough to provoke these walking brand names with their dogs. But I'm not going anywhere near a kid I'm certain no one wants me to be around.

"Mom's oder-der." She points at a big, white house framed by columns, reminding me a little of the White House. It's not more than eight yards from the park, but I don't care how close the house is or how fancy this park is. *Who the hell leaves their kid alone in a park?*

"She has a head ouch," Maddy continues.

"A headache?"

"Yeah! She lets Petunia take me to the park."

"Where is Petunia?" I ask a little worriedly. I do *not* want to get in trouble for talking to a kid, but I'm relieved she's at least with someone. I look around us, but everyone seems busy catching their dogs or has left already.

"Der she is!" She points again to the Dane.

"Your *dog* is Petunia?" I ask in disbelief.

"Your dog is in love wiff my dog and der going to get married."

"What?" Startled from my thoughts, I look down at her again.

"Our dogs! Der getting married!" She points again with a big, gappy grin.

Looking over at them, it's as if Petunia can feel my eyes on her. Her head goes up and her eyes reach mine instantaneously. Spinning off from Ugly, she runs to us, breaking into a trot as she nears. Ugly follows closely behind. While Petunia isn't quite as tall as Ugly, she's still huge and intimidating up close.

She approaches me slowly, and I have the feeling she's behaving because her girl is right next to me. I bravely let her sniff my hand and a good portion of the rest of me. When her nosy wet nose finds its way to my neck, I giggle, and Petunia sits back, apparently satisfied with her search.

Ugly comes and sits beside her and we now have two massive dogs grinning and staring at us. *Some guard dog you are.* I roll my eyes at him.

Regarding Petunia again, I think maybe she's not such a bad babysitter after all.

"I'm Alex," I tell the girl. "Do you know Ugly?

"Yeah, our dogs play in my yard. He doesn't come *here!*" She is laughing at me before she finishes what she's saying.

Looks like I actually have broken some unspoken rule. "You know Dill?" I ask her. She looks at me in question. "I mean Pickle?"

"Yes! I like Pickle. He brings Ugly to play!"

"How old are you?"

"I'm five!" she tells me proudly.

I feel protective of her and I really don't like that she's only here with Petunia. "How often does Petunia take you to the park?"

"I come wiff her on school days and play wiff my brothers on weekends."

Oh, lovely. More spawn for these parents to neglect. I look over to the fancy, white house and contemplate how abuse can take on all forms. "When do you usually come to the park?"

"We go when the clock hits the twelve and the five."

"Great! How about you ask your Mom if Ugly and I can meet you in your yard tomorrow to play, or go to the park? Tell her I'm Dill's—sorry—*Pickle's* dog walker, Alex." I have to exercise Ugly every day anyway. Letting him play with his wifey and making sure this girl has an extra pair of eyes on her is an easy decision.

"Tomorrow? Or always?"

"If it's okay with your mom, on weekdays for as long as I can," I say, smiling at her.

"Okay! I'm going to ask her now!" She hops up to leave, and I stand too, securing Ugly back to his leash.

"How about I walk you home and meet your Mom?" I loath to meet the kind of woman that leaves her kid to play out in a park alone, but I know it's safer if she meets me.

"No, she can't be disturbed wiff a head ouch."

"Okay, well, how about I just walk you across the street then, and you can ask her later like our first plan?"

"Okay!" And with the trust of a kid that has never faced evil, she grabs my hand.

CHAPTER 4

The days have sped into months, and I have found a rhythm at the manor. My weekdays consist of organizing, books, gardening, music, food, and walks with Maddy. My weekends are more chaotic with tagging along to occasional gigs with Dill, barbecues with his endless stream of friends, jam sessions, and learning my way around Green Mont.

I'm surprised to find the ease at which I've settled into this new life. I never pictured myself in a fancy manner. Let alone feeling at home in one. But then again, I never knew I liked dogs or kids or bikers, but I'm liking these things an awful lot lately. And oddly enough, they seem to like me too.

I was finally able to get in touch with Vic in July using a burner phone. She promised everything was back to normal and said everyone missed me. For her safety, I didn't tell her where I am, and she never asked. I have missed her and Shells every single day since leaving and even though I am surrounded by new friends, I still feel the loss of having confidants my own age. Though most of the time I'm able to push the melancholy away with work.

I have never much trusted adults before, but Dill is a rare breed and our personalities complement the others in a surprising way. He doesn't ask me too many questions, and we give each other the space we need to let our guard down. Most nights are spent with sub-par food, beer, bad jokes, and jamming.

He thought it was pretty cool I could play the piano and guitar. I can actually play most things pretty well once I learn the machinations of them. But with no real purpose other than to relax me or make a buck on the street. I never thought too much of it. But Dill seems to love it, so our nights have become ritualized by jam sessions and trading music.

Dill's friends and bandmates are over most weekends. The front yard used to get littered in bikes, but I finally started making the pack of animals park them on the driveway or down the street, like civilized folk. I just figured it would be a shame to have a grand house with a mud lot for a front yard. Especially when the back is so spectacular!

It turned out there is, in fact, a pool in the back and it's been my saving grace. With the serious heatwave happening this August, nothing has beaten the pool in terms of cooling off. There is also a pond, eighteen rose bushes, four orange trees, three bonsais, two bridges, one gazebo, tons of flowers, and tons more I can't name. And now, thanks to me, another hammock so that even Dill hangs out in the back more. The place was an over-grown mess when I started working on it, but now it's my little slice of paradise.

Kind of like all the work I have been putting into the office. Only, instead of paradise, it's more like hell. I can totally see why Dill was overwhelmed. I have been going extra hard on it because until I can get the paperwork organized for everything Dill wants to sell, I can't make any money. And that would be no BFD except that I need to get the final repairs done on Marty. I'm two hundred dollars shy. And even though

Dill knows a couple of guys at the garage and got me a friendly discount... It's still a major lack of independence that I'm missing.

Dill and I have taken to alternating meals. He's a decent chef, and I'm getting better, even though breakfast for dinner is still my specialty... And he usually cooks something involving red meat and sauce—even for breakfast. And weirdly enough, it works for us both.

Ugly has slept in front of my door every night since I arrived. In the mornings, I find him sitting there waiting for me like I'm the best thing since mac 'n' cheese. He's definitely grown on me... In-fact, I might actually be trading in my obsession with unicorns for this Wolfhound. Turns out he's way cooler.

∞

It's my day off and it's sweltering out. I just finished with the pool and am getting ready to take Ugly out. Dill has a show tonight and I am running into town to pick up a cord for him at the music store. It's too far to walk in this heat, so I'm strapping Ugly into his harness. It's a rig I constructed myself to meet Ugly's *demand* that he goes where I go. And my need to travel farther than walking distance.

Before the harness was born, Ugly and I experimented with a series of tether systems. At first, I tried riding a bike while having him on his leash. That was a disaster that ended in scraped knees and one very traumatized Ugly who thought he had hurt me. After that, he wouldn't go anywhere near the bike, so that was out. Then, I tried the scooter one of Dill's friends loaned to me. I ended up having to pay for the busted thing on the first day.

Another friend of his donated a skateboard thinking that would be harder to trash, and it would be hilarious if Ugly became the next skateboarding sensation. The idea being that I could trail behind him on my own board. But Ugly thought it was a chew toy, and out went that bright idea. So, his board became mine and though it had been a while since I had been on a board, the moment it was under my feet it all came back. The next step was keeping us together and utilizing his speed and energy. Skateboarding with his leash around his neck didn't allow me to maneuver properly and didn't feel good to him. I figured out a back harness was a much better option, and the rest came pretty naturally.

It's our game now to communicate through subtle tugs of the leash with as few words as possible. And we have gotten pretty good at it too. These days we go *fast*. I'm learning to take the curbs tighter and tighter, and it feels natural when we catch air or need to come to a swift stop. I have total trust in Ugly, and he does me. And that's how we ride the wind and get into town in record time.

We slow down as we arrive at Main Street. "Music store" is all I say to his perked ears and in that direction we go. I'll never really know if he's a genius that understands English better than most... Or a genius that reads minds better than most. Either way, he's a total genius, and there is no hesitation as he leads us to the front of the shop then stops. Kicking up my board, I rub his ears. "Good boy! How are you so damn smart?!"

He looks at me with a big toothy grin and attempts to lick. "No! You know that's against the rules! You give me cooties, and you don't get treaties!" He barks at that, and I laugh while I secure him to a light post.

"Don't frighten any of the customers, and I'll get you ice cream after this."

He eagerly wags his tail, and his ears perk back up. I have just uttered two of his favorite words. "Yes, *ice cream*. *Two* scoops if you're good and don't bark when you get bored."

I give him my serious face but it's hard because he's still giving me his dopy grin. Reaching in my bag I pull out his bowl and fill it with water. He huffs out his version of "thanks" and attacks it.

I don't take long in the store. For once they have the right cord in stock. Walking out as I stuff the supply into my bag, I find Ugly right where I left him. He stands and starts to do a little impatient foot dance thing. He knows exactly where we are going next. It's become our ritual to get ice cream together when he takes me to town. He may actually love the stuff more than me and I *love* ice cream!

I immediately recognize the fancy cars parked out front and sigh. I was bound to cross paths with them at some point. I've been avoiding these particular cars because of who they belong to. The other teens here make me nervous enough as it is. But these teens? These are the beauty queens, prom kings, and their entourage of the most popular and privileged. And next to them? I feel like yesterday's leftovers. Every school in America has this group of name-brand terrorists. And I am very familiar with exactly how welcoming they can be.

But... I can't deny Ugly his ice cream treat. Letting out a breath and completely on edge, I secure him outside the shop. He must sense my change in mood because instead of his usual hopping happy dance, he's subdued. I look down at him and try to stand taller. "We got this."

Walking inside, a blast of cool air hits me and I'm immediately aware of how sweaty I am in my damp, sticking tank top. Then I start thinking about all of my other little malfunctions. My wild, wind-swept hair that I wish I had pulled into a bun. My tattered jean shorts that are barely holding themselves together with *actual* wear and tear. Not the kind you buy for a statement. My dirty hand-me-down Converse sneakers. I don't know if every eye in the room is actually on me, or if I'm just being paranoid. But it feels that way.

With my shoulders back, I remove my sunglasses and walk up to the line before the counter and studiously ignore the eyes boring holes into my back. There are only two people in front of me but being surrounded by students from the other side of the fence, has my teeth grinding. It's not that I care so much what they think; it's just that I know how they operate. They find insecurity you have, and they pull at it like a thread, and they keep pulling until you eventually unravel. And I'm just here trying to lay low and not punch a tool in the face today.

Sweat drips between my shoulder blades and absorbs into my tank top. I try to relax my jaw and then the rest of my body and not adjust my shirt or hair. Because how pathetic would that be? Besides, anxiety is blood in the water to these sharks and I need to calm the fuck down. *Why should I care what these people think anyway?* The mental unpacking of my discomfort halts long enough for me to step forward as the next customer moves up to the cashier. Only one more ice cream loving fool to go, and then I can make my order and get the hell out of here. I inwardly cringe as the lady in front of me starts counting out a pile of change.

Above the quiet snickering and whispers behind me, a voice rises above. "Hey."

I know it's for me, I know it. But I ignore it anyway, feigning ignorance and wishing I had thought to pop in my headphones before walking in here. Unfortunately, he doesn't give up. "Hey you. Red hair." The woman in front of me spills some of her change. Relieved at the reprieve, I kneel and start gathering it up for her. One of the quarters leads me to a foot. *Don't look up.* A hand reaches down for the change just as mine reaches across for it, and we collide.

"I have it." That voice... I instinctively look up and am greeted by two of the greenest eyes I have ever seen. We only pause like that for a second. But it's a *long* second. Unexpected heat blooms over me and a new layer of perspiration beads over my skin. His blond hair slips forward and full lips pull into a smile. Not wanting to stare, I mumble, "Thanks," and stand up, quickly moving away from him, to give everything back to the lady, who loses the count she was in the midst of, and starts over again. *Damnit!*

"What's with Master Splinter out there?" One of the guys wearing the universal Jock jacket hollers at me. With no other reasonable options, I turn fully around and finally check out the two tables that have been doing the same to me. And sure enough, it's the poster board for teen vogue. I focus in on the fellow ginger who asked.

"Master Splinter?"

"You know," He nods at Ugly through the window, "The talking jumbo rat from *Teenage Mutant Ninja Turtles*?" He's already chortling at his joke.

Make fun of me. Make fun of my clothes or my hair or even my miserable life, but *do not* make fun of Ugly.

"You actually watched that?" I try to keep the challenge out of my voice but can't help the somewhat condescending grin that spreads across my face just before I turn around to order my ice cream. A couple of the others are snickering now. I wonder if it's Green Eyes.

"Yeah. Along with everyone else on Planet Earth. Where have *you* been?" I turn back around and see that his cheeks are growing splotchy. Point for me.

Before I can respond, Green Eyes speaks up. "I didn't see it." And just like that, the tide shifts. All of the focus going back on Ginger Jock and the teasing begins. ...The thing about sharks? They're cannibals. They eat their own kind.

Still smiling, I take my cone of ice cream and Ugly's cup and pause before exiting. "Oh, and the *rat* you're referring to? He's a pure bread Irish Wolfhound in his prime. Where have you been?"

The door jingles behind me as I step back out into the heat feeling vastly better. "Look what I have for you!" I adjust Ugly's leash so he can sit with me on the bench outside of the shop. With the jacket-wearing crew's attention diverted, I'm able to sit back and relax. Who wears jackets in this kind of heat anyway? Is making a statement really that important?

I'm holding his cup for him in one hand and licking my cone in the other when the Jacket Crew comes out, unfortunately it seems, to join us.

"Is he friendly?"

I'm surprised when Ugly stops licking long enough to check out the guy who asked. I follow suit and see nothing but beautiful, caramel skin and matching caramel eyes. This guy is a hulk! And sexy too.

"If he likes you."

He makes no move to come closer as his friends pile behind him. Ugly goes back to licking the cup and ignores him. I know he's down to scoop two when I hear him snort. I got him hazelnut for the second flavor, his favorite. I feel oddly calm with him, even though I'm basically surrounded.

As if from a distance, I note the peculiar way in which my body reacts to this group. Chills race over my arms and down my back and legs. As they close in on me, my hackles rise even further. But even as the primal end of my instincts go haywire, the giant ice cream monster next to me has me grounded and secure.

Green Eyes steps forward and speaks up, "I haven't seen you around here. Are you new?"

Crap. And here comes the inquisition within minutes of meeting these people. Nosey *much?* "Relatively."

"Oh my god! He's so *big!*" says a cute blonde in the name brand version of my shorts.

"That's what she said." Ginger Jock rebounds quickly, and the guys start laughing while blonde just rolls her eyes.

"Are you going to school here?" Ginger Jock asks while Hulk reaches in slow to pet Ugly.

I don't think Ugly will do anything but still...

"Not while he's eating," I warn. And then look back at Ginger Jock. "No."

He puts up his hands at my terse response. "Okay, just trying to be friendly."

A girl with cotton candy pink and pale blonde hair with a purse too small to fit a phone in, comes forward, "It's too hot out here, and *that's* totally grossing me out!" She gestures to the ice cream dripping down my arm from Ugly's current assault on what's left in his cup. In perfect timing, he finishes with it and starts licking my wrist.

Normally at this point I would stop him. But the horrified look on her face is priceless. I look up at her with a smirk, "Problem solved." Then lick the sides of my own cone to keep it from dripping. Ugly whimpers, drawing my attention, and he licks his lips at what's left of my ice cream. "Don't be a pig! You already *hoovered* yours." I chuckle as he huffs, and the Hulk goes in again to pet him. *Brave guy*. I'll give him that.

"I don't think so." The girl responds snidely, giving me an intentionally slow once over with her eyes as if to say my problem is totally *not* solved.

If I show her weakness now, I might as well be giving her permission to run all over me. "Do I know you?"

"I should think not."

"Then what's with the attitude?"

Ginger Jock guffaws at that. "That's not an attitude! That's her!" A few more of the crew laugh at that but they stop when she looks at them. Turning back to me, a creepy smile settles across her pretty face.

"What school are you going to?"

I have no idea where she is going with this, but I'm sure it's nowhere good. "Not to your school."

"Well *obviously*. The wait list to get into *my* school is a mile long."
She flips her hair. "I meant what *public* school are you going to?"

Riiight. I was wondering how long it would take someone from this
Jacket crew to bring up money or start digging for information on the
new girl in town. The first of which is only mildly annoying, but the latter is potentially dangerous. Time to shut this social hour down. "To be
honest, I don't know what school you go to and I don't care. I wish I
could say I'm flattered that you do, but I don't like you and I don't want
to get to know you. So how about we cut this little meet and greet short
and you go back to... Whatever it was you were doing, and I'll go back
ignoring you?"

Ginger Jock might as well be a paid commentator with his commit-
ment to narration. "Whoa, she's feisty. ...And I like it. Look out Sarah!"

Sarah's smile goes cold at the round of laughter that ensues and she
steps up and leans over me. —Like she's actually trying to intimidate me
or something. But then the most unexpected thing happens as her stick-
thin body gets closer. My already hyped up instincts go into hyper drive
and every intuition I have is suddenly blaring; DANGER, RUN, DAN-
GER... I can now smell her overly sweet perfume... And maybe something else... Just underneath it all...

"It's a shame you're new."

Thrown off balance I immediately take the bait. "Why?"

"Because someone would have warned you there are two things you
never do in this town." She ticks off her fingers in front of my face to
illustrate. "One, you never drink the tap water. Because grrr-oss. And
two... You never, and I mean *never*, make an enemy of anyone in my
circle. ...It's such a shame th..."

Ugly sneezes, ice cream and snot spray all over Sarah. My eyes bulge, and after a beat of shocked silence, all of my non-sensical instincts are forgotten as I burst into laughter. She's still frozen in horror, which just makes it funnier. I glance over at Ugly who is smiling, and I would bet *money* he did that on purpose! Without ceremony, I give him what's left of my cone.

"Oh. My. God!" She wipes her face then looks down at her outfit, holding up her soiled pink handbag. "This. Is. *Gucci!*" she spits the brand name at me like it's a weapon.

"Yes. And I'm pretty sure that was Karma," I serenely respond.

The cute blonde pipes in before Sarah can commit the murder her eyes are promising. "Come on Sarah, Joel can get that out before it stains. It smells here anyway," she says, lifting her nose at me.

"It's not the dog," Hulk says. "You smell like hazelnuts." He's now scratching under Ugly's cheeks with both hands. "Don't you? Hazelnuts." He looks at me. "Strawberries." Uncomfortable, I glance at Ugly who is leaning into Hulks massive hands. *Traitor.*

"We *know* it's not the *dog.*" Sarah seethes, glaring at me. And for just a second I swear I see her eyes flash at me as bright as an LED. What the hell!? But as soon as I blink her unnatural eyes are back to normal and she's turning away to storm off with the cute blonde. I look around to see if anyone else noticed, but more of the mob is following her lead and dispersing.

"What's his name?" Hulk distracts me.

"Ugly," I absently respond, still watching Sarah's retreating form as she gets into an SUV with jerky, angry movements.

"Seriously?! And you had a problem with the *rat* reference?" Ginger Jock asks incredulously.

I repeat my earlier question, "Do you *know* him?" I gesture to Ugly.

"No..."

"Then you don't get to tease him."

"His name is really Ugly?" Green Eyes has a sultry voice, and it's honestly hard to look at him for too long.

"Yeah, I didn't name him, but he seems to like it." I chuckle when Ugly looks over at me adoringly. He's finished my cone.

The white SUV pulls forward to stop across from us and the passenger window comes down. Shining pink and blonde waves spill out as Sarah directs her gaze on green eyes... "*Ash*, are you guys *coming*? We're going to Ella's."

Green Eyes turns around to face her. "Yeah, see you there."

I take that moment to get up and prep Ugly for our trip back, and for some reason I'm feeling a little self-conscious about the harness.

Green Eyes, -*Ash*, turns back around to regard me. "What's that?" he asks.

Hulk leans in closer to get a look.

"It's how we leave." I step on my skateboard and without having to ask, Ugly takes off and saves me from any awkward goodbyes or commentary from Sarah.

∞

The manor is filled with the sounds of hustle and bustle as Dill, his bandmates, and I organize for tonight's gig. Double-checking my reflection in the mirror, I de-clump a bit of mascara. The insecurity that I look younger than I want to only ever bothers me at Dill's gigs. It's not that they card me. They always leave me alone when I'm with him. It's standing around next to everyone else who is at least four years older, that stresses me.

I figured out that by pulling the sides of my hair behind my ears and leaving the top with volume to fall back, I look more sophisticated. Add in a smoky eye and some light contouring and my age becomes vaguer. I don't own a lot of clothes, but Dill never noticed until his last gig that I wore the same thing every time. He told me I could wear whatever I wanted from around the house. So today is the first time I'm taking him up on the offer. Feeling oddly hesitant about going through his grandmother's things, I opted for his Grandad's instead. That man honestly had style.

I'm wearing his black blazer with my white crop top, jean shorts, and black combat boots. The jacket is oversized on me but just like my worn-out shorts, I think it looks intentional in a good way.

Dill shouts the same question I have heard a hundred times from a floor up. "You have the cord?"

"Yes, it's already packed. You ready to go?"

"I've been ready! I'm waiting for *you*..."

"You're worse than a *girl* Pickle!"

"I resent that!"

Arch, the drummer downstairs pipes in and yells... "Nooo, you *resemble* that!"

Rolling my eyes, I shout at both of them, "You guys are adorable! Now can we get the hell out of here?"

CHAPTER 5

The familiar smell of cigarettes and beer greets me as we start unloading equipment onto the stage. It's been years since anyone was allowed to smoke inside, but the scent has soaked deep into the wood and walls from decades of reveling. The scent is now a signature of "The Bar".

"Put that down," Dill instructs over the din of chattering customers, clanking glasses and crooning indie pop. He has some old-fashioned notion about me lifting things. But still, every show I do what I can to help. And every show he insists I go mingle and enjoy myself. I'm a feminist at heart, and I know his notions should offend me more—and from anyone else they would—but deep down, the discarded kid in me preens at his misguided, if not sweet, consideration.

I also know he's begun to notice the lack of friends my own age and cares enough to want me to make some. What he doesn't understand, and what I can't explain to him, is that I can't afford to have any close friends. The *last* thing I need is someone digging into my personal life.

Dill's band, The Givers, is a favorite amongst the locals, and so is The Bar, making for a packed Friday night. I move to the stairs, wanting to get to our booth before it becomes any more packed. But the booker of The Bar, Colin, meets me at the top with a waitress in tow. She has a tray full of drinks, and before he opens his mouth, I'm already talking.

"Gin and tonic there. Whiskey sour there. The beers are for Dill and Marv over there. And this is for me," I say, plucking the mojito from the tray. "Water?"

"On the way. You want some for your booth as well? Chief Nanas are up next, and I know you guys will want to stick around and check them out." I have to lean in to hear the last part.

"Sounds good! You guys are already packed!" I shout, over the tuning and testing of instruments on stage. I'm not a big drinker but holding one helps to blend in and ward off the older creepers who would otherwise offer to buy me one. "Same booth as last time?"

"Yea! And no problem!" He says with a wink and passes me with the waitress.

Since moving in with Dill, music has become a surprising force in my life. I always appreciated it, but it's different now. Somewhere along the lines, it's become a passion. Which is a strange thing to consider when I think about how focused I was just on surviving. Not that long ago I was the girl that made fun of dream chasers. Though as impractical and useless as these budding fantasies are, I can't help but wonder about it as I look at Dill tuning his guitar.

He told me once that he and the boys don't play because they think one day they will hit big or get rich. He said they do it because in a crazy world it's the only thing that makes any sense to them.

I like it, my friends like it, and so we keep doing it. If that ever changes, I'll stop doing it. His humble words resonated for me because he made it sound so simple—practical even—to share something he loved.

And it's not just about the music for me... It's the honesty of a loud, belligerent crowd quieting down because suddenly something bigger than the individual connects them all and compels them... Holding them suspended in the motion of sound. Sometimes it looks as if a big invisible hand reaches out and softly pushes a milling crowd towards the stage. I would never say it out loud but to me, there's something magical about how a single person, or a handful of people, can hold and enthrall countless beings.

And then there is the transformation that comes over the musicians themselves. When Dill plays, a different part of his spirit rises and comes out onto the stage. An otherwise soft-spoken and humble guy turns into a confident, charismatic heartthrob in seconds. It's like any doubt, any worries he might have had, just disappear for the span of his set. He's himself up there in a way that he can't be otherwise. It's inspiring to see.

It makes me wonder what it would *feel* like to be free like that in front of so many people. To be sort of naked in a way and not care. I've *always* cared. I've always been embarrassed, and I've always felt uncomfortable in my own skin. My friends have told me I'm beautiful, but they are my *friends,* and most of the time I just feel awkward and like I don't belong. But up there, on stage, it's like you can be anyone and hold the world in your hand for just a moment.

Shaking myself out of my reverie, I look back over the crowd and can't believe what I'm seeing. There, by the entrance, is the Jacket Crew filtering in. But how? *Oh right*, they can afford fake IDs and are just confident enough to pull them off. Dodging them for the rest of the night is going to be such fun!

Still, at the top of the stairs, I have a decent view and can see which of them have come. Searching... I go still as a pair of green eyes ensnare mine. And there is that inexplicable charge between us. The kind that drowns everything else—*everyone else*— out.   Swearing under my breath, I force myself to look away and sip my mojito. It goes down wrong and I rush the rest of the way down the stairs to sputter and cough without his eyes on me. *Smooth Alex.*

Winding my way through the crowd, two things are clear. The first being that tonight has taken a definite turn, and the other that green eyes, -Ash... My mind gets caught on his name and the thought abruptly ends.

I make it through the crowd to the band's booth and pocket the little "reserved" sign as I slide in. It's the best seat in the house and no one usually bothers me from here. Taking a deep breath, I relax a little. I pull out Dill's camera from my bag and double-check that the battery is fully charged. I am checking the band out through the lens and messing with its settings when a familiar voice halts me.

"We meet again."

I slowly turn away from the stage and set the camera down. I'm prepared this time for the jolt his nearness sends through me, but no less affected as it happens. My thoughts are interrupted when I realize he's talking to me.

"So what is it?"

"What is what?"

"Your name?" He's smiling at me now.

"Sorry, it's hard to hear in here."

"What?"

I move to the edge of the booth and stand up so he can hear me. "It's hard to hear in here!" I say next to his face.

He moves in so our bodies are almost flush and his lips brush against my ear as he softly asks, *"What?"*

Okay. I am in sooo much trouble. Unnerved, I think to move back but there is nowhere to go. He has expertly trapped me between him and the booth. And the *smell* of him! This close, his effect on me is not even fair. But my stupid pride won't let me back down. I risk looking up into his face.

"It's Alex." I'm trying my best to sound confident in the midst of his sheer beauty.

"Alex." He says it slowly. Testing the name out while he searches my face. His lips line up perfectly with my eyes and my gaze gets caught there.

"Ash! However did you win us these seats?" Sarah comes up behind him and runs her hand over his shoulder before seeing me. The moment she does her voice changes. "Are you *serious*?"

Ella and another girl I don't recognize come up behind her. "OMG, *stalk* much?"

I decide not to mention that *they* came to *me*. It's too easy. "You guys take this whole mean girls thing a little too seriously." I sit and scoot back further into the booth behind me just as the rest of the Jacket Crew crowds around. Deja vu much? "This is actually my booth."

Scooting into the other side, Sarah lays her chin on her linked fingers and says sweetly, "No, I'm pretty sure this is *our* booth. You're confused, honey. This space is for hot bitches *only*."

A deep voice cuts through our convo. "You're out." I look up and see Jake, the bouncer, eyeing Sarah, who falters. I'm a bad person for enjoying this. But it's nice to have something this entitled snob wants.

"*Who* are you?" she says looking at me in question.

"I'm their manager," I say, casually gesturing to the band. I'm more like their lackey, but she doesn't need to know that.

"*You're* the manager of The Givers?" One of the guys moves forward to get a better look at me. "*They're lit!*"

"Yes, and this is our booth," I add, looking back at Sarah, trying—and probably failing—not to look smug.

"You are so full of shit." Sarah starts laughing at me along with the other girls who join in just a tad late.

"*No...*" Jake's bored voice interrupts Sarah once again. "*S*he is with the band. *You* are not. *You* can leave her booth now, or you and your friends can leave The Bar. Your choice." I know Jake from Dill's occasional barbecues and jam fests. Like so many others, he detailed Jake's bike and they formed a friendship. I have only ever known Jake to be a big teddy bear but tonight he is all business.

Sarah draws my attention back to her. "You know what? I don't like the view here anyway." She flicks her manicured hand at me while simultaneously swishing her perfect hair and leaves the booth.

But before they completely disperse, Jake mutters "Sexy bitches only." I crack up... Until I see Sarah leaving with her arm around Ash. I guess that's, that. I want to be relieved, but the little ache in my chest is impossible to miss. I give Jake a little wave goodbye with a nod of thanks.

Just then the band starts their first song. I grab Dill's camera, happy for the distraction.

"You really don't care, do you." Hulk is leaning on the table.

Sighing, I set the camera back down. "Where did you come from?"

"Oh, I was here. Your bouncer friend just didn't see me."

I take note of his size and find that hard to believe. "Care about what?"

"About any of it. ...Sarah. Her crew."

"You mean the Jacket Crew?"

He falters for a moment, then starts laughing. "You're calling us the *Jacket Crew*?"

"Oh come on! Wearing your Letterman jackets during the hottest part of the day was already a statement. But *here?* You all just got in with fake IDs and you're wearing your high school jackets! I can't tell if it's stupid or ballsy. Either way, you guys earned the moniker!" Taking no offense, he chuckles and looks a little too proud.

"So *those* are your friends huh?" I know it's a lame question but even though he looks like the scariest of the bunch, I am getting the impression that he might actually be the nicest. Even Ugly liked him. It begs the question, why those jerks?

"Yeah. We all grew up together. Our parents did the same." He shrugs it off like growing up together and parental relationships are synonymous with friendship. But far be it from me to judge how family's and normal teens operate. "What's your name?"

"Alex. Yours?" I make sure to say it loud enough for him to hear.

"It's Nicholas but everyone calls me Nick."

"Nice to meet you, Nick." He nods and looks at me for a moment. "What?"

"Nothing it's just... Usually, Sarah reduces other girls to tears when she doesn't like them. But with you ... I swear, I think she might be the one to cry first." He shakes his head, with a mystified expression on his face.

I get what he's saying and that he means it as a weird sort of compliment... But I can't shake his comment about Sarah making other girls cry. I *hate* bullies. Probably because I had to deal with so many growing up. And I am not a big fan of those that stand by and watch it happen either. It makes me want to distance myself from him and dims some of the glow around Ash.

"Sorry to disappoint you. I'm not much of a cryer. And girls like Sarah? She's just another insecure twit, trying to make everyone else feel beneath her so she can act like she's above it all. That's not cool. But honestly? Neither are you for standing by while she treats people that way. You actually seem nice, but at the end of the day you're just as guilty as she is."

Stunned silence greets me, and I guess I'm a little stunned myself. I mean, why even bother? I don't know this guy.

"You talk like you know her," Ash says. Surprised, I look over and see him. *How long have you been here?* But I'm undeterred.

"I have met lots of Sarahs in my life, and this one is no different. I stare at him silently for a moment, oddly disappointed. And then flick my eyes back to Nick the Hulk. "You guys should go. Jake is circling the room and will be back. If he sees you here, he will kick you out."

Ash's voice pulls me back to him and I see an odd smile has softened his features. "Sarah is more different than you know. You would do well to avoid her. ...To avoid all of us." With that stinging comment landed, he nods at Nick and some kind of unspoken communication passes between them. Without even looking back at me, Nick leaves just as silently as he came. I can't tell if I made him mad or hurt his feelings. I doubt it was the latter. I have no idea why I gave him such a hard time. But if it keeps these guys away from me and out of my business, it's for the best.

"That was harsh."

Feeling angry and defensive, I look back at Ash.

"You're *still* here?" When he doesn't respond to my barb, I take a breath and steel myself. "No. *That* wasn't harsh. That was *truth*, and it's not personal. Harsh would be if I told you that you have shit taste in women. That I don't even *know* you, but I think less of you for hanging around her."

A moment of silence passes, and then he laughs. His smile too sharp. "No one gives a shit about what you think! You're right. You don't know me. You don't know Nick *or* Sarah. It's weird that you would have any personal thought about any of us at all." His eyes grow intense. "Why do you care?"

I'm all out of steam and feeling completely unsure of myself at this point, so I do what any self-respecting girl in my position would do. I stall. "What?"

He leans in closer so I can hear him, and an idea catches me. "Why do *you* care?"

"What?!" I yell above the music.

Frustrated now, he gets into the booth with me and right next to my face, asks, "Why do you care?"

Leaning in very close to him, just like he did with me, I whisper in his ear in the same seductive way he did, "I... Don't."

He pulls back and looks at me then, and I can't help the audacious smile that spreads across my face at his startled expression. But then, something in his face changes and I forget about everything as heat erupts between us.

A throat clearing pulls both of our attention away from each other and I see Jake has made his round. "Is he bothering you?"

"He was just leaving." Forcing my smile back in place, I move back into my booth as Ash retreats without a word. "Thanks, Jake."

"Any time."

As Jake also leaves, I muse that my "fuck it" attitude has gotten more pronounced over time. Somewhere along the line, I stopped pissing myself every time someone didn't like me or came at me. And I have always been an unstoppable shit talker, but now... I don't know... I actually *feel* some of the confidence to back it up. Maybe that's just what happens when you go through real-life struggles; the small things become less and less significant. I have never been an optimist, but the realization that there might be some silver lining to the hell that I have been through makes something inside me feel like it's beginning to shift.

Shrugging it off, I take a sip of my mojito and reel it all back into logic. It's a lot easier to fight Goliath when you know there is nothing he can do to hurt you. I don't go to school with the Jacket Crew which means there is no backlash. I don't ever have to see them again if I don't want to. Not soon enough for them to even remember me anyways. Ash will have forgotten about me by tomorrow I'm sure. That thought, which was meant to be reassuring, totally deflates me.

∞

Dill's set is well into their most popular songs, and I'm absorbed in my self-made role of photographer. I'm taking shots that include the room when I catch something through my lens that has me faltering. Zooming in, I curse and look for Jake.

Sarah and her friends, who normally stick together like glue, have left one of their compatriots passed out at a table. Normally passed out patrons are woken up and asked to leave, but Jake is nowhere in sight. And this girl, Ella, I think it is -has two guys that I'm certain she doesn't know, holding her limp body up and posing it while taking pictures. *Creeps!*

It doesn't look like they have moved on to anything lewd yet, but if they have crossed this line, I don't doubt they will get to the next line soon enough. Scanning the room again for Jake I find he's MIA. Worse yet, everyone else is slammed. Looking back at Ella, I see one of the guys is now touching her leg. Without any thought, I throw myself into the crowd and move through the room as quickly as I can. But for every two people I push past, one pushes back. I'm not tall enough to see what's going on at the table anymore, and I'm trying not to panic. All the while I keep looking for Jake, or anyone of this girl's so-called friends.

Right now it doesn't matter how rude this girl was, or who her friends are. Only that they are not there and she is alone. Right now, she might as well be my best friend or any one of my sisters from my group home. She could even be me... Or any other women who are not impervious to this kind of bullshit! I'm furious enough to forget all common sense by the time I reach her table—her *empty* table. *Shit!*

Fear spreads through my body as does the panic I was fighting. This is not happening tonight! I dash the rest of the way to the table not caring about the people I'm moving over. I climb up onto the chair she was just in and once again scan the room, praying that I can find her or someone to help.

There! Just by the exit, I see a flash of pale blonde hair and the familiar outline of one of the guys just before the door closes behind them. With my heart in my throat, I make it to the exit in record time and burst through the door. I run down the empty alley and straight into the parking lot. I am so relieved to see them still there; I don't even assess the danger.

The two guys are half lifting, half dragging her little body. The horrible scene has me instantly nauseous. And I hardly register the angry tears stinging my eyes. Other than us, the lot is completely deserted. And not for the first time, I wonder where the hell her friends are. Feeling utterly helpless now, I look around me for something, *anything*, that might help. Then I remember my camera! It's still around my neck.

Wasting no more time, I shout at them. "Hey *perverts!* Say cheese!"

They stop in their tracks, and with Ella still held up between them, they turn around just in time for me to snap two shots. *Flash, flash, mother fucker!*

"I'm going to make sure my Uncle Cole and his friends at the local jail here take *real* good care of you. After I send copies to the police, your work, your family, and your friends! Thank you Facebook facial recognition!" I'm not even fully aware of everything I'm saying, the bullshit is flowing out so fast. All I know is I need to stall them while a better plan forms or someone else comes outside to see what they are doing, and maybe even help. I continue with my litany of shit talk with all the gusto and confidence of a born politician.

They are still blessedly frozen for a moment, and the look on their faces is almost comical. Almost. But the sight of Ella's vulnerable form between them is anything but.

"Give me your fucking camera!" The one that shouts at me lets her go and takes a threatening step towards me. Thundering footsteps sound behind me on the gravel and I can only hope that it's help and not more friends of theirs. Not taking any chances, I use the precious moment of distraction and run at the pervert full speed ahead. I flash my camera as many times as I can to disorient him even more, just before tackling him to the ground. The first thing I do is put my street skills to work, nabbing his phone and wallet.

Before I am able to do anything more, big hands drag me off of him like I weigh nothing. I am just beginning to struggle when I see Ash has replaced me. Unfortunately for Ash, the element of surprise has been lost and now the guy is up and holding a knife. Fear clutches me for Ash and I turn around and see it's Nick holding me.

"Help him!" Ginger Jock is already chasing after loser number two and I shout at him next. "Make sure you get his phone! They were taking pictures of her!" Not taking my eyes off of Ash and knife guy I try to shrug Nick off. "Let me go! I'm good!"

As soon as his grasp loosens, I'm running to Ella's crumpled body. Quickly checking her for injuries, I pull her into my lap when I find none. The guy holding the knife lunges at Ash and my heart leaps into my throat. Ash spins out of his way with such grace my mouth falls open and somehow the knife winds up in Ash's hand. I'm so stunned by the speed that it takes me a moment to realize Ash's eyes have become impossibly bright. Almost glowing. *No*, they are definitely glowing. Remembering Sarah's eyes, I furiously blink and wonder what the hell is in the water here.

Ella makes a pathetic little whimper, capturing my attention. And in the split second, I look away from Ash, the sickening crunch of breaking bones sound. I look back just in time to see knife perv hit the ground. Ella's hand reaches for mine and as I gently hold hers and look down at her, the most embarrassing thing happens. Useless tears start running down my cheeks. I don't know if it's relief or sadness or old traumas that are best left forgotten. But I can't stop them as they drip from my chin. Ginger Jock joins us, out of breath and red in the face.

"He got away, but I got his phone." He proudly shows us.

The sound of sirens reaches my ears, but I'm too full of rage to care. Furiously, I look at the three of them and yell, "Where the hell were you? She was alone! Passed out at a table and discarded with your coats! What the *hell* kind of friends, are you? What kind of *men* are you that you don't look after the girls you came with! Do you have *any* idea what they were going to do to her? *Do you?*"

I scream my last question at them. More tears are falling now and a flashlight shines in my face.

"Is she okay, ma'am? Do we need an ambulance?"

I can't see anything behind the light, but the unmistakable authority of a police officer is in that voice and now it's my turn to freeze. *I am completely and totally screwed.*

CHAPTER 6

Why is it that all police stations look and smell exactly the same no matter *where* they are? With enough florescent lighting guaranteed to bring on the mother of headaches... Set against yellowed brick surrounding islands of metal desks crammed together and littered with piles of files. And the smell of sweat and burnt coffee permeates the air in each and every room.

A cup of said coffee sits untouched between me and the detective currently clicking away at his computer. I can't see the screen, but I know what he's looking at. I have been told that my pictures coupled with my fast thinking to get the phones, has this case closed before it's even started. The two losers are going to jail, no question about it. But my sense of justice is not put to rest in the slightest. It would have been far worse for them had I been able to get their mugs on the net. But now, Ella will be lucky if they don't post bail in 72 hours.

Meanwhile, my life is now *over*. Helping Ella means I forfeit the first real home... Job and... Dog... I've ever had. I can hardly *think* of Ugly or Dill now without completely *losing it*. I force the thought away before the tears come back and dig my fingers into my palms. ...It didn't take me long to screw everything up.

"Okay Miss Walker, I have confirmed your identity... And your *age*..." He looks over his computer at me with a frown etched into his tired face. "You have a list of priors..." He clicks more on his computer. "Petty theft..." More clicks. "Assault and battery?"

"That was in defense. Believe me, he had it coming. And... I needed that coat more than they did." I strive to look calm even though I'm freaking out. At any moment, what happened in the group home is going to come up and I am going to spend the rest of my life behind bars. While those two perverts are free to walk the streets. *How's that for justice?* But nothing in my life has ever been fair.

"How did all you kids get into that bar?"

"What?" I'm totally confused now. This is *not* where I saw this going.

"How did minors get into The Bar?"

"I'm not with *them*," I say a little sharply. "I'm with the *band*."

"Right. A mister Dillon Brennon. Is that correct?"

"Yes."

"And Is *he* the one that escorted you into The Bar?"

I don't like where this is going... My concern suddenly shifts into worry that I've somehow implicated Dill in all of this. And for some unexplainable reason, that thought upsets me more than the looming prospect of my jail time.

"Dill has no *idea* about my age! I gave him a fake one, so he would give me a job! I'm like... His personal assistant... He takes me to those gigs to *help!* And what I do when I'm not working, is *my* business."

"You're saying he's not your legal guardian?"

Why would you think he's my legal guardian?? ...Unless they don't know about what happened...

"I am her guardian. And I'll ask you not to question her anymore. ...Unless you're arresting her?" I have never heard Dill sound so angry or full of authority. I swing around to see him. *Yep! Definitely mad.* I guess he heard all of that, I realize with a sinking stomach.

"I don't have you listed under guardianship sir."

"Do you see anyone else here claiming her?"

"That's not how it works."

"He is my guardian," I interject.

"Mam, you just said he was your employer."

"That means he can't be my guardian too?"

A man clears his throat and we all turn around.

"Chief..." The detective asks more than states.

The tall, older man behind us looks only at Dill and cracks a grin. *"Pickle."*

"Hey, Joe." Dill responds with a small, tired smile and a nod.

"Detective Cooper, I can vouch for this man. Dill, why don't you bring her back here tomorrow afternoon and we can sort this out."

"What is there to sort?" Dill asks in his no-nonsense way.

"She's a minor in the system that is listed under missing persons." The chief holds up his hands. *"I know* you had nothing to do with it Dill... But I would like to know how Miss Walker here, made it all the way from Hammond, Louisiana to our neck of the woods. And what we need to do to get her back there without raising a bunch of red flags for you, and more issues for us. ...So tomorrow, after we have all had some rest, Miss Walker, you're going to tell Detective Cooper the whole story.

And we're going to get this all sorted. Cooper, we're hitting pause. You understand?"

"Yeah, Chief. No problem."

"And Dill? Do me a favor and clear out your friends from my reception. They're scaring my criminals."

∞

The sight that greets us in the reception room has my eyes widening. But that's nothing compared to everyone I see when we reach the parking lot. The place is filled with bikers. Despite that, it's now raining. Despite the very nervous looking officers that clearly don't want them constipating their lot... It seems like everyone I have ever met at gigs or barbecues or jams, is here, holding their bandanas in their hands. Their solemn eyes following us. Dill's band greets us first. I'm speechless as they surround me in a silent hug. All the tears I have been holding in, come spilling out.

I can't believe that I am blubbering in front of all of these proud men. But the feeling of being enfolded and cared for is my undoing, and I'm powerless to stop my weeping as hands and arms I've come to trust surround me and gently support me. Whiskers are brushing my face and the smell of leather, tobacco, and aftershave soothe me.

"You guys make a great mother hen." I chuckle and sniffle at the same time and they laugh, breaking the tension. Pulling back, I wipe my eyes and nose as best as I can.

Four bandanas are pushed at me and I indiscriminately grab one and blow my nose in it. More laughing ensues and I feel a little better.

"Why are you all *here*?"

Arch, whose beard I had been crying all over, looks at me with kind eyes. "Word spread about what happened and what you did for that girl... And we didn't want you to be alone. ...Plus, since you're our *manager*, we couldn't just leave you here." Laughing at that, I feel more steady. Looking around at all of them I give a little nod of thanks. Arch gets red-cheeked smiles and nods back. And just like that, everyone breaks ranks and begins to disperse.

Dill is quieter than usual on the drive to the Manor. The pattering of rain on the windshield is the only soundtrack to my mounting anxiety. I wish he would just yell at me or say something. *Anything*. I know I have disappointed him and betrayed his trust. But the silence is excruciating because I don't know what he is thinking. We pull up to the house and I'm still trying to figure out what to say when he gets out, shutting his door firmly behind him. With no small amount of trepidation, I watch him pass the front of the car to wrench my door open. Holding it there, he leans on it and still doesn't say anything. Either oblivious or not caring that the rain is beginning to soak him. We both end up trying to speak at the same time.

"You okay?" and "I can go." -in a jumbled mess.

"What?" I ask.

"Are you okay?"

"Yeah, just tired. Listen, I'm really sorr..." Dill holds his hand up and gives me a firm look.

"No. No..." He shakes his head. "I *knew* you weren't twenty-one. And I know something set you to runnin'... I just thought..." He's scratching the back of his neck and the familiar gesture calms me a little. "I just thought that you would tell me when you were ready. And you seem so capable and beyond your years... That I just... I let you, *do you*. I see so much of myself in you and I... I just wanted to *help,* you know? ...But I don't know if I did." He looks so lost in that moment, that it cuts through the shock of what he's saying.

"But you *have* helped me! More than *any* adult, in my *entire life,* has ever helped... You *have*! Before you and Ugly, I had *nothing*. I was... *Nothing*. No one cared about me. I had an enforced curfew, but no one cared where I was. *If* I ate, *what* I ate, if I was okay. Most of the time I *wasn't*... Other than the girls at the community home, I had *no one*... But for the first time in my miserable life... I *had* someone. And now I've *ruined* it!" I can't believe I am crying again. This never happens to me, but I can't stop.

"Look at me." Dill lifts my chin. "Look now, all those friends out there in that parking lot? You *see* that family? I was married into that family." He pauses at the look I give him. "That's right. I was married... But I lost her… And I lost the son she was carrying... And I lost *myself.* I pushed away everyone that stood together for you today and then some. And when I finally started to feel kinda normal again? ...Started to pick up gigs again and let people back in? ...GranDad died. The only father figure I ever had... Just… Gone. And I didn't get to apologize for cutting him out after taking care of my sorry ass for so many years. The *only* thanks he got was not having to look at my sorry mug the day he died. And it was dark times... *Man, it was.* But then you came out of *nowhere.* Out of the biggest storm I have seen this year... There you were. And you woke me right up Alex. I *didn't* have barbecues before you. There wasn't any *jamming.* I hadn't done any of that since before... Before I lost *her*. I let that family in after you gave me some of that sunshine of yours. You get me? You can't ever be *nothing* Alex... Because you're the girl that changed *everything* for me. You're my family now. You got that? And I'm yours! And I'll be damned if I let them take you back to Hammond where you don't belong. So get your ass inside now. I have some calls to make."

His hands roughly wipe away my tears and he pulls me into a cold, wet hug that leaves me breathless. Sometimes in life... There are no words. Even though I'm *reeling* and I need time to process everything. I don't know the *first thing* about family... As the rain washes over us and he doesn't let me go? I think... Maybe I can.

∞

The last two weeks have gone by in a flurry of activity. I still can't believe that Dill filed an emergency petition for guardianship and that he actually got it! That a judge was willing to see us before I was shipped back to Hammond, was nothing short of a miracle. But the fact that the judge *met* Dill, in person, and granted him even temporary guardianship, has me walking around in a floaty state of disbelief. We meet her again in sixty days for a final interview and hopefully a more permanent guardianship.

On the downside, one of the judges stipulations was that Dill enrolls me back into school... Which I start, *next week!* I want to be pissed about it- I know I should be-but I never thought that I would have someone able to make a difference in my life, ever fight for me; let alone as hard as Dill has. Even the school was something he went to battle for. *Appar-*

ently, the school in this district is as notorious and exclusive as it gets. But after meeting the principal and finding out that she's is a Harley enthusiast, Dill made some kind of deal that got me in. I *still* haven't been able to get him to tell me what it was.

I've already begun the online courses that are catching me up to my grade. I'm speeding through those bad boys without a hitch. My teachers used to hate that I could miss thirty percent of a class and still get a ninety percent on a test. They used to always say if I would just apply myself, I could achieve so much more than passing grades. This time, I'm determined to do it all differently with my new start. Though I would *never* say this out loud... I want to make Dill proud.

My relationship with him is the total opposite of what I thought it would be after leaving the police station that horrible night. It's crazy that my flaws and weaknesses, of all things, are what he relates to the most. The very parts of me I thought would repel others are what have us bonding closer. Oddly, it's the same on his side. After learning about the hell he has been through, I trust him more.

Much to my dismay, the judge also stipulated that I could no longer be an employee of Dills. But that worked itself out too, as now I have a manageable level of chores and Dill is still letting me keep my fifteen percent of whatever I sell. He finally gave me the green light on some of the excess antiques in the basement. And I *still* can't believe what it auctioned for! It's mind-boggling what people will pay for some crusty, old stuff!

I was *finally* able to pay off the rest of the repairs for Marty, and I still had leftovers for school supplies. Luckily, uniforms are required so I don't have to worry about my pathetic lack of wardrobe. With the way things are going, I can remedy that soon enough. It's actually thrilling to think about buying something with my own money instead of nicking it. But my next goal is to pay back the money my girls loaned me, *with interest*. I will never be able to thank Vic and Shells enough, but at least I'll be able to do this.

Familiar sadness washes over me at the thought of them, but it's not as sharp anymore. Though Dill has been gone a lot lately, I don't feel as isolated as I used to. It probably helps that Ugly is with me constantly. I still don't know how I'm going to get my stage-five clinger to relax enough to let me go to school without him. But Dill has assured me, he has it taken care of.

Marty is three days late in coming, but Dill is finally driving him home today! The first thing I'm going to do is pick up another burner phone, and get in touch with Vic. I need to know how it's possible that nothing new is on my record, and why I'm not in jail. There's *no way* I'm getting out of that madness scot free. I just need an idea of when not if, it's going to catch up to me so I can be prepared.

I cringe at thinking about driving Marty to school. My new classmates are going to have a field day with that rusty, antiquated hunk of screeching metal. But if I'm totally honest, I can't wait to be reunited with him. I went through a lot with Marty and he's a big part of why I'm here. Looking back at the computer screen, I complete another session. If school here is as easy as these courses, then I'm going to have some sexy report cards to show Dill.

The unmistakable sound of motorcycles has me headed outside with Ugly to the front porch. What are all the guys doing here? I'm looking at the band riding up when I notice what's behind them and my jaw drops.

No. Way. Dill is following behind them in Marty... Only it's not the Marty I left in that shop. No... This is freaking Marty 2.0! And I *cannot believe* the transformation!

The guys park their bikes and Dill hops out of the coolest truck I've literally ever seen in my entire life.

"What? ...You ...*How?*"

The guys look proud and Dill is beaming. "Happy birthday kid."

It's not my birthday!"

"It was last week but we were too busy to celebrate. Now we're not."

"Is this *real?*" I'm unable to keep the emotion out of my voice, completely choked up. "You did this? ...*For me?*"

"We all did. Plus some friends that owed me, paid me in parts. And the crew at the shop is now even with me too. Took a lot of manpower, but I personally did the paint job. You bought yourself a rusty 1955 Ford F100 truck. Damn near un-salvageable but good, good bones. You know who else has that truck? My man, Sylvester Stallone. They used it in his movie, The Expendables. It was Arch's idea to do it up like his and we resurrected the fuck out of your Marty." He looks so proud in that moment I just want to hug him. "Notice those iridescent flecks you see by the nose and fenders? That was my special touch."

Completely overwhelmed, I feel dizzy as I slowly approach Marty. He's painted an amazing velvety black. Somewhere between glossy and matte. And all the rusty metal has been replaced with sparkling chrome. The fiery iridescent flecks Dill painted around his nose and the curves above his tires remind me of opals, and the effect is *unreal*. I open the door with shaking hands, and it moves smoothly with none of the old creaks. Looking inside, I blow out a breath. *Wow.* Black on black with stainless steel accents and a brand new sound system? Marty looks like a million dollars!

"This is for *me? The whole truck?*" I have to ask because I'm still not able to comprehend it.

"Well, I'm not taking it apart after all of that. So yeah, it's yours." He throws a set of keys at me and I catch them noting that even they look new, save for the old Ford fob. They left that untouched. Incredibly moved, I run at Dill and wrap my arms around him. He gives a little *oooff* and then puts his arms around me. "Happy birthday Alexa. I hope this makes up for some of the birthdays you never got to celebrate."

And that's all it takes to bring on the waterworks. I feel more arms enfold me and I smile at the second group hug I have had inside of a month. Then my face turns red as I hear Arch start to sing and the others join in. "Happy birthday to you..." All I can do is laugh and cry as I listen to them sing.

We break apart as they finish, and I wipe my face and smile at them. "For a band, you guys are really *off*-key. You should practice more." They laugh and a couple of them look almost as emotional as I am. The sound of more bikes coming our way breaks the moment and has me looking at Dill in question.

"What's a birthday without a party?"

CHAPTER 7

Laying in bed unable to sleep, I stare at the ceiling. I can't remember ever having so much fun. I even sang at one point in the jam session that broke out towards the end of the evening. Big, burly bikers telling me I have the voice of an angel is something I will not soon forget. The cake was so good and I got more presents!

Chuckling, I recall the loot of the evening. Two wicked-looking pocket knives, mace, a new pair of combat boots, and a black pair of vintage styled shades that are going to look amazing with my truck. A studded leather harness for Ugly and a gift card to the mall. I couldn't have asked for better gifts if I had tried! Rolling over, I feel butterflies erupt in my stomach as I think of my old, new truck. Marty is going to get attention at school alright, but not for the reason I had thought.

∞

Pulling up to the school parking lot, I tell myself for the hundredth time that it's totally fine I don't know anyone here. It's senior year and cliques of friends have been years in the making. But I have always been an outsider and being the new girl shouldn't bother me at all by this point. Circling, I search for my assigned space and am surprised to find it near the front between a rockstar worthy collection of wheels.

There are way more students loitering outside than I expected. In my previous school, the parking lot was the last place anyone wanted to be; even the teachers rushed indoors. But here, everyone seems happy enough to catch the sun and reunite with their friends. Taking a slow breath, I open my door. Determined to look as confident as I wish I felt.

Almost immediately a guy passing me yells, "Sweet ride!"

And I relax realizing it's Marty everyone is staring at. Not me. *Thank you Dill.* Stepping back from the astounding row of luxury vehicles, I am secretly thrilled to see my truck is by far the coolest one there. But that feeling is shattered the moment I recognize the white and chrome hummer with all the frills three cars down. *Shut. Up.*

There is *no way* the Jacket Crew goes *here!* But in running through my conversation with Sarah, I realize that it should have been obvious they would be here. Glowing eyes flash through my mind and I feel a little sick. Logically, I know I could not have actually seen what I re-member, but it's just one more reason to avoid them.

I'm almost to the front doors when the girl before me in impossibly high wedges, is shoved as two guys giving chase, push past everyone filing in. I go to help her pick up her books when another guy behind us reaches for her ass. *Nuh uh.* Popping my foot out, I watch him go down right in front of the girl.

She turns around sharply just in time to see me snatch my foot back with a guilty smile on my face. "Better watch that spot. It's pretty slimy." I say it loud enough for Romeo to hear.

"Thanks." She smiles at me and checks me out at the same time. "You're new."

"Yeah," I say as I help her collect her books. She has the most amazing waterfall of long jet-black hair and stormy grey eyes. As we stand up, I'm impressed with how well she managed to dress up her uniform with accessories. "How did you get this ugly uniform to look like that?"

Her smile reminds me of a feline, slow and relaxed. "It's what I do. I'm Jade."

"Alex," I tell her as we walk inside.

"Where is your first class?"

"Actually, I have no idea. Would you mind?" I hand her my class list.

"AP Calculous first thing in the morning? *My* people." Like it's a sealed deal, she wraps her arm around mine and begins leading me down the hall.

"You have Mr. Williams too?" I struggle to keep up with her long strides and look as graceful walking. She's tall enough to be a runway model and she walks like one too.

"People are staring. Is my uniform on backward or something?"

"No, that's not why they are staring, but you could use a little help. We have fifteen more minutes before class and I only need ten. Down?"

"Sorry, down for what?" I hate how lame I sound.

"My help? *Believe me.* I don't offer it to just anyone. But you're a perfect canvas and I like you."

I haven't decided if I like Jade or if I'm scared of her. She's already pulling me to the lady's room before I have a chance to agree.

"Your hair is amazing. But it's a crime to get a color job that good and then do nothing with it." I try to look like it's not totally weird that she just pulled a dryer from her bag because who knows, maybe that's normal here. She pulls out other products too and I wait for the rest of the salon to follow. "Flip your hair over like this and keep your head down." I do as she instructs and stare at my knees while she blow-dries and heats up my already dried hair. I want to ask her the logic in drying dried hair when she adds in a product that smells like citrus. Before I know it, I am standing again and she is twisting one half up into a bun. She repeats on the other side. The buns actually look kind of cute but get even better as she pulls out random strands.

As she works with the efficiency and speed of a seasoned bank robber I have to ask, "How do you get all of that to fit in one bag?" Before I am even finished asking, she is pulling out a makeup kit!

"Talent. And my bag is an intuitive, smart bag with strategic compartments for everything." I don't know what that means but I nod and file it away for google. She's moving like a video on fast forward as she dabs on lip gloss then adds some kind of bronzy blush around my face. "Look down with your eyes and keep your head where it is." I do as she instructs and try not to blink as she adds the same bronzy blush to my eyes and then mascara. She eyes me critically while she tucks all her toys away. "Perfect!" I'm about to move when she leans into me and snaps a selfie of us. "Love how you're not trying too hard. This is a keeper." She clicks away on her phone as she grabs her bag and leaves the bathroom. I turn to look in the mirror, but she sticks her head back in. "Coming?"

"Yep! And thanks." She *is* good. I look misty, sun-kissed and my blue eyes look more intense. "I have never done this with my hair before but it looks great!"

"It's going to look even better when you take your hair down after class." She takes my hand and pulls me through a door just as the final bell rings.

Most of the tables in class are taken and I am disappointed to see there are no paired seats left. Too bad. I have decided I like Jade. She's a unique flavor of strange badass that I haven't been acquainted with. and I want to get to know her better. I suddenly realize we have stopped moving at the front of the class and everyone is staring at us.

Jade is leaning on the first table closest to the door, staring down the guy sitting there. She slowly leans towards him. "Do I need to say please?" His chair screeches back and he hustles to the back of the class without a word. Waving her hand to a seat with an elegant flourish, she looks at me. "Shall we?" My first friend in school is terrifying. *Yep*, I like her.

My class with Jade goes by fast. I don't know how she manages to be so smart and gorgeous without being a total twit about it. While she's assertive and powerful, I suspect she has a softer side somewhere in there. We're walking down the hall and I'm just shaking out my hair as Jade instructed when I hear my name. Thinking I must have heard it wrong I flip my hair back. I can't see the loose, wavy curls Jade assured me I would have but I can feel the volume and bounce.

I have never had another female primp me before and I'm definitely finding it more exciting than when I do it. Jade smiles at me. "You look hot. Is that... Ash Hartford calling you?" Goosebumps rise across my flesh at hearing his name. I look around, unsurprised at the electricity I feel when our eyes meet.

"Alex... You're a student here?"

Jade saves me from my laps in speaking coherently by responding for me. "I should think it's obvious, no?" She gestures to my uniform then wraps her arm around mine. "We were just leaving. Don't want to be late." She pulls me along and I once again attempt to keep up with her as we get lost in the crowd. "Don't turn around. Let him watch you leave. You either don't speak much or Ash caught your tongue."

"No..." *Hell.* "Was it obvious?" I ask her worriedly.

"No. It wasn't. It was Ash who actually looked off his game today." She sounds thoughtful as she says it. "And he's never off his game."

We come to a stop and she gestures to a hall on our left. "This is you. That way is the English department."

I want to ask her if I'll see her at lunch but then I get shy. "Thank you," I say instead. "I mean it. You didn't have to do all of that."

Jade eyes me and again I'm reminded of a cat. "You're not from around here, are you?"

"Is it that obvious?"

She smiles at my recycled comment. "Yes. Meet me at lunch. Through the cafeteria, you will see the exit to outdoor seating. I'll be at the table under the big tree. You can't miss it."

Leery of thanking her too much, I give a little nod and turn to find my next class. All the while marveling that I may have just made a friend.

Everything about AP English is pretty cool. My teacher Mrs. Eldridge is funny in an unintentional way and passionate about the subject. Her syllabus outline actually sounds interesting and I have my own table. There's just one thing that's ruining it for me. Glancing over my shoulder, I see Nick is still staring at me. *Ugh.*

When the bell rings I rush from the class, not daring to look back. Detouring to the Ladies room, I'm finally able to really look at my reflection. I look like a different person. It's not that Jade's makeover is over the top... It's not. It's just... Someone else bringing out my natural features paired with my styled hair and uniform. It's like looking at a fantasy version of myself.

Sultry, light blue eyes heavy with lashes look back at me. My lips that I have always thought were too big, seem to have finally grown into my features. The soft, bronzy rose tint Jade gave them highlight the matching hues in my sharp cheekbones, and even they look softer. I have always hated my porcelain skin that's incapable of tanning. But right now, with the bronzer, I look a little more normal, I guess. *Pretty,* even. Jumping at the sound of the door swinging open, I head out and in the direction I was given for the Drama department.

I make it to the theatre just after the bell rings. Everyone is staring at me from the stage as I make my way there through the rows of seating. Trying not to focus on the fact that I'm the center of attention, I instead note how this school is nicer than most of the buildings I have ever been in. A remodeled mix of very old meets very new and modern. The theatre being one of the older spaces they kept and restored. Stepping onto the stage I try to channel Jade's serene confidence. All of that crumbles as I hear *that* voice and look up.

"Why don't you take a little longer. We have nothing better to do." Looking over, my eyes confirm the warning signals my brain is throwing out. As if seeing Sarah is not bad enough. Right next to her is Ash. *Crap nuggets. Of course, we would share a class!* Keeping my mouth shut, I sit next to a guy with messy blonde hair and a nice smile. I'm thinking he looks harmless until he opens his mouth.

"Oh come now Sarah, you can't *always* be the center of attention. I'm sure you can arrange your schedule so that next time you can be the late one."

A few snickers sound and he turns his gaze on me. "Don't worry about her. She's all lime and salt with no tequila. I'm Aron."

Smiling at his unusual choice of words, I give him my hand, startled when he brings it to his lips.

"Alex."

The teacher walks in and cuts off the chatter. She strides onto the stage and manages to have both presence and flair in just her walk. This is definitely going to be an interesting class.

"Get in a circle. Let me see what I'm working with. Hurry up. Come, come. There. You..." She gestures to me. "I don't know you. Who are you?" She asks me directly without any rank.

"Alex. I'm new to this school."

"And *how* pray tell, did you make it into *my* advanced class Alex?"

"Bribing the principal." I tell her truthfully. She has a fluttering laugh that ends as she literally swallows it.

"I don't doubt it. *I...* am Miss Waverley... And as everyone else here knows, one of my *many* great gifts is *honesty*." She enunciates each word to the degree that I could swear I hear extra syllables. "And I will *honestly* tell you if you deserve to be here in... one week. For now, you are temping." Her hands seem to move as much as her lips. "If you don't make the cut, that won't be so long that you can't make up the time in an alternate elective. *Everyone* in this room has earned the right to be on this esteemed stage, and now you too shall have your turn."

All I can do is nod so she knows I understand. The gravity of her words and the implication that it's possible I won't be good enough has me all of a sudden, very nervous, and interested in this class. I didn't choose it and I wasn't particularly thrilled about it. Now that my worth is on the line, I am hanging on to her every word. The series of exercises she has us run through is embarrassing and silly, but everyone seems to take it seriously so I follow suit and give it my best.

Lunchtime doesn't come soon enough. Who knew drama would be so physical? Between all the stretching and sound-making, we hardly did any acting! And now I'm *starving* as I enter the cafeteria. The food offerings here turn out to be crazy, and I go all out at the organic salad buffet. My mouth is watering by the time I make it outside. The lunchroom looked state-of-the-art, but I much prefer the outdoors. And apparently, so do the other students because it's already getting packed.

I see the tree almost immediately. Following the winding walkway, I'm too shy to observe my schoolmates in the way I feel them observing me. I would be relieved to have reached Jade's table if she were there, but no one is. The only thing worse than being late is being early. *Ugh.* Resolutely sitting down, I put down my tray and go to work on its offerings.

"Pig out much?"

"Every chance I get. What do you want Sarah?"

"You will *never* make it past."

Looking up at her, I am a little surprised when I see Ella standing next to her looking uncomfortable, and another girl I recognize from The Bar. "Never make it past what? Bigger sentences please..."

"You think you're *so hot*. Do you even know whose table this is? It's none other than Jade Elliot's table." I stare at her with a schooled, bored expression. *Wait... Elliot... As in Elliot Electronics?* The rest of the Jacket Crew has arrived and my cheeks heat as I see other students taking notice. I intentionally do not look at Ash and instead see the offensive little shooing motion Sarah makes at me. "You don't belong at this table. Run along now."

Losing my patience, I shake my head. "This again? *Seriously?* Haven't you learned anything?"

"*This* is not your table. *This* is not even your school! *That's* not your drama class. Because you have *no class*." She smiles at her own cleverness. "And *This* is *my* school and you're not welcome here."

Ash puts his hand on Sarah's shoulder to either calm her or support her and Nick nods to him about something. "Come on Sarah. Let's go."

"Oh, but I'm just getting started." She says sweetly.

Before I can say anything more, Jade's voice cuts through the tension like it's butter. "I always knew you were bad at math Sarah. Since when did you get bad at reality?" Jade's voice stays perfectly level as she takes a seat next to me and slowly starts arranging her food. Laying it out in a beautiful way as she raises her voice just enough for everyone around us to hear. "Until you buy this school, it doesn't *belong* to you. Until you speak with me first, you don't know who's invited to sit with me. Until the week is over, you won't know if she's better at drama than you... And your estimation of a class is... Shall we say, *questionable*. After all, that's *last* season's Gucci bag. Try your mother's Chanel if you can't afford something relevant. Classic Chanel is acceptable year-round. And here's one more free piece of advice; try not to be so obvious about the fact that Alex threatens you. It's not a good look." She finally looks up from her feng shui'd food. Her direct feline stare seems to pin Sarah where she stands. Without even looking at her, Jade has just undressed the Jacket Queen with just a few seemingly casual words.

"This *bag* is limited edition, complete with custom painting. It's practically priceless." Sarah says through clenched teeth.

"Yes. And maybe you can wear it again *next* year in the spring. Which is exactly what your custom *daffodils* painting, so clearly suggests."

"Are you seriously going after my bag when you have that frump sitting next to you? Just look at her Army surplus backpack!"

Jade's laugh is as sweet as Tinker Bell's. "Catch up Sarah. Alex is sitting with *me* which negates any question of her class or otherwise. As for *her* bag? That's Canadian Army, circa 1960s. It's collectible. I lost bidding on one last week." When Sarah doesn't immediately respond, Jade loses patience and picks up her fork. "You can go now." She doesn't say who she's talking to, but everyone starts to disperse like she waved a magic wand. And Sarah? She actually looks like she might be ill before leaving in a huff.

"You have to teach me that trick," I say in lieu of thanking her profusely.

Ella stays behind and when she reaches us, she speaks quietly so only we can hear. "I know what you did at the Bar. You stopped those guys." I don't know what to say but she saves me from having to figure it out when she goes on. "I wanted to thank you... But... Why did you help me? I was so rude to you."

She looks like she might cry, and I hurry to form a response that won't sound as awkward as I feel. "There is no comparison. I wouldn't want those losers around my own enemy. Let alone you. What they wanted makes them evil. And all I saw was a girl facing my worst nightmare. There is just no way I would ever passively stand by...No one deserve it." I am up before even consciously making the choice and hug her.

"I didn't lead them on. I didn't even know them! I didn't." She mumbles into my shoulder and begins to cry. It's strange that I went from hardly any human contact for so long to hugs almost every other day now. I think I'm getting pretty good at it. I rub her back the way the guys did mine and tell her the things I wish someone had said to me. "It wasn't your fault. You have absolutely nothing to do with their choices." Pulling back from her I look into her eyes and say softly, "It's not your fault. You didn't deserve to have that happen to you."

"Thank you." She whispers.

"I'm glad I helped. But honestly, it was Ash that did the heavy lifting."

Jade passes her a tissue from her enchanted bag of tricks and Ella immediately dabs at her pretty silver eyes. "No. *You* saved me. You saw what they were doing before anyone else, and you had the guts to confront them alone. *You* saved me... And I really just wanted to say thank you." With that, she leaves and I am left a little dumbstruck in her abrupt absence.

"I want to know all about you miss Alexa Walker." Jade's silky voice sounds from next to me.

Aron from Drama class slides in across from us. "I do too. This is the most entertaining first day of school I have had since the second grade when Nick kissed Miss Marten on the mouth." He looks at Jade. "You weren't there that year but it was history in the making!" Jade says nothing but quirks a brow at him then goes back to her salad.

"How do you know my full name?"

"I know everything. But I caught that tidbit on your schedule."

"*Right...*"

"Can I join you?" We all l look up to see Nick standing near Aron. No one responds but I'm a little shocked to find Jade looking to me for an answer. *OK...*

He puts up his hands. "There will be no more crying girls. Not on my watch." He says the last part so sincerely that I giggle.

"Sure."

Aron whistles. "Yep. A historic first day indeed."

CHAPTER 8

The rest of the day goes by without event. Other than the fact that everyone keeps looking at me. Biology is a snooze. History, far more interesting and Ella is in that class. My request for the piano chair caused a little stir as the new girl out played the previous chair holder to win the position. But Nothing has fully distracted me from the events of lunch. I keep replaying how Jade stood up for me, and then the fact that Ella thinks I *saved* her. My brain feels overheated as I walk out to the parking lot.

Just at the end of the walkway, parked front and center is none other than Sarah in her fancy convertible along with her girls, and Ginger Jock. They are heckling passers-by and laughing like their jokes are hysterical. I *sincerely* hope this is not a ritual for them. Seeing no way to avoid what's coming, I channel Jade and walk like I mean it.

"Hey Alex, need a ride? The school busses are *that* way!" Sarah points across the lot and laughs like she can't handle how funny she is. I don't even slow down as I pass her.

I make it to Marty and am thrilled all over again that *this* is my truck. I start him up and hear his new engine roar like a badass, and I'm ready for battle. I pull up alongside Sarah's little convertible and people have already begun checking out my truck. I roll down my window but before I can have words with her, a guy from my History class interrupts.

"Yo! Can I get a selfie with this baby?"

"No problem." I *know* it's just killing Sarah that she's all but invisible now. Waiting for the photo ops to finish, I look at her and smile. "My ride can eat that cute little thing for breakfast. But... *Thanks* for the offer." I give a little wave and rev the engine a bit for good measure and people move away. Just as she opens her mouth to say something, I take off.

I know it's small of me, but I don't care. That felt great! I literally *never* have the upper hand in anything! So, I take a minute to bask in my little win. Having a bully is proving to be more fun than I thought. Actually, so was my first day of school.

∞

Ugly is all hyped up when I get home. The moment I open the front door he is all over me. You would think I left him for a week the way he's snorting and whimpering and barking. Giggling at his theatrics, I do my best to calm him down. "Sit!" I finally demand. Without question he obeys. "Good boy." I had let him sniff my school bag before I left and now I take it off and let him smell it again.

He wastes no time in checking it out. His tail wagging as he moves his snout all around it, pausing in certain spots. I patiently wait for him to finish. This is important because I want him to understand through scent, where I have been. He already knows the smell of Dill's gigs and accepts that he can't come. I'm hoping the new smells will communicate that I have gigs now too.

He finishes with his sniff-a-thon and I sling the bag over my shoulder. I look him in the eyes and repeat what I said to him in the morning. "I have to go to school every day, five days a week. But we are still going on our walk *every day*." The word *walk* has his tail wagging double time. He's still sitting as I haven't given him permission to relax. What a stellar dog. I give him a treat before we go and we rush our walk so we're not too late meeting Maddie.

∞

Jade pulls out the buns I twisted my hair into last night after my shower, and blow dries out the dampness. "This is a great idea. Your hair is all silky and shiny now and the body and waves are going to last all day. I def need to try this. By the way, what salon are you getting this multi-toned red from? It's magic." Coming from Jade that's high praise. Smiling I tell her my secret.

"I was born this way." I shrug, helping her finger comb the waves out, and flip the long locks back. It has way more volume today and she's right, the shine is lustrous. I try to see my color through her eyes. The under layers are a deeper red hue and the top is a blended watercolor of gold, copper, and red mixed with a few subtle sun-kissed streaks of blonde. I was always made fun of for being ginger. But today, maybe because of my new friend, I feel it's beautiful.

Jade is already onto my makeup when she responds. "That's some good genetics at work. Was it your Mom or Dad who was a redhead?"

Trying to keep my eyes from blinking as she applies the mascara, I use the moment to figure out how to respond. This was bound to come up, but somehow I feel no more prepared even with expecting it. Jade comes from one of the most illustrious families in America. How is she going to look at me knowing I come from nowhere? That no one wanted me?

"What's wrong?"

Crap. Too late to guard my features. I look at the girls behind her and she reads my mind.

"Some privacy." She doesn't even look at them as she says it, but they leave without saying a word.

"How do you *do* that?"

"It's a gift."

When she says nothing more and waits for me, I quickly decide ripping off the band-aid is best. Though I can't quite look her in the eyes as I say it out loud. "I don't know who my parents are." My throat feels too tight to say anything more.

"The mystery surrounding Alexa Walker thickens. You could be a rockstar's secret offspring or descended from royalty."

I look up at her to see if she's joking but her face remains as serious and direct as ever. "Think about it. Your ability with music, your aptitude with numbers, and public speaking. Your incredible bone structure. You don't get a combination that good without some serious lineage. Now come on. We're going to be late." She shoves everything in her bag in record time and pulls me along. Stunned, I say nothing and try to keep up.

Nick sits next to me in English and I can feel, more than see, the disruption it causes the class. No one says anything to us and we say nothing to each other. I'm too caught up thinking about what Jade said to care. In my *whole life,* I had not once ever looked at being a foster kid as anything more than abandonment and rejection. That she would insinuate it adds to my character in some way and suggest I come from more than trash, sparks something inside of me.

I'm on time for Drama today and relieved to see Sarah isn't around. Ash is there, blatantly staring at me when Aron saunters in and sits next to me. Relieved to have a distraction, I smile at him.

"Hello Red."

"Red?"

"Yeah. I give anyone who's anyone a nickname around here." He says it proudly as if he's bestowing some great honor onto me.

I chuckle at his arrogance and have to ask, "What's Jade's nickname?"

"I once tried to call her Jules and I thought she was going to gut me right then and there."

I bust up laughing because I can totally see it. "What nickname did you give Sarah?"

"In all the years I have known her I never came up with one that stuck." He looks thoughtful now. "Any ideas?"

The girl in question walks past us and wrinkles her nose at me. "Bathe much?" She taunts as she goes to sit next to Ash.

Smiling as inspiration strikes, I look at Aron mischievously. "Isn't it obvious? Satan Sarah."

I have seen Aron chuckle and I have seen him smile. As I look at him losing his shit so hard the class is staring, I decide I like this version of him best. I suspect he doesn't laugh like this often enough.

"*How* was this not my idea?" He's wiping tears away when we both look at Satan Sarah and see her glaring at us. This time we both break down laughing just as Miss Waverly walks in.

"Circle everyone! I want you to start making one before I come." She peers at Aron and me as we catch our breaths. "Anything amusing you would like to share with the class?"

I studiously keep my eyes away from Satan Sarah knowing I'll lose it all over again if I see her face. She couldn't hear us, but it's obvious we're laughing about her.

"Your time is far more valuable than ours Miss Waverly. We wouldn't dream of wasting it." Aron smoothly responds.

Nullified, she runs us through yesterday's stretches and some new exercises. The class is back in a circle and taking a beat when she addresses me. "Alex, I want you to choose a monolog no more than 5 minutes long and have it ready by Friday. Consider it your audition for this class."

Sweaty dread courses through my body. I nod at her, not daring to speak. After class is over Aron walks with me to lunch. "Not to worry. you happen to have the schools most gifted thespian at your service!" He gives a fancy bow and I finally smile. We're setting down our trays at our table when I finally respond.

"She's only given me *three days* to memorize an entire monolog and I don't know the first thing about acting!"

Jade sits down across from us. "Miss Waverly?"

"Yea. She *hates* me." I drop my head into my hands.

Aron cuts in. "No. You would have been sent to the office for a new class day one if she didn't want you there. She wants you to prove to her and the class that you belong with us, so you don't get shit for the rest of the year. What are you doing after school?"

"Walking Ugly and doing my homework..."

"*Ugly*? What is this *Ugly*?"

"He's a dog," I say chuckling. "You have to meet him to understand."

"Perfect. I'll follow you home after school, meet... *Ugly* and help you find the best monolog and rehearse it."

Before I can respond, Jade chimes in. "I'll cancel my driver."

Looking at them both I know I'm out voted. "*Fine.*"

Nick sits next to Jade and joins us. "What's fine?"

Aron looks at him. "Our new nickname for Sarah."

"What?" Nick looks resigned.

"You won't have to wait long to find out. *I promise.*" Aron wiggles his eyebrows and looks at me with an evil grin and I giggle. Which turns into full-blown laughter as I recall Sarah glaring at us in class.

None of us ask Nick why he has started sitting with us but at some point, we all need to talk. He's been part of the Jacket Crew for years now. I need to know he's not spying on us and reporting back. If he ever uttered more than a few words at a time it would be easier to get a sense of his intentions. He's been broody and quiet from the first day I met him. Glancing at him, I catch him looking at Jade.

∞

We meet at the front of the school. Jade and I walk to my truck while Aron splits away after seeing where I'm parked. Sarah is in front of the school again, surrounded by more friends than last time. At least today she's distracted and not jeering at anyone. As we make it to my truck Jade smiles. "I was wondering whose this was. I thought it would be a guy's, but it makes perfect sense that it's yours. Sexy Alex." If she only *knew* Marty's humble beginnings!

"*My*, but aren't you just *full* of surprises," Aron says from behind us, in a sleek set of wheels.

"What is *that*?"

Jade gets in the passenger side. "Ashten Martin."

"You mean Aston Martin?" I ask, impressed.

"No. I mean Ashten Martin. Aron customized it so much that he gave it his own last name. Let's go before he starts talking car. *Ew.*"

I'm a little nervous to bring them to the Manor. I have never had a place to bring friends before. This feels vulnerable in a way I wasn't expecting. I love where I live, and I'm proud to have Dill as my guardian. This is a big first for me, and I don't know how I will feel about them as my friends if they don't like some part of it.

"You're quiet." Jade looks at me. "More than usual."

Relaxing my fingers on the wheel I go for nonchalant. "I have never invited anyone over before." And fail. I sound as insecure as I feel.

"You might be as reclusive as me. How long have you lived there?"

"Going on three months now. It's a pretty new situation but... It fits. Nothing ever has before now."

"Understandable... You have more odd corners than most and I imagine it would take a rather complex puzzle for you to click in with."

Jade has such a unique and practical way of looking at the world. It seems like every time we speak she challenges me to look at everything differently. "You're going to do something amazing in the world one day Jade."

"I know."

I pull my truck to the side and wave Aron past me to the garage. I'm thinking about how to handle introductions with Ugly as Aron joins us and we start walking to the front.

"I can't believe you're at the old Library!" Aron exclaims. "When I was a kid we used to imagine it was haunted! I have *always* wanted to see the inside."

I look at him in mock surprise. "You had friends?"

"Hard to believe anyone could be good enough for all this. *I know.*"

"I have never been to this area. It's nice." The way Jade says *it's nice* makes me laugh.

Aron looks at her as I go for the front door. "Your attempt at being polite is making me uncomfortable."

Chuckling, I crack the door and shout my demand through the slit. "Sit."

I look back at my two unlikely friends. "I should warn you this place actually is haunted." Jade shows zero reaction while Aron looks a little worried. "By a furry *beast* that will eat you up if you're not nice to him!" I open the doors. "This..." I step aside. "Is Ugly."

His tail is moving so fast that his whole body is shaking.

"*No way! You have a Wolf Hound?*" For once Aron loses all pretense of civility and with zero fear goes right for Ugly, letting him sniff his hand.

"Hey boy! Look how big you are! You're such a big, big boy!" As soon as Ugly smiles at him, Aron goes right in for a hug. I look at Jade. "This would be cute if it were not so weird!" I go back to watch Aron, now fully on the floor with Ugly who's exposed his belly and is doing a hilarious happy wiggle on his back.

"What the hell's going on here?" Dill asks as he walks into the foyer with Ugly and Aron.

"I brought Ugly a new toy. I think he likes it." Aron gets up as quickly as he can, but Ugly tries to get up at the same time and they trip over each other. "Oh my god." I'm now laughing and trying to introduce my friends. "Dill, this is my friend Jade and that's.."

Aron finally is on his feet, and he rushes out his hand. "Aron Ashton sir, at your service." I have never seen Aron so flustered and it's oddly endearing.

"Hmph. You sure about that? Looks like you're more at his." He gestures at Ugly and I see him sitting politely, holding up a paw for Jade. She genuinely smiles and gives it a dainty little shake. I feel like my heart just melted. I look back at Dill and see a funny little smile on his face too. I think he's just as charmed.

"What are you doing right now?" I ask him.

He looks at me and crosses his arms. "What do you want?"

"I have a really important project to work on and very little time. It's due Frida-"

"Yeah, yeah, I'll take him." Dill is already reaching for the leash. "Do you kids need anything?"

"We're good. Thank you so much!"

"Yeah. You can thank me by not letting your friends steal anything." And out the door he goes.

I look back at my now very quiet friends. "It's a joke! You get used to him. Let me show you around." I turn my back hoping they haven't noticed my beet red cheeks.

I have never seen Jade so animated. I wonder if anyone has. She's totally *in love* with the Manor. and Aron... He's dissolved into a 10-year-old before our eyes. He's opening drawers and doors and looking under rugs and beds as we move through each room.

I finally ask him, "What are you doing?"

"You *cannot* have a place like this, and *not* have hidden treasure."

"Are you serious right now?" I ask him a little too loudly.

Jade chimes in. "I know right?"

"Because I *totally* think there has to be a secret passageway or hidden room somewhere."

Jade is now looking at us both funny. "I didn't have you pegged as the fanciful type."

I'm now leading them to the North Wing. I look over my shoulder at her. "I'm not. But just wait until you see this. I am about to make a believer out of you! This house is enchanted and I'm going to prove it." Stepping aside, I allow her and Aron to see the beautifully painted door. "A great and gifted woman used to live here. She was a painter in an era where there were very few female artists, and even less that were recognized. She painted that door and it is..."

"Spectacular." Jade finishes for me.

"Yea," I say, a bit giddy now. "Open it."

I follow behind them and watch as amazement and wonder fill their features. And I imagine that's what Dill must have seen in my face when he walked me in here. It's nice to share this with people who mean something. I look over at Jade. She's speechless. Just as I was. Aron and I follow her up the winding staircase. I watch them look all around. At the stained glass and into the room. At the mirrored ceiling and the 360 views of Green Mont.

"This is incredible," Aron speaks softly, reverently. I have to agree.

"I thought the exact same thing. This whole place is such a trip. But the towers..."

"There's another one," Jade says a little breathlessly.

"Yes. It's just a slightly different theme. Sunrise, instead of night."

"Let's go!" Aron is already going down the stars.

Jade stands by the windows, looking out and turns to me. "A complex puzzle indeed. I'm starting to see how you fit here." She passes me and I follow her down the stairs, oddly moved.

We are back in the living room when Dill arrives, arguing over monologs.

I fold my arms and let out a frustrated breath. "But none of them are working! I'm a *lost cause*!" I huff and fall back into the sofa.

Ugly comes up and lays his head in my lap, instantly upset when he sees I'm upset.

"It's ok. The world of theatre will forever remain a closed door. A path never wandered. A hidden sea. But I'm fine. My hopes and aspirations are dead. But no big deal." His tail gives a little thump in what I think is solidarity and I ruffle his head before flopping back into the sofa, defeated.

Aron drops the book on the coffee table. "Well, no one can accuse you of having no drama. You cannot honestly tell me there is not a *single* piece in this *whole book* of monologs, that you *don't* connect with in some way?"

Dill saunters in holding pizza boxes. "Why not do a musical? She sings." Then he disappears into the kitchen and I hear the pantry opening and closing. "Pizza!" Dill belatedly shouts. Like we didn't get that when he walked in carrying the two aromatic boxes.

Aron and Jade seem to get it at the same time because they both say, "You sing?"

I make an ugly noise in the back of my throat and throw a pillow at the door Dill disappeared through.

CHAPTER 9

The lights of the stage seem brighter than usual. For once, the class is seated in the front pews. Satan Sarah is sitting right across from me like she can't wait to see me fail. Ash is with her, as per usual. Miss Waverly is standing to the side and she gives me a little nod. I don't know what lunacy has lead me to this moment... Standing alone on the stage before them, when all I want to do is run away...

"And what monolog will you be performing?"

Nervously pushing my hair back, I try not to let my voice shake as I respond. "'With You' from *Ghost The Musical*."

I know this is a big gamble. I discussed it in depth with Aron and Jade. After finding a number I connected with and giving it a chance, we all agreed it was the only way to go. I just wish I felt that certainty now. I don't know what my friends did to get the other dethroned pianist in my music class to agree to this. Sure enough, the haunting notes of the familiar melody pours from the piano behind the curtain.

My heart is beating so hard and loud that for a moment I panic, and I think I can't hear the music anymore, or my cue. But then... I think of Dill on stage with the guys. I think about how they step up under the lights and they lose themselves only to become greater. I remember how badly I wanted a moment just like this one. As the last notes before my cue drift over me, I shed my everyday skin and decide to live in the light.

I *know* what loss is. I *know* about longing and misery and trying to be brave when I'm *not*. I feel everything *she* feels. I walk in her shoes and tell her story like it's my own and I bleed my heartache into her song until it's my song. As I hit all the notes, I'm not seeing my classmates anymore, or even the great theatre that holds me. I'm seeing the apartment that once held everything I ever wanted and needed. Now hopelessly empty because he is forever gone.

I let the last soul-wrenching note hold just a moment longer before I let it go. Let *him* go. My voice gently drifts off as the last of the piano notes chime around me. I become aware of the embarrassing tears slipping down my cheeks. For one heart-stopping moment of silence, I think *Oh no. They hate me.* But then I hear it. The applause. I wipe my eyes to see my classmates moving to stand and holler in my support. A magical kind of wonder fills me at what I just did.

It's strange that in one way I have never been so present. And in another, I have zero perspective on my performance. It's like I gave myself up to something else and took the back seat. If it were not for the room's response, I wouldn't know how I did. Miss Waverly comes onto the stage with me and takes my hands in hers. I'm shocked to see her eyes look wet. "That was very, *very* good. You are a natural Alex." She tells me with feeling.

I feel his eyes before I meet them through the lights. For once, I hold them. I'm still riding the wave of confidence and what feels like magic. So I give myself up to his pull and surrender. Just for this moment. The intensity of his gaze is nothing short of wildfire. Heat suffuses my skin and I don't understand it... Can't comprehend it... I don't even *know him*. But here it is anyway, inexplicable and no less true.

Satan Sarah steps in front of him, abruptly blocking our view and ending the spell. The look she gives me over her shoulder is pure, undiluted hatred. Whatever I feel for Ash, it would never make sense out in the real world. The most personal thing I know about him is who he has chosen to surround himself with, and it's the least flattering thing about him. Shaking my head, I turn away from them, resolved that I'm finished with my crush on Ash Hartford.

∞

Lunch has become my favorite time of day. I half-listen to Aron sing my praise to Jade as he gives her a play-by-play of my audition. Our table is under the shadow of the tree at this hour, so I'm perched on the lone corner that still gets dappled in light.

Jade takes my hand and my eyes slit open as I smile at her. "I should have skipped French. *Merde*. Sorry I missed it."

"You missed nothing. I'm going to find the guts to do it again and you can see me next time." My statement miraculously has Aron finally shutting up. I let out a contented breath at the silence.

Aron stands up. "You want to do that again? But you said..."

"I *know* what I said, and I *was* terrified. But that's a part of what made it... I don't know... *Real*. I get why Dill and the guys do it. And I want to get better at it."

"In that case..." Aron does his eyebrow wiggle thing. "You ladies are coming with me Thursday night." Aron eyes Nick. I still don't know why he is with us. We haven't included him in much. Apparently, Aron takes pity on him because he invites him too.

Nick looks as surprised as I am. "I have practice Thursday."

"Too bad," Jade says, and I can't tell if she means it or not.

"Maybe I can come after. What time and where?

"Daily Dose. 6 pm, but you can be late."

I look at Aron quizzically. "Why would we be going to a cafe in the evening?"

"Hmmmm... I could tell you. But I could also surprise you..."

"He's bringing us to the open mike night." Jade shrugs one delicate shoulder at the exaggerated betrayal on Aron's face. I love her so much right now.

"Not just *any* open mike night. *THE* open mike night. People travel as far as Hollywood to perform there. Most go extremely early just for a *chance* to register for the evening's lineup. It is the *only thing* worth doing here on a Thursday."

Nick, who never says anything, clears his throat and we all look up. "What about tonight?"

We stare at him dumbly.

Nick sighs and does his best imitation of Aron. "Football is the *only thing* worth doing on Friday!"

A moment of shock goes by and Jade and I burst into laughter.

"I sound nothing like that." Aron sniffs. Jade and I laugh even harder.

Wiping my eyes, I look at Nick. "You have a game tonight?"

"First game of the season. It's going to be big."

"We will be there," Jade confirms for us.

I think Aron is as surprised by Jade's immediate response as I am. I look back at Nick, realizing this is the most we have spoken to each other since he started sitting with us. I hate to put him on the spot, but I have to know, and I have waited long enough.

"How come you left the Jacket Crew and are hanging out with us now?"

Aron pipes up before he can respond. *"Jacket Crew? You call them the Jacket Crew? How have we been friends all this time and I don't know this? It's genius! But this is momentous. There is a new nickname whisperer in town. Have I been dethroned? My gift eclipsed?"*

I pointedly stare at him until he shuts up. *"Fine... But we are talking about this later."*

We all look at Nick and he takes a moment longer to respond. "It was something you said to me back at The Bar... About the quality of people I was choosing to hang around and how it reflected on me... And then what you did... For Ella. And what almost happened to her. If you hadn't been there... It would have happened, and it would have been my fault. You were right. About everything. When I saw you were going here, I realized it was a chance to start over. To try and be the kind of guy who would never let that happen and... To surround myself with better people." He finally looks up at us then and even Aron is shocked into silence.

It's Jade who finally breaks it as her eyes land on me. "I'm glad you started going here too. I have trouble with... Relating to other people. But you were so... Refreshingly honest. I never had to guess with you or look for social cues. You're just... You. And it's easy to be me, around you."

"What she said." Aron chimes in.

I'm so moved and surprised that I can't speak. "Awe, look! She's blushing!" Aron coos.

"Shut up." I give him a little push and then look at Nick. Trying to see him for who he is, rather than the assumptions I have been projecting over him. He's a handsome guy. No question about it. Beneath that gorgeous, caramel skin and his piercing light eyes, is a quality of character I hadn't recognized before now. "Looks like I'm going to my first football game!"

∞

For the first time ever, I'm going to Jade's house. She insisted that the game called for the big guns and that we go to her place to get ready. It's a good thing too because I have no idea what girls wear to football games and probably wouldn't have the right things even if I did. I'm secretly relieved she wants to do a makeover and I can't wait to see what she does.

We left Marty at school and I am sitting in the back of a fancy black car with her, drinking soda. I lean even lower in my cushy leather seat and smile at her. "I could get used to this."

"It's not quite as exciting as your truck but it has its perks. I'm usually able to get most of my homework done before I get home this way."

We have been driving for a little while. At the moment, we're going up a canyon into a beautiful wooded area I have never seen before. We have passed a few side streets and gates, but I haven't seen a single house. "It's really pretty up here!"

"Just you wait. It gets even better." Just then we crest a hill and the main road gives way to a cul-de-sac with a massive wrought-iron gate at its center.

I can't be certain, but it seems like Jade might be as shy as I was about sharing her home with me because she's gotten really quiet, more so than usual. If I'm being honest, she looks a little constipated. The gate opens and we ascend a long driveway that winds around pristine plots of grass, artfully decorated with beautiful exotic looking trees, statues and... Wow. "Is that a fountain?" As we pull closer, I see it is! A beautiful and massive fountain big enough to swim in, shooting water from every level to combine into a glittering cascade. Just past it, nothing but sky and hills beyond the sheer drop of a cliff face.

Wanting to ease Jade's discomfort, I look past her to the modern monster just beyond her window.

"We are arrived." The driver says with a slight accent.

As he gets out to open our doors for us, I give an obnoxious whistle. "*Wow*. Swanky digs Jade. ...I liiike." I try to imitate Aron's eyebrow wiggle and fail. Luckily Jade cracks a grin and we both get out.

"I promise to give you the tour later but we're pressed for time and I called a few friends in for assistance."

We're fast approaching the imposing front doors and before I can ask her what she means, they swing open. A tall, elegant looking Asian man comes out and I instantly recognize him as Jade's dad. "Ah, you have finally brought a friend over! Let me get a look at her."

"*Dad.*" Jade sounds closer to her age in a single word then I have ever heard her sound before.

"Steven! Don't be rude in front of our new guest! This *cad* is Jade's father, and I'm her mother Sandra. You must be Alex." She holds out her hand for me and I take it. "We have heard such great things about you." She smiles at me warmly and squeezes before letting go. She's on the short side but her regal posture and voice make her seem taller. She has a lovely Spanish accent, curly hair, and Jade's grey eyes.

Her dad looks back at me. "I do apologize. But it is not every day our daughter brings someone home. It's quite the event around here."

"*Dad...*" I see Jade giving him *the* look and I giggle as her dad puts up his hands in surrender.

"Alright, alright... But you girls tell me if you need anything else. Jade, we've had the staff arrange a little snack service for you on your patio."

"Can I take your jacket miss?" I look behind me, surprised to see a fully attired maid. I unconsciously grip the sides of my hoody to my body. "No thank you." I step a little closet to Jade.

She grabs my hand and eyes her parents. "We're running late. Thanks!" And off we go. We're moving too fast for me to really see everything. It's all wide-open spaces with lots of natural light, concrete, marble, rustic wood and art. All the trees indoors make it feel warm and the hard surfaces seem softer against the green.

"Your home is beautiful." We dash up another flight of stairs.

"My father designed it." We finally draw up to a door and she pulls me through. A little out of breath, I look around and can't believe my eyes. Jade's room is more like an apartment! With a sunken in sitting area and a wall of windows facing an incredible view that opens up to a patio currently featuring a feast-worthy spread of food.

Another maid pops in behind us. "Good afternoon. Jade, your 4 p.m. is here."

"Send them in." Jade waves her hand and like magic, a small troop of uniformed staff walks in carrying trays and pulling luggage. Within minutes her room is transformed into a spa and I have someone working on my nails while another is cleaning my face and still another is doing something with my hair.

"What is happening right now!?" I try looking at Jade without turning my head and messing up whatever they are doing to me. Nervous excitement has erupted in my stomach at all the attention.

"We're getting ready for an important evening."

"But it's just a football game!"

"It is not *just* a football game. It is the first game of the *season* and the entire student body will be there. When we walk down those bleachers, all eyes will be on us. You're fast becoming the new *it* girl and that makes you a target as well as an icon. You need armor Alex. Sal, who's at your hair, Mary, who's on your face, and Aleta, doing your nails, are in effect, your fairy godmothers. And from now on, when we have an event, they're your new best friends who are going to armor you up. Oh, and I almost forgot to mention, we're going to a party after the game."

My head is literally spinning as I try to digest everything she just said. I can't even think about the rest until I break down her first point. *It girl?* "I'm not an *it* girl. The popular kids hate me. Especially Satan Sarah."

"Sarah is not the queen bee in our school. She never has been."

Much to my fairy godmothers dismay, I swivel at that. "Then who is?"

Jade laughs. "Seriously? You are so oblivious sometimes! *I* am the queen bee Alex. And *trust* me. You are not just the new it girl. But *the* girl. Haven't you noticed the way people stare at you in school?"

"They are looking at you! And the *only* reason anyone is looking at me is because I'm the new kid."

Jade is openly laughing at me now. "You're the first girl that has gone head to head with Satan Sarah and lived to tell the tale. And on your first day of school! *No one* gets away with that... No one other than yours truly anyways... And most of the girls in my athletics class are *still* talking about how you saved Ella. *Everyone* knows who you are. And it's important that you realize that because it means the power dynamic at our school is finally shifting. It means that I'm not the only one keeping Satan Sarah in check anymore. You're going to have new clingers and wannabes, who are not your real friends, clamoring for your attention. It also means enemies, haters, and rumors. The *only way* to fight that is to see it coming and remain two steps ahead. Oh, and let's not forget... To look amazing while you're doing it."

I can't help but laugh at Jade's dramatic take on things. It's all very teen drama TV. But some of her warnings ring true and it sends a chill through me. I have never aspired to be anyone of note. I have spent most of my life believing that I'm no one. It's hard to believe anyone might look up to me or come after me because I might be *someone*. Shaking off the lofty notions, I try to relax into the surreal experience of extreme pampering. Mary is massaging something that smells like spring onto my face and I inhale a deep breath, relaxing.

I wake up to something soft sweeping across my face. "There she is. wake up, love. I have been holding off on your eyeliner and mascara but we're just about ready for it." I nod at Mary and try to come fully awake. The heavenly smell of coffee teases me and a cup is placed in my hands.

"Drink that," Jade says. I automatically begin gulping down the caffeine, only to stop short. The foamy, creamy texture with the sweet and smooth flavors is *divine*.

Looking over at Jade I let out a contented sigh. "Damn that's good."

"I know." Jade looks like royalty! Her eyes are glittering against sultry, smoky shadow and her skin seems to be glowing. Her hair is French braided on the sides and pulled back tight into a ponytail sitting high atop her head with incredible volume and shine. I'm not used to seeing her dressed in anything but a uniform and it's weird and intimidating to see her now in a cream, short lace dress and a matching tweed jacket emulating the shape of a biker jacket and her signature wedges.

"You look incredible."

She smiles back at me and does a little spin and curtsey. "Mary, we're short on time."

"Just... About done. Look down for me love." I do as she says and in record time eyeliner and mascara are completed. "Just a bit of setting spray... And... Done." Jade comes before me and surveys the results. I reach up to touch my hair and discover it's pinned in multiple twists.

"Perfectly done Mary. Thank you."

"My pleasure."

Everyone leaves the room but Sal, who is sitting on the sofa facing opposite us, watching what looks like a soap opera on an obscenely big TV. Jade grabs my hand and pulls me into a boutique.

"You didn't tell me your house was also a shopping mall! That explains so much!" I gush at her.

Jade laughs and tugs me through the largest closet I have ever seen, as she selects a few things for me to try on. When it's all said and done, we settle on jean shorts with a killer corset waist. The faded peach crop top compliments my coloring perfectly. The tan, suede booties she gives me look too cute to be comfortable, but I am pleased to find not only do they fit, but I can walk in them! I move to step in front of her mirror, but Jade puts a hand on my shoulder, halting me.

"Not yet... Sal we're ready for you!" She gives a little shout.

"You girls look stunning. Come with me." I sit back in the beauty chair and let him unpin my hair. Jade calls her driver and hands me a sandwich as he finishes up and I wonder if she's a mind reader as well as a genius. She disappears for a minute and returns wearing pearls and hands me a pair of silver, turquoise earrings.

Sal sprays on the final touches while I slip in the earrings and finally, we're done. I cross over to a full-length mirror and check me out... *No way!* Staring back at me is a beautiful girl. She has long, big wavy hair with romantic loose braids pulled back and lovely wisps falling free that frame her heart-shaped face. Her blue eyes are incredibly vivid against orange and gold tones that pair nicely with bronzy blush and golden highlighter. Her lips are a natural rosy hue and her long lashes seem fuller and longer than they have ever been. I look down to her amazing ensemble and back up at her face again. I can hardly believe it. I do a little twirl like Jade did and note how long my legs look in heels and how tiny my waist looks in these shorts. Even my butt looks amazing!

"This is me?" I look over my shoulder at Jade.

"This is how I and the rest of the world see you every day. Can you see it now? How beautiful you are?"

"*Do not* make me cry! I will tell Mary you ruined her makeup!"

She walks to me and stands beside me so that we're both in the mirror. "Tonight is going to be very interesting. You should call Dill and let him know you're sleeping over."

"I am?"

"Trust me."

CHAPTER 10

The football game is already in progress as we move through vendors and throngs of people to get to the bleachers. The distant roar of the crowd growing louder as we get closer sends excitement coursing through me. Jade is ahead, pulling me behind her as per usual. She always seems to have a confident sense of where she's going. I think not for the first time, *I want to be like her when I grow up.*

Finally, we step out into the bleachers and without missing a beat Jade heads down. I notice she has slowed the pace and I want to push her to go faster, but I know what she's doing. This is her catwalk. The hundred or more sets of eyes on us that would otherwise have me ducking for the nearest seat, have her *living.* I push past my insecurity and look back at a few people as I walk with her. Trying to discern their interest rather than shying away from it. I'm surprised to see open curiosity and some smiles, as well as hints of hostility. *Could Jade actually be right?*

"Finally! Aron stands up and yells at us from below with no regard for everyone he's now blocking. He is in the *very* front and I can't imagine what he had to do to get those seats!

Jade eyes him cynically. "How long have you been waiting?"

"About five minutes. ...*What?* Braxtons don't wait... Or go to football games for that matter."

We walk the rest of the way down to him when I notice the Jacket Crew a few seats back and over. Satan Sarah is looking at us and whispering something to Ella who looks worried. Aron has seated himself by Jade and I sit down on the other side of him and do my best to ignore everyone but my friends. "How did you get these seats?"

"I had people hold them," Jade responds to him.

Whoever said being rich doesn't buy happiness, wasn't rich enough. Because I'm beginning to feel like 'a day in the life' has given me a whole new insight into the power of the dollar.

"You two birds look like you stepped right out of Teen Vogue. We should be posting this!" I look over at Aron and am impressed with his transformation as well. He looks dapper in a grey tee with a low slouching neckline, grey rolled up slacks and a colorful sweater jacket that shouldn't match, but gives the outfit a fun, high fashion vibe.

"Alex isn't on socials." Jade looks at me as she says it. This has been the only subject she and I have disagreed on. I know she's telling Aron to gang up on me.

He's played into her hand perfectly because he's looking at me like I'm from another planet. "I'm sorry, but did she just tell me that you are not on socials?"

"It's not my thing," I say, in leu of telling him that no one want's to see my sad life, only, it's not so sad anymore.

"Being too cool for socials is no longer chic. Your online presence is a bank account you invest in. It's an opportunity that costs you nothing but time that you already have. As a friend, I can't allow you to hide that pretty face from the world when I know one day it will bring you options."

"But what..." Aron holds up his hand to stop me.

"I'm making you an account right now."

The old me would have stopped him, but the new me gives Aron my email address and gets up and cheers when I see Nick steal the ball. I look over to see Jade smiling at me. *Bitch*, I silently mouth to her. She cheekily winks and we go back to enjoying the game.

Between some decent shots Jade has taken of me, a few of them I wasn't even aware of, plus a couple Aron took during my audition, my page is off to a solid start. They curated my images along with some quotes I like plus related images for texture, and I'm amazed at how good it all looks. Feeling excitement over something that had previously caused me dread is just another example of how quickly my life is changing, and not just from the outside. I am changing too. Looking at my friends, I'm beginning to think it's for the better. I came to this town looking for a place to hide and instead it seems I'm doing the opposite. It's weird to find that I'm not only okay with it... But I might actually be enjoying it.

We lean in for another group shot and I make a funny face feeling less self-conscious than I ever have. I laugh when my friends do the same and it's a perfect shot. I get up, wanting to hit the bathroom before the halftime rush.

"Do you guys want anything while I'm up?" They nod at me and I head up the bleachers. It really is a different experience when you feel cute and kind of confident. Someone by the Jacket Crew whistles at me and I keep going, not bothering to look over. Maybe I wouldn't mind helping to dethrone the sorry lot of them. But there are more of them than there are of me, so for now, I stick with ignoring them.

I get sidetracked after the bathroom when I see a cotton candy vendor. I have seen the stuff in movies and even in a park once, but I have never actually experienced it myself. Looking at the developing peach-colored cloud, I'm momentarily mesmerized.

"That flavor is the best." A boy's deep voice from just behind me has my fine hairs prickling. If his voice is any indicator, he's going to be nice on the eyes. I decide not to turn around and enjoy the mystery a bit longer.

"I wouldn't know. I've never had cotton candy before."

"Inconceivable! Why now?"

Still facing the vendor, I try not to smile. "Because it's a day of firsts for me. This is my first football game for example. I'm discovering I like trying new things." I signal to the vendor that I want one. "Lucky me that I'm getting the best flavor for my first time." The subtext of what I am saying is not lost on me. I'm enjoying this game very much.

A hand reaches around me and I feel nothing but heat where his body brushes mine. He lays bills on the counter. "Add a couple waters to her order please." He tells the vendor. Even though it's hot out, I feel cool when he steps back from me. "Your first time is on me." He whispers in my ear. *And... I'm hot again!* I hate myself for giggling, but I can't help it. He is way better at this game than me.

The vendor hands me a beautiful wispy cloud of golden peach and my mouth instantly salivates. Mystery boy finally steps beside me and takes the two waters and his change.

Deciding it's more fun to leave him a mystery, I start to walk away with the massive ball of fluff held between our faces.

"Hold up." He's laughing now as I turn around with the fluffy sugar still hiding my face. "I have to see the girl who has never tasted cotton candy." His hand covers part of mine as he pulls the peach cloud down to reveal my face. It's as if I just stuck my finger into a live outlet. A quick zap followed by static electricity that has my nose twitching and face itching. *What the what?* The well-defined chest that comes into view distracts me from the absurd reaction of our physical contact. I look farther up... A pair of unusual gold and tawny colored eyes greet mine. So heavily lashed it almost looks like eyeliner, making his eyes seem brighter and more vivid. With his long, wavy dark hair and aristocratic features, it's a striking combination. My stomach does some weird dipping thing like I'm on a rollercoaster that just dropped.

"You are beautiful." Strong, arched eyebrows pull together and he looks just as unsettled as I am. His hand flexes over mine and I remember it's still there. Stepping back, I pull my hand free just as a couple of other guys approach us.

"Caden! You take too long man! We volunteered as search and rescue. The whole team almost came looking for you." I can just make out a built blonde guy resembling a Ken doll from my periphery, but Caden doesn't take his eyes from mine. I want to break our staring contest but I can't seem to pull myself from his grip. *The force is strong with this one.*

"Who's your friend?" A new voice asks as they reach us.

Finally pulling my eyes away from his, I look to see who just spoke and I'm surprised to find that he is also crushable. With high cheekbones, heavily lidded hazel eyes, and sexy mussed brown hair. I give a friendly smile and try to be chill. "I'm Alex."

They pull up short as they notice me. It's thrilling to have these guys check me out when I'm feeling so good. *Thank you, Jade and Fairy Godmothers.*

I look back at Caden. *Yep. Still gorgeous.* "Do they speak?"

Before he can respond, brown-haired hottie chimes in. "I'm Gabriel, and this is Luka." *Oh my gosh... That English accent is so not fair!*

Luka cuts Gabriel off. "And no one has ever accused us of not speaking."

Caden laughs. "Usually I can't get them to shut up."

"You guys are on a team together?"

Luka puffs up a little. "We are in a mixed martial arts dojo together."

"I thought you were going to say basketball or something. That actually sounds pretty useful. What school do you go to?"

Luka nods his head in apparent approval. "I couldn't agree with you more."

Caden manages to look even hotter when he crinkles his eyebrows. "There are only two schools here. Wouldn't our school be obvious?"

He definitely has some wise-ass in him. *My people.* "It would if the land of assumption were the land of reality." I chuckle at his discomfort and let him off the hook. "I'm new to Green Mont. And I haven't familiarized myself with everyone at my school yet."

"I'm new as well" Gabriel's accent is *killing* me.

"Hey Red. Already run out of boys to harass from our school?" Sarah's voice has become as grating as nails on a chalkboard to my ears.

I know it's purely in my head, but it's all I can do not to cringe. With a sinking heart, I look up to see her approaching us with Ella and her other minion in tow. Ella gives me a small wave and mouths, *sorry*. I kind of feel bad for her and have the urge to snatch her away from the darkness of Satan Sarah's shadow.

Letting out a resolved sigh I get the introductions over with as fast as I can. Because all I want to do now is leave and finally get a taste of my cotton candy. Without consciously meaning to, my eyes slide back over to Caden's. "Satan Sarah... Meet my new friends." I purposely do not give her their names. "Guys, meet my favorite neighborhood bully. Oh, and that's Ella, and... I'm sorry..." I look at her other friend that has done nothing but glare at me since my first encounter with her and throw back her shade. "I have no idea who you are." The girl looks at me and squints her eyes shooting more venom my way while she crosses her arms. *Oooh... Scary.* She wouldn't last a day in my community home.

I look back at the guys who are now smirking. "I should have mentioned, making people go speechless is a gift of mine." The guys chuckle and Sarah turns my favorite shade of pink.

"What are you even talking about? Kristen's not telling you her name because she doesn't want you to have it!"

This has me and the guys laughing. It's gratifying to know she hasn't completely turned this crowd against me. Students begin funneling out in streams and I realize it's halftime. I rock back on my heel, ready to make my escape before this can escalate but Sarah has other ideas.

She tilts her head at me and shakes it with a sympathetic look on her face. "It's so brave that you can laugh given how completely pathetic your life is. A concerned friend of mine did some digging." Other members of the Jacket Crew join us, but I hardly notice them as acidic dread pools in my stomach. "Foster home after foster home. *No one* who could stand you for longer than a few months at a time. You were practically homeless before you came here. ...A discarded piece of rejected trash... Some might say."

"Stop," Caden says it with a kind of dead calm that has my head turning and Sarah freezing.

Her spit from passioned words has already sprayed my face. And the damage is done. Everyone has just heard the one thing I never wanted another human to know. This was my new life. My chance to start over, where no one knew me or the dark hole I crawled out of. Once word of this spreads? - And it will. *Everyone* will know my secret. I might be all dressed up. I might even have an amazing car and a couple cool friends. But beneath all of it is exactly what Sarah says. A piece of trash.

I glance around me looking for an opening to get the hell out of this mess but all I can see is a large crowd of classmates and strangers surrounding us. This is the stuff of nightmares. I don't know how she got that information, but I can't worry about it now. The last thing I am going to do is give this bitch the satisfaction of crumbling before her. With that thought in mind, I stop looking for places to run and meet Sarah's eyes. I let the horror I'm feeling give way to anger and feel it burn through me like fire, making me bold.

"Say it. Don't spray it Sarah," I exaggeratedly wipe my cheeks and flick my hands as if their dripping in her drool.

Jade steps up behind me and gently places her hand on my back while she addresses Sarah. "I know an excellent vocal coach who can help you with that... Issue."

Laughter breaks the silence and I force myself to smile back at Sarah. "I'm just going to go clean off." But the wrath in me demands an outlet and I turn back to Sarah pausing my exit. "Have you ever wondered why it's so easy for you to treat everyone like they are beneath you?"

She looks at me in confusion. "What-?"

"Come on Satan Sarah... You know exactly what I am talking about. Why do you get off on putting everyone around you down?" I look at the Jacket Crew, no longer caring that even more people have crowded around us. "Even *them. Even your own friends*, you treat like trash."

"What the hell are you talking about? I do not!"

"Really?" I step up to her. "*Where were you* that night?" She goes utterly still. We both know exactly what night I mean. "While I was looking out for *your* friend... Where the *hell* were you?" My voice has raised and it's all I can do not to shout at her. This anger has been bubbling beneath the surface ever since I saw Ella trapped between those creeps. There is no stopping it now. I look at her friends. "You guys were *seven people...* Seven! And not a *single one* of you so much as checked on her!" I glance at them and notice some can't meet my eyes. *Good.* I look back to Sarah. "*You*, of *all* people, have *no right* to cast judgment on anyone after what you did!" I point at Ella. "She is supposedly your *best friend!* You're calling me trash but what kind of a soulless pit do you have to be to leave your *best friend* alone and passed out at a bar full of drunk strangers!?"

"That's not how it happened." Sarah frantically looks around us for backup, but it doesn't come.

"How would you know Sarah? You weren't there! *This piece of trash was! This piece of trash* took care of *your friend* when it should have been *you!*" I look back to Ella then. "You didn't deserve that and you don't deserve *her!*" I look back at Sarah's shocked face. "Do you know *why* I have won every round that you have thrown at me, *Satan Sarah*? Because you care so much... And I don't."

"I don't give a *shit* about you!" She's yelling now and it completely undermines her point.

I shrug my shoulders doubtfully. "You're a petty stalker Sarah. You just admitted in front of everyone that you went so far as to look into my personal past."

"No, it's not like that... You have totally twisted everything!" I hold my hand up and cut her off.

"You are *constantly* coming at me, unprovoked... Following me just like you have now. You're so interested in who I'm talking with, how I do in my classes, where I sit, what I drive... I have never met *anyone* so obsessed! And *Everyone* sees it. So I have to ask you again... Why are you so quick to call others trash when it's you who insists on acting like it?"

Total silence. "Ella..." She looks at me and I feel a little bad when I see tears running down her cheeks. "If you want to know what real friendship feels like, you know where to find me." *Now* I can leave.

∞

Claustrophobia clutches at me as I push past the crowd of people. The smell of burnt popcorn is suddenly nauseating. I don't know where I'm going but I need out. Aron comes up behind me and swings me around. "That was amazing you were..." He stops when he sees my face and I see Jade over his shoulder. I don't even need to say it. She just knows.

"Keep your head down and breathe. I know a place." She takes my hand and I take Aron's. We weave through throngs of people and I focus on deep breaths. Trusting Jade makes the wait bearable but just barely. By the time she pulls me through a door, I'm suffocating. I don't look up to see where we are before I bend over and try to gulp in air. Jade rubs my back in slow circles and leans down with me.

Tears are dripping down my nose and chin when I hear her taking long slow breaths beside me. She doesn't speak, she just breaths beside me and keeps the rhythm up on my back. Then Aron is at my other side, copying Jade like we're in some kind of demented Lamas class together. Time goes by and my short, gasping breaths slowly begin to match theirs. As soon as I can breathe, I slide down the rest of the way to the concrete floor and look around.

We're in a storage room. Something about seeing them impeccably dressed in this dirty, dingy place with me makes me smile. "I love you guys." Aron looks so relieved that I chuckle. "I'm okay now. I swear."

"I would get down there with you but these slacks are Gucci and even friendship has its limits."

Jade pulls me up. "You don't belong on the floor either."

I blink at her for a moment and then, "Did I ruin my makeup?" I know I must look horrible when she bursts out laughing and Aron joins in. "*Thanks.*" My droll words just make them laugh harder. She pulls out a compact mirror and hands it to me. One look at my raccoon eyes and red blotchy face has me in hysterics right along with them. It's a good cathartic laugh, and I feel a little better when we finally stop.

Jade looks at me. "Don't worry, I have just the thing." She pulls out a little Chloe backpack. I giggle when I see the miniature makeup kit she whips out. "Mary is really good... But I'm better. When I'm finished, we are going back to our seats to enjoy the rest of this stupid game. And then, we're going to party."

"But you don't know what she said to me... *In front of everyone.*"

Aron starts to say something, but Jade is already talking. "I have a good idea of what she said and in the end, it makes absolutely no difference."

"Why?"

Aron cuts in. "Because you handled her *like a boss!* I mean... I don't know where that came from, but you got her *good.* Even her own friends don't have the guts to have a real talk with her. And you called her out on *everything!* It was so epic and that is all everyone is going to be buzzing about. ...Who were those sexy specimens by the way?"

"Who? The guys?"

"Um, yesss..."

"And you owned the narrative so she can't use it against you without it directly reflecting on her." Jade stops applying makeup to look me in the eyes. "It was brilliant and I'm so very proud."

"Me too," Aron says and squeezes my hand. He lets out a happy sigh. "*Oh* the look on her face. I'm going to think of that the next time Prada is out of my size. So about your handsome company?"

"Wait... You're into guys?"

"It's not gender... It's all about the soul for me."

"As long as it's by an Italian designer." Jades says drolly and we share a smile as I decide to pepper him with more questions later.

∞

We make it to our seats just after the game has started, luckily *before* the Jacket Crew. So no one is the wiser that I needed a cleanup crew in the wake of Satan Sarah. Jade squeezes my hand to signal their arrival and I don't bother looking back. I hate that a scene like that went down in front of those cute guys. They actually seemed pretty cool and it's upsetting to have left them with such a messy, drama-fueled impression of me. On our first, and last, meeting no less! *Ugh.* I try to focus on the game and shrug off the embarrassment. I'll never see them again anyway.

A familiar, sexy-as-sin voice startles me from my self-pity. "You forgot something." I look over to see Caden holding up a new cotton candy with Jude and Luka in tow. It's impossible to stop the smile that overtakes me. I had all but forgotten mine.

Caden takes back my attention. "I couldn't let you miss out on your first cotton candy."

I stand up and move into the aisle with them. Accepting the tasty cloud. "Thank you..."

Luka looks over my shoulder and I follow his eyesight to see him regarding Sarah who looks blotchy and red. Too bad she doesn't have a Jade. I also notice that Ella isn't with her. "Satan Sarah suits her."

"Right?" Aron stands up and holds out his hand. "I'm Aron and that goddess there is Jade."

Jade smiles at them but makes no move to get up.

"Sorry! Cotton Candy here is Caden, and this is Luka" I gesture over, "And that's Gabriel."

I notice Gabriel openly staring at Jade like she's the peach cotton candy he's never had. I have to stifle a laugh, and suddenly a football goes whizzing past his head.

"I've got it!" Aron shouts, but he is nowhere close to the ball. Some guys in the row behind us begin wrestling for it and I look down at the field to see Nick glaring at Gabriel. *Oh... OK, Wow.* I look at Jade to see if she's seeing what I'm seeing; a puffing, angry, jealous bull. She definitely does because now they are staring at each other. Nick has taken off his helmet and is striding with a purpose to us. *What the actual hell?*

I hear skin pounding skin and look behind Jade, surprised that the scuffle for the ball has turned into a fight. *What the hell is going on today?* Gabriel pulls Jade out of her seat and moves to stand between her and the fight while Caden and Luka work to break it up. The ball fumbles out of the mess and Aron uselessly shouts again "I've got it!" though still he makes no move to go near it. Gabriel leans down and plucks it up amongst the chaos.

Nick, who is tall enough that he's clearly visible over the bleacher divider, says in the deepest voice I have ever heard him use, *"That's mine."* He's talking to Gabriel, but his heated gaze is squarely on Jade.

Holy... Is Jade blushing?? Gabriel fully turns around to face Nick, and he hesitates! *Hesitates* before he gives him the ball. *Showdown much? What was in everyone's kool-aid today?*

"This might actually be one of the best days of my life." At Aron's ecstatic face I start laughing. Nick sends Jade a last smoldering look and then winks at me.

"I'll see you guys at the party." With his helmet in one hand and the ball in the other, he jogs back to the field.

"*Did that just actually happen?*" Aron ecstatically whispers at me.

"What party?" Caden says, looking at me.

It's hard to believe with everything that's already happened, the night is still young.

CHAPTER 11

Jade's driver picks the three of us up after the game. As soon as the door shuts and the three of us are alone, I'm on her. "Okay. *What was up Nick?*"

Jade shakes her head and, for once, she looks completely unsure of herself. "I have no idea? You saw it too?" She's looking at Aron now.

"Hell yes, I saw that! *Everyone* in the stadium saw that! But what I did not see, was that coming."

"Me either!" I look at Jade and see a Mona Lisa smile on her lips and suddenly get what that painting is about. "You did too know!"

"No! I swear I didn't!" She's giggling now. Actually giggling. "But I kind of hoped." Oh my god, records must be breaking because this is the second time I have seen her blush.

Aron takes over for me as I am too stunned to say anything. "You like Nick? Big, surly, jock boy Nick?"

Jade looks out her window and I swear it's to cover up her red face. "Did I wake up today in an alternate reality? Why didn't you say anything?"

"Because... It's nothing serious. He was only ever eye candy up until he finally said why he's been hanging around us. And then... I don't know." Jade looks back at me and I'm surprised to see anxiety cross her features.

Aron chuckles. "Well, I think h*e knows* because he looked at you like a priest to his favorite pew boy."

That sends us rolling into laughter. "I don't know what kind of porn you have been watching, but that's just..." I can hardly get the words out between my laughter. "That's just *wrong!*"

"That's your line? *Really?* Fine... He looked at you like Michael Jackson..."

"Stop! Stop! Okay! *We get it!*" I dab my eyes trying not to mess up my makeover for the second time today. Even Jade is smiling. "You know who else was looking at you like water in a desert?"

"Okay, that's not funny at all." Aron pouts.

"But it works! You saw the way Gabriel faced off with Nick over Jade!"

"Noooo..." Aron's eyes grow round. "It's a love triangle!"

Jade huffs. "Are you done yet?"

"Not even close." He smiles at her.

Jade looks super uncomfortable, so I change the subject for her. "Can you believe today? Sarah came after me so hard! How do you think they were able to dig into my past?"

Jade's head snaps up. "*Wait. What?*"

"She said she had a friend of hers do some digging. She brought up all this stuff about how I was moved to a bunch of different homes, but those are private state records."

"She had a hacker do it. " Aron says now, all business. At least he can be serious when it's important.

Jade perks up. "That's a federal offense. She could go to jail for that."

"Hacking is incredibly hard to trace. If she had even a basic hacker do it, they would know better than to do if from a private server." At our blank stares, he amends, "From her own computer."

Jade waves that away. "Then we find out who did it for her and we get the evidence we need. My Dad has the best cyber defense team money can buy. A few scones and some coffee for the nerd heard and we should have it sorted."

Aron tisks at Jade. "*I* will be the only *nerd* herd you need. I'm better than your dad's team anyway. I guarantee it."

Startled, Jade and I both look at him.

"What? I have a few tricks up these gorgeous sleeves. And besides, if plan *A* doesn't work out we always have plan *B*."

"What's plan *B*?"

"We beat her at her own game." Jade finishes for him with a vicious smile on her face.

∞

I can hear the bass even before we enter the house. Jade told me whose house this was, but I have already forgotten. Teens are littering the yard and I guess it's a good thing this vacation home is out in the boondocks. I have been to parties before, but they were always more on the adult side and had a feeling of danger. As nervous butterflies erupt in my stomach, I realize this could be dangerous too.

I doubt the sanity in going to a party just after Sarah aired all of my dirty laundry on the streets. Jade convinced me that we lucked out with a big party tonight because it immediately gives me the chance to face any fallout head-on. Oh, and also to show everyone *zero fucks given* as Aron put it. I square my shoulders and move to cross the yard when Jade stops me.

"Wait!" I hear a pop and see our driver pouring an expensive-looking bottle of champaign into the three crystal flutes Aron and Jade are holding up.

"You two are crazy!" I tease but actually, I'm really excited. I take the extra flute Aron passes me and try not to look too thrilled as we clink crystals. "What are we going to do with these glasses?"

"Oh, this all goes with us. Benson will be parked just down the street if we need a re-fill. My father doesn't mind me going to parties so long as he knows I'm not drinking anyone else's crap, I have my own cup, and Benson is on site."

"Well, that's very modern of them," I say as I hold up my flute and admire its golden contents. The color reminds me of Caden's lion-like eyes, and I wonder if he's going to show. They had their own party to go to which we are now invited to. Jade insisted we go here and face the music. With my friends at my side and a crystal glass of bubbles in hand, I feel as ready as I'm ever going to be.

We cross the yard and I can already see people staring at me and speaking in low voices. A couple of them hold up their cups to us in salute. *Great.* I take another sip of mine and step into the house. The music is so loud it's hard to hear myself think, and it's a relief. Letting out a sigh, I take Jade's hand and nod at Aron to let him know we're moving. Into the lion's den we go.

Classmates are covering every surface. Talking, laughing and hollering over the music. Another school's jacket passes us by us and I realize this party is packed because it's not just our school. We pass a table of body painting and everyone is filming a girl in her bikini getting covered in hearts. From a distance, it looks more like a bad rash all over her body. Something crashes to my right and I see Ginger Jock yell and start chasing someone through the house. I move out of their way just before they run me over.

"Hey!" A girl shouts behind me. I swing around to see I spilled her drink, but before I can apologize, she puts her hands up in a conciliatory gesture. "Oh! OMG! I didn't see it was you! Don't even worry about it!" She gives me a huge grin that instantly makes me nervous. *What the actual fuck?* But Jade pulls me along before I can investigate the girl's odd behavior.

She leads us to a sofa in the living room that's been pushed back to accommodate a dance floor. This house is not as big as Jade's palace but for a vacation home, it's massive. I kind of recognize the classmates currently sitting there but they vacate as soon as they see us. Jade takes their place like it's all business. Shaking my head and chuckling, I perch on the back of the sofa for a better view of what's happening around us. Maybe, just maybe, we're the lions here.

"Yo! Alex! I'm so glad you guys could make it!" *Wait. Whaaaat? Why is Ginger Jock smiling at us like a happy puppy dog?* Then it hits me.

"This is your place?"

"Yuuuuup! Best party of the season!" He faces the crowd and *whoops* at them and gets greeted with a few *whoops* back. "We slayed it out there tonight! Am I right?"

"Yeah... Yeah, it was a good game." I'm still trying to figure out why this virtual staple of the Jacket Crew would be happy I'm at his party. Maybe he doesn't know about what went down with Sarah yet?

"I heard you did some slaying of your own." He poses like a boxer and playfully mock punches me.

I have to yell to be heard over the music. "Aren't you friends with Sarah?"

"I'm a free agent!" He turns back to the crowd at that and yells, "Who's your boy?" A bunch of cheers greets him, but I'm tempted to yell something random like *peanut butter!* Just to test my theory that they will respond to anything. Ginger Jock looks back at me "See?" He leans in a little closer, "Besides, us gingers got to stick together!" He gives me a little fist bump and addresses Jade and Aron, "Holler back if you need anything. I got the key!" Then he disappears into the crowd.

I look at them in confusion. "What was *that* about?"

Aron rolls his eyes. "He means the key to the *VIP* bathroom so you don't have to wait in line with everyone else. He has a power-gasm every time he hands it out."

"No, not that! The fact that he's being so nice to me!"

Jade just looks at me and smiles her knowing smile, while Aron shrugs and leans back into the sofa, looking so at home that one might think this is actually *his* party.

"Wait, what's his name again?"

"It's Eddy but we call him-"

"Ginger Jock!" I yell, before he can finish.

"Whaaaat??? You are literally stealing my *thunder!*"

"But I'm so good at it!"

"I hate you! But yea... That *is* good... Like perfect!"

"What was yours?" I ask him.

"That's so yesterday."

Two cute girls approach us and draw our attention. When they reach us, they eye Jade warily and then look at me.

"Alex, right?" *Crap. Here it comes...*

"Hi." I give a half-hearted wave.

"This is totally random but... Sarah has been nothing but terrible to me... And her too." She points to her companion. "I have a large scar she noticed freshman year in the locker room. She was so relentless about it that everyone started calling me Tara Scar-a." Even over the music, I can hear the pain in her voice. Without meaning to, my eyes unconsciously do a sweep of her body to identify what she's talking about, but I don't see anything obvious. "Anyway, when I heard about how you stood up to her... For the first time, it made me feel like I could too." She turns around to reveal an open-backed shirt, and a massive scar over a good portion of her back.

Oh no. I have seen a fair amount of this kind of thing in my community home and even some of my foster homes. For some reason, it's shocking to see it here. How she got a burn so severe is nothing good. The fact that Sarah would terrorize her over something that must already be incredibly traumatic, sets my blood to boiling. This girl's bravery leaves me humbled and makes me want to do something more for her. The fact she's telling me that I might have *inspired her in some way?* I can't really wrap my head around that.

Before I can think of an adequate response, her friend speaks up. "For me, it was always about my weight. I was too fat. No matter how much I dieted. She just wouldn't stop, and I hated myself for it. But then, I was there today when she called you trash in front of all those people. I thought, there goes down another girl by the venom of that witch's mouth. Only, you didn't go down. And *I swear* when you said; *This piece of trash took care of YOUR friend.* It changed the whole meaning of the insult." She huffs out a laugh. "I mean, I had never imagined not apologizing for who I was until today when I saw you challenge her." She holds out her arms and looks down at herself. "I haven't worn a dress in two years! Can you believe that? And I look fucking fine in silk!" She takes off a beautiful wrap revealing the rest of the dress and her gorgeous curves. Then she's handing it to me. "I want you to have this because I'm not wasting one more day hiding from Satan Sarah or anyone else."

Oddly moved, I run my hands over its ultra-smooth surface. "Thank you... You really do you look amazing in silk." The girl smiles huge. "What's your name?"

"It's Gabby."

"Thank you for telling me your story. It means a lot." I look at Tara to say something to her but then I have a crazy idea. I gulp down the rest of my drink and stand up. "Wait here. I'll be right back!" I take her wrap and get through the crowd as fast as I can. When I make it to the body painting booth I stand as tall as I can and do my best Jade, while checking out all the paints on the table.

"Hey! I saw your video!" The painter's eyes light up as soon as they land on me. *What?* "Hey!" He's now addressing his audience, "It's the girl from that vid! The bullydozer!!" *Bullydozer?* "Satan Sarah! That was killer!" He gives me a wonky fist bump and I try to keep up. "You were bad!" But I think he means good. "You want to be painted? You don't have to wait or anything. I'm just finishing up here."

"What video?" I ask with mounting dread.

"It's dope! You got like 2k views already!"

Feeling sick, I try to keep my cool. *Why would anyone even care about a stupid girls exchange?* "Where can I see the video?"

"Instagram. Hashtag bullydozer!"

Of all the hashtags I could have gone viral with, *this* was so not what I had in mind! If my girls from the group home ever see it, they would never let me live *BullyDozer* down. *Like ever.* Taking a deep breath, I do my best to shrug it off. There is nothing I can do about it now. At least for some weird reason, people actually seem to be taking the whole *I'm trash* notice pretty freakin' well, all things considered.

Looking back at the paints, I remember why I came here, to help liberate someone. Maybe I can do the same now that my worst fear has been realized and no one seems to care... *Yet.* "Hey, can you do me a favor?"

"Yeah! Anything!"

"Can I borrow some of that?" I gesture to the paint and brushes.

"Of course! Take whatever you need!"

"Thanks! I'll just be over there." I point to the sofa.

"What?"

I shout. "I'll just be over there!"

"Dope! Everyone! Follow her over there!"

"That's not what I meant!" I shout at him, but everyone is already shifting to move with me. *Fuck it.* I dump a bunch of the paint and brushes into the wrap. Time to be a lion.

Coming back to the sofa with so many people packs the room even tighter. I don't know how everyone manages to fit, but they do. My heart is beating so hard and I'm sweating. Seeing Tara, Gabby, and my friends, I feel a rush of support and confidence. Like a mind reader, Aron hands me my full glass and looks at all the people around us with questions on his handsome face.

There is no time for that now. "Thank you." I take a quick gulp to steel my nerves and pass it back to him.

To no one in particular I yell, "Help me move these drinks off the coffee table." Within seconds it's cleared, and I smooth Tara's wrap with all the paints and brushes over its surface. I take a deep breath, look at Jade, and let it out as I get up and stand on the coffee table. As soon as I see the DJ, I wave at him to turn it down. Amazingly, he does so without question. I can't believe I'm actually doing this... But I must be drinking the kool-aid here too because I hardly hesitate before I address everyone.

CHAPTER 12

I shout as confidently as I can so that everyone can hear me. "Some of you may know me." I pause when I see a few cameras go up, recording. *Crap.* Taking another breath, I resolutely push myself to finish what I just started. "Some of you already know me. For those of you that don't, I'm Alex. And to some, I'm *trash!*" I relax and smile as soon as several people cheer, and others shout *Hi Alex!* "I'm up here..." *Making a fool of myself.* "Because I just met two of the coolest girls who also have been harassed and bullied."

I look down at Gabby and Tara and they are clearly freaking out. Leaning down I am praying I can make this work. "Tara, will you please come up here with me?" She looks like a dear caught in headlights. Getting my Jade on, I yank her up before she can argue. "*Trust me,*" I whisper in her ear. Turning back to everyone and holding Tara's hand so she won't bolt, I swallow down the knot in my stomach and remember to be a lion.

"I want you all to meet Tara. Some of you might already know her as Tara Scar-a." A few hollers erupt and someone shouts at them to shut up. "I hope that none of you ever have to suffer the way Tara did the day she got the scar that she now lives with." I squeeze her hand to let her know it's going to be okay. "It's amazing to me that there are *people* out there that can look at pain and turn it into an amusement or worse, something to be ashamed of." A few *boos* sound and I nod in agreement. *"Exactly.* It's messed up! But when I look at Tara's scar, all I see is her incredible strength. Not just to get through what she did, but to come out the other side a sweet and kind person. So I have just one thing I want to say..." At this point, I have everyone's attention, and I use how pissed off I am to drive my next words home. "NOT TODAY SATAN SARAH!" Laughter, hollers, and even some stomping meet my shout and I know I've got them.

I let go of Tara's sweaty hand, to pick up a brush and squeeze some paint onto a little wooden board. I'm hoping no one will notice how much I'm shaking. Getting back up with my tools in hand, I say to the crowd what I wanted to say to Tara and Gabby. "Tara Scar-a is not just *brave,* she is a *survivor,* and her battle scars are beautiful." It's a major relief that in a party full of drunk teens, I'm somehow still getting mostly support.

"So I'm taking this brush." I hold it up for everyone to see. "And I'm turning Tara's scar into wings!" My heart warms at the cheers and I have to wait for them to settle down before I can finish. "Whoever has been harassed or bullied, whoever here is a survivor, you're invited to come up and sign the fabric at our feet." I point down at the wrap we're standing on with the paints. "And if you have been the bully and you want to start over, come up and sign a name, a message, leave your mark and come say hi if you want."

I begin painting giant wings on Tara's back as the hollering dies down, and people immediately crowd around us. I fill in feathers as I listen to one person after another tell Tara and Gabby their own stories. While others give them some love. The wings I paint along her scar are as big as the span of her exposed skin. When a couple of people that had perpetuated her nickname tell her they are sorry, the emotion is so palpable I have to reign in my own reaction. It could be the bubbles talking, but I think her wings come out pretty damn good.

Aron stands up next to me and hands me my flute as I finish up. "You're the best." I warmly tell him.

"Any time... BullyDozer."

"Crap! You saw it?"

"Oh yea! Congrats. Your first day on socials and you're viral. That has got to be some kind of record. Check this out."

I step down from the platform to get a better look at his phone screen. I snatch it from his hand, not believing what I'm seeing. I look up at his smiling face and over to Jade who's still sporting that same knowing grin.

"1,580 views? In one night?"

"Wait for it... That video is just beginning to make the rounds."

I don't know if I'm elated or terrified. I look behind me at several people filling in the gap that my feet left with messages and signatures. I guess this can be a good thing. Even with an incredibly embarrassing nickname like the BullyzDozer. ...Wait a minute...

I round on Aron. "You did this!"

"Did what?" He innocently asks.

"That horrible nickname! The BullyDozer? That has *you* written *all over it!*"

Jade starts laughing and an evil grin spreads across Aron's face. "Payback's a bitch!"

"No, *you're* the bitch! Get over here!" I reach for him with a paintbrush and cannot believe the high-pitched squeal that leaves his lips as he hops over the couch and hides behind Jade.

"I'm going to nickname *you* if you're not careful!"

His eyes round and he gasps, pointing his finger at me. "*Not today Satan Sarah!*" I look around mystified when several other people holler the phrase back in support. I drop the brush. "Is that now a thing?"

"It is." The deep voice behind me has me squealing myself.

"Finally!" I throw my arms around Nick and give him a big hug. He's stiff with surprise at first but then he relaxes into it for a second before pulling back. "What took you so long!?" I yell at him. He's smiling now too.

"Some of the guys and I got tied up with something at school, but it's taken care of now." His gaze goes past my shoulder and I know exactly where he's looking. Turning around I see Jade, suddenly looking for all the world like she's hanging onto Aron's every last word. *Bullshit.* Smiling, I pat the big guy on the shoulder. "Here, you deserve this." I hand him my bubbly knowing I have probably already had enough and not caring. "It was a great game. I'm going for the next bottle."

I take another look at the wrap. A boy from Jade's and my first class is writing really small to fit his name in a tiny space between messages. It's almost completely covered now, and it looks incredible! Pride... Foreign but not unwelcome washes through me. As I cross the room and classmates greet me with smiles and a few hugs and fist bumps, I finally accept it all with joy.

I managed to start something good in this room. I hope for people like Tara and Gabby, it goes beyond these walls. Stepping out into the cool air I lean my head back and let out a deep breath. Shoving my hands into the miniature pockets of my shorts, I kind of wish I had taken the shawl with me.

It doesn't take me long to find Benson. He's parked just down the street. Jade must have notified him I was coming because he hands me an already opened bottle in a bag. It feels weird to have an adult hand me booze, but her parents are right. It's far safer than the alternative. I have seen what can happen to girls who don't have that kind of support or honesty with their family.

Thanking him, I turn back to the house but get distracted by a side road with a clear view of the moon. In this part of town, there are so few houses and light pollution that you can really see the stars. I walk down a little way and stand there, taking it all in.

"I'm glad I came." A wave of elation hits as I recognize his voice. A heavy jacket is dropped over my shoulders before I can turn around and the amazing smell and heat of him hug my senses. He leans in so close I feel his breath tease my ear just the way it did at the cotton candy vendor. "This view is spectacular." Chills race over my flesh. "Can I have some?"

"What?" I say, a little shakily.

Warm hands glide down my arms and one brushes over mine to gently take the bottle I forgot I was holding. I'm no blushing virgin, but with just a few words and a caress I'm losing all my cool. My heart is ready to gallop straight out of my chest and the skin where his breath is touching me feels like it's buzzing. How is it possible to *feel so much* given so little?

I break our game to turn around and look at him. He regards me quietly as he takes a sip and passes the bottle back to me. I put my lips where his have been and slowly tip the bottle. Daring to keep my eyes on his. We are locked on each other and suddenly it's too hot for his jacket. I pass him back the bottle and put my hands in the pockets only to find one is already full. I move my hand around a little to be sure the fabric is what I think it is. Sobering instantly, I pull it out.

Yep. Sure enough, held aloft between us from the edge of my finger waves a bright pink thong.

"That's not..."

I let it drop to the concrete between us. *Whoops.* "Not my business." In one move I'm out of his jacket. Quickly tossing it at him, I grab my bottle and start back towards the house.

"Wait. Look..." He jogs to catch up with me. "I know how it looks okay. *Fuck!* I get it! But hear me out...." We're approaching the lawn of the party when he puts his hand on my arm to stop me. "Let me explain..."

"I don't think she wants you touching her." Ash has appeared from out of nowhere and is walking towards us. *What the actual hell? First Ginger Jock and now him?*

"I'm fine," I snap, pushing past them and rushing inside. The sight that greets me in the living room has my foul mood evaporating into wonder. The shawl has been hung over the large flat-screen TV above the fireplace and tons of guys are shirtless with big wings painted on their backs. Some of the girls have fashioned their shirts in such a way that they have little wings too.

I find Jade sitting on the back of the sofa where I was with Nick standing silently next to her. "Where's Aron?" Jade lights up with an open warmth I have never seen in her. She embraces me and says into my ear "Look what you did!" Startled, I step back from her and she's pointing at a line of kids back at the painting table. The artist and one other girl are furiously painting wings. Aron is one of the current back canvases, and it looks like he's arguing with the artist about something. Probably what color.

A little dazzled I look back at Jade's flushed face. "You have created the slogan and symbol against bullying."

Dumbfounded I ask, "Slogan?"

Nick shouts "Not today Satan Sarah!" And a bunch of people holler back at him.

Just for fun I give in and yell, "Peanut Butter!" And laugh at the shouts that greet me. "Looks like they're not too choosy about the slogan." Nick laughs and Jade reaches for the bottle.

"Allow me." He takes the bottle from her and pours her a glass. Then he pours another and hands it to me. "I'm more of a beer guy myself."

"Thanks." I take a sip and notice Tara and Gabby in the middle of the dance floor shaking and twirling about, surrounded by all of those wings. The room does feel different. It feels charged and open.

I take Jade's hand. "Do you want to dance?"

She giggles. "No, you go ahead. I'm at limit." She sets down her flute between the couch cushions and waves me off. I look at Nick.

"I've got her."

"He has me." Jade adorably parrots, and I almost don't want to leave. I haven't met buzzed Jade yet. I notice Nick's hand hovering just behind her to silently support her from falling and I see that he does in fact, have her. He's surprised me and not many people do.

I wind my way around the crowd to join the girls in the middle of it all and It's not long before I lose myself to the music. There is so much to dance out. I do my best to let it all go as I raise my arms and move to the beat. I used to sneak out with my girls at the home and charm our way into clubs. Dancing was our favorite decompression from the shit life constantly threw our way. I forgot how good it feels to have bass so strong you feel your skin hum with it. Nothing but music and heat pushing you to move and sweat.

But there it is again, that *feeling. Damn.* I open my eyes to find Ash standing in front of me. "Did you kick his ass?" I shout above the music. He smiles at that and relaxes a little. I don't like the way his smile affects me. The way *he* affects me. Maybe having feelings you can't control is a part of being a teenager. I'm suddenly overwhelmed with them because I never got to be one before now. In my world, control is another means of survival and I don't want to be so quick to give mine up.

"What are you doing here?" I ask. He leans in to hear me better, but I don't want to play that game. I know he heard me. I step back and his smile fades.

"Can we talk?"

"I'm busy." I take another step back, raise my arms, and sway my hips back in rhythm. I know I'm teasing him... *Just a little.* But he deserves it. I have spent the better part of this party listening to the abuse Sarah has put countless classmates through. While I am a believer that most people deserve a second or even third chance, cutting off hair, stealing clothes, laxatives, shaming, every way to torment and terrorize have been perpetrated by that demon. This guy was at her side through all of it. How could I ever trust someone like that?

When he doesn't leave as I expect him to, I make sure to speak loud enough so he gets every word. *"You're. With. Her."*

"She's not my girlfriend!"

"You're with her." I shrug and turn around to dance. Not teasing him this time as I move to ignore him. Only his hands pull my back against him and my traitorous body loves it. "What if I want to be with you?" He asks at my ear. Before I can respond he's suddenly yanked away from me.

"I don't think she wants you touching her." Caden taunts Ash with his own words and they go chest to chest. *Hello testosterone.* The sight of the two of them all puffed up against the other is something I will think about later on when I'm alone. But for now, I'm not liking all the agro energy on the dance floor. Everyone is moving back from the heated pair and the room has gone quiet as everyone else begins to sense the tension even before they see it.

Thinking fast, I shove myself between them and shout as loud as I can, "Not today Satan Sarah!" Much to my relief, the room erupts into laughter and more than a few people shout it back. The party atmosphere rebounds faster than a rubber-band as most people go back to what they were doing. I look over to Jade and see her leaning against a very conflicted looking Nick. Who clearly is worried his friend might need backup. I give him a nod to let him know I've got this and look back at the two idiots to make sure I have their attention.

"I don't know what is going on with either of you." They both try to speak but I cut them off. "No!" It's awkward trying to glare at them as the crowd closing in pushes us tighter together. I'm about to tell them they go or I do, but I'm getting a little distracted with being sandwiched between them. It's impossible to stop the stupid look that comes over my face as the beat changes into something more sultry.

"Are you smiling?" Ash asks perplexed. I cover my face so he can't see how red it's turning as I grow hotter. Much to my dismay, Caden chuckles. *He knows. Oh god.*

"I think she likes where she is..."

"What?" But Ash must catch on because no one is moving, including me. The music is still going and most of the people around us are dancing now. The guys get pushed against me even closer as the dance floor fills up and it's like some sort of a wet dream come to life. *Now if they had their shirts off like most everyone else in here, then it would really be... Oh god!* I move my other hand up so I'm completely covering my mortified face. *Thank god they can't hear my thoughts!*

I feel hands move onto my shoulders. "You like this?" Ash asks huskily from behind me. Another pair of hands reach up and take mine away from my face.

"She likes covering that beautiful face of hers way too much," Caden tells Ash as his hands move down to my waist. *What is happening?* I feel dizzy with nerves and yearning.

"Wait..." I put my hands against both of their chests. "You guys *hate* each other. Remember? You were literally just about to fight."

"My bad man." Caden nods as Ash who is now grinning back at him. *This cannot be happening. This doesn't happen in real life. Not to me.* I

166

move my hands up to cover my flaming face again, and this time Ash takes my hands and pulls me against his chest. I'm not even close to processing that when Caden comes back in tight behind me. *Oh my god* I can feel both of their hard bodies pressed against mine!

I don't know if I need to faint or run five miles. We're not really dancing so much as being jostled but it feels way too good. I am very, very aware that several people are still watching us. I'm just glad we're not bumping and grinding and making a scene like some other kids on the floor. But still, I know we make a serious picture. I should leave. I know I should. But also, I don't want this to end.

"Don't be scared." Ash pulls my attention back to him.

At my ear, I finally feel Caden's lips brush against it. "Just one dance, ok?" Ash's eyes move past mine and I know he is acknowledging some unspoken truce with Caden. *This is crazy.* But as Caden's hands begin to slowly roam my body I lose all sense of time and space. Ash moves his hips a little to the music and my last coherent thought is *fuck it.* Before I surrender to them both completely.

They slowly explore me. Rubbing over the goosebumps that have rippled across my flesh. Over my arms. My hips. Even my thighs. Caden gently pulls my hair and my head falls to the side to let his lips brush my neck. My eyes close for a blissful, perfect moment. He doesn't do anything obscene in front of anyone. He just rests them like that and torments me. Ash's eyes find mine as his hands roam over me. He's so close to me now his lips are almost touching mine. Just when I think I can't take it anymore, the song ends.

For one heart-stopping moment, I stay planted where I am. Rooted between two virtual strangers who, for no good reason, completely intoxicate me. In that single heartbeat, we hold onto each other. It's too intense for me and I don't understand it. The amount of strength it takes to leave their heat is Herculean. I reluctantly pull away, confused and a little achy at their absence. I know if I don't leave now, we would definitely make a scene, and I'm at my limit for dramatic scenes today.

"I have to go." It's all I'm able to get out as I give them one last look before making my way to Jade. She's curled up in Nick's arms, fast asleep. If they were not so cute, I would be mad at her for missing all of that!

"Oh my fucking gawd! *Did that just happen?*" Yes!!! Yes, it did! Aron is my witness, but I can't freak out with him like I want to. There are too many onlookers.

"Are you guys ready to go?" Aron nods. I think he gets that I need to make my escape.

"Yeah. Let's get this one home." Nick responds.

"Great! Aron, can you get the shawl?"

"Done deal."

CHAPTER 13

Jade, Aron, and I spend most of Sunday drinking smoothies and hanging around her pool while we regal each other with stories from Saturday. The events have already taken on a fuzzy dreamlike quality. We keep having to remind each other that it all actually happened. Jade refuses to talk much about Nick but she keeps finding stealthy ways to cajole more information out of us about how he couldn't take his eyes off of her and the way the big guy took care of her. Even if she doesn't want to show it, it's plain to see that she really likes him.

My social page has taken on a life of its own and Aron has expanded my network between several other platforms to funnel some of the traffic. New videos have surfaced and I'm now tagged in all of them. "#bully-dozer" *Yuck*. But my favorite is the one from the party with everyone wearing wings. I hardly recognize the confident foolhardy girl on the screen, but in the best way. I silently promise myself to do my best to be that brave more often. We take and post a few more pictures and then it's time for me to pick up my car and head back home. I know Ugly must be wondering where I have been. I'm eager to take him on a walk and tell him about everything, so I thank Jade and her parents one last time before Benson and I head out.

∞

I'm surprised to see my school's parking lot almost a third full. I hear a whistle blow in the distance and shudder. *The horror!* The weekend practice is just another reason why I don't do sports. I feel like you have to be a sadist to work students out on a sunny Saturday afternoon, and you're probably a masochist to agree to it.

I'm almost to Marty when I notice that someone has fingered the outline of wings on my passenger window. It's hard to believe that it actually is becoming a thing, but the proof is on my window. When I drew those wings on Tara's back, I did it to make a point. It made me sick to think about her getting taunted for something she is forced to live with. I couldn't stomach the thought of her facing that kind of cruelty one more day.

It seems Tara has now moved others just as much as she moved me. If anything, the topic has only grown since the party. Maybe now that people seem to have united, Sarah won't have the same power over others which enabled her to hurt and mess with them in the first place. *That will be the day.*

"Alex." *Not possible. Nope. Ash is not behind me.* I don't have to see him until the third period tomorrow. I still have time to figure out how the hell I'm supposed to act around him now. "Alex, c'mon..." Damn! *That's definitely Ash.*

Slowly, reluctantly I turn around and find that sure enough, he's right behind me. "Whoa..." My arms fly up between us, my hands landing on his rock hard chest. "Personal space much?"

He looks down at the hands I have on him and I yank them back as if he's burned me. "You didn't seem to care much about personal space at the party."

Ugh! So I guess we are not avoiding the topic! I turn back to Marty and forcefully pull on the door handle, but Ash pushes the door shut before I can open it all the way. Pissed off, I whirl around but he's caged me in. Up close his eyes are even more compelling. It's like he has some kind of power over me that causes my brain to short circuit.

"*Look*, I'm sorry. Okay? I don't know how to be around you. You make me..." His eyes drift to my lips and he trails off.

I expel a breath and his eyes flick back up to mine before he squeezes them shut like he can't bear to look at me. "I don't know what to do." He sags a little bit and his forehead drops down to meet mine. I have no idea what he's talking about, but I'm still unable to say anything coherent. "I have tried to stay away from you. Tried to leave you alone. I know you don't belong in my world..."

Wait, what? Hurt burns through whatever spell he has me under. I shove him away, but he only moves back a little. "You think I'm not good enough for your world?" I regret how raw my voice is and that I can't hide the way he makes me feel. "You think *Sarah* is right and that I'm trash? Is that it?"

"No! No, that's not what I mean or think *at all!*" He presses against his temples in frustration and turns away from me. *Finally, I can breathe!* With his back to me, he says so softly I can hardly hear him, "It isn't *safe* for you..." I'm assuming he's talking about Satan Sarah and suddenly my hurt turns into jealous anger I can hardly control.

"*What do you see in her anyway?* I mean, *other* than the fact that she's a walking talking Barbie doll?" Is that all it takes for you? *Beauty?* I don't get it. I don't get you! Why are you here Ash? Can't you just leave me alone?" I instantly want to take that last part back. Especially as his whole face goes cold and remote. At the end of the day, he's right. I don't belong in his world. I'll never be a part of the Jacket Crew, and I wouldn't want to be anyway.

He looks at me wordlessly for a moment and reaches a hand up and cups my cheek. His face is still un-readable, but some part inside of me recognizes a goodbye when I see one. I suddenly want to hold his hand to my cheek and make him stay with a desperation that leaves me shaking. Letting his hand drop, he closes his eyes and turns away from me.

Refusing to watch him walk away, I get in my truck and speed out of the parking lot. I have no idea why I'm crying. No understanding of why I suddenly hurt so much. The only thing that calms me is knowing I'm going to see Ugly in a matter of minutes. He always cheers me up and I miss him.

My walk with Ugly is extra slow but by the time I have caught up with Maddy and we're headed home, I feel like I have a better grasp on my emotions. It would be so much easier to compartmentalize if I could understand where all these feelings for Ash are coming from. I have no context, not even a conversation between us that accounts for some of this wild chemistry. It's the same thing with Caden... Maybe it's actually me who's shallow and only into looks.

I'm completely dejected as I step into the manor and unhook Ugly. Sensing my disquiet, he rests his head on my shoulder and I give him a big hug.

Dill walks in and catches me before I can move away. "You okay?"

"Fine."

"Did your team lose or something?"

"No, we won."

"Was the party crap?"

"No, it was actually kind of amazing."

"You get in a fight with your friends today?"

"*No...*" Annoyance bleeds into my voice. "*We had a great time!*"

Dill throws up his hands. "I give up. We're doing a BBQ for dinner." And he's gone.

"Sorry," I shout as his back but I don't think he heard me.

∞

I feel like I'm in some kind of an alternate reality. School is the same. All of my classmates are the same, but everyone is acting differently. Wings are appearing everywhere around campus and people I don't know are greeting and nodding at me between classes. I keep wanting to check my face and my hair to make sure nothing is on it, so many people are looking at me.

Sarah and Ash are inconspicuously absent, but so is Nick and other members of the Jacket Crew. I try not to worry over it as I meet Jade and Aron at our table. "Are you guys noticing how weird things have gotten around here?"

"In what way?" Jade absently asks.

"In *every possible way imaginable!*" Aron laughs.

"*Right?* Are you getting stared at too?"

"No one has been able to stop staring since I hit puberty sophomore year."

Never mind. I look back to Jade. "What about you?"

"I don't notice things like that."

"Are you kidding me? You notice a knockoff a mile away, but you can't see when the entire school is on its head? You guys are *not being helpful.*"

Aron puts his hand on my shoulder. "Yes. Things have definitely shifted around here, but what's life without a little chaos and change?"

"Since when did you become an anarchist?"

"Since Jean Paul Gaultier made it look good. *Obviously.* So, when are you and Ash going to seal the deal? I have heard like ten people say *Not today Satan Sarah!* I didn't know how fast that would start to annoy me. But Sarah is probably going to transfer to a new school if she hasn't already. *She's* def out of the picture..."

"Nothing is happening between Ash and I. That dance was a *one-time thing and it* was just the bubbles talking."

"Excuse moi, but *no one* was talking. I could feel the heat coming off of you guys from the other side of the room! I grew up with Ash and Sarah and I have *never* seen him look at her, or anyone else that way. It's the kind of look we all want to feel some day, like you're the only thing that matters in the world. And never mind the fact that he danced with a guy he was ready to *murder*, just to be close to you! *Come on Alex! One of us needs to get some! And* you guys would be the hottest thing since Brangelina! *Think about it...* You could be *Alsh.*"

"That sounds like crap and you know it!"

Jade pipes in. "True."

"Riiiight. Okay, fine. Then what about tall, dark, and mysterious bachelor number two?"

"No! I'm not going for *either* of them!"

"Why the hell not?" Aron asks me incredulously. "I would give my left nut for either of them!" He grabs my hand and slams pistachio in it.

"Gross!" I throw it at him, and I accidentally hit him in the forehead.

"Oh! You could have blinded me! I would have been stuck wearing an eye patch! Which we all know is *not a good look* with fair skin!"

"*Sorry!* But you might look good with a custom glass eye."

Jade looks up at that. "True."

"See?"

Aron gets quiet and I can just make out a little cloud above his head with a multitude of eyeballs selections, rotating before him. He grabs a handful of nuts and holds them out. "Oooh! I could have a new eye for every day of the week!" *Yep. Call me the Aron whisperer.* "But seriously. Why neither guy?"

He's like a dog with a bone! "Because... *Caden* already has at least one *someone.* Have you forgotten about the pink thong I found in his pocket? And Ash... He has the kind of shit taste in friends and women that I just can't get behind."

"About that..." Aron stops there and gives Jade a look.

"About *what? Ash?"*

"The thong," He says and looks back at me.

"Okay... What about the thong?" I say trying not to lose patience.

"Homecoming is coming up."

"*Oh my god Aron*, if you don't start to make sense or get to the point, I'm going to make your glass eye fantasy come true!"

Jade takes pity on me and explains. "We talked about it after you left Sunday. It's a tradition between cheerleaders and any jock with a letterman jacket. If a cheerleader wants to let a certain jock know she's interested in going to Homecoming with him, she puts her underwear in his pocket. Usually a bright color so when she flashes him during the game wearing its match, he will know who it belongs to and hopefully be persuaded to ask her."

"You're making that up." They shake their heads at me. "But that's horrible!"

Jade taps her lip thoughtfully before responding. "Not really. I see it as empowering and taking charge."

"I see it as sexualizing and demoralizing."

Aron huffs at me. "Okay, Madam *tight ass*. Do I detect some jealously?"

"Over *miss thong?* ...Hardly." I scoff, but I'm already feeling hope bubble up inside of me.

∞

It's Thursday and *still* most of the Jacket Crew hasn't been back to school. We finally got a hold of Nick and he said their parents got wind of the bullying and the school strongly advised counseling before any of them are allowed back. I feel sorry for him but worse for Jade. I know she was hoping to hear from him at some point after the party and even I don't think his change in schedule has anything to do with his lack of contact at this point.

We're at my house, getting ready for the open mic night and she is rummaging through my non-wardrobe. "This makes no sense. Where are your actual clothes?"

From anyone else, I would be offended. But coming from Jade, her very real concern is kind of funny. "For the last time, *I swear*, I am not holding out on you. This is *all* I have."

"But there is nothing here! What are we going to do?"

Jade is one of the toughest cookies I know. It takes a lot to shake her. Which is why I walk over to her and rub her back instead of giving in to the laughter that wants to take over. I know exactly why she is over-reacting and it has nothing to do my crap wardrobe. "It's okay. You know what? Dill's granddad left a lot of..." At her sharp look, I amend my words, "*Grandma*, left several trunks of clothes. Do you want to check it out?" She nods her head and for once, I take her by the hand and lead the way.

Dill told me a long time ago that I was welcome to go through these trunks, but I never felt comfortable with it before. Having Jade with me helps, and she takes no time to pop those suckers open and start digging. She's making a lot of noise and I can't tell yet if it's good or bad noise. I do as she says and move her choices to the bed and try on several pairs of shoes and boots. She hands me with a couple of exceptions and most of them fit. The small pile on the bed is now a mountain.

Jade finally stands up and stretches after all said trunks have been thoroughly looted. She approaches the bed with a discerning eye, I trust implicitly. Looking at me, she puts her hand on her hips and gives me the same level of consideration. I can't stand the silence anymore. "*Well?*"

She fingers one of the dresses and looks up at me. "Dill's grandmother had exquisite taste. You have original Dior, Balenciaga, Balmain, Chanel, Oscar De La Renta... Just to name a few! Some of these embroidered pieces here, are by designers I don't even recognize." Even I know a couple of the names she's listed. What excites me the most is her excitement. "And all of it is in superior condition. It just needs to be aired out. This beaded vest here... This will look amazing with your coloring and hair. You can pair it with something casual for an upgrade."

"Is that what I'm wearing tonight?"

"No. *This* is what you wear tonight." She hands me a creamy blouse that has a million tiny buttons going up the front and the wrists of the billowy sleeves. "Try this one with your jean shorts and those brown over-the-knee boots, and don't tie the neck shut. Let it hang open so the 'V' shows some cleavage. Do you still have those earrings from the party?"

"Yeah."

"Okay, once we take those rollers out and finger-comb your hair, those will look perfect. Everything on the bed goes in your closet. And the next time you're at my place, I am going to have a bunch of stuff for you to take home. Also, those are some serious gowns you have in that wardrobe. You should try some out and see if any will work for Homecoming. As long as the fit is close, I have an excellent seamstress. Otherwise, there is always my personal collection."

"I can't take your clothes!" The very thought mortifies me.

"My mom won't take me shopping again until I weed my collection out. It's a process I go through twice a year and it's about that time." At my look, she shrugs. "I don't wear most things more than a few times. After that, it gets donated. So trust me, you would be doing me a serious favor." A part of me is ecstatic at the idea, but another part of me still feels weird about it. Sensing my discomfort, she takes my hand. "How about a trade?"

"I don't have anything nice enough to trade you."

"I have been drooling over your backpack since the first day of school. Remember how I mentioned I lost one in an auction?"

"I thought you were just saying that for Sarah's benefit because she was giving me a hard time."

"I never lie about fashion, even for you. I want your bag." She says it so seriously I have to laugh. I got it at Goodwill for nothing. But if she says it's collectible and she wants to trade the thing for her throwaways, far be it for me to deny her.

"Okay then, it's yours." A rush of excitement courses through me. I am going to have my first real wardrobe!

CHAPTER 14

We get to the Daily Dose on the early side but it's already packed. We find Aron at a little table near the front with his headphones on, typing so fast I can hardly see his fingers move. I tap him on the back and he jumps like a firecracker was just lit under his ass. "Ahhh! Do not sneak up on me like that!" He pulls his headphones down.

Jade is impassive. "She could have kissed your ear with a feather and it still would have seemed aggressive. You were zoning. What are we coding today?"

"*Oh*, never mind that. You two look lovely." He pulls out a seat for Jade and snaps his laptop closed. "If you want any food or drinks, now is the time to get it. *Damn* Alex. Where did you get those boots?"

Jade answers for me and I turn around to check if I can see what's left in the pastry display from our table. "Dill's grandmother was a fashion goddess. Those boots are legit 60's Chanel."

"Shut the front door! They are hot as fuck."

"Thank you." Both Jade and I respond and start laughing. Sure enough, the place is filling up quickly now and there is already a little line forming at the register. "Do you guys want anything? I'm going to grab a snack."

Jade looks at me funny. "How do you stay so small. We literally *just ate.*"

"Muffins and scones don't count."

Aron chuckles. "Get me on that diet *please.*"

Leaving them to their bickering, I head over to the line and hope the blueberry scone is still there when I get to the front. I am impressed with the size of the crowd this early. Aron wasn't kidding. This is the thing to do on a Thursday. Looking at all of the notebooks, sketch pads, instruments, and even a puppet, I wish I had Dill's guitar with me, but we came too late to sign up anyway.

My scone is still there when I make it to the front and I'm about to order when an unforgettable voice interrupts. "Got any cotton candy back there?" Trying to school the goofy grin on my face, I turn to find Caden next to me and he is even more attractive than I remember. Abruptly self-conscious, I have to control my hands from checking my hair in front of him.

The guy with a million piercings behind the register is not impressed. "No."

"The blueberry scone and a chai tea please." I look at my favorite stalker. "Do you want anything?"

I hate that he wrecks me with his smile. "Yes." He looks at me deliberately.

"*From the bar.*" I chuckle, with embarrassment.

"That will be $6.35." The barista interrupts. Caden reaches into his pocket and says to me conspiratorially, "I don't think he likes me."

"Imagine that!" I pay before Caden can and collect my scone and change, but not before I catch the sullen Barista wink at me.

Rattled, I hightail it to the waiting area with Caden.

"What do you have, that I don't?"

I'm chuckling as Luka and Gabriel join us. "Hey, Alex."

"Hi, Luka! Gabriel... What are you guys doing here?"

Luka smiles at that. "We come here most Thursdays, but I've never seen you here so the more appropriate question is what are *you* doing here?"

I nod at my friends. "I came with them."

Gabriel lights up at seeing Jade. "Can we join you?"

There is little I can imagine more uncomfortable than sitting next to Caden for the next two hours, under Aron's microscope. Even the possibility that Gabriel might cheer up Jade and get her mind off a certain someone is worth it. "If you can find some extra chairs, sure." I take my tea and head back to the table, stopping myself from checking to see if Caden follows.

Before the guys can join us, I warn my friends. "Heads up. We have company."

Aron looks disgruntled. "But this table is just for- *Hello.*" His upset evaporates as quickly as the guys join our table.

We scoot our chairs to accommodate them and I glance at Jade to check her temperature. She hasn't glanced up from her Physics book and she hasn't moved her chair an inch either. *Okay...* I'm grouped together with her and Aron and Gabriel waste no time getting his seat wedged up to hers. Caden's voice distracts me.

"Great table."

"Thank you," Aron responds for me. "I usually work here after school so I get VIP seating."

Surprised, I look over at him. "You do?"

"When I'm not hanging out with you witches, this is my home away from home." Looking around the room, I find it hard to imagine sophisticated, modern Aron hanging out here in this rustic, bohemian setting.

"You guys hang out a lot?" Caden looks like he is measuring Aron and it makes me want to laugh.

Aron's eyebrows do that wiggle thing and I know nothing good is about to come out. "Oh, we hang out in *every way* you can possibly imagine." His lewd expression has me bursting out in laughter and Jade chuckling from behind her book. *I knew* she was paying attention.

I give him a little shove. "You're disgusting."

"But you love me anyway." The other guys are laughing at his antics when the host steps onto the stage and gives an introduction. Looking around once again, I see that it is indeed packed. The first act is a spoken word poet that blows me away. Most of the artists that follow him are just as good. The acts are as varied as they are compelling. The guy with the puppet turns out to be the world's worst ventriloquist but he knows it and his jokes have us all in fits of laughter.

I catch Caden watching me laugh and if that's not flustering enough, I look over and see Aron watching *him* watching *me*. *Damn!* I'm about to tell Aron to stop being weird when Caden and Luka are called up. *This should be interesting.* Looking at Aron I suspect he knew they were going to perform because he has that annoying know-it-all smug look covering his face.

Caden and Luka pick up guitar cases that are already by the stage and pull up another chair so that they can sit together. When neither of them reaches for a microphone, I lean back ready to be bored. No singing? I know it's bitchy of me, but anyone can jam out. Looking over at Jade, I see Gabriel say something to her and she nods. A small smile on her lips. *Hmmm.*

My hair prickles and I look past her shoulder to see Ash with his hand on Nick's shoulder. Nick looks like he wants to eat Gabriel for breakfast. *Shit.* Ash is watching me as he says something to Nick who gives him an almost imperceptible nod. I'm about to kick Jade under the table when a beautiful melody from a single guitar captures my attention.

Caden is leaned over an impressive looking Flamenco Negra guitar. But I can still see his eyes looking at me through the curtain of his hair. *Holy hotness.* His fingers deftly fly over the strings and Luka seamlessly joins in while Caden begins to tap his guitar in rhythm to a romantic Spanish tune. My mind is a little blown as he pulls, plucks, and flicks the guitar in deft, swift moves I have never even *seen* before. All the while he doesn't take his eyes off me.

My heart has begun to beat fast enough that I could be running a marathon right now. His expression mirrors the demand and passion of his playing. I am completely terrified and utterly transfixed. Someone kicks me under the table, momentarily snapping me from his thrall.

Aron nods his head at me and mouths *HOT* as he dramatically fans himself. I look up and catch Ash still watching me and my face flames up. I have no idea *why* I feel like he's caught me with my hand in the cookie jar. As the melody picks up to go impossibly faster, I remind my-self that I have done nothing wrong and look back to Caden who is now in an intense staring contest with Ash.

I'm not a fan of guys getting into pissing contests. I would *never* admit this out loud, but it's pretty impressive that Caden can play his guitar at this level while keeping rhythm *and* going agro on Ash. *Multi-task much?* The fact that he is smiling with his mouth and threatening with his eyes? All the while, his playing is becoming more urgent and tinged with violence. None of that should be a turn on because *that* would be all kinds of wrong.

Just before the song ends, a string breaks and the spell is broken. Letting out a breath I automatically clap with everyone else and become aware that Aron has been gripping my knee under the table. I shrug him off but can't ignore his elation. "Where is popcorn when I need it?!"

"*Shut up,*" I whisper to him as the guys rejoin our table. I give him my own little kick as a prompt to *behave.* I still want Jades attention so I can warn her but it's no use now that everyone is here. Pointedly ignoring Ash, I look at Caden and Luka. "That was amazing!"

I expect an egotistical response but instead Caden surprises me by looking away and mumbling, "Thanks." I could swear his cheeks have reddened but that wouldn't make sense. Not when he just masterfully made love to that guitar and seduced the entire audience at the same time! Looking back at Jade as the next act goes on, I try to see if I can get her attention without gaining any notice but it's not happening.

Giving up, I elbow Aron and hope he can play it cool. Putting my *Aron whispering* abilities to the test, I direct my eyes where I want him to look. I place my hand over his leg, signaling restraint. I continue to pretend-watch the poet all the while. I know when he's seen Ash and Nick because he squeezes my knee back. A full-on stealth convo ensues between our eyes. Wherein we agree he will be the one to give Jade the heads up since he is closest to her.

My phone begins to vibrate just as the host introduces the next act. It only vibrates for emergency calls. I signal that I have to take it before ducking out of the cafe. I can feel something is wrong even before I pick it up.

"Alex?" The sound of Shells' voice does nothing to alleviate my dread. She would *never* call me unless it was serious.

"Tell me."

I hear muffled sobbing and somehow I know what she's going to say before she chokes out, "It's Vic."

Gripping the phone with both hands, I slide down the bricks behind me. Neither of us says anything. I just listen to her cry and hate myself for not being there. "Coke?" I numbly ask.

"Heroin." More silence. I feel a part of me split in half and I'm so full of shame and regret. It's a bitter taste in my mouth. "Don't." Shells snaps. "I can hear you blaming yourself. *Don't.* We always knew this would..." More sobbing. "I have to go. This isn't my phone."

"I'm coming back."

"There is nothing to come back to. After you left, we got the hell out. I'm... I'm going to go home."

"But your stepdad!"

"Had a heart attack two weeks ago. I'm staying to see Vic get buried and then I never want to see this place again."

"*Shells.*" I try to say more but my throat has locked up on me.

"I have your number. I know where to find you. *I want to go home.*"
She sounds like a little girl and I have to blink back more tears.

"I love you."

"Always."

The line goes dead. I stare at my phone for I don't know how long
before a voice interrupts.

"Alex..."

I look up at Ash's worried expression. I shake my head no at him, still
unable to speak. I get up and brush past him to go inside and get my bag.
Hardly aware of the people I'm pushing past, I make it to the table when
Aron puts his hand on my arm. I look at him and he's smiling at me.

"Just in time! That's your name he's calling."

"What?" I'm unable to compute what he's saying to me.

"Is Alex in the house?" The host has his hand shielding his eyes from
the over headlights and is peering into the audience.

"She's right here," Caden speaks up. Startled, I look at him and his
amusement fades the moment he sees my face.

Aron, who is still oblivious, pushes me forward. I stumble a few steps
towards the stage. And as people clap, I walk the rest of the way like a
zombie. The lights are not as blinding as they were in Drama. I can still
make out the faces of my friends. Nick. Ash.

I lean into the mic and say the only thing that comes to mind. "Give
me a minute." Turning away from the audience I see a collection of instruments and try to clear my head. The audience starts to chatter behind
me but all I can think about is Vic. *What am I doing up here?*

Someone is touching my arm. It's the host. "Are you ready?"

Just like that, I know exactly what I'm going to do. What I *need* to do. "Yeah. Can I use that?" I point at the keyboard. Looking a little putout, he signals for me to wait before leaving the stage. Presumably to ask its owner for permission. I'm already setting it up when he comes back looking even more annoyed and gives the okay. With the mic now hovering above the keyboard, I scoot in. I'm kind of facing the audience, but it hardly matters.

With my heart in the midst of breaking, I lean into the mic and talk to my friend. "This one is for you Vic." My fingers start moving before I'm even totally conscious of it. The first notes to *Medicine* pouring out as I see memory after memory flit by. Our rocky beginning. The first time she came to bat for me despite herself. Late nights sharing, laughing, and opening up in ways we never could with the rest of the world. Getting our asses beat by the older girls over and over again until the cherished day we were finally big enough to turn the tables. Teaching me to dance, to be alive in the shittiest of circumstances.

Leaning back into the mic, I pour my heart and soul into this last goodbye. I have never sung this way before. It's the best I have ever been and I know it. But it *has to be*, because I need her to hear me. I need her to *know* from wherever she is. *All* of my regret, my frustration, my devastation. The song ends but I can't move. I hear them cheering, but I can't look at anyone.

The host is touching me again. I look up at him, completely empty. "That was incredible. You're welcome back here any time you want." He helps me up and leads me to the stairs. I put one foot in front of the other until I'm at my table. People are talking to me, but I can't hear them over the buzz in my ears that seems to be growing louder and louder. I take my bag and keep going. I'm almost to my truck when Jade steps in front of me. I shake my head at her on the very edge of a total breakdown. "I can't." Is all I am able to get out. She looks behind me, to who, I don't know.

"Give me your keys. I'm driving." Without thinking, I fumble around in my bag until I find them, but tears have already begun to leak down my face and it's hard to see anything. Grabbing my hand, she takes the key then opens my door for me and tucks me inside, wasting no time with getting in herself. I have a pretty good idea that my whole table is outside with us, if not Ash and Nick too. I pull up my knees and bury my head in them, feeling too exposed and too raw to meet anyone's eyes as we pull out.

When we drive up to the manor, Dill is already waiting outside with Ugly. I stumble out of the truck even before it's fully off and I jog into his arms. I instantly crumble the moment he wraps me into his safety. Big heaping sobs choke me and he holds me up. I hear him thank Jade and he takes me inside. How overwhelming it all is at the loss of my best friend and sister.

He leads me to the sofa, and I settle down enough to sit next to him and lean my head on his shoulder, still crying. Ugly is licking my hands and nuzzling me but I can't bring myself to comfort him. It's like singing my heart out took away everything I had left. No longer sobbing now, I gulp in shaking, hiccupping breaths.

"If you don't tell him you're going to be okay soon, he's going to stroke out." Sure enough, Ugly is looking incredibly upset.

Petting his head, I finally get out "I'm okay." But I'm not and another wave of overwhelming sorrow hits me and I'm sobbing against Dill again. I feel his beard tickle my face as he rests his head over mine and something about the feeling of his bristles against my skin soothes me. As soon as I slow down a bit, I register that Ugly is howling and I'm pretty sure he's been crying with me this whole time. I blink past the tears and see that while Dill has one arm over my shoulders, he has his other awkwardly reaching over to comfort Ugly. *Poor Dill.* Next to Jade, he's the least emotiional person I know.

His chin moves over my head as he speaks. "Just this once, I am going to let the dog on the sofa. I have never seen him this upset."

I mutely nod. Grateful to be able to really hold something. I pat the sofa next to me. Ugly stops whimpering long enough to crawl into my lap. It's an impossible fit. When he's all situated, most of his weight is on me. Instead of it being uncomfortable, his warm pressure, fir, and beating heart sooth me. I feel bad when I notice him trembling. That's what gets my voice back. I start stroking him and rubbing his back.

"Shhhhhh. It's okay. I'm okay. You're such a good boy. Yeah. Good boy." I look over at Dill and finally get it out while still petting Ugly. "A good friend of mine, my best friend from the home. She overdosed."

Dill looks in front of him at nothing, nodding his head. "I'm so sorry." I'm grateful he doesn't look at me when he says it, or else I might start crying again.

Even though Ugly is on top of me I'm freezing. "I'm cold."

Dill gets up and starts a fire even though it's a warm evening, and he makes my favorite hot cocoa. "You hungry?" When I nod at him, he rubs the back of his neck. "Yeah, yeah, stupid question." He sits over in his leather chair and I stretch out on the sofa, laying across it. Somehow

Ugly fits himself over my legs and beside me, and we all stay like that. Watching the fire as Dill occasionally feeds it.

CHAPTER 15

*I*t's too bright. Turning away from the offensive light, I find my legs are numb and trapped. Shielding my eyes, I try to move them again and a familiar annoyed groan responds. Blinking, the first thing I see is Ugly draped over my legs. I'm on the sofa? Looking around I try to gauge the time. My phone is MIA and the cuckoo clocks are too far away. If the light is any indication it's definitely later in the day, the school day. *Shit!* Sitting straight up, I squint at the cuckoo clocks willing the blurry numbers to crystalize. The pounding in my head intensifies with the effort.

Looking away, I notice a scribbled message on the coffee table right in front of me. Grabbing it and moving it close enough to kiss, I peer at Dill's chicken scratch. I have to scrub away the grit from my eyes several times before the jumbled letters finally become words:

I'm at the shop if you need me. Leftover pizza in the fridge. You're excused from school.
-Pickle.

Then I remember why I'm on the sofa, sleeping in on a school day and in come my useless tears. As if sensing my distress, Ugly comes awake all at once. He somehow manages to stretch his entire body across the sofa and kick me in the face. Momentarily startled from the depression that's wrapped itself around me like a heavy wet blanket, I shove his foot away.

"Ouch! Ugly!" But he just curls his massive body around, grumbling and huffing the whole way through like a thousand-year-old senile man and then settles his giant head on my chest. His wet nose tickling my neck as he breaths out a contented sigh. I stop sniffling long enough to hug him. He lets me hold on while I let go and cry into his fur. Trying not to be too loud because I don't want to upset him and make him cry too.

I don't know how long I have been at it when the doorbell rings and Ugly stiffens. I debate on getting it for a moment, but lethargy wins and my head droops back into Ugly's fur. The annoying doorbell rings again. Moaning, I find Ugly's ear. "Tell them to go away." Ugly scrambles to look at me and I end up pushing him off the sofa. "Tell them to go away," I repeat, looking directly into his eyes and making my command more serious. Incessant knocking replaces the ringing and I could kiss Ugly when he trots over to the entrance and growls low in threat.

That gets whoever it is to stop. Satisfied, I flop back and pull the blanket over my head. *Good boy.* I'm already halfway asleep when sudden tapping at the window has me throwing back my blanket and glaring daggers. Two pairs of worried eyes stare back at me. Without even thinking, I launch the first pillow my fingers reach and watch it sail to the window at Jade and Aron with an unsatisfactory *thump*. "Go away!" Ugly comes running back to the living room full of aggression but the moment he sees it's Aron and Jade, he enthusiastically barks and wags his tail. *Traitor!*

When I don't move to get up, they start back in with the knocking. Cursing, I wipe the snot from my face and stand up on shaky legs. "Alright! *Cut it out.*" I hobble my way over to the door in yesterday's clothes and a quilt wrapped around me. As soon as the door is open, Aron starts in. "You look like hell."

"You are hell," I say without any rank. We move to the living room where I reclaim my place on the sofa. Ugly hops up next to me and leans until I'm forced to move over and make room for him. Jade perches on the coffee table and Aron takes Dill's chair.

"Spill," is all Jade says.

Sighing, I lean on my knees and put my head in my hands. "I'm fine. Do you guys want water or something?" I get up and move to the kitchen, not waiting for their response and fill a glass of water. I gulp the whole thing down and fill it back up again searching around for the bottle of aspirin that's normally by the stove. When I finally turn around, both of them are staring at me. The same worried expressions they wore on the other side of the window reflected back at me. "I'm *fine*, okay?"

Jade looks at Aron who looks me up and down. "It's two-thirty in the afternoon and you just woke up. You are wearing yesterday's rumpled clothes accessorized with grandma's quilt. You slept on the sofa, smell like a dog, and your hair is a nest. Not to mention this whole... Thing." He waves his hand in the general vicinity of my face.

"Fine."

"*Fine?*" He looks like he's ready to go another round with me.

"FINE! I'm not *okay...*" My voice hitches and I unceremoniously plop down. The shock of the cold floor feels good and from down here the worried looks on their faces are more comical than upsetting. I pat the floor. "It's clean."

Jade gracefully sits next to me and nods at Aron. "Do you know how to work that thing? She needs coffee."

"I'm not completely incompetent." He mutters and begins working the machine.

She smiles and whispers at me conspiratorially. "I know." And then she reaches out to me and takes my hand. Hers is warm against my icy skin. She looks worried again. "Do you need a bigger blanket?

"No. I'm just... Tired." Without any thought, I lay my head in her lap. I let out a shaky sigh as she begins to stroke my hair and Aron comes back with a steaming cup. "Thank you." I balance it over my bellybutton.

"Do you want tissue?" I have never heard him sound so gentle. It makes me look at him.

"Why?"

"Because you're crying." *I am?*

He looks so upset now that I want to comfort him, but I feel so empty.

Jade intercedes. "My bag's by the door. The second pocket from the front, you'll find a tissue pack."

Wordlessly, Aron leaves us. Jade is still stroking my hair when he comes back and sits next to me. I let him wipe my cheeks and close my eyes. I know it's twisted but for just a moment, I pretend I have parents who love me and are holding me through the worst agony I have ever been through. Breathing out and letting the fantasy fade, I note the wipe Aron pulls away, stained with inky dark makeup.

"I really must look like hell."

"Yeah." Aron huffs out a soft laugh. "Close your eyes again? I want to get the rest."

With my eyes shut and Jade's hands moving softly through my hair, I let the words spill out. "I was living in a state home before I came here. I couldn't get adopted so that's where I landed. If you're lucky, or not lucky depending on how you look at it, that's where you go if no one wants you. It's a rough place. You have to be tough. Me and some of the girls... We connected. Out of necessity at first. But then... They *got me* and I got them. We learned each other's story and ways and we just became our own little family. I was especially close with..." I have to swallow a couple of times. "With Vic. She saved me more than a couple of times. This one time, she took the fall for me when it was my fault we missed curfew. She almost got kicked out for that." I chuckle at the memory. "I was *so* pissed at her. But she kind of thought she was my big sister." I choke back the sob. I need to get through this. "She always had issues with addiction, but most of the time she seemed to have it under control. At least compared to some of the others. I found out last night she..." I take a deep breath. "She overdosed. It was a heroine."

I roll over then, curl up and sob into Jade's lap. Clinging to her as if she is the life-raft that will keep my tears from drowning me. She doesn't stop stroking my hair and I feel Aron's warm hand rest over my shoulder. Shame and guilt wash through me and I don't know how to sustain this level of anguish. As I cry with my friends, it's like letting steam out of a balloon. I don't know how long we stay like that, but after I settle down, Aron hands me a tissue. I push myself up to a sitting position and blow my nose as hard as I can. Making an embarrassing amount of sound.

I throw the crumpled tissue aside and see Aron looking at me funny.

"What?"

"You're... An ugly cryer."

"*What?*" Both Jade and I shout.

"Like *bad* though. Like Kardashian level *bad...*"

The serious look on his face snaps me in half. I start laughing so hard my ribs hurt. *"You're such an ass! I hate you!"* I say between laughter and tears.

Smiling, he picks up my cold, discarded coffee, dumps it out and makes a new one. When he passes it back to me, I take a sip. "How do you know how I like it?"

"Some things are important enough to remember." I set down the coffee and take his hand. Jade already has my other. They grasp hands too and it's a real moment.

"Now you know where I really come from," I say on a shuddering sigh.

"No." Jade simply responds.

"No, *what?*"

"*No.* That's a place, but it's not where you come from Alex. You come from loyalty, from integrity, and from resilience. You come from pure talent and adaptability and *kindness.* You come from so much strength it intimidates me sometimes. If you think your past would make us look at you any differently, you're *wrong.* If anything, I just admire you more. And... I want to be like you when I grow up."

"What? *No!* I want to be like *you!*?" I shout back at her, completely incredulous and touched.

A very upset sounding Aron chimes in. "Then *who wants to be like me?*" Jade and I go silent at that and then we all burst into laughter.

Taking my coffee, I pick myself up off of the floor and peer at Aron as he gets up with Jade. "I am *not* an ugly cryer."

"Ew. You *so are*. I wish I could erase the faces you made but it's stuck *here*." He taps his head and I laugh and push him.

"Shut your mouth. I am not."

I still hurt from the inside out. My whole body aches, and all I want to do is sleep. But somehow my friends have made the weight bearable. Before they came it felt like I was never going to be able to catch my breath. But here I am, somehow smiling. "What now?"

Jade stretches and looks me up and down like Aron did. "Now you shower and for the love of all, brush your teeth and your hair. Get dressed and when you're ready, we need to talk about some things."

"Can't I just go back to sleep?"

"No." They both respond.

"Jeez, *okay*. Make yourselves at home then. I'll be out soon." I gulp down the rest of the coffee before I go and can't decide if I'm annoyed or relieved that they are staying and bossing me around.

∞

Armed in sweatpants, a hoody, and a pair of Dill's woolen socks, I make another cup of joe and head to the living room but find it empty.

Walking over to the library wing I shout, "Guys?" Nothing. It takes only a moment to figure out where they are. I move up the stairs slowly. I feel like I'm ancient and my bones are so brittle they might break. The closer I get to the wing, the more buoyant I start to feel. Coming up here is a good idea. It's harder to be depressed when you're covered in glowing colors.

I pause to admire the door before I push it open and finding them sprawled out on the bed with Ugly. I didn't even bother with checking the other one as for the moment, this has been our wing of choice.

"Ugly..." I say in an admonishing tone. *Getting to be on the sofa with me must have really gone to his head.*

Aron moves to hold him in place. "This bed is like one hundred years old and these moth-bitten sheets have seen better days since the Bible was written. He's practically a service dog... *Come on.*"

"More like a service horse. It's amazing we have any room at all." Jade grumbles still looking up at the stained-glass ceiling.

"You know you love him." Aron challenges.

Jade looks over at Ugly, who is staring at her with adoring warm brown eyes. His tail gives a lazy thump. "True."

They look so angelic. For just a hair raising second, they are angels. Their golden bodies glowing apart from the jewel-toned light spilling across them. Their eyes looking *different.* But what has my heart ready to explode in my chest is the shimmering wings, tucked against their bodies. I have never seen anything so fantastical or impossible in all of my life, but the undeniable reality of what my eyes are signaling to my brain settles deep into my consciousness. It's like that inexplicable feeling of relief you get when someone finally tells you the truth. Aron looks over at me then and his eyes are like looking into the sun. My headache takes on a new dimension of pain and my legs crumple beneath me. His massive wings stretching out and fluttering in agitation is the last thing I see.

A tongue is frantically licking my face and Ugly's agitated mumblings bring me awake. "Oh my god! Ewwww! Get him off of me!" I shriek at my useless friends.

"I'm trying, but he's too big!" Aron's dramatically groaning with his lame-ass attempt and Jade is still on the bed watching us with a bemused smile on her face.

So over all of the disgusting slobber on my face, I shout as clearly as I can, "Ugly! SIT!"

Finally, I can breathe again as Ugly snorts and immediately sits back.

"Ahhhh! Not on me you wretched demon!" Aron yelps in a manner that has me chuckling as I move to sit up myself. "What happened?"

Aron crab walks away from Ugly until he can finally stand and then comes back over to help me up. "You fainted."

"What? No... No way! I do not... Faint." I huff, completely embarrassed now.

"Um, yeah. You do. Because you did. Just now actually." I cross my arms and glare at him. As if looking tough will somehow dispel the truth. "Remember that one time you were on your back and only loves true kiss could wake you from your slumber? Well, that was you, Beauty and your Beast right here just woke you."

I look to Jade for some support, but she just scoots over to make room for me. I'm adjusting myself next to her and Aron is doing the same when I remember. "Wait. I saw..." I look up at them then. Both beautiful in their own right. Even more so under all the stained-glass colors, but totally and completely normal. Human.

"You saw?" Jade asks, raising an eyebrow at me and glancing at Aron.

"I saw... Well for a moment you guys looked..." At their critical gazes, I let out air I didn't realize I was holding. "Nothing. You guys just looked like a work of art for a second."

"A second?" Indignation immediately replaces the worry from Aron's gaze. "I am a walking, talking masterpiece! Puuulease. ...A second. Psst. Are you okay now? Or do you require sniffing salts to keep you lively?"

"I'm.."

"FINE." They both interrupt me.

"We know." Aron finishes.

Despite everything, another smile cracks my face. I take a deep breath and let it out slowly. Willing my brain and body to come back and start working right. "So what's up?"

They glance at each other, sharing another look and Jade begins. "Last night, after we left, Ash and Nick followed me to your place. Ash said he wanted to walk home, and Nick drove me home."

"Wait... Nick drove you ALL the way home?" Relieved for the distraction from my head, I latch onto that juicy bit and dig in. "Was Benson not available? Or you just... Preferred to go with Nick?"

A shy smile covers Jade's face and I find her hand and squeeze it. "Come on. *I need* this."

She huffs. "Fine. But then I need to get back on topic because Nick and I, are not it."

"Deal."

"Nick insisted on driving me, so I sent Benson home." Aron and I exchange smiles at that but stay quiet. Jade is not a big sharer and neither of us wants to spook her. "We mostly talked about you." She looks at me and I roll my eyes. "And then he explained why he never called. He said he *wanted to*. But... And this is a part of what we wanted to talk with you about... Apparently, he and Ash are already promised to other families." At my confused look, she shakes her head. "As in, *arranged marriage*."

"*Excuse* me?" *Nu-uh*. I look to Aron for support and he just looks down at the sheets.

Jade looks more flustered then I have ever seen her. "I know. *Believe* me. *I do...* But when it comes to old money, family names, and big business? Advantageous marriages are more commonplace than anyone realizes. And anyway, he said he didn't know how to tell me or explain it. Especially because we were only just beginning to really get to *know* each other. So he just thought it would be better for me and less painful if he just disappeared."

"I have so many questions I don't know where to start. Why would you lump Ash and Nick together? I mean I know they're friends but..."

Aron's eyes grow large and disbelieving, stopping me short. "*Everyone* knows they're brothers...."

Jade squeezes my hand. "I thought you knew."

Aron shakes his head. "*We* thought you knew."

"But Nick is..."

Jade sits up. "They adopted him."

The realization has my eyes rounding. "They are brothers... *Wow.* Okay... And they're both in arranged... Situations?" I can't bring myself to say marriage.

Jade shakes her head. "Not exactly. They have not been promised to anyone specific. As long as they marry within a particular set of candidates that reach their family's standards, they will carry on their family legacy and retain all privileges and inheritance."

Shocked I sputter, *"And if they don't?"*

"They will be cast out, disowned, and shamed. Not to mention the certain retribution that would result."

I sit up at that and rub my arms at the sudden chill. "What do you mean? *Retribution?*" I say the heavy word like it's a joke, but Jade's face remains serious.

"I have met their parents and other parts of their... Family. My father has had business dealings with theirs in the past. Things seemed to be going well when he abruptly ended their connection. He never spoke of it after, but there is something not right with their family. I can't explain it. But their Dad always scared me. And Nick told me life would become very difficult for them if they were to fall out of line."

"Oh my god." I breathe. Hardly believing the archaic nature of what she's revealing but finally getting so much of Ash's weird behavior around me. And why he said I wasn't a part of his world. Suddenly another thought occurs to me. "And Sarah?"

Jade lets out a frustrated sigh. "Is one of the acceptable families."

I get up and pace around the room. No longer able to sit. *"That's* why they're always together? This is *bullshit!* They shouldn't have to marry someone just because of their name or money or whatever... And when do they have to marry? Right after high school!? This is so messed up! No wonder Nick didn't want to tell you!" *The poor guy! And what about Ash? Have I been judging him wrongly this whole time? Has he been with Sarah because he has to be? Not because he wants to be?*

More questions are reeling around my head when Aron clears his throat. "No teen weddings. It's not about *when*, but *who*, and this is only a part of what we wanted to talk to you about."

"There's *more*?"

"Yes," Jade says resolutely. "Ash said he wanted to walk home last night. They don't live that far from you so it was a no brainer for Nick to agree, but Ash never came home last night."

Alarm replaces all other emotions. "What do you *mean* he never came home? No one has seen or heard from him since last night?"

Jade and Aron nod and suddenly I feel wide awake. "We have to find him."

Aron stands up. "I thought you would never ask."

We go downstairs without debate and an idea hits me. "Ugly can help." I turn around and look at them. "I need something of Ash's for him to smell. I can put him in his harness and we can track where he went on foot." I have no idea if my idea will actually work, but there is nothing Ugly hasn't been able to do so far and it's worth a shot.

Aron looks dubious. "He can do that?"

"Hell yes, he can," I say with forced confidence.

Jade takes out her phone. "It will be faster if I go over to his place and pick something up."

"I'll get ready to go with Ugly."

Aron looks at Jade. "I'll go with you."

I'm already heading to my room when I hear the front door click shut. I change into something good for running, because you never know, and pull my hair up into a ponytail. I put Ugly into his harness but he's not jumping around in excitement as he usually does. He senses something is wrong, and he calmly lets me strap him in. Grabbing my skateboard, I open the door and slam into a chest.

"Ash!" Relief floods into me and I wrap my arms around him without thinking. "*Thank god,*" I whisper into his neck. His arms wind around me and he feels *so good* and his smell is everything that's right in the world.

Pulling back from him but unable to let him go completely I demand, "Where have you been? Everyone is looking for you!"

"I texted you. I was worried about you."

"Worried about *me?*" I laugh at the absurdity of the situation. "I was just about to track your ass, on foot, with my dog as search and rescue!"

"He can do that?"

"Where have you been!?"

"I just needed to know you were okay and I couldn't go home until I did, but you weren't answering your phone."

Looking behind me I see my discarded bag from last night on the floor. I pull out my phone and see a million unread messages. A few of them from an unidentified number. I show him the screen and point. "Is this you?"

"No. *That's me.*" He points at another number with no contact saved. "Who is that?"

"I don't know." *But I have an idea.* Pocketing the phone, I hear a car pull up and look over Ash's shoulder. Jade, Aron, and Nick get out.

Ash's head falls to his chest. *"Shit."*

Nick jogs over and doesn't slow down when he reaches us. It looks like he is going to charge Ash, but he tackles him into a hug instead. When they pull apart, Nick just shakes his head at him.

"I'm sorry," Ash mutters and finally looks up into Nick's face.

A beat of silence goes by and Nick roughly pulls Ash into another hug. "I know." He steps back and looks at him. "You're still a complete asshole."

Ash looks a little worried. "Dad?"

Nick let's out a breath. "Still out of town." He pulls out his phone and messages someone as he speaks to Ash. "I covered for you." He pockets the phone and his voice takes on a sharp edge. "But don't do that again! Not without some kind of warning! *At least* give me that."

Ash looks away. "I know. I have no excuse. I Just..."

Nick puts his hand on his brother's shoulder. *"I know."*

It's amazing so few words can pass between them when it's clear they are sharing a wealth of communication and understanding between each subtle look. Vic, Shells, and I used to be like that.

As Jade and Aron join us on the porch and it becomes clear that no one is leaving, I say the only acceptable thing I can think of, "There's leftover pizza."

CHAPTER 16

No one wants to leave me alone and I have to push them out of the door. If it were not so sweet, I would be annoyed. I have to take Ugly for a walk and I can't have everyone over at Maddie's without her parents' permission. Giving one last wave I shut the door behind me and lean against it. I'm so drained I don't know how I'm going to have the energy for this walk. But looking at Ugly's eager face, I can't deny him. I'm still leaning against the door when someone knocks, startling me.

I pull it open and for the second time today, Ash is on the other side. I get a feeling kind of like vertigo when I see him. The nervous dip in my stomach making me a little queasy. "Did you forget something?"

"I'm not convinced."

"*What?*" I look over his shoulder and see that everyone is gone. Even Nick.

"That you're *fine*. I can't leave until I know you're okay." *Why do you care? Why are you here?* I want to ask him but think better of it. "How did you convince Nick to leave you here, *again?*" I say, distracting him from the invasive tangent he's on.

He chuckles. "Promises were made."

"Are you good at keeping your word?"

"The best." Ugly *woofs* from behind me.

"I need to take him out."

"Let's go then."

My whole world has been toppled, and I am never going to get over losing Vic. *Not ever.* But for this one shining moment, I feel warm joy spread through me at this boy's attention.

I should say no, "Fine."

We are silent at first. Each of us lost to our thoughts, but then my fine hairs tingle and I know he's looking at me.

"Why are you smiling like that?"

Busted. Letting out a breath, I shrug. "It's going to sound strange."

"Go ahead."

Peering sidelong at him I see nothing but open curiosity. "...I can always *feel* when you're looking at me." He pauses from walking for a moment but resumes when he sees my obvious anxiety. We are passing through the park now near Maddie's, but I would really love to find an empty bench.

"What do you mean?" He still sounds relaxed and casual, but I can't help feeling self-conscious.

I look ahead of me instead of at him. "I don't know. Like the fine hairs on my neck and even my arms sometimes, they go up. Kind of like goosebumps but more..."

"Primal?"

"Exactly. Almost like a warning. I can sometimes sense when other people look at me too. But with you, it's a body thing." I risk glancing at him to see if he thinks it's stupid, but he still looks relaxed and interested.

"Is there anything else unusual that you notice around me?"

As if I would ever share how all of my senses seem heightened around him. How his scent can affect me like a physical touch, or how the chemistry with him is so strong for me that sometimes I can't speak, or think. "Do you feel anything unusual around me?" I ask instead.

"*Lots* of things."

I stop walking and look at him sharply. The heat that is always between us erupts the moment our eyes lock and I get the craziest urge to nuzzle him. *What the hell?* I take a step back, *not kiss him* or *hold him,* but *nuzzle him?* Shaking my head at my errant thoughts, I take another step back.

"Alex." Ash begins to close the gap between us.

"No. I don't know what this thing is between us, but I know you must feel it too. Or you wouldn't be here..." When he doesn't respond right away, I take that as an affirmative. "And it's so much... Most of it... *All of it...* I don't get!" Still shaking my head, I take another step back. "And I am *dealing* with way too much as it already is. How am I supposed to process this too? When I don't even *understand* it? You know this is the most we have ever talked? *Ever?*" Another step back. "Doesn't it strike you as strange to be worried about me? To *care* when you don't even know me?"

"But I *do* know you! I know that you like speed. A *lot* of it. I have seen you skateboarding with your dog and it's *insane.* And I know you love pistachio ice cream, hot summer days, and writing." Before I can ask him how he knows these things, he continues. "I know you're *brave*. Sometimes stupidly so! I know you are willing to risk yourself for what you believe is right. I know you can't stand seeing anyone get hurt because you have been." He takes another step closer to me. "And I know your heart is as deep as the ocean because of the way you care about *everyone* around you. The way you speak only when you have something worth saying. And the way you *sing*... My god when you sing it's like I can *see you* so clearly because you make me, and *everyone else* who's listening, *feel, everything you feel*. And you feel *so much Alex!*"

He takes one last step, closing the distance between us. His hands, that have somehow found their way to my shoulders, travel up my neck, over my face, and gently into my hair. It feels like pure, undiluted energy is being passed from his hands, into my body. Leaving a trail of incandescent pleasure. His stormy eyes dive into mine and I am anchored to him. "I know you're more beautiful inside than you are outside, and your outside is *impossibly* beautiful Alex." His face comes closer to mine. "I know the way it feels when you watch me too."

He leans his head against mine as he did before. His lips mere inches from my own, and I need him so much right now that I'm trembling. Gripping his wrists as he holds me captive, I try to catch my breath. "I know you smell like roses in bloom." He leans in, his lips grazing my neck as he inhales. "Dirt after rain and something else that's totally undefinably you." His mouth is now hovering just over mine and I can feel his breath whisper across my lips, as intimate as a kiss. "And I know I *want you*. More than *anything... I want you!*" He pulls me the rest of the way to him and we crash and meld together like breaking waves in an ancient sea.

It's like I was never kissed before now. *Now*... As his soft, demanding lips arch over mine and clash, in a symphony of sensation. I open for him, unable to deny him anything, and wanting to give him *everything*. The pleasure builds and cascades around and through us. And my heart. *My heart*, that I thought couldn't take anymore, is pounding furiously in my chest, alive and strong against his.

My hands move up to tangle in his hair, to stroke his ears and his cheeks, as his lips conquer mine. He's holding me so close, but I want to be *closer*. His tongue reaches for mine and as I meet him that way for the first time a moan escapes me and I feel my legs go rubbery as he responds in kind. It is the hottest, most passionate exchange I have *ever* experienced. But there is something more, something so much *deeper* to it all. A taste of perfect belonging.

My senses are now in a state of hyper-focus. His incredible scent intoxicates me further and I greedily inhale him in. The most addictive drug in the world, with a high beyond anything I have ever felt. I'm soaring as another moan escapes. My eyes open wide as it becomes overwhelming. As *he* becomes overwhelming. But his open at the exact same moment as if he feels it too. This epic, undeniable connection between us. I can see every tiny fleck of gold. All the veins of brown woven around his iris that bleeds out into the most amazing shades of green. There is a whole universe there that I could easily be lost to forever. If I would just let go and surrender.

His kiss becomes hungrier and suddenly I'm against a tree. Its rough bark cutting into me and pulling me back to the present, and there is Ugly's warning bark too. I don't want this to stop. I really, really do not. But I don't know what Ugly will do if he feels I am being threatened, and his snarling threat is growing louder. Ash takes a small step away from me as if that's all he can bear. His forehead once again rested against mine and we're both breathing heavy. I let my hands drop from him like weights and turn my head to Ugly.

I try to keep the frustration out of my voice as I treasure him. "It's okay. I'm fine." He sniffs the hand I offer, then licks it; instantly calmed. Ash has finally stepped back, but it looks like he might be struggling just as much as I am. That makes me feel a little better. Then the realization that we are in a public place, with kids around, hits me like a splash of cold water. I look around. Paranoia has me expecting to see a crowd, but it's just us.

How does he do this to me? Make me forget about everyone and everything? "This is crazy." I finally say. "We can't be doing this." Anxiety and defensiveness smother me as vulnerability sinks its claws in. "You're practically *engaged!*"

His head snaps up at that. "Who told you that?"

"Does it matter? It's true, isn't it?" He can't look at me in the eyes and I know then, with certainty that it's true. *Shit.* Deflated, I shake my head at him. "I *can't* Ash. I *can't* do whatever *this is* with you. You're going to break my heart okay? If we go any further, you're going to crush it. And it's already too broken to survive more! This is selfish and we *can't.* You need to go."

Ash looks pained and like he wants to say something, but nothing comes out. I can't blame him. But I can't help him either. Whatever this is, it's not a casual thing. Nor could it ever be. There are no options for us and he knows it. Unable to look at him anymore, I move away from the tree. Away from him. Resting my hand on Ugly's warm shoulder for the support, I meet his eyes.

"I get it now. Everything you said. Why you're always around Sarah. It's a *horrible* position to be stuck between politics and family..." I start walking backward, towards Maddie's house in slow deliberate steps, as I speak. "And I'm sorry. *I am*... But you coming around... Checking up on me... It's not fair. I'm all mixed up. And I need you to just..." I can't get the words out. I can't bring myself to tell him one more time, to s*tay away* when every piece of me that's true, wants the opposite.

I don't feel strong or brave. I am lost and wrecked. And now that I know how it feels? How *he feels?* I desperately want to cling to him and beg him to stay, to fight for me. But that's selfish too and either way, one of us loses. *Why is this so hard?* It shouldn't be. But leaving him is ex-cruciating! Walking away from him when I feel magnetically pulled to him is like trying to swim upstream against an impossible current.

My damned fine hairs tingle again, and I look up, unable to resist his call. I struggle to take another step, but he looks so hurt and alone and I see myself and so much more in him. Unable to go any further and un-able to reach out to him, I stand there and feel useless tears begin to run down my cheeks. As we say nothing, I try to memorize the sound of his voice as he speaks. I try to take in everything about him because we can't ever be this close again.

"I have never wanted my life and responsibilities less than I do right now." His voice is low and thick. "I wish more than anything, that things were different. And I *know* I'm being selfish Alex. I'm not *trying* to mess with your head *Okay?* I just... I haven't been able to fight this need as well as I should have. But it's like the more that I'm around you, the harder it is to stay away."

I hear everything he is saying, and each word hits my heart like a physical blow. But I become distracted as his eyes grow lighter and lighter until it looks like they might be glowing. A familiar memory is triggered. Aron's eyes. Blazing like the sun. Ash's glowing eyes behind the bar that night. I blink my eyes to clear them.

"Alex?" Maddie's voice sounds from behind me and I turn around to see her standing there uncertainly. "You're late. Do you still wanna play wiff us?" She lifts her red leash and Petunia pounces against the earth, giving Ugly a clear challenge.

"Yes... Just a sec." I turn around to where Ash is... Was. I look all around, but he's gone. Looking at the ground I try to clear my pounding head and wonder how the hell he was able to make no sound and move so fast. And his eyes.

"Weady?" Maddie sounds exasperated and I don't blame her. Not wanting to stand in this spot any longer, I take her hand. "Let's play at your house today." I look behind me one last time, but he's still gone. Desolate and unnerved, I walk with Maddie and try my best to plaster a smile on my face.

CHAPTER 17

I stay home for the rest of the week. Aron and Jade are over every day after school with homework and the latest gossip. Jade has been notably subdued but has refused to talk about it. I can so totally relate. I don't talk about Ash either and we don't push each other. No one from the Jacket Crew has been back to school yet but apparently, the guys in the football team still make every practice.

Aron begged me to go to open mic on Thursday. He said I was the standout performance last week. But with as good as some of the other acts were, I think he just said it to get me to go. I refused on the premise of needing more time to recuperate and he couldn't argue with that. My walks with Ugly and social time with them and Dill has been the only thing getting me out of bed during the day. Otherwise, I spend a lot of time hiding underneath the sheets.

Except at night. Nightmares plague me so much now that I no longer even try to get rest. Instead, I have taken to going into the gardens and laying in the hammock to stare at the stars with Ugly or sometimes we go to the bench swing on the front porch with a book. I do everything I can to avoid the dreams. It always seems to be varying combinations of the same ending. My best friend getting murdered.

The state wound up cremating Vic, and Shells collected her remains as she had no family other than us. She promised me that one day we would spread Vic's ashes together and hold a real ceremony, but we haven't made any solid plans. Neither of us is ready to officially say goodbye. I have been sleeping more during the day over the last week then I can ever remember but I'm always tired regardless. My body aches never went away after getting the horrid news. These days I'm almost used to the constant pain and fatigue.

My court date with Dill is just around the corner and I promised him I would go back to school on Monday. If nothing else, to make things look better for the Judge. I was hoping to feel better by then but there's this raw gaping hole inside of me that makes even breathing hard at times. I eat for everyone else's benefit, but everything tastes like sand. I keep telling myself it's only been a week and things will get better. But deep down I know they can't.

The doorbell rings and Ugly trots into my room and *woofs* at me. It's Friday and too early to be Jade or Aron. Rebellious hope suddenly takes root in my chest and a second later I am flinging off the covers and running to the door. Seeing my reflection in a window I realize I have no pants on and run back to my room.

"Just a second!" I shout, and stumble over my pants as I try to pull them on and get to the front of the house simultaneously. I quickly finger comb my hair before I swing open the door and try not to look out of breath.

"*Ella?*" I'm too surprised to be disappointed.

"Hey... I know this is weird." She looks completely flustered and anxious.

"Come in." Dizzy and out of breath, I lead her to the living room. "Can you wait here? I just need to do something real quick. Do you want anything? Water?"

"That would be great. Thanks."

I rush to the bathroom and quickly brush my teeth and smear on deodorant. If I can smell myself, she *definitely* can. Glancing in the mirror, I notice for the first time how sickly I look. *Wow, don't you make a picture.* I give myself the finger and hustle back to the kitchen. I fill us both a glass of water and find her on the sofa with Ugly at her legs.

"Sorry, I should have warned you about him." I hand her the glass and sit in Dill's chair.

"No. He's great." She holds her water but doesn't drink it. I don't say anything while she gathers her thoughts. She finally sets the water down and meets my eyes. "I heard about what happened. With your friend. And I just want to say that I'm sorry. I have never lost anyone important to me before, so I don't know what you're going through. But I know it's got to be an indescribable feeling." She trails off, looking uncertain of what else to say. "*Oh,* I brought you something!" The way she suddenly perks up reminds me a little of Ugly and softens me towards her. She pulls up her bag and rummages around. Pulling out her laptop and opening it on the coffee table, more confident now she pats the space next to her. "Come on! It will be easier to show you from here." Curious, I move over to sit next to her and push Ugly over. Chuckling at his grunt, I watch as she clicks to open a folder with thumbnails of artwork.

She clicks on a thumbnail of wings, opening the image so it covers her screen. Amazement renders me speechless. It's an iconic and bold, black ink drawing on a white background. She looks over at me, hope-ful.

"I saw the video of you painting Tara Scar-a..." She turns beet red. "-*Erm..* of you painting Tara's back, and I've heard about how the wings are all over the school now. And how it's united most of the student body together. And I thought it was really cool... And I got inspired to do *this*." She gestures at the screen. "A symbol is more powerful when it's undiluted and consistent. So I thought I'd give it a shot and I think it came out pretty good..."

Incredibly touched and humbled I stare at it. "You *did this?*"

"Yeah. It's kind of a thing I do. Just a silly hobby. "

"No! This is *really good* Ella! "

"Honestly? Thank you!" She looks down a little shyly. "I just thought you should have it. But I didn't know your email, so I got your address from Nick. I hope you don't mind. "

"*No*, I don't mind. This is amazing, Thank you!" I look back at the screen. "I don't know what I'm going to do with it, but I love it!"

"I'm already on that. Posters, stickers, even pins!"

"Seriously?"

"Yeah! What good is a symbol if no one sees it? And what good is a gift if I have nothing solid to give you?"

"I always thought gifts were about the gesture but this is *so cool*." I look back at the screen. "You really didn't have to do all of this..."

She pulls out a big, round sticker and hands it to me. "In my world, a gift is something you can touch." She sounds a little sad as she says it and reaches down to pet Ugly. "It's just as much for the rest of the school

I guess, as it is for you. I pretty much owe everyone a major apology. And nothing I say is ever going to make up for the way I've..." She trails off again and remorse and sadness cover her features.

Understanding, I take her hand in mine and truly look at her. "Ella, I can't pretend to understand what has led you to stick with someone like Sarah for so long, but I do know a thing or two about survival. And I know what it's like to ban together with people that at first, you wouldn't have chosen. I also know how important loyalty is. But the fact that you want to change and that you recognize it wasn't healthy or good is *major*. Most people can't change. They are too afraid, but *you're trying*. And if it's any consolation I forgive you. So I'm sure everyone else will too."

Tears fill her eyes and if anything, the shame on her face has only increased. "I don't deserve anyone's forgiveness, but that's not why am doing this. I'm doing this because it's the right thing to do. And someone special reminded me that being brave isn't supposed to be easy." She looks back up at me then, and I feel an unexpected kinship sprout up between us.

"I haven't felt very brave lately." I'm surprised to hear the truth come out.

"Are you *cereal?* I hardly know you and you're the bravest person I've ever met!"

"*Cereal?*"

"Of course! *Nothing* is more serious than cereal." At her *cereal* face, I burst out laughing.

"So what are we doing with this?" I wave the wings sticker.

"That's just the start, I already have people passing them out and putting them up. But this..." She pulls out a piece of paper from her bag and hands it to me. "Is phase two of my plan."

I look down at the flyer, hardly comprehending it. At the top in bold, fiery lettering, *NOT TODAY* stand out, with wicked devil horns above it. Below is the date for the homecoming dance with the quote: *Sorry Devils and Sexy Angels welcome* with the striking wings symbol taking up the rest of the page.

Ella smiles proudly, "I head the homecoming committee, and everyone agreed, this is the theme for this year. It's getting posted at school on Monday. Do you like it?"

"Like it? Ella, this is huge! And it's perfect! The play on words, the symbol. You are majorly talented!"

She is preening under my praise when Ugly lets out a *woof* and trots to the door. "Is someone here?"

"That's just Aron and Jade." I shrug.

Ella jumps up at the sound of car doors slamming and shoves her laptop back in her bag while she talks at light speed. "Think of me as a double agent. The fewer people that know, the better. Sarah and everyone else are back on Monday. I will give you a heads up the moment she is up to something." The sound of their feet on the porch has her going even faster. "For now, I need an exit!"

Grabbing her hand and laughing, I pull her through the kitchen and shove her into the garden. Shutting the door behind her, I go to meet Aron and Jade in the living room.

"Who was that?" Aron asks and the hope in his voice is way too obvious.

"Not a boy." His blatant disappointment makes me smile and I debate for only a second. "It was Ella. She fancies herself a double agent now."

Jade lifts Ella's glass and eyes the bright pink lip gloss lining the ring. "A spy huh? She's off to a great start." She sets the incriminating glass down.

Aron plops into Dill's seat and scratches Ugly's head. "Do we trust her?"

"That will be something she has to earn."

"Is this what I think it is?" Jade lifts the flyer.

Aron's eyes go wide. "Those wings! They were all over school today! I was going to tell you!" He snatches the flyer from Jade. "Oh my god, it's the theme for the dance! This is Major!" He gasps as he thinks of something and looks at Jade. "Tell me you know what this means..."

Jade smiles. "Your custom Maleficent horns will rise from the sashes of your closet?"

Aron sits back on the Arm of the chair. "Like a Phoenix, they will rise. And with my Armani suit? They will *live*." He dramatically falls into the chair and smiles wistfully. "Wait, are you telling me Ella had something to do with that?" He gestures to the flyer.

"Ella *made* that. Including the wings symbol. She's the one that had them passed out this morning."

Aron looks delighted with the idea. "*For real?*"

"Cereal."

"Oh my god, it *was* Ella! That little Barbie doll really *is* a double agent!"

I'm laughing at his freak out when I notice the suitcase Jade has with her. "What's that about?"

"Oh, this little thing? It's just the first installment of our trade." I had never considered myself much of a girly girl before meeting Jade. It seems that in no time, she has converted me. Because it's possible that I'm more excited about the contents of her luggage then Aron just was about Homecoming.

"Let's go!"

True to her gift of fitting copious amounts of items into tight spaces, Jade's suitcase is no exception. As she pulls out another pair of jeans for me to check out, I wonder if a rabbit will come out next.

"Is Ugly in there? I haven't seen him in a while."

She smiles at me with obvious pleasure and the next item she pulls out is a super cute white sundress. I fall in love with it instantly and reach for it, but then I noticed the tags. "Is this one new?"

"New is a relative term."

"You didn't buy any of this for me, did you?"

"No. Sometimes I'm just not in the mood anymore."

I can't tell if she's lying so I'll accept it, but as I hold it up and admire the embroidery around the top my greedy little mind is made up. "Lucky for me then because I *love* this!"

"Try it on. Let's see the fit"

I hurry to my closet and do just that. The top half is like a bathing suit. Tying at my neck and back for an extra complimenting fit. Other than the tie, my back is fully exposed. The embroidery gives way to flowing tiers of skirting that fall just below my butt. It looks innocent and sexy as hell all at once. *It's perfect.* I have spent the better part of a week looking like hell froze over, then melted. I can't remember the last time I wore a dress. I'm thinking years! Stepping out, I do a little spin for Jade and Aaron. They both clap, looking way too excited.

"What?"

Jade gets up from the bed and moves to her suitcase. "Nothing, it's just, that dress is going to look amazing at the football game."

I see the ambush too late. "*No*. There is no way I'm going to the football game. Have you *seen me lately?* Besides, we would *never* be ready in time." I trail off as Jade pulls out a curling iron and makeup bag from the pocket of her suitcase.

∞

We're back in our previous seats and people are going crazy over the game. It's not even halftime yet but most everyone is already standing and shouting at the field. I debate getting up to have a little school spirit myself, but Aron distracts me. He has his t-shirt pulled out from his chest and is peering down through the neck hole.

"What are you doing?"

He doesn't look up as he responds. "It's so hot my nipples have inverted. I want to make sure they're not going to disappear."

Jade looks over her shades at him. "You get weirder with every year that passes." And then goes back to cooling herself with a red fan that matches her lipstick, hair-tie, and handbag. She looks utterly flawless in a navy-blue romper with military-style pleats and short shorts.

Aron drops his shirt and smiles at her. "And you get shadier."

"You're too kind." She responds, not slowing down with the fanning.

So far whatever magic product she used has beaten the heat and kept my hair full of body and waves. The open toe wedge sandals that tie around my ankles with a matching purse to complete the look are also super beachy and cute. But the real feat is how she was able to turn my pale, lifeless skin into a bronzed shimmery, sun-kissed dream. If Jade were not so damn smart and going to change the world with mad science, she would definitely change it with fashion.

I have been trying to ignore the fact that Ash is down there playing like a beast. Unlike me, Jade has hardly taken her eyes off the field. I ultimately agreed to come with them because I wanted to cheer her up. But it seems more like she needed support in stalking with style than a distraction. I'm not mad though. I'm too busy resenting the Hartford family and maybe it's not fair, but the brothers most of all.

Unable to watch the game any longer I stand. "What can I bring you back?"

Aron looks at me with a pitiful expression. "A bucket of ice?"

"Something I can actually carry back?"

He pulls his vintage straw hat forward to shield his eyes. "Something cold."

Jade chimes in. "*Anything* cold."

I make my way up the bleachers. Smiling and returning waves and nods with my schoolmates. *Maybe going back on Monday won't be so bad. It might even be a decent distraction.* I make my way to the vendors and go straight for the ice-cream truck, but the line is already long. Two familiar faces have my heart skip a beat.

Given the abrupt way I parted with them at the coffee shop, it's a little awkward to approach Caden and Luka now but my feet don't slow down. It's actually kind of empowering to overcome my anxiety by confronting it. The old me would have run in the other direction. Caden is next in line looking at the swirling smoothy flavors when Luka notices me. I put my finger to my lips, signaling him not to give me away. He smirks and resumes looking at the offerings with Caden. I get close to Caden's back. My heels help me reach his ear a little better. Before he can turn around I say as saucily as possible, "That flavor's the best."

He whirls around and surprises me by pulling me into a tight hug. "Alex." The way he says my name combined with the way he is still holding on has my knees feeling weak. Growing uncomfortable with the intensity between us, I pull back and force my smile in place.

"Surprise!"

Before he can respond a guy behind us interrupts. "Is this reunion with the hottie going to take a while? Some of us have a game to get back to."

The change that comes over both Luka and Caden is instantaneous, like someone just flipped a switch from casual to lethal. The looks they shoot the group of guys behind us is chilling, to say the least. While they are outnumbered two to one, there is no question in my mind who would walk away from this fight. Before that theory can be tested, I turn to fully face the group of guys and grab Caden's big, warm hand in mine.

"Sorry. This hottie is taken. But even if he weren't, you are *so* not his type. I turn my back to the guys and pull Caden with me as the immediate sounds of the guys' friends teasing him hit our backs. I look up at Caden then and cheekily demand my order.

"Three blue Gatorades plus three cold somethings. I'll pay you back."

Caden's demeanor melts in my presence and Luca follows suit. They are both beaming at me now and I feel oddly proud that I can command such incredible specimens of the male gender.

"Coming right up."

He starts to turn to the register when I tug on his arm. "*Oh!* Can you make sure one of the cold somethings is red?"

He chuckles at that but gives nod and proceeds to order a heap of goodies. I'm about to ask how we are going to carry it all when Luka starts placing it all in a cooler at his feet. I pull out some bills for Caden and hand them to him as we walk over to the grass in the shade of the bleachers. Gabriel is waiting there with a large blanket covering the grass.

"You guys have done this before." I snicker at the thought of the three of them having a picnic together.

"Alex!" Gabriel pops up as soon as he sees me and gives me a big hug that feels very different from Caden's. The boy in question's aggressive throat clearing from just behind us has Gabriel chuckling and spinning me out into a dip.

"Care to give him something to really choke over?"

"Not on your life!" I laugh and stick my tongue out at him while still in the dip.

Unruffled, Gabriel smoothly moves me to stand again and bows at me, bringing my hand in for a kiss as he openly smiles at Caden. Before my hand is anywhere close to his lips Caden is tackling him to the blanket. The two of them make a mess of it as they wrestle around. The sounds of laughing and grunts mingle with Luca's heckling and suddenly

I'm laughing too. This is exactly what Jade needs right now. Aron too if he's not already become a puddle of sweat. Before I can over-analyze it any further the words come out.

"Can my friends and I join you guys?" I'm looking at Luca but Caden responds from under Gabriel's legs.

"If you want your treats, that's number one on our list of demands." The guys fall out of their hold and breath heavy as they start a new debate about who won.

Herding Jade and Aron back is easy with the promise of shade, sweets, and beefy guys. Jade makes a total picture with the red popsicle Caden got her and I can't help but laugh at Gabriel who is completely mesmerized. Aron snaps pictures. His dapper straw hat falling off in his excitement to capture the scene. Caden picks it up and places it on my head.

"It suits you." And just then, with Caden's hands still holding the hat atop my head and the two of us looking into each other's eyes, Aron snaps another shot.

"Cut it out! This is a patch of grass, not the red carpet!" I chide, but as always, he remains unfazed and continues snapping shots. Caden chuckles from beside me.

"What?"

"You. You're just funny."

"Is that a compliment?"

"It is. But if you want something more traditional, I will tell you how insane you look today. Like sunshine and honey. All bright and shiny..."

I shouldn't be dependent on a guy's praise for validation. I should know my worth enough that his words don't heat me up and completely melt me into a mushy useless mess. I tell myself this even as I'm glowing and have to look away so he won't see how much he affects. "Thank you," I mutter.

Luka passes me a Gatorade and I gratefully take it. He sits up from his reclining position and speaks for the first time like he has just been waiting for the opportunity. "Can we please talk about your performance now?"

Aron finally stops taking pictures. "*Thank you!*"

Luka smiles at him and looks back at me. "You can sing, like really sing. And you play too?"

Aron cuts in. "Hell yes, she plays. So far I have seen her crush on the piano and the guitar."

Embarrassment and surprise mingle in my gut. "When did you see that?"

"I passed by your music class and saw you with some other girl playing something fast."

"You are such a nosy brat!"

Caden interrupts us, "You can play more than one instrument?"

Jade's popsicle is almost completely finished when she takes a break from it to join in the conversation. "She's a musical prodigy." And then she's back to finishing it up.

Annoyed at all the attention I clarify, "I am not a *prodigy*. I can mess around on a few instruments is all. But I'm a master of none."

Jade looks up at that. "Not. True."

Refusing to argue and make it any more of a thing I change the subject and look between Luka and Caden. "You guys, on the other hand, have mastered those Flamenco Negras like no one's business."

Luka is delighted. "You know what they are!"

"My... *Uncle* has friends over every other week and we usually jam out at some point. One guy that comes a lot loves Flamenco and he told me all about his guitar, but he wasn't as good as you." I look up to see if Jade or Aron takes any notice of me calling Dill my uncle, but they say nothing.

Caden reaches for my drink and I pass it to him. He nods his head at me, smiling. "So fast to change the subject..." He takes a long pull from the bottle and makes quite the picture all sweaty and tussled. Setting it down he regards me again. "When will you be performing again?"

"Next Thursday," Aron answers for me.

Before I can say anything Gabriel cuts in. "That song that you did..." I feel my chest tighten at the memory. "It made me think of my mother." All of us look at him then. He speaks softly. "She was one of the world's great lights. And she loved a good party. Too much so. I lost her when I was just a lad. But your song got to me. It hit home, yeah? I haven't let myself think about her in a long time, but I felt her when you sang. And I remembered... It's the right gift you have... And well, anyone who can do something like that, is a master of something."

"Thank you." I have no idea what else to say but I'm rescued from responding further by Gabriel.

"So when is your next jam session?"

I'm encouraged to see Jade finally checking Gabriel out as she responds for me. "I have actually been wondering about your *Uncle's* infamous BBQs.".

I have come to know Jade well enough to understand there is a whole conversation of subtext there. Chiefly, that Gabriel has captured her attention and she wants a neutral setting to get to know him better and also I have been hiding for long enough and it's time to occupy myself with something positive. I look over at Caden who is staring at me with enough heat to the rival fire. Maybe I could use a distraction too.

"BBQ?" Gabriel says like it's all he heard.

Fuck it. "This Sunday." *Dill will be thrilled.*

CHAPTER 18

The thought of mixing my friends with my biker family had me full of anxiety. The two just didn't fit in my head, like peanut butter and cheese. I love them both. *Separately.* Yet watching Aron stretch his teenage muscles in Arch's leather vest to the great amusement of the band? And Jade showing the three bouncers manning the grill, how to make Japanese barbecue? It all kind of makes a weird sort of sense.

The house is packed as we haven't had a barbecue since my birthday, and the tone is jovial and celebratory. Jade and I put up fairy lights and lanterns all over the backyard. While the sun hasn't completely gone down yet, the lights and candles have begun to twinkle. The gurgling water from the fountain, acoustic music, and bursts of laughter set the backdrop. It all has a dreamy quality that makes me want to capture it, in a way that my memory cannot.

Aron invited some of his friends from the open mic crew and it looks as though they invited some of theirs. The whole crowd is as diverse in age as they are in style, with many faces I don't recognize. Thankfully, Dill seems to be enjoying it as much as I am. I catch him smiling at the scene of a girl with feathers and fringe putting a bindi sticker on the forehead of a red-cheeked biker. I realize he needed this just as much as I do.

Meandering to the front yard, I see that bikes are once again sprinkled everywhere. Smirking to myself I imagine the guys' reaction when they arrive. It might be a little wicked of me, but I didn't tell them about the crowd tonight. It will be far more fun to see how they swim or sink in the unexpected water. I'm just turning back to the house when a bright, chirpy voice sings my name.

"Alex!" I turn around just in time to almost get mowed over by blonde hair and glitter.

"How are you so petite and so strong!?"

Ella giggles up at me. "Ten years of gymnastics and two of Pilates will do that. I'm *all* muscle baby. Here! punch my stomach!"

"No, no...I'm fine," I nervously chuckle. "I'm so happy you came! I wasn't sure if you would."

"If you trust your people enough that you know it won't get back to mine, that's good enough for me." I laugh at that, not really sure if she's being serious or not.

"Come on, I'll introduce you around."

A deep, sexy voice stops me in my tracks. "You waited for us out here? You shouldn't have."

I turn around and smile at Caden and the boys. *Does he get better looking every time I see him?* I gesture to the conspicuous driveway and yard loaded with bikes and cars. "We're easy to miss as you can see."

The sound of an explosion and shouts have us freezing, then running along the drive to the backyard where it came from. I see the smoke billowing up before I'm able to break through the crowd and find ground zero. Jake, our beloved bouncer from The Bar, is in front of the grill that is now engulfed flames. He's lifting a bucket of ice water towards it when Caden who I swear, was just behind me, is now knocking the bucket from his hands.

Before Jake can react, Caden is yelling, "It's a gas fire! Water makes it worse! We need salt! As much as you can find!"

Dill shouts at Caden from the buffet table, "Behind you!" And tosses him the large container of Morton Salt as soon as he turns. I'm already running for Caden and pass him my favorite pocketknife in his free hand. He's a mind reader because he doesn't hesitate to slice off the top and dump all the contents over the flames. He then gives some kind of signal to Luka who kicks out faster than my eyes can track and snaps the grill lid shut. The fire has gone down but it's still blazing through every vent and crack.

"We need to starve the fire and close the vents!" Caden shouts to Jake, who passes him a heat protective glove seconds later. As soon as they can get to the vents safely, they are pushing them closed at either side. And the fire becomes manageable enough so that the imminent threat of the whole house burning down passes. Someone hands Jake more salt and people start cheering and clapping like the whole thing was a show. I bend over and take a deep breath.

"Forget to breathe?" I look up at Aron who is fanning himself and looking at Caden. "I know *I did*... There is nothing more breath-taking than a man who likes to play with fire."

"My house almost burnt down." I grouch at him.

He has the decency to look chagrined. "Right. ...Yeah, that too."

"I believe this belongs to you." Caden is pulling off the mitt to get to my pocketknife when I see a massive burned hole in it. A flash of raw melted skin jolts me into standing before his hand is moved casually behind his back.

"Caden, your hand!"

"It's nothing. I'm fine."

Dill is joining us when I nearly shout, "You're not fine! Your hand is cooked!"

Dill looks concerned. "I can get you to the hospital in fifteen minutes."

Caden shakes his head looking flustered now. "*Trust me*, it's not as bad as it looks. Do you have a first aid kit? We can bandage it and if it gives me any trouble, I'll have it looked at."

Dill chuckles and looks to me. "I like your friend. Introductions after you make sure his hand doesn't need amputating. First aid kits under the sink in the kitchen. You need any help finding it?"

"No, I've got it," I tell him. Even though I don't, because the sight of Caden's melted skin has me feeling faint. I honestly don't know how he's even standing and vaguely wonder if he's in shock.

"Follow me."

"Alex!" The sound of Ella's shaken voice has us stopping. "Oh my god, that was *cereal!* Are you okay?" She asks Caden.

Feeling an unexpected surge of jealousy as his eyes find her baby blues, I step between them. "I'm taking care of him now. Why don't you check on his friend?" I point to Luka.

"Don't mind if I do."

The tone of her voice has me momentarily relaxing enough to chuckle. "We'll be back soon."

Taking Caden's good hand, I pull him quickly into the kitchen so no one else has the chance to stop us. "Hold on." I grab the first aid kit and pull him behind me through the house and up the stairs for immediate bathroom access.

"The bathrooms downstairs will be occupied for the rest of the night. This is faster." Pulling him through the first room and into the adjoining bathroom, I switch on the light and seat myself on the toilet, opening the kit in my lap while he leans against the sink.

"I thought I was the damsel in distress. Shouldn't I be the one sitting?"

"You sit there. Don't be a baby. Show me your hand."

"Bossy."

Steeling my nerves, I look up from the ointment and bandages I have organized to the hand he has offered and see angry-looking red skin.

"Your other hand. The one with the burn." I say briskly. Even though I could have sworn it was this one.

"This *is* my burn." He laughs at me. "*See?* You over-reacted about nothing."

"What? No... I..."

I take his other hand gingerly and turn it this way and that, looking for the melted, charred skin I saw earlier. But there is nothing. Goose-bumps ripple across my flesh and my equilibrium goes wonky even though I'm sitting. Forgetting about the first aid kit, I stand up, hardly noticing its contents toppling to the floor. Disregarding the mess, I take the reddened hand he first gave me and flip it over where I originally saw the worst of his burn, but it's only swollen and red. Looking up at him with wide eyes my stomach dips.

"*How?*" I demand.

He's obviously a bit taken back by my bluntness, but I couldn't care less. When he doesn't respond right away, I pull his hand up again and look at it in the light. I could swear it's even *less* red now! Blinking, I abruptly let go and take a step back only to almost fall into the toilet. His arms snake around me to hold me up.

All at once, I'm aware of how small this bathroom is, and how close we are. With my heart pounding, I start to feel like I can't breathe. And that's before I notice how bright his eyes have become. *Impossibly bright.* Dizziness rushes through me. I doubt I'd still be standing if he were not holding me up. I want to run but I feel frozen. He abruptly squeezes his eyes shut and drops his head, taking in a shaky breath. He looks so lost and the conflicting urge to comfort him wars with my flight instinct. Slowly, tentatively I reach up my shaking hand to lift his face to me. He's still squeezing his eyes shut and his chest is heaving too. It takes every ounce of bravery I have to say my next words.

"Caden. Open your eyes."

But instead, he pulls me the rest of the way to him and rests his head on top of mine. "I can smell your fear. Don't be afraid of me Alex." He takes in another slow, deep breath and lets it out. "The glove protected my hand. It looked worse than it is." I try to step back from him, but he refuses to yield. "Wait. Hold on a minute. I *hate* fire, okay? I just need... Can you just hold on for a minute?"

Almost instinctively I wrap my arms around his waist at his vulnerable tone. Before I know it, I'm surrendering to his embrace. My heart is still pounding but heat is flaring up between us. I can smell him too, and his scent is *so good* I feel a little high. But then again, I could also be hyperventilating. It seems like everyone's eyes have been glowing lately. I'm either completely losing my mind, or something is seriously wrong with the locals here. Caden pulls me in even tighter so that there is no space left between us. Chest to chest. His hot breath now on my neck, and I am now very aware of his hardness pressed against my belly. And we just stay there like that. Him gripping me close and breathing heavy, and me, completely overwhelmed by everything. Then he is nuzzling my neck and suddenly all the chaos in my head dims as an avalanche of white-hot need courses through me. I should be terrified. Something about him isn't... *Right*. Or natural. Every instinct I have is screaming it. But instead, my anxiety melds with desire. Before things get completely out of hand, I pull back just enough to see his face.

"Look at me. Let me see you." When he doesn't move, I bring my hands to his cheeks. "Please. I just... I need to know." Caden shakes his head and opens his eyes. Familiar eyes, that are still bright but not glowing. He steps back to lean against the seat and his face grows remote.

"There is nothing to know. Hand me that?" He motions to the roll of gauze at my feet. I automatically pick it up and offer it. "And here I thought you were going to nurse me back to health." He gives me a forced smile. Conflicted and confused, I stupidly stare at him as he does my job and wraps his own hand. That doesn't actually *need* any wrapping.

Swallowing, I try to speak over the roar, ringing in my ears. "I *know* what I saw... Your burn... It looked like raw hamburger meat." Emboldened by a sense of growing hysteria the more I start to think about all his weirdness, I grab his halfway bandaged hand and pull the cotton away.

"What are you doing!" Caden snatches back his hand and lifts it away from me, but the bandage has shifted enough. I can clearly see his perfectly flawless hand. He follows my gaze and looks at his skin that's not even red anymore, and mutters something under his breath. Abruptly pushing out of the bathroom while he re-works the gauze. I stumble to catch up and follow him, finally grabbing his shoulder before he can leave the room.

"Your eyes... They were..." I feel crazy saying it out loud but what else can I do? He stiffens and turns around enough to look at me with his normal eyes.

"What about my eyes? Are they red from the smoke?" He sounds so rational. It's crazy-making! Looking at him now, all I see is the handsome, concerned face before me. "What's the prognosis doc? Will I be blinded for life?" Shaking my head at his cocky grin, I look down and push back the need to cry. *Am I going crazy?* "Alex?" Lifting my chin, Caden gazes into my eyes a bit more serious now. "Is it that bad?"

Unable to ignore his concern any longer, I let out a frustrated breath. "No. You're fine. It's just..."

"What?"

Still shaking my head, I force back my anxiety and meet his beautiful eyes. "*Nothing.* It's... Nothing. I'm just worried about you." I stammer. Then realize how intimate that sounds. "What I mean is..."

"No." He stops me. "I like that you worry about me. I worry about you too." His smile is so sweet and disarming. Something weird is going on but I don't know how to wrap my mind around it just now. His proximity and incredible scent are invading my brain so that every part of my body feels aware of him. Almost like my skin is holding its breath in anticipation of his touch.

It's oddly similar to my insane reaction to Ash. *Ash*. Suddenly feeling skittish, I finish wrapping his hand and tuck the gauze in. I go to squeeze by him, but his hands come up to rest on my shoulders, stopping me. He's so close and there is nowhere to look but up. I'm caught again in his fathomless eyes. And heat. More heat is building between us.

"Thank you." He says after a pause.

"For what?"

He glances at his wrapped hand. "For making my nurse fantasy come true."

I sputter out a laugh, breaking some of the tension and he finally lets me pass. Following me back down the stairs and into the thick of it. By the time we rejoin everyone outside, the sun is almost completely down and the party is back in full swing. I'm even almost able to convince myself that I must have confused what I saw. I'm slightly more relaxed by the time Dill joins us. He rests his hand on Caden's shoulder and gives him a warm smile. I notice they are the same height.

"You okay?"

Caden smiles at him. "Yeah, I'm solid. You must be Uncle Dill?"

Dill looks sidelong at me and I smirk at him. "I'm her guardian." He winks at me. "And what's the name of the kid who saved my yard and possibly this house?"

Mentally slapping myself, I fumble. "Right! Sorry. Dill, this is my friend Caden. Caden, my guardian *and Uncle*, Dill." I wink at Dill. "But you can call him Pickle. Everyone does."

Caden's grin widens, "There must be a story there."

Dill chuckles. "There is indeed."

"There is?"

Dill just smirks at me. "You don't get a nickname like *Pickle* without good reason." Before I can ask him more, he goes on. "I saved some ribs for you both. They're in the microwave. *Hey,* wait a minute. Are you the one with the Negra guitar?" Dill looks at Caden hopefully.

"Yeah, I brought it along."

Dill rubs his hands together and his eyes glitter as he smiles. "Tonight's jam is going to be *interesting.*" Someone gets his attention then, and we're left alone. Wrinkling my nose, I nudge Caden.

"You smell like BBQ."

His smile turns wicked. "Am I making you hungry?"

"Hardly."

"Your lips are moving but your eyes are giving me real talk."

Flushed, I swing said eyes to the door behind him where the ribs are hiding and glare at him. "What are my eyes telling you now?"

Caden bursts out laughing and several heads turn. It's the first time I have heard him sound truly carefree.

"I'll load a plate and find you."

"What?"

"You want the ribs?"

"Right! Yes."

I watch the back of his tall built frame disappear into the kitchen.

The party goes on with no more problems and gets more packed as the night goes on. Ella and Luka have been attached by the waist and even Jade has warmed up to Gabriel. The jam session becomes one for the history books. It's like every other person at the party has an instrument of some kind or has rigged one out of things around the yard. We are all in a loose circle around the dead grill that's become a fire pit. The music styles that ripple through the crowd are as eclectic as the players themselves. But somehow, they have all synced up and the resulting beats and sounds that follow are inspired. At times, impossibly beautiful, and others the drum player's so passionate and fierce that my whole body feels compelled to move. Some of the braver revelers are up and dancing about, hair flying and spirits soaring. It's the moments when everyone quiets down to let a certain musician have a solo that is especially magical.

I pass Dill's guitar over to his friend so he can have a turn at it, and sit back with Jade and Aron to take it all in. And like them, I'm completely in awe. Looking across the flames I meet Caden's glittering eyes and wonder how long he's been watching me. He hasn't stopped playing his guitar with Luka since they sat almost two hours ago, and I wonder if their fingers aren't ready to fall off. He smiles then and my heart stutters. Suddenly flushed and shy, I glance over to Ella who is contentedly sitting next to Luka and smiling like so many others. I have always wondered at people who find it so easy to share their affection and feelings.

"Do you want to dance?"

Stunned I look at Jade. "Cereal?" She laughs at me and nods her head. Unable to pass up my first chance to groove with her, I look at Aron. "You coming?"

"If I'm dancing I might miss this, and you couldn't pay me to miss *this*." At my hesitation, he waves us off. "Next time. I promise." I let Jade pull me into the circle and feel relief at finally allowing my body to do what it's been wanting to do since the music started. Watching Jade, I forget my self-consciousness and let go. It turns out Jade's a great dancer. She has more of an exotic sinuous style that's mesmerizing. Mirroring some of her moves and blending them into my own, we find our own frequency of synchronicity, and soon enough we are dancing our asses off.

CHAPTER 19

I am literally dragging myself to school. Dill kicked out the last of the stragglers around 2 am. Even though we left cleanup for later and I passed out almost immediately, nightmares plagued me. I'm too late for our morning makeover session and instead meet Jade in class. She's wearing a fabulous set of shades and has two Starbucks cups sitting in front of her.

"You *angel!*"

"Better believe it. Nothing but the best for my girl. That's three espresso shots. Sip with caution." The way she says it makes me chuckle.

"Are you wearing those all day?"

She peers over at me. "I wish. Looks like you could use a pair too."

"Thanks," I say drolly. "Did you get into any trouble last night for going home so late?"

"No. Benson was parked down the road and reporting back to my parents the whole evening. Though I did have to get on the phone with them and explain I hadn't died in a horrific explosion." I snicker at that. "Benson heard it from all the way down the street."

"Oh my god! I'm surprised he didn't come and get you!"

"I texted him the all-clear as soon as he messaged me. Otherwise, he might have. Explosions aside, my parents are just thrilled I have actual friends these days."

"Wait... How did you manage to become the queen bee here without real friends?"

"The three A's."

"Come again?"

She ticks off her fingers looking as cereal as ever in her shades. "Acquaintances, Appearances, and Associations. Four if you add Aron. Though we were not as close before you. "

"Is that a bona fide Jade-ism?"

"True."

"The three A's. You are something else." The way she looks back at me over her shades only underlines my point.

∞

I let out the breath I didn't know I was holding when I find that Ash and Sarah are not in Drama. Class feels different without them. Lighter. And maybe it's just me but everyone seems more relaxed. I'm surprised to find at lunch that all the buzz isn't about the Jacket Crew's return but my own. For some reason, the reality of popularity is only now just hitting me. As more people than ever wave at me and smile, it's become impossible not to see the change. True to Ella's word, wing stickers are everywhere in lockers, on backpacks, and even in the bathroom stalls.

The dance theme is a major hit, and everyone is talking about it as I finally make it to my table.

I'm a little sad to see Nick is still MIA, but Jade seems happier than I have seen in some time and I take that as a silver lining. The erosive hole that has punctured my spirit is ever-present. But since last night's festivities, I am feeling more myself. I know Vic would kill me if she knew I was crying over her every night and suffering over a boy I hardly know. I'm doing my best to look forward and carry on.

The rest of the day passes uneventfully and as I pull up to the manor, all I can think about is taking a nap. Even if I could convince Dill to walk Ugly, there is still the party to clean up. Feeling like roadkill, I shuffle through the front door. The sound of voices and the lack of Ugly slobbering all over me in welcome distracts me from my pity party. Dropping my bag, I follow the noise through the kitchen and to the back yard and cannot believe what I'm seeing.

Ugly gives a happy *woof* in greeting and lopes over to me for pets. *Oh, now you want to say hi.* I absently ruffle his head, bemused as I watch Caden, Luka, Gabriel, and Dill work together to clean up last night's fallout. Just then, Caden straightens and with his back turned I can't be sure... But it looks like he's sniffing the air. Silently snickering at the thought, I abruptly stop as he swings around to look at me.

It's almost like he *smelled* me in the air. But the thought is quickly forgotten as I take in his sweat-slicked skin and white shirt plastered over hard muscles and *holy abs!* He chuckles then like he knows what I'm thinking. Mortified, I look away. He totally caught me checking him out! "What are you guys doing here?" I don't mean to sound so accusatory but Caden has me feeling off-kilter. As per usual.

"Oh hey Alex!" Luka nods as the others notice my arrival.

"Um, hey."

"I called them here," Jade says from behind me. "I figured you guys could use the help." She smiles winningly at Dill. *Yeah, because you totally weren't scheming to see Gabriel again or for me to see Caden.*

Giving her a look so she knows I *know*, I smile sweetly at her. "*Thank you* Jade. How very *thoughtful* of you."

Aron pushes past us. "Are you okay Alex? You look a little overheated."

Oh, I am so going to kill them. "And you look... Annoying!"

Aron shrugs, "Only because you're so cute when you're flustered."

At the chuckling behind him, I turn my glare to Dill who puts his hands up. "I'm just going inside. If you need me, I'm on dish duty." He slides past us.

Gabriel drops his full garbage bag. "See, now you've gone and scared him off."

"I'm getting pretty good at that," I mutter. "I'll be out to help in a minute. I need to get out of this uniform."

Caden stops what he's doing then and blatantly checks me out. "*Must you?*"

Jade laughs. "Another boy lost to the school girl cliche."

Gabriel smirks at her. "Make that two." The heated look they exchange has my eyebrow raising. I look at Caden to see if he's noticing the fireworks but instead, I find him still watching me with an inscrutable look on his face.

"What?"

"Nothing. ...You're just full of contradictions." With an uncomfortable shrug, I pull my friends back through the house with me to change.

Aron wearing a pair of Dill's rolled-up ripped jeans and a faded rocker t-shirt is maybe the best thing I have seen this year. We're out in the yard with the guys, and every time I look up and see him, I start laughing all over again.

"It's not that funny." Aron huffs.

Jade snickers, "Yes, it actually is. It's a whole new you."

"Well... I for one, think I look pretty damn good in vintage Calvin Klein."

Trying not to laugh, I look over at Ugly and take pity on him. "It's time for this ones walk, do you guys want to take a break and come along?"

Jade stretches, "I'm going to stay here and finish up. Aron, would you help me?"

"Sure." He gives a half-hearted wave from the hammock and it's obvious he going to be zero help.

Gabriel saunters over to her. "I've got you."

Luka chimes in, "We'll get this done in no time."

Gabriel looks to the sky and breaths in deep through his nose. "Thanks, Luka. You're the *best mate!*"

Before I can dissolve into laughter, Caden calls to me from the door. "Ready?" My stomach does a nervous flip as soon as I realize it's just going to be the two of us. Looking back at Jade, I bark out a laugh when I see her knowing smile. *Devious little witch!* I don't know why I'm so nervous, but as I grab Ugly's leash with clammy hands, I take a calming deep breath and try to steady myself.

Caden breaks the silence of our walk when he gestures to Ugly who is marking his hundredth tree. "You do this every day?"

"Mostly. Dill does sometimes. Other times I put him in a harness and he pulls while I skateboard."

"Now *that* I have to see."

"He can go *fast*. Like *car, fast*." Ugly seems extra perky as I talk about him and I wonder not for the first time, how much he understands.

"It's good to see you out and about. I was worried. ...After open mic..."

I look up at him, squinting my eyes against the sun. I guess this was bound to come up. But still, I don't feel prepared. Anything involving Vic is still too painful to think about. Trying to distract him, I remember our conversation from last night in the bathroom. "So now *you're* worrying about me?"

"From the first day I met you." He says without hesitation.

I smile at that until I see his solemn face. He rubs the back of his neck in a gesture that reminds me of Dill. After a moment he looks away from me. "There is something I want you to know... I was an addict. ...*Am* an addict..."

"What?" I can't help the shock that's in my voice.

He hesitates before continuing. "It's not any kind of substance..." He's quiet again for so long that I wonder if he will finish. "It's pain." He finally says and looks at me. "I'm addicted to pain and it led me down a dark path. But then I found my chosen family. Luka, Gabriel, others you haven't yet met. Finding them, finding my purpose, it saved me. But... I *still* think about it... And sometimes... I still *want* it. And I think it might just always be that way for me."

I don't interrupt. Hoping if I keep quiet, he will explain. "Now... I can't go down that hole when so many others that matter, are depending on me." He stops walking and I follow suit. "In a weird way it's like loving them, and having them love me, means I don't just belong to myself anymore." He looks down at his feet and starts walking again. "And at first that was terrifying and also frustrating, but it also meant that my burdens were not my own either, and I didn't have to carry all of that weight I was holding alone anymore. They kind of forced me to share it..." He looks up at me then. His eyes full of intensity. "So I understand addiction. And I understood the song you chose on Thursday. And I know... I know that you lost someone to that same battle."

I inhale sharply. Desperate to hold in the emotion that's ready to escape. "I can't... I can't talk about this." We have stopped walking again. Caden lets out a ragged breath. I doubt many people are privy to his addiction. I bet even fewer have seen his dark side.

"Look, I don't know what I would do if I ever lost any of my brothers." He turns back to me. "But... I know if you keep this inside? If you don't talk to someone about it? It's going to haunt you, and you will *never* be able to get past it." I lean against a tree under some shade, feeling like all the energy has been drained from my body. I try to calm myself before speaking. And what I mean to tell him, is that its none of his business. But...

"It was opiates for Vic. She is... *Was*, my best friend. And we were a part of that kind of family but I left." I choke on my last words and have to swallow down a swell of pain so I can continue. "I had to leave, but she *needed* me. And when I could have gone back? I stayed here. In the big old manor with the fancy school and my fancy new friends. And... And I left her there to die!" Hot, angry tears stream down my face. Rivers of shame that keep coming no matter how much I swipe at them. I end up with my head in my hands and shoulders curled in. Defeated.

Caden's warm hands cover my own and he gently pulls them from my face. When I finally look up at him, the kindness in his face that I know I don't deserve, makes me want to lose it all over again. "Alex... Addiction is *impossible* to fully comprehend when you are not an addict. So you *have* to believe me when I tell you that I *know,* there was nothing you could have done to change the path she was on. There or not there." I move to speak but he shakes his head. "*Listen* to me. At most, you might have been able to slow her down, but it was always going to be *her* choice and *her* demons."

"But you just said that your chosen family helps you hold up weight and that with them, you couldn't be selfish. I *failed* Vic. How could I carry any of her weight when I wasn't there?" I suddenly realize I'm shouting. Taking a deep breath and huffing it out, I shake my head. "She overdosed... *After* I left!"

"I need you to *get* this." Caden takes back my hands. "*How* and *why* a person becomes an addict? Is different between all of us. And the answers to those questions are the foundation of our addictions. *Meaning,* what works for some of us? Does not work for *all* of us. And what motivates me and helps me? Isn't going to be exactly what would have for her... But even if she was *exactly* like me? Then she could have been another continent away from you... But *still,* she would feel closer to you than the people she's standing next to. Just knowing you existed in the world. That you cared. Would have been a game-changer for her. My point is... You *cannot* take accountability for her addiction and her choices. Her demons started before you and were always going to be there whether you were in her face or not. Blaming yourself for her personal battle does not honor her or help her." He pulls my chin up, forcing me to meet his eyes again. "Do you understand?" But I'm unable to speak or even fully see him through all the tears still swimming in my eyes. "*Alex*, you were never going to be able to save her from herself. Your support of her was the most meaningful gift you could have given her. Knowing you, I am sure she knew she had that regardless of where you were. She had your love." Stepping back from me, he scrubs his face a little. Like talking about it has taken something out of him too. Looking at me with a sad smile, he tugs at his shirt. "I would give you this to blow your nose on, but it's sweaty and probably grosser than your boogers." I cough out a laugh and feel something release inside of me. I don't know if I can fully get behind everything he is saying but he has definitely given me a lot to think about.

I give him a small smile and push off the tree. "Is your tee grosser than I look?"

"Of course not! You're definitely worse."

"You ass!" I don't know how he can make me smile after all that, but here it is. As we start up walking again, I want to ask him more about his addiction. I have never heard of anything like it. Is it like cutting? Or something else? But I'm afraid to ask him. "You're about to meet Maddie and Petunia," I tell him instead as we cross the park.

"More friends of yours?"

"Yes," I say, biting back a grin. "Petunia is Ugly's girlfriend. And Maddie was my first friend in this town." I'm relieved to find the dog park is nearly empty and we can use it.

"Ugly has a girlfriend?"

"Don't sound so surprised!" I say defensively. "All the bitches love him, but he only has eyes for his Petunia."

"I guess he's smart enough to know something special when he sees it." I give him a side-long glance at his tone, but a familiar bark distracts me.

"Alex!" Maddie yells at me from across the street in her yard. Petunia starts hopping around and yipping excitedly.

Caden huffs out a laugh. *"That's* Maddie?"

"The one and only." As we reach her, Ugly and Petunia greet like they haven't seen each other in years. Feeling lighter, I run introductions. "Maddie, this is my friend Caden."

Caden smiles warmly at her and puts out his hand. "Nice to meet you Maddie."

She giggles at him. "I'm not old enough to shake hands."

Undeterred, Caden nods in acceptance and does a little curtsey instead. Both Maddie and I laugh and she happily does a little curtsey back. But then she tells him in all seriousness, "You should bow next time cause you're a boy."

Before Caden can respond to her sage advice I gesture to the park. "How about we take them to the dog park today? It's pretty empty."

"Okay!" Maddie's excitement for the change in plans is infectious and as we spend the hour chatting and watching the dogs, more weight is lifted. I'm surprised at how good Caden is with Maddie. And am pleased to see he's visibly upset when he learns that she was playing alone in the park before I came along. As more people begin to crowd in, we corral the dogs and walk Maddie home. Caden promises her he will join us again sometime and I fail in my pathetic attempt to mentally trample down the butterflies that erupt in my chest.

We talk a little bit on our walk back, but I'm distracted and still thinking about everything he told me before we met with Maddie. Caden is nothing like the care-free jock I thought he was when I met him. He has darkness within him and he's a bit twisty. It's hard to understand how I can be even more attracted to him than I already was. But I'm still hurting and raw over Ash and I'm not ready to be so vulnerable. It's crazy I could feel so much for one guy, but now it seems I can for two?

As we cross my front yard Caden halts our progress. "What are you thinking about? You have been somewhere else ever since we left the park."

Letting out a rush of air I shrug, "Honestly? I'm thinking about everything you said. It's going to take me a minute to process. And when it comes to your personal battle I just have more questions, but I know it's personal and I don't want to press..."

Uncertainty covers his features and he looks away. "Maybe... I want you to press. Maybe I *want* you to know me..." Unused to seeing him anything less than confident, I feel my heart squeeze at glimpsing this side of him. The front door opens then, and I turn to see Dill.

"We got pancakes and eggs in here. Get it while it's hot."

Caden's self-assured grin pops back in place. "Blueberry?" He says with undisguised hope.

"Better believe it," Dill says before disappearing back through the door.

Breakfast for dinner is a hit amongst my friends and Lucas' pancakes are to die for.

"Ella should be here for this."

I smile at Luka across the table. "She would love it." At his soft smile, I go on, "I'll be sure to tell her about your mad pancake skills."

"She likes pancakes?" He asks.

Dill looks up at me. "Ella Hearst?"

"Yes..." I say slowly.

Dill's surprise is obvious for the whole table to see. "You're friends with Ella Hearst?"

Feeling uncomfortable I shrug. "I guess I kind of am."

He chuckles, "Ain't that something."

Lucas' chair groans in protest as he shifts and we all look at him. "Why is Ella and Alex being friends *something*?" The silence that follows and the closed look Dill gives him, have the opposite effect of closing the subject. I note the guys exchanged glances and realize we're only making it more interesting by *not* talking about it, so I throw them a bone.

"Before I joined our high school, there was some trouble over the summer." I trudge on at their expectant expressions. "I helped Ella out of it. It's just a funny coincidence that we would end up at the same school and become friends."

Luka slowly nods, but I can tell he's dying to know more. Unfortunately, Caden isn't as reserved. "What kind of trouble?" He looks between all of our faces, but I don't worry about Jade or Aron breaking ranks. Straightening my back a little, my voice comes out a bit more defensively than I mean. "That's Ella's business to share if she wants to." I look at Luka and he nods in understanding.

Caden corners me as everyone gets ready to leave and I square my shoulders, expecting him to ask more about Ella. "What is it?"

"Well, I'm wondering if you're going to your homecoming dance?" Completely surprised I don't immediately respond. "Never mind." He shakes his head ruefully. "I'm sure you must have already gotten a date weeks ago." There is an edge to his voice that definitely sounds a little jealous.

"Is this your way of asking me if I want to go with you?"

He lets out a massive breath and looks back at me. "I was just wondering what your plans are."

"I haven't made plans to go with anyone. I've been so distracted with things. You know..." With my heart thundering in my chest, I press, "Why are you asking me this now?"

He steps in close to me, looking into my eyes in a way that has my whole body feeling all fluttery. "Because I haven't been able to stop thinking about dancing with you, ever since we did. And I want to know what you would feel like when I'm not sharing you with someone else. Alex... I want to know what it would be like to have you as my own for a night." His admission has me lighting up like a Christmas tree. I feel beautiful and powerful beneath his gaze. "And so, now that I know that no one had the balls to ask you, I humbly offer you my own to step on or hopefully not."

"*What!?*"

"Wait." He grabs his hair, messing it up. "Let me try this again." He takes both of my hands in his. "Alex, will you go to the dance with me?"

The smile that spreads across my face is unstoppable. I *know* that this is exactly the kind of thing I should be avoiding if I want to spare my heart from any more disasters. But my mind wonders to Ash who would never invite me to the dance. Who would never invite me to *anything* because I'm not good enough for him, or his family or whatever. Even though it's not totally his fault, some part of me that I can't ignore feels like it kind of *is*. Because I want to be a girl that's worth fighting for. Looking at Caden now, I feel like he would fight for me. Is fighting for me, I realize. I'm honored that someone so exceptional would want to go anywhere with me. So I *know* I should say no. But...

"Yes. I would love to." The smile that comes over his face has my joy spiking into thrill.

He lets my hands go and steps back so he can fully regard me, "*Really?*"

"Really."

"Okay then. How about you finally give me your number and we can work out the details later? I'm sure Gabriel has already asked Jade by now and Luka wants to ask Ella, so we can all go together if you want."

"That would be amazing! If they say yes."

"Gabriel can be very convincing. And Luka-"

"We will see... For their sake, I hope you're right." Giving him my number, giddiness makes me want to fidget. It rushes through me in a combination of nerves and excitement. "I'll see you later then."

He shakes his head. "I honestly can't wait." Too embarrassed to stand there, I move to the door to see everyone out and say my goodbyes. As soon as the door is shut, I text my people.

"I like your friends," Dill says from behind me. Turning around to smile at him I nod.

"I do too."

CHAPTER 20

The weeks before the dance breeze by. The Jacket Crew has finally come back to school but so far, they have kept to themselves. Ash and I have somehow managed to avoid each other altogether. Not so much as a glance in the halls. It's like the kiss never happened. All of my feelings for him have shifted into ugly festering anger.

I have slowly begun healing from the loss of Vic. It turns out Caden's words were exactly what I needed to hear, and I feel a little less like her blood is on my hands. While my guilt has reached a healthier plateau, my nightmares about her have only gotten worse. Much to my friend's dismay, I have taken to napping in my car at lunch and after school. We don't see each other nearly as much.

To my excitement, Jade finally agreed to go with Gabriel to the dance. He sent her an exotic flower each day until she said yes. Even my un-romantically inclined heart was cheering for them. But I suspect her willingness had more to do with finding out Ella was going with Nick. Which shocked all of us. Poor Luca most of all. Nick is another person I'm really upset with. Firstly, because I don't let that many people in and now he is back with the Jacket Crew. Secondly but most importantly, because he hurt Jade. The first offense might have been forgivable but the second is a *hell no*. Aron has a date but in typical *Aron style*, he has refused to reveal with whom.

I haven't had any more gatherings with Dill or invited the guys over again, but we see them every Thursday for open mic. I had thought that not making any plans other than seeing them for a few hours once a week, would slow whatever is developing between Caden and I, but if anything, the anticipation for the dance and keeping our distance has only served to build the tension between us.

At night in the early hours of the morning, as I waver between drifting off and daydreaming, I deviate between thoughts of Caden and Ash until they seem to merge into the same fantastical being. In my hazy musings, that entity is both incomprehensible and familiar. Though clarity remains elusive and the more awake and conscious I become, the less I remember of my visions.

Another crap change I have been trying to adjust to is crazy intermittent states of awareness. I noticed it first with Ash and then Caden too. But now it seems to be a random, recurring predicament. It reminds me a little of when I was in a car accident. As adrenalin shot through my body, my perception of time slowed down in a way that had everything before my eyes moving extra slowly while I was able to react and function in record time.

I remember observing my hands and hair in front of my face, gracefully waving through the air as if submerged underwater. When in reality, the trajectory of spinning out at ninety plus miles an hour, created a gravity so strong, I was violently moving this way and that. Even so, I was able to easily and calmly catch my flying seatbelt and strap myself in, which ultimately saved my life.

But now, while everything is not necessarily moving in slow motion, my instincts spontaneously flicker on, and in those moments, they are just as sharp. I can sense things and hone in on them in a way that I know is not normal. It goes just as quickly as it comes. One minute I'm suddenly sponging up and retaining information from my classes and schoolbooks like a computer. Another, I'm having panic attacks due to an overloaded sensory experience.

What should be background noise, is abruptly grating and loud. Small gestures and body language between my classmates and teachers is now a clear and defined form of communication. More complex than words and yet much easier for me to understand. I have gotten so adept at reading signals, that sometimes I'm able to anticipate things before they happen or know what someone is going to say before they do. It has me feeling absolutely insane!

Not to mention my growing sense of smell. It's become totally overwhelming. I'm gagging over scents no one else even picks up on or I'm in ecstasy over the incredible flavors of banal processed foods. Just as quickly as these spells hit me, they're over and I'm left wondering if it's all in my head and I just made it up; or if I might actually have a brain tumor.

But amidst all the chaos is Aron and Jade, an unlikely duo. Made all the more implausible when matched up with me. But somehow we do fit. They have kept me grounded and sane at times when I otherwise would have lost myself completely. Ugly and Dill, my other great equalizers, have been rocks - constant when nothing else feels certain. So much has changed over the last months, I can hardly keep up with it all, but they are my constants.

Somewhere between the crazy and the security, I feel more of *me* coming to the surface and unfolding. Like I am only just now beginning to learn all the potential I might have. My musical inclinations have been evolving. For the first time in my life, I am actually beginning to feel confident and worthy. It's all had a profound impact on my day to day.

Right now, I'm approaching Jade's room for pre-prep on the dance. A notion I have never heard of. I mean, who needs to *prepare* for preparing? But I'm trusting her and going with it. Whatever *it* is. As we enter her room, the answer glares at me like a neon sign.

Three long racks of dresses are waiting for us. Half in varying tones of black and red. The rest in a gradient of white to the palest blue and pink. A few silver and gold dresses are sprinkled in as well. And on the third rack is more avant-garde offerings. Utterly floored, I say nothing as I follow in Jade's wake.

The massive assortment of headpieces ranging from crowns to horns covering almost every surface in her room is impossible to miss. Then by her bed is a smaller rack holding every kind of wing imaginable and what didn't fit there is splayed out on her bed. Passing Jade and descending into her seating area, I see that her sofa and coffee table are also littered with accessories and jewelry.

My wide eyes reach hers. "Since when did your room become a department store?"

At that moment, Jade's mom Sandra comes sweeping in with a tall blonde woman trailing behind her. "Oh good. You're here! Girls, meet Mia, my personal stylist. When I'm not lucky enough to have her, Vogue, the red carpet, and royalty do. So you listen to what she says and know you're in good hands."

"Mom..." Even I can hear the emotion in Jade's voice.

Her mother approaches her and tucks a stray hair behind her ear. "Too much of the time I'm not here. And this is the first time I have seen you really take an interest in something outside of the usual and I just..." She drops her hand from Jade's cheek and looks around the room. "Well, we may have gone a bit overboard, but I wanted it to be just perfect for you." She looks from Jade over to me. "For both of you. Jade has been..." She takes a moment to search for the right words. "Changed since meeting you." Her face transforms with such love as she looks at Jade that it leaves me feeling a bit awed. "And it's a beautiful transformation." Seeming to shake herself, her face and posture become more composed. "So, Mia will ensure that the two of you feel and look as stunning as you should." Smoothing her already flawless dress she sighs. "Your father and I have an engagement this evening so I can't be here for this fabulous moment you're about to share, but I want to hear all about your selections tomorrow! So be home for dinner Jade." At Jade's nod, she heads for the door and turns a last time to give a delicate wave. "Do enjoy!"

Jade finally gets out, "Thank you..." But it's to an empty doorway.

The next two hours are spent sipping champaign, trying on dresses, accessorizing our top choices, and having *way too much* fun. Mia is assertive without being overbearing and a genius at knowing what fits with what. She has picked out several dresses for me that I would never have picked for myself and they ended up being my favorites. Jade jumped at the role of devil with an enthusiasm that almost made her seem her own age. A rarity for her. So I went the route of angel.

I am standing in front of Jade's full-length mirror, in the last of Mia's selections. A metallic, pale gold confection that sweeps the floor and hugs my body in all the right places. It's one of the simpler of the gowns, but the draping neck and low back with the two slits in front make it sexy as well as elegant. The shimmering tones blending in perfectly with my skin and hair so that it looks as though I am glowing too.

As Jade and Mia come behind me they smile and they don't even have to say it. *This is the one.* The delicate diamond straps that hold up the front, meet at the center of my open back, to form a thin "Y" and then disappear provocatively beneath the fabric set low on my waist. As I turn around to look at them, I can't help but admire the new angle in the mirror. When I finally look at Jade she nods in satisfaction.

"You're *everything*, looks amazing in that."

Mia comes up behind me and reviews my reflection in the mirror. "This dress was made for you and I have just the thing." She disappears and Jade comes up next to me. We look at ourselves in the mirror.

She is wearing the sexiest mini dress I have ever seen. The entire thing is made up of Swarovski crystals. Starting up high on her neck in fiery red and continuing onto her shoulders in a ruby hue. Only to bleed down her arms and torso, into the darkest black. The long, tight glittering sleeves turn into fingerless gloves that cut off at her knuckles. And the dress ends at the same length as her sleeves. She has paired it with skintight over-the-knee boots made of the same black crystals that blend into red at the tips. And the effect is devastating.

"Gabriel is too young to die of a heart attack. Don't you think?"

Jade snickers. "Maybe I want him to suffer."

I look at her knowingly. "Are you sure it's not *someone else* you want to suffer?"

Her face becomes imperious. "Maybe I want *all* the boys in our school to suffer! You *can't* say they don't deserve it."

I shrug at that. "You won't hear any arguments from me."

Mia comes back and places a headband that looks like a half sun with spikes of rhinestones shooting out of it, atop my head. It has the effect of a shimmering halo that matches my dress straps.

Jade puts her hand on my shoulder and smiles at me through the mirror. "I'm glad you don't because you would be a hypocrite otherwise. This is bound to make him suffer." We both know she's not talking about Caden. Though he will definitely suffer too, and the thought has me smiling slyly back at her.

Jade has been teaching me all along about the inherent power of being a woman. But I'm finally starting to understand her meaning. She puts on a set of crystal black horns that fade into a matching ruby red at their tips, just like her boots, and she suddenly looks dangerous.

Mia is obviously pleased with her work. "I'm opting against the wings. Why mess with perfection?"

Jade takes a quick selfie of us. "Why indeed." And I can't wait for the dance.

∞

I'm having the strongest deja vu as Sal styles my hair around my headpiece. He's happily chattering about something and I'm only half-listening as I watch Jade transform before my eyes.

His tone of voice now implies this isn't the first time he's asked. "Are you agreed?"

Guiltily, I shake my head. "I'm sorry, what did you say?"

Thankfully he chuckles instead of taking his frustration out on my hair. "I said, I'm going for a Grecian style with the top half loosely up around your crown and the rest down over your shoulder, leaving your back exposed."

"UmHmm..." I absently nod.

Sal huffs. "Hellooo?"

Feeling bad, I give him my full attention. "I'm sorry it's just... Look at her." I gesture to Jade who smiles at the awe in my voice. "I have never seen anyone made over like that... Like she's out of a movie!"

Jade's eyes have dramatic ruby red shadow that blends into the new red streaks at her temples. The dramatic black liner around her eyes have them looking especially exotic against skin that is milky pale. She is wearing black-out contacts that have the effect of glittering bottomless chasms. Her lips are done in a geisha style with the same ruby red as the matching streaks in her hair. Her hair has tons of volume at the top and falls in a silky straight line down her back. Ruby earrings and black crystal claws glued over her fingertips complete the look. She is terrifyingly beautiful.

Sal grunts in agreement. "Hunny, you be the light and she be the shaade. You just wait until we're done with you."

True to his word, I'm an ethereal marvel. My soft curls and waves are lustrous and romantic with a sheen of glitter and crystals dotted throughout. My halo crown is perfectly framed and the hair twisting down the side of my neck makes it seem longer and more delicate.

Anywhere I have exposed skin, I am covered in opalescent gold shimmer and my back is show-stopping.

Mia got her hands on the wing design Ella made and blew it up to make a crystal stencil. It is now proudly displayed between the delicate crystal chain running down my back. My shimmering crystal shoes tie the whole affair together. My eyes, which have always been blue, stand out tonight in a way they never have before. If I saw myself on the street I would definitely think I was not of this world. As Jade comes to stand next to me, I notice we make the perfect Yin and Yang.

Looking at her I nod my head. "You know, we are never going to be able to out-do this right?"

She smiles at me wickedly and I notice little fangs in her mouth. "There is always prom."

Sal scoffs from behind us. "She's right. This is just a warm-up." I start laughing until I hear the doorbell. A second of pure panic hits me. "They're here!" I whisper shout.

Jade's smile never leaves her face. "Sal? How about you open that bottle of Dom I was saving."

"I thought you'd *never* ask."

My eyes are big as I address her. "You're having them come up *here? To your room? Now?*"

"Relax!" Jade chuckles at my nerves and she looks so evil and beautiful it distracts me. "They can wait. You and I are going to have a moment. My father is going to need a minute to get acquainted with Gabriel and Caden anyway. Never forget, the best things in life do not come easy or fast."

Sal hands us each a flute brimming with bubbles and we toast to that. He pours himself a healthy glass and winks at Jade. "My tip."

She smiles at him sweetly. "The rest of the bottle is yours. We have a long night ahead of us."

Our moment was a sweet one. Jade and I made toasts until our flutes were empty and we dissolved into laughter as they got to be sillier. Sal took pictures and we posed until my nerves settled down. I imagine I felt a little like Cinderella did, just before entering her pumpkin coach. I was ready to see my prince, slay the haters, and open myself up to all the mystery and possibilities of the night.

CHAPTER 21

Making sure to wait the full thiry seconds Jade insisted on after she went down the stairs, I begin my descent. I remember to keep my shoulders back and my head high. I feel naked in the silk. It whispers across my skin as light as a feather. Cool air brushing up my glittering thighs between the slits, I slide my hand along the banister. Not gripping it, but ready to catch myself if I trip. *I'm definitely going to trip.*

My nerves are back tenfold because I know in the next second, I'm going to see Caden. The boy who has filled my thoughts, countless nights. Slowly letting out a nervous breath, I look down the stairs and meet his gaze as Jade's mom happily snaps pictures. It's a breath and an eternity but as I reach the bottom step and accept his hand, I know it's going to be an unforgettable night.

"You are exquisite." His breathlessness as he says it has my inner Christmas tree set to glowing again.

Jade's mother sniffles and I look over, catching her dabbing at her eyes. "This world isn't good enough for the two of you."

Jade's dad is brimming with pride and insists on pictures with her after she gets some with Gabriel and then her mom. It kind of makes me wish that Dill was here even though this is so not his scene. But he is the closest thing to a parent I have ever had and if I could share the joy of my first formal dance with him, I would.

Caden and I are next and my skin ripples with goosebumps as his hand connects with the bared skin of my back. "Is this okay? I'm not going to mess up your wings?" His low voice at my ear only sharpens the sensation of his hands on me.

I shake my head and try my best not to smile like an idiot. He smells more like the woods tonight and it has me wanting to shove my face into his neck and breath deep.

Standing back from him I admire his black tuxedo. "You look like a James Bond villain."

"High praise." He smiles broadly at me as Jade's parents snap a few more candids.

"Be still my heart."

I swing around at the sound of Aron's voice. True and undiluted giddiness overtakes me. And I realize all at once that this must be what care-free teenagers with nothing to worry about but tests and fitting in, feel like. This ecstatic high that makes me want to make a complete fool of myself by running at Aron and squealing in glee. I see him all the time. But now, my circle is complete and we are dressed to kill. A united front ready to take on the night.

Even better, his "date" is none other than Tara and Gabby, who are draped on his arms and beaming. The three of them look amazing together with coordinated outfits. Aron looks every inch the Demon with blackout contact lenses like Jade's, smokey eye shadow, and fangs with gold rings on each of his fingers. His Maleficent horns are *full-on*. He has black glittering body paint from the collar of his matching black but-ton-up, to his jawline. And his face is sharper with subtle contouring and paler makeup that enhances his features.

Like Aron, the girls are body painted gold from fingertips to jawlines. Where his wings are gold with black tips, theirs are white dipped in gold. And with long sequin burnt-gold gowns, smoky eyes, and large golden halos above their heads? They manage to accent Aron perfectly while standing out and being striking on their own.

"You guys are smashing." Gabriel grins at them.

"Naturally," Aron states and makes Jade's parents titter.

We spend twenty more minutes on pictures and then Benson has us filing into a massive limo that has my jaw unhinged. Caden goes ahead of me and takes my hand to help me inside. I would be more touched by his old school moves if I were not so distracted by this marvel mobile. My eyes go even rounder as I take in the interior that looks more like a dance club, than a car. Our crew only adds to the crazy scene. Everyone looks more creature than human. Even Caden's eyes are brighter and his skin has a glowing sheen to it. Looking at Gabriel, I realize they both must be wearing a bit of makeup as he glows too.

Jade picks up a remote and music pours from the speakers. It's a song we all know and as Aron starts to sing, I join in until everyone is belting out the words and laughing. I don't know who started it but pretty soon we're dancing. Flashes are going off as pictures are taken and we are in full-on party mode. Tara and Gabby look a little mystified and I don't blame them. I know exactly how they feel. When you spend most of your life on the outside looking in, it's a revelation to suddenly find yourself on the inside.

"You two look amazing!" I smile at them.

Tara laughs. "I would accept that compliment from anyone but the people in this limo! You guys don't even look human!"

I grin at her. "I was honestly just thinking the *same thing*!"

Caden captures my attention with a little nudge. "Why wouldn't we look human? I was just feeling bad that Gabriel and I didn't put in as much work as the rest of you."

I lift my brow at him. "You mean apart from your bright as hell contact lenses, smoky eyes, and glowing skin?" At his uncomfortable look, I roll my eyes at him.

"Welcome to the future! Where even the manliest men can wear makeup!"

His shoulders go down and he smirks at me. "You notice everything, don't you?"

"More now than ever," I say it under my breath but he catches it.

Leaning close enough to send more nerves skittering through my system he quietly asks, "What do you mean?" He looks too serious for the teenage revelry surrounding us. But before I can tell him about the bazaar changes I have been going through, Jade shouts my name from across the car.

Looking away from Caden I shout back. "Jade!"

She laughs. "We're doing a shot before we head in. Want to join?" She's holding up a neon tube that glows blue in the black lights.

"Gimme!"

She looks at Caden and hands him one at his nod. Passing them out to everyone except Gabby who admits she doesn't drink in apparent embarrassment.

When Jade gets to the last tube, she dumps out its contents and fills it with sprite. Looking back at Gabby with a wicked grin. "You do tonight. We are not going to have a single toast without you so long as you're with us."

Gabby looks so happy and relieved I want to hug her. She accepts the tube and holds it up. We raise ours with her and Jades' black glittering eyes meet each of ours. "There is only right here, right now. And this night is the last of its kind. In your whole life, there will never be another exactly like it. For this reason, I propose a challenge to you all. Each of you is allotted a single wish for the evening. You can ask it of one of us, some of us, or all of us. I trust everyone here enough to know your wish will not be harmful or in bad taste. If you make this toast with me, it is a pact to honor every wish as the participants will honor your own."

"Hell yes!" Gabriel clinks his tube and the rest of us don't hesitate in following suit.

Feeling Caden's eyes on me, I look over at him and meet his smile. The night feels charged with magic and possibility. And the unity and jubilation filling our limo have me realizing we could go anywhere and it would be amazing. The next song that plays is a favorite of mine. Meeting Jade's eyes she gives me a pleased nod. She knows.

I sigh contentedly and lean back in my seat, right next to Caden, allowing all my nerves to do their worst. There is nowhere else I want to be. And nothing more thrilling, than boldly staring back at the gorgeous boy next to me. We reach the dance too soon and all of us seem a little hesitant to leave our limo party.

Except for Aron. He's out in seconds and turning around and reaching up to help his dates out before Benson can. "Ladies..." The concern that crosses Benson's face over Aron doing his job, makes me giggle. When it's my turn I pointedly ignore Aron's hand and eyeball Benson. He stands a little taller and replaces Aron who is already distracted with his dates.

"Thank you," I say, taking his hand and stepping out. The weather is so good, we could have had the dance outside. I kind of wish it was. Stepping back with Aron I wait for everyone else. The look on Caden's face when he finds me standing before him is like he's seeing me again for the first time, and my whole body warms.

He takes my hand in his and I don't have time to react over how much that single gesture affects me before we are all walking together. A boy I recognize from the yearbook committee is on the sidewalk before the red carpet with a camera and crew. He instantly starts filming us even before we make it to the sidewalk. I imagine what we must look like walking up to them. In my mind, we're in slow motion, and the drama of the image has me laughing out loud.

Aron looks over at me. "What?" Never one to miss out on a joke.

"I'm just imaging us in slow motion. So epic."

Gabby giggles. "*Best* night *ever.*"

No one disagrees. We walk onto the red carpet and pose for our school's paparazzi.

Once inside, Tara grabs our attention. "Guys! I have my wish..."

Aron smiles in delight. "So soon?"

She looks a little nervous but goes on anyway. "I want to go back to the red carpet and get a group shot together."

Jade smiles approvingly. "Your wish is my command."

We make a commotion going against the line and taking up the red carpet again, but no one stops us. I hear Gabriel ask Jade if she would say that to him when he makes his wish and belts out a laugh when she just winks at him. We do multiple poses including one with Tara and Gabby right at the center. And the school's newspaper crew has a field day. By the time we make it back inside, I feel like a movie star. Looking at the elated faces in our group, I get the feeling we all do.

I give Tara's shoulder a little squeeze. "Good wish!" She looks so happy her joy is infectious.

The gymnasium is decked out in fluffy cotton clouds and paper stars hanging from the ceiling with twinkling lights. The walls of the gym are ringed in cut out flames with red and yellow fairy lights. I'm surprised to see a band I recognize is playing instead of a DJ and make a mental note to say hi to them later. Jade finds us a table with a few discarded cups and a single person sitting alone.

"Mind if we join you?" The kid takes one look at her and stumbles away. Jade looks back at us as innocently as she can, given the black eyes and fangs. "Was it something I said?"

I stifle my smile in case the poor guy is close enough to see. We sit down and Jade sweeps aside the cups, which Gabriel diligently takes away from the table for her. She pulls out a tube of red lipstick and in large letters facing the dance floor, writes on the white paper covering it: *JADE'S TABLE.*

I seriously doubt she needed to claim the table. From the moment we walked in, it has felt like all eyes are on us. But she takes a picture with all of us sitting around the lipstick sign and its perfection.

"Ready to dance?" She seems to be asking all of us. And I don't think I have ever seen her so jaunty.

"With pleasure," I say as Caden moves to pull my chair out for me in a show of amazing speed.

I look over at him as we stand with everyone else. "What era are you from?"

His eyes take on a gleam and he smiles secretively at me. "Pick one. My gentlemen skills are *no joke*."

I'm about to ask him about whatever inside joke has that particular smile on his face when we suddenly come to a stop at the edge of the dance floor. I look up to find the Jacket Crew blocking our path. And now I don't just *feel* like everyone is watching us. I *know* they are. But Sarah looking glorious in a red sequin gown and tall red horns does not intimidate me. The traitorous telltale sign lifting all my fine hairs is what has me faltering. Refusing to meet his eyes, I lean back into Caden for support and zero in on Satan Sarah.

Jade faces off with her. "Jessica Rabbit called and she wants her dress back.

Sara looks her up and down but comes up with nada. Looking over the rest of us, her eyes land on me and they are smoldering. "So good of you to make it to *my* dance."

"*Your* dance?" Gabby sputters.

"Haven't you seen the flyers? They are basically all me." She flips her hair and rolls her eyes like it's the most obvious thing in the world.

In a brave show of support, Tara steps up to draw Sarah's attention. "*Right*. Because '*not today*' with the inferred '*Satan Sarah*' at the end, is a positively glowing review for you."

Sarah giggles evilly. "All press is good press. But I guess you would have to *be someone* to understand that. Now, step aside and let the adults talk."

Aron surprises me by subtly angling his body between Sarah and his dates. "It's so cute you think this dance is about you! I mean... Considering the girls who inspired the whole movement this dance was built on, are standing before you." Sarah bristles and moves to say something but Aron cuts her off. "You must have missed the entire point of the wings that have been, oh, I don't know... Everywhere? But look, if you don't have the sense to recognize royalty and bow down, then it's you who can step aside. Have fun playing the adult. With yourself."

In an audacious move, he links arms with his dates and brushes past Sarah and the rest of the Jacket Crew. We follow suit behind them, and I concentrate on ignoring the burning sensation of Ash's glower. I'm filled with pride when I realize that not a single one of us has given Sarah and her ilk a second glance. I lean back so Caden can hear me as we walk. "Brush-off touch-down, point for us!" And as we all make it to the center of the dance floor, I speak loud enough for everyone to hear. "*That* was fun!" I look at Aron. "And what a surprising display of chivalry!"

He shrugs. "One should never be too predictable." And with that said, he turns around and spins his two dates to the slow song the band has switched to.

We all start dancing then and I turn around to give Caden my full attention. He looks slightly unsettled.

"What is it?"

He shakes his head and smiles at me. "How is it that you can read me like a book when no one else can?"

"Don't change the subject."

"When I asked you to the dance, I was worried you were already going with someone else." He nods over his shoulder to where I know Ash is still watching us. *Ugh.* He breaths out a laugh. "But the fool's taken that evil skin bag."

"*What?!*" I laugh at his outrageous depiction. "Evil s*kin bag?*"

"Yes well, that's about as deep as her beauty goes and the rest is just... Empty." Caden's hands glide from my shoulders, down to my hips. The tips of his fingers lightly brushing against the bare skin of my back then squeezing. His large hands almost encapsulating my entire waist, and it feels *so good* I barely register his next words. "But enough about them." He gently tugs me against his body. "I want to focus on you."

All thoughts of Ash melt away as I inhale the scent of Caden. He fairly vibrates against me as I lean my head against his shoulder and blatantly breathe him in. It almost feels like he is purring. I lean up on my toes to whisper in his ear. Even with my heels, he's still taller than me. "… I've been wanting to do that all night."

He leans his head down and buries his face in my hair. Taking a massive inhale of his own. I swear I hear him groan. "A coincidence then, because I have too. I just didn't want to weird you out."

"I'm good with weird."

" I should never underestimate you." I lean my head back on his chest and become aware of his racing heart. Smiling big, I feel my own heartbeat pick up speed.

Caden is a caliber of the guy that I *never* would have gone for. Not that long ago, I was far too insecure to think someone like him could ever be interested in someone like me. But right beneath my cheek is the hard evidence that I'm wrong. Because while faces can deceive and words can twist, the heart doesn't lie. And his is beating *for me*.

With the warmth and scent of him wrapped around me and the steady pounding of his heart a melody at my ear, a spell is cast over me. Something inside of me breaks open. I'm about to be lost to this boy and I don't think I want to fight it any longer. The song changes and I step back from him, swaying a little and smiling up into his face.

He takes a second to look at the ceiling then looks back at me, beaming. "You keep stealing my breath. You're so damn beautiful Alex." Before I can respond, Jade grabs my hand and pulls me away. She shouts over my shoulder to Caden. "Gabby's made her wish! She wants us to start a dance circle!"

Within seconds we're a part of a circle that is growing larger until it seems half the dance floor is a part of it. I'm surrounded by celestial beings, demons, and devils. I feel transported into another dimension where even *I* feel different but more apart than I ever have. Everyone takes turns dancing within the circle. When Aron steps out with his two angels and does the robot between them, I'm laughing so hard my ribs hurt. Someone pushes me in after him. I have a momentary flash-back of dance-offs with Vic and Shells and my heart constricts painfully but it's bittersweet as all those good memories flash before me. *This one's for you guys.*

I spin into the center of the circle and let the music take me over. I go from a liquid style body role that moves into my swaying hips. And then I'm merging into a seductive pop and lock. I shift from there into a belly dancing hip shake that I ripple throughout my body. When It reaches my hands, I move them to form shapes with precision and speed, I let the moves loosen up in rhythm to the music until they become liquid again. Until I am liquid again, rolling my neck and my shoulders to the waves only I can feel. And then I'm arching my back farther and farther with each hip roll until my hair brushes the floor and I'm looking upside down at a stunned Caden. As the move takes effect on the crowd, I roll my hips in reverse to roll back up until I'm standing again to the thrilling backdrop of shouts and cheers, and best of all, Caden's apparent stupor.

I spin off the floor and into the only arms I want to be in. Without meaning to, my eyes find Ash's in the crowd, and for just a second my whole body freezes. I quickly look back to my date, breathlessly leaning into the hard length of him. I let out a happy sigh as he speaks into my ear. "You are *extraordinary* Alex. What the hell am I going to do about you?"

I stand up straighter and look into his eyes. "Get me something to drink?"

"As you wish."

"That wasn't my wish!"

"Don't worry Alex. As long as you're with me, you get unlimited wishes."

It's not the first time he's struck me silent. And it won't be the last time I watch his beautiful form depart before I can whip up a coherent comeback.

∞

The line to the lady's room is longer than I expected, but as I approach the sea of girls miraculously parts for me. Unlike Satan Sarah or even Jade, no one seems to be afraid when they step aside to let me pass. Most of the girls are smiling at me or nodding in hello.

"Oh my god, you look amazing!" A cute girl with black hair and fairy wings comments as I move past her. I stop and admire her outfit.

"A fairy at an angel party. How punk rock of you." She looks uncertain at my compliment, so I smile. "I love punk rock."

"Oh! Me too!"

"What's your name?" She seems surprised that I'm asking, and her face turns rosy as the other girls in line listen in to our conversation.

"I'm Beth. One of Tara's friends. I saw that she's with you guys tonight?"

"Yeah, feel free to stop by and say hello."

"Really?"

Shaking my head at her I try not to laugh. "Yeah, of course!"

"The girl in front of her gets my attention. "I'm not in any hurry, you can go ahead of me."

Not one to look a gift horse in the mouth, "Are you sure?"

The girls in front of her wave me in front of them too. I feel a little bad, but not so much that I'm going to pass up the royal treatment. "Thanks!" As soon as my stall door is shut, the whispering begins. But to my shiny new heightened senses, they might as well be yelling.

"Were you at that party where she stood up for Tara?"

"No, but my bestie saw her at an open mic and said she can honest to god, sing. *And* I have it on good authority that she can play any instrument... And she speaks five languages."

Ha! I wish! Chuckling to myself, I flush and wait a second longer to give them warning before I step out. The girls awkwardly step around me. Looking up at me through lashes and around phones, and I have to wonder if this is kind of how celebrities feel? I mean, I'm sure after a while it would be awful. But at the moment the newness of it all, of having anyone consider a reject like me as special? If I am being totally honest with myself? It's nothing short of miraculous.

Going to the mirror to wash my hands I glance up. And stop. The girl in that reflection is someone I hardly recognize. And though it's not the first time some makeup and a new outfit has made me look completely different... There is something in my eyes, my face that is changed. I lean a little closer to try and figure it out. I realize what it is as soon as I realize I am still being watched. I blink my eyes furiously like I have an eyelash stuck and am trying to find it. Which is good because I'm not in control of the sudden feels I'm having.

I look different because my mouth isn't drawn tight in stress. My eyes are not squinting in a perpetual sneer from needing to look tough and ready. The worry lines in a face too young for them have begun to fade. I look different because *I am* different. My clothes and hair and makeup haven't changed me. I have. The soft smile my reflection gives me as recognition clicks into place, has me still smiling as I leave the bathroom.

CHAPTER 22

" We need to talk." Ash grabs my arm and pulls me down the wrong end of the hallway from where I'm going.

"What? No!" I'm too surprised to be freaked as we pass through a set of doors that lead into a darker hallway of lockers. What I do feel? *All* I can feel? Is unchecked anger at the incredible nerve of him. "I said... *let me go!*" I dig my heels in and yank my arm from his grasp. Unless he plans on dragging me, I am not going another step. To that end, I put a few feet between us.

Ash looks more out of sorts then I have ever seen him, and it almost stems some of my anger. Almost. "*Alex...* It's not secure here, people might hear us."

Incredulous I scoff at him. "Are you kidding me right now? I don't want to hear anything you have to say, and I could give two shits if someone hears us!" I look around me at the empty hallway. "And I think it's in my best interest to be where people *can* hear us."

He turns away from me and hits a locker. The loud bang startles me and makes my voice louder than I intend. "What is *wrong* with you!? Why am I here Ash?"

He turns back to me. "That's what I'm *trying to tell you!* But... I can't talk about it here. It's too open." His eyes land on something behind me and I look up to see the red light of one of the many cameras at our school.

Uncomfortable, I take another step away from him. Begrudgingly noticing that he looks incredible in his tux. But his actions and now words, are giving me the creeps. "Look, I don't know what this is about. And honestly? *I don't care.* You have been the ultimate mind fuck and I'm *over it!* And besides... You made your choice!" I hate the hurt that bleeds into my voice and I quickly let my anger trample it down. "You're acting *crazy*... OK? And this?" I lift my arms up to gesture around me at the dark empty hall and nod at the camera. "Is *weird.* Even for me. So take your absurd, melodramatic, cloak and dagger bullshit, somewhere else."

He visibly deflates. All the aggression leaving him. He barks out a hollow laugh that sounds more desolate than amused as he shakes his head, looking down. "My cloak and dagger bullshit?" The smirk on his face as he looks back up at me doesn't reach his eyes. He heaves out a breath. "Believe me... *I wish.* ...I... I *know* how I sound, okay? But there is *so much* that you don't understand." His head snaps up to the doors that we came through. But I don't see anything there. "I'm running out of time." He sighs and then slowly approaches me. I mean to move but he stops like he knows that he's spooking me. "I know I haven't given you any reason to. But I *need* you to trust me. Okay? That guy you're with? Caden? And his friends? They are not...." He buries his face in his hands and scrubs it, looking wild and agitated.

Some of his urgency passes through me. "*What?* Tell me? They are not *what?*"

"They are not *safe!*" He yells out the last words and I take another step back at the dangerous look on his face. "...They are not *safe* Alex." He says it again with a little more composure. He looks at the door once more than gets in my face. *"There's no more time,* but you *have to trust me!* He's *dangerous* and I want you to stay *away* from him!"

His last words hit me like a bucket of ice water. Before I can even think about it, all of the fury and desolation over the last weeks harden into a shove that sends him flying back into the lockers. One minute he's in front of me. The next, the doors burst open. Not even bothering to look that way I take a threatening step closer to Ash. *"That's* what this is about? You're *jealous?"*

The school's sweetheart actually stutters. *"No!* ...It's not like that!"

I take another step closer to him. Power and something darker pulsing through me. I want to hurt him the way he's hurt me. "If you think, I give a flying fuck who you want me to be around? You're even crazier than I thought!" Without looking, I know Caden is now standing behind me. "You lost your right to say *anything* to me!" Ash's shocked look at my violence is finally what pierces through my anger. Stepping back towards Caden, I heave out a shuddering breath. Shaking my head to rid it of that thunderous pulsing. "Stay the hell away from me. And if you think I can't make you? My *dangerous* friends will."

Before I can do or say anything I'll regret, I turn my back on him and take Caden's hand, giving it a little tug for us to leave. He intently searches my face then glances down at Ash, who is glowering at him from the floor. Caden sends him a glare that promises violence. But I tug his hand again and he seems to shake himself, squeezing my hand back. Finally letting out a massive sigh before he leads us to the lights without a word to Ash. We say nothing until we are alone at our table.

"I was ready to murder him." He confesses, as soon as I am sitting. "But it turns out, you're not a princess in need of rescuing." Resignation relaxes his features and he huffs out a laugh. "I didn't even get to *threaten* him before you did that too! And the way you sent him flying into those lockers! I couldn't believe it! Do you have any formal training?"

Embarrassed by his flattering and still heated from my exchange with Ash, I am grateful for the subject change. "Um, no. But I have kind of always had to look out for myself. It's pretty instinctual at this point."

He gives me a considering stare. "You should come to the dojo with me and the boys some time. You have a lot of untapped potential, and *rage*." He says the last part in a way that has us both chuckling. "It's a good place to get it all out and learn some cool tricks while you're at it." At my dubious look, he smiles and shrugs. "Just think about it."

There's a commotion on the stage and the music stops. My group materializes and sits around us as the crowed falls into murmurs. I lean over to Jade as the principal takes the mike. "What's going on?"

Jade looks board. "They are announcing the homecoming king and queen."

Ignoring the prattling of the principal, I take the opportunity to look around the crowd. I can just barely make out another table through the crush of students to see the Jacket Crew. I don't see Ash. But Sarah's focus is glued to the stage and Nick is glaring daggers at Gabriel's back. *Why are boys so dumb?* Even if he had to one day marry someone else, like in his twenties or thirties, or even *later*, does that really mean he couldn't take Jade to our high school dance? Instead, he and Ash are running around with other dates acting like tools.

Rolling my eyes, I cross my arms and finally focus on the stage. The principal takes on the voice of a game show host. "And this year's homecoming king is... Nicholas Hartford!" *Of course.* I look over to him, surprised when he doesn't immediately get up. He just sits there like a lump. When no one comes to the stage the principal raises her voice over the dwindling cheers. "Nick Hartford? Please come to the stage!"

I can't hear what his friends are saying to him but they push him out of his chair and he finally, if not reluctantly, makes his way to the stage. The principal lights up when he sees him. "Ah! There you are! Okay, everyone ready? And this year's homecoming queen is... Tara Davis!" *What!?* The crowd erupts and Tara looks more shocked than even Sarah.

She whispers at no one in general, "Did he just call *my name?*"

"Yes!" I laugh. "Hurry up and go!"

Ever the gentleman, Aron stands and escorts Tara onto the stage. Not letting her trip or fall. We shout and clap for her and by the obvious enthusiasm of the student body, I have to wonder if this is the first time the most popular kid wasn't chosen. On that thought, I look back over at Sarah who has a scary glint in her eyes as she watches Tara. Nudging Jade, I direct her gaze to Sarah. She nods at me and just like that, we have an unspoken understanding that Tara is now officially under our protection.

The sound of Tara's strong voice draws my attention back to the stage. She holds up her crown. "This is the last piece of evidence I need to know for sure, that it's a *new era! Not today satan!* Because it's *our* day now!" She makes a show of putting the crown on her head and the student body loses it. She just publicly threw down the gauntlet to Sarah and we all know it. Apparently, most people have been waiting for this day because it's loud enough one might think we just scored a touchdown.

The rest of the dance goes by too quickly. We don't see much of Tara, Aron, and Gabby since her queendom was announced. But the boys keep Jade and I busy on the dance floor and the night has been fully salvaged. I'm delighted to find that Caden *can dance* and for a while, I forget all about my worries, Ash and the Jacket Crew.

∞

As we pile back into our limo, Aron is the first to speak. "I have my wish..." We all go quiet in anticipation of his ask. "I *know* we have a party to get to. But it's only 10 pm and I have *never* approved of being on time for *anything*. Least of all parties, which don't even get interesting until people hit the *fr*unky."

As the limo takes off, I have to ask, "F*runky?*"

He looks at me like I'm an adorable little puppy dog. "Sometimes I forget you're not from this planet." He takes on the tone of my calculus teacher. "*Frunky*, is *fun*, *funky*, and *drunk*, all in one. Said *drunk*, is not exclusive to alcohol, it can also apply to any form of inebriation, including sugar high to life high. But *any party* that's worthwhile, has a period of time where most people collectively get *frunky*. And that's the sweet spot." He looks at Jade for support. "Am I right?"

She smiles at him. "True."

Karaoke is a blast! Somewhere between a Cher impression and Aron going 90's rock, I get misty-eyed. I never fully realized how much I was missing out on. I can't remember a time before Green Mont where I didn't feel too old, too tired, and too scared. But I didn't understand the weight and the toll of it all until now. In the light and sheer joy that is now radiating through my being, I am can fully recognize the darkness in my dreary existence before moving here.

The recurring dreams that led me to this town, don't seem like such a coincidence anymore. This is too good. Too *right* to be accidental. But the thought is lost as I get caught up in Caden's song. U2's, *With or Without You*. His eyes never leave mine and my friends make childish little taunts. Completely unfazed, he sings to me about a passionate, tragic love. His voice as he croons out the chorus is sexy as hell and I know he's telling me something through the words but I'm not really sure of what. All I know is that this charismatic, beautiful boy is singing to me and I'm having a true movie moment. The air around him practically sparkles as I go tunnel vision and my heart does something funny in my chest.

Then Aron gets up with him and picks up the other mic. Supporting him in a confident, off-key harmony that has Caden losing his rhythm and messing up. We all bust up laughing and Aron shrugs. Luka shows up and completes our happy posse. He picks at our leftovers and makes the perfect heckle partner. We spend a good amount of time making fun of everyone and cracking up at our cleverness.

∞

The party is almost anti-climatic. *Almost.*

"I've got my wish!" We all look over at Gabriel who is sitting next to Jade. This might be pressing it right, but the most powerful things come in threes. "*My wish*, is for each of you, to find three things to say yes to from three different people. Hopefully, they will be things you normally wouldn't be open to. The point is to get out of your comfort zone. In one hour, I want to meet you all back here and find out what sort of mad adventures and trouble you've found, yeah? And if you're havin' trouble findin' trouble, then I'll help the trouble find you. Right?"

When no one responds, Jade speaks up. "He wants you to say yes to three random things you wouldn't normally do from anyone that asks. We meet back here in one hour. Sound good?"

Aron chuckles. "Well look at you, a regular *Gabriel* whisperer. I'm in." His dates both nod their assent and I worry for them when Aron's smile turns mischievous. It's a good thing we can choose what to say no to.

"Yes, yes, and yes!" I smile at Gabriel, excited for the challenge.

Caden shifts in his seat next to me. "Good one mate."

Gabriel looks at Jade, who in typical fashion, makes him wait. "You're killing me love."

Her face breaks into a smile. "Your wish is my command."

He dramatically falls on his butt. "*Oh... you're absolutely destroying me. Dead. I'm so dead.*"

I feel Caden's chest rumble behind my back and I turn around to see him laughing with a hand covering his eyes. "I know exactly how you feel." And he looks back at me and winks.

I don't know when "killing" a boy became a good thing, but I'm happy to learn I'm doing it. Eager to start the festivities I stand and make sure everyone hears me. "I bet I can complete my threes first!"

Gabriel perks up at my proclamation, and Aron looks close to rubbing his hands together like a true villain. He looks over at me. "Care to wager on that?"

"A moment." Gabriel sits on the arm of a love seat and I almost laugh at his serious face. "Before we take this to the next level, *no cheating*. And you cannot ask a single soul for your challenge. It must be freely offered, and they cannot know about our game. You can cheat, but I promise you, I will *know*. And besides, what's the fun in that?"

Aron stands. "Agreed. Ladies? Do you want in?"

Tara speaks up first. "If I say yes... Does it count?"

Aron looks impressed. "Clever."

We all look at Gabriel for the answer. "Right then, one of your three yeses can indeed be given from this group. But only after this discussion ends and again, it should be something you wouldn't normally do."

Debby makes a little squeal, "I'm in!"

Tara smiles at her. "Me too."

Caden nods, his eyes on me, and a wicked smile on his face. *Lord.*

"The wager?" Aron asks.

Jade moves to the edge of the seat. "The winner gets one additional wish from each member of our group. To be used any time till the end of the school year. With all the same rules."

Aron lifts his eyebrows. "Works for me. And the loser? The last one to get three?"

Gabriel answers, "Has to say yes to one challenge from each member of the group, before the end of the school year."

Aron nods his head. *"Perfect.* How do we find each other when our three are completed?"

"Message me."

As soon as I have his contact information, I'm off. Not even waiting for Caden. They are all going down.

Drifting through the hallways and rooms, I wind up following a girl into an entertainment room. My eyes lighting on a piano. As the door shuts behind me, the sounds from the rest of the party grow muffled and I hear a boy playing his guitar before I see him sitting on the floor. He's leaning against a large chair that has three girls piled in it. One of them has a little drum. On closer inspection, I notice most of the kids in that area have instruments as well. *Perfect.*

I recognize a girl from my band class and a boy from open mic. The girl notices me and excitedly waves me over, just as a guy on the sofa with a violin picks up where the guitar left off on *Love the Way You Lie,* by Rhianna. He plays the same cover but with his own flair and he's actually pretty good. As I move to sit on the edge of the sofa, the boy who played the guitar nods at me, "If you're sit'n you're join'n."

"*Yes,*" I say with relish.

Almost to the end of the song, the violinist shifts the cover into *Chandelier,* by Sia and when he's partway through, the girl with the drum picks up the beat and begins singing the words as the violinist drops out on the chorus. Getting the gist of it, I stand up and move to the piano. I don't want to waste any time getting my first yes.

The girl switches to another song by Zayn, *Dusk Till Dawn* featuring Sia. When she's about partway through, I start playing the chords on the piano and harmonizing with her until she drops out and it's just me.

Where her voice was soft and whimsical, I'm a little self-conscious that mine is so much stronger. But Gabriels' wish isn't about being comfortable.

I look up when the door opens and my stomach flips as almost the entire Jacket Crew crowds in. My anxiety kicks up to the point that I'm certain I'm going to bomb this as Sarah steps forward. She casually saunters up to me and leans on the piano, popping her ass out in a provocative pose. Her eyes never leaving mine. That malevolent grin of hers never dropping. Only I don't falter. I get pissed as I realize who she's posing for.

Almost by instinct, my eyes slide past hers to Ash. He's leaning across the back wall, his hands in his pockets. The picture of a solitary brooding bad boy. And just like that, I know my next song. I mix it into my current one until there is nothing but the melody of *Elastic Heart*. I meet *his* eyes in challenge. I want him to *know*, and I want him to *feel* because it's not fair how he played with me and this is the *only* revenge I have. As I open my mouth to sing, the words come out clear. The notes, pure. My confidence builds back into me as I reach the soaring heights of the song. I take a break from my stare down with Ash and glance at Sarah. For once it looks as if it's her confidence I stole.

But then I'm lost to the song. Its words mirroring my heart. "And I will stay up through the night. Let's be clear, I won't close my eyes. And I know that I can survive. I walked through fire to save my life. And I want it, I want my life so bad. And I'm doing everything I can. Then another one bites the dust." I'm not just seeing Ash anymore. I'm seeing my journey. My past, the home... *Vic*. Too much emotion to fight bleeds its way onto the words, "It's hard to lose a chosen one."

Thankfully, the guitarist picks up the song and I'm saved from a public meltdown with Sarah sitting front and center. Not wanting her or Ash, or any of them to see my vulnerability, I stand. As casually as I can, rejoining the seating area and studiously ignoring my haters. I find a place at the feet of my bandmate and focus on arranging my dress.

"Hey! That was really good! I mean like, *wow*." I look up at an auburn-haired boy with hawk-like features and a million freckles sitting behind me. I'm surprised to see he's holding a xylophone.

"Thanks. You play that?"

"*Yeah* I play it!" He has a slight defensive edge. "Everyone thinks this instrument is only for kids' music and fairytale shit. But I have reinvented the xylophone and it's *real*." I bite back my smile at his *cereal* tone and simply nod instead. I am actually curious to hear him play. He opens a plastic bag and pulls out a cookie. My stomach rumbles and he looks up at me smiling. "You want some?"

This isn't my first rodeo. "What's in it?" I ask with a saucy grin.

"Mostly just sugar, butter, and weed."

I have smoked before and know I'm a pretty big lightweight. Two drags from a blunt was kind of like drinking too much. But on the upside, it wasn't like that nausea-inducing spinning that comes before a monster hangover kind of drunk feeling; it was the relaxed, loose, and giggly side of drunk. Looking over at Nix, I decide a little escape and another *yes*, might be just the thing for tonight's adventuring.

"Yes, thank you, I will." Taking the cookie from him, I shove the whole thing into my mouth before I can change my mind. It spreads out my cheeks and I realize too late my inner cookie monster is showing and it's not a cute look. I somehow swallow the whole thing before I have even chewed it. Guiltily looking around to see if anyone noticed the massacre that just took place. Thankfully most eyes seem to be on the guitarist. Save for my new friend who is a bit wide-eyed.

"What?" I sound more defensive then I mean.

"Oh. Well I was just going to tell you a quarter is more than enough. And you know, you should eat it slowly and stuff."

My stomach drops. "But you just watched me eat the whole thing!"

"Yeah?"

Incredulity colors my voice. "Yes! Just now!"

"Oh right. *Oh man*," He has the grace to look distressed but then suddenly honks out a laugh. Literally, he *honks*.

I look at him closer now. "How much have you had?"

"A quarter. Why? You want some?"

Shocked, I try to see if he's messing with me. "No I don't want one. ...You just gave me one."

He chortles at that. "For real? The force is strong in this batch!" I watch him laugh with mounting dread and stay frozen only a second longer before I'm up and moving. I need to find Aron. *He* will know what to do. Otherwise? I am in way over my head.

CHAPTER 23

Moving down the hallway, a hand on my arm pulls me to a stop. And I know exactly who it is. *"Not this again."* I let out an exasperated sound and meet Ash's eyes. He looks conflicted. *As usual.* *"What?"*

"What did he give you?"

"Enough weed to tranq a horse, in the form of a cookie. Can I go now?"

Ash smiles despite the worry in his stupid perfect eyes. "Eat as much as you can find to dilute it and have some beer to counterbalance it. You should be fine."

"Thanks." I tersely respond.

"Ash!" A familiar grating female voice calls from behind him.

"Hope to you never."

He looks at me for a moment, hesitating. Then, predictably, he lets me go. I turn away before I have to watch the sorry sight of him following Sarah like a dog on a leash. *I hate him. I hate them both.* Grumbling, I go back to looking for Aron who I'm certain will give better advice. A door opens close enough I almost stumble into it. Florescent pink light spilling into the hallway along with a pumping beat. As people pass me by, I look through them to see a stairway going down.

That is exactly where Aron would go. Descending the stairs, I read the lit up neon lettering that follows me down the rabbit hole: *ALL WE HAVE IS NOW.* Bass amplifies with each stair I pass, and I let the vibration move through me. I'm grooving out in a dance party of one, by the time I reach the last step. To my right is a large room packed with dancing teens in pink lights with a DJ.

To my left is a smokey dim hallway lit up in colors by the lights of open and cracked doorways. The music is beckoning, but I know Aron would have gone for something a little more VIP. And time is of the essence. I turn away from the crowded room and head down the vaudeville hallway. The first door is locked. The door is barely slit and has red light seeping out.

I peek through the crack and find three girls bathed in the fiery lighting, dancing, touching, and kissing each other. This is not what I expected from a high school party. But I remind myself that these are the privileged I'm walking among. Their world is one I am still just beginning to learn. Their movements are slow and seductive. I shouldn't be watching this. With a pounding heart, I turn away from the scene, but something stops me. I move back to the crack and swallow. My throat suddenly dry. Unable to deny my interest, I gaze through the slit again. One of the girls is looking right at me. I freeze. She beckons with her finger. And I realize they wanted to be watched. I am the fly on the wall that was led into their trap.

I push away from the door, feeling shaky and embarrassed. Now *that* is one "yes" I am not ready for. Clutching my chest, I move to the next door that is wide open. Peering inside and hearing laughter, I try to see through all the thick blue smoke. Teens in various states of undress are bent over a large blanket on the floor. Their tangled hands and feet over different colored dots. The smoke I realize is coming from a machine. And paired with the blue light the colors are near impossible to discern. A girl tumbles over and they all crash into a laughing mess of limbs and hair. "Hey!" One of them spots me and shouts. "Want to play?"

I project my voice so they can hear me. "How can you tell what color you are looking for?"

A boy shouts back "We can't!" And they all start laughing again.

"I'll come back," I say to appease them. *Now I know what frunky is.*

Back in the hallway I turn the corner and am met by a crowd of teens in a loose line for what is undoubtedly the bathroom. Not seeing any other doors, I turn back and head for the music. Maybe there is a seating area in that room and Aron's there. Just before I reach the end of the hallway, the locked door swings open. A girl stumbles partway out and heavily leans on it, gripping the nob for support.

She squints up at me. "I need *help*. Can you help me?"

I know if I don't reach Aron soon, *I* will be the one that needs help. But looking her over, I know I can't leave her. "Yeah, if I can. What's wrong?" *At least I got my final yes.*

"My friends left and it's hitting me really hard."

"What's hitting you?"

"Molly."

Damn. I'm pretty familiar with molly because of Vic. She always danced more and drank lots of water when it hit her wrong. But when it was too much? It was bad. "Do you trust the person who gave it to you? You're sure it's molly?" She nods her head yes and weaves a little on her feet. *At least that's something.* "Do you dance?"

"You're asking me if I can dance right now?" She looks back at me like she might have made a mistake in asking me for help.

"It will get out of your system faster if you sweat it out. Plus, you'll feel better as soon as you focus on the beat."

"I can hardly move though."

"Hold on. I'm going to get some water. That will help." At the worried look she gives me, I touch her shoulder reassuringly. "What's your name?"

"Blake."

"I'm Alex, and I accidentally ate a *very* strong pot cookie. That at any minute, is going to hit me. So you and I? We are about to be in this frunky boat together. And that means that we are going to be eachothers *not* sober companion for the night. Because *you're* not going to judge me. And *I'm* not going to judge you no matter *what* happens. Deal?"

She smiles in relief and gives a little nod. "Yeah, deal."

With that out of the way, I know the two of us are going to be okay. "Secondly? I know for sure that dancing and water will help. Those two things? Are basically the answer to *life*. So I am going to go to that room right there..." I point at the blue smoky doorway. "And I am going to ask them if they have any water. And you are going to wait right here. Okay?"

She visibly relaxes and nods. "Yeah, okay."

I let go of her shoulder and waste no time asking everyone from the Twilight Zone if they have any water. A guy sitting on the bed reaches under it and pulls one out. "Any chance you can spare another?" I try subtly batting my lashes at him the way I have seen Jade do on occasion but the effect is ruined as all the smoke agitates them and I start furiously blinking to clear them. Still, when I'm finally able to look at him again he's holding two bottles and smiling at me.

"We have tons so if you need more, just ask." He tosses them over to me.

"Thanks!"

Waters in hand I go back to Blake and find two guys crowding her. *Cereal?* "Do you know them?" I ask coming up to her. When she shakes her head no, and I see the anxious look on her face, I wordlessly turn to them and stare. *Hard.*

The taller one shrugs. "We were just checking on her and trying to help..." While he's talking, I hand Blake a bottle. She immediately starts gulping it down, and I pull my phone from my bag. When he's finished with his bullshit-a-thon I click a picture of them both. This trick is an oldie but a goodie and it hasn't failed me yet.

"If I see either of you trying to '*help*' any more girls, this photo is going *everywhere. So everyone* can learn what *good* Samaritans you are. Understood?"

"Fuck... I mean yeah, but you got us wrong."

"*Bye.*" So not caring, I put my hand in their faces and turn back to Blake. I hear, rather than see Tweedle Dee and Tweedle Dummer leave her personal space.

"That was chill. Thanks." Eyeing her empty bottle, I hand her mine. She gladly takes it and drinks even more. "We have a stop to make before the dance floor. Are you okay to walk?"

"I think so. The water helps."

Taking my new best friend's hand, I walk her to the bathroom. Praying the effect I had at the school's bathroom line will hold here. I try walking her to the front, but a girl stops me. "You can't just cut in front of everyone."

Blake speaks up, sounding remarkably sober. "I can if it's *my* house. And by the way? I *love* your hair. Your head literally looks like my favorite kind of rose." Before the girl can respond, Blake grabs my hand and pulls me to the front. We stealthily slip inside the bathroom just as a guy comes out and she slams the doors to the sounds of a pissed off crowd.

Blake cracks the door and pops her head out. "Sorry, not sorry! *My* house, *my* bathroom. *You're* welcome!" And slams the door in their faces once more. Turning to me she takes a few more gulps from the water. "What are we doing here?"

"This is your house?" I ask with surprise.

She smiles brightly at me. "Of *course not!*"

"My people." Laughing, I point to the toilet. "You first. Once we're on the dance floor, we are going to be there for a while."

The music is blaring and in the pink light everyone's horns and wings look more real. I know the cookie is finally starting to do something because the vibrations from the bass start to feel really good. Almost like a physical touch over my body. I look at Blake who is dancing her ass off already and I yell at her. *"Can you feel that? The bass?"*

She blasts me with a grin so big it feels like she's hugging me from the inside out. *"Hell yes I can. It's amazing! Thank you for taking me here!"* Like I have just taken her out for a girls' night at the club instead *of the next room over.* I laugh out loud and cheerfully nod my head. My tongue suddenly feeling too thick to speak.

Dancing *is* helping. It's channeling sensations that would otherwise be way too overwhelming into good vibes. Letting my head fall back and my arms raise I move my hips. As yet another guy takes the liberty of grinding against my back, I *accidentally* bury my heel in his foot.

"Ow! Shit!"

Without turning around I yell, *"Sorry! Two left feet."* And wave him away with zero fucks given. Latching onto Blake who is snickering at my obvious brush off, I give her a stupid toothy grin and we burst out laughing. Finally settled she smiles goofily back at me and runs one of her hands down the part of my hair that is down.

I moan too low for anyone to hear. My lids slam shut and I live in the minute sensations that reverberate through my being like expanding, rolling rings of water. *"That feels so good!"*

"I know, right? Me next!" I laugh at the childlike quality to her voice and bury my hands in her hair, at the back of her neck. I gently pull and twist and it feels so good it's like *I'm* the one getting my hair pulled. More laughter bubbles out of me at the pure ecstasy that washes over her face. I lean in to hear what she's saying.

"Oh, that's sooooo goooooood!"

She starts laughing with me and I have enough presence to appreciate the freedom of diminished personal boundaries and restraint. It's like I'm doing things before I have a chance to filter. And as someone that normally overthinks *everything*, it's totally liberating. As we notice the people around us looking, we laugh even harder. I dab at the tears running down my cheeks.

The music changes and Blake's eyes light up. *"This is my jam!"*

She leans down and flips her hair out as her arm follows the motion. It's a weird move followed by even weirder ones but she's so into it that to my mind, she looks amazing. I like Blake. She reminds me a little of Vic. I mirror her moves a little and laugh at how ridiculous I know we look. We end up jumping and laughing like a couple of loons and I'm having the time of my life. It feels like my heart is too big for my chest and the jumping is beaming love from my chest into the crowd around me, so I jump harder to shake out more love. I finally open my eyes, expecting to see people staring at us like we're crazy but several groups are actually jumping with us and I'm totally ecstatic!

I point them out to Blake. *"Look!"*

While she's still jumping, she beams at me. *"I know! It's magic!"* Looking around us, I have to agree with her.

I have lost all sense of time when I realize my feet are *killing* me and I'm totally out of breath. I was supposed to be doing something, but I can't remember what. "More water?"

She gives me her hand. *"Yes!"*

I pull her through the crowd and back to the hallway which looks darker now. The blue rooms' door is shut. I open it wide and find a couple making out on the bed. I don't even hesitate. *"Sorry*, just need to grab something." They don't so much as glance over as I rummage under the bed for the water. Taking the last three with me, I pass one to Blake. "Bathroom?"

"No, I'm good. Let's go back to my room!" I let her pull me to the door I originally found her at. In the back of my mind I know I'm forgetting something, but I don't want my adventure with Blake to end. Taking out a hair clip, she works at the little lock mechanism and has the door popping open in under a minute.

"Blake! You little clever delinquent you!" I shout with admiration.

This room is smaller than the others and the only light is a soft golden pink glow in the corner. It's a laundry room and there is a sleeping bag on the floor.

"Is that where you were hiding?"

"Yeah. The salt lamp helps it feel less depressing."

"How did you find this place?"

"My friends did. They left me here and said they would be back, but they never came. And people kept knocking on the door that wasn't them and it really freaked me out, so I set it to lock."

What bitches! Don't girls know better than to leave a man down... Er -Girl down? Whatever. Still a little deaf, I shout, "That's totally lame." Looking around the room I note the boxes and stacked chairs in one corner, and the shelves full of blankets and towels on the other side. "*I have an idea!*" Putting down the waters I open one of the boxes and am delighted to find another sleeping bag and pillows. *Excellent.* "We're building a fort!"

"*Fuck yes!* I want to build a fort!" The way she yells back has me dissolving into hip slapping, eye-watering, unhinged laughter. Which causes her to laugh harder.

"Look for anything soft!" I shout.

By the time we're done, I'm *pretty sure* we have just made the world's best fort. Blake dives into the pillows and lets out a happy moan. "*Oh my god,* I want to *live* and *die* here! In my final will and testament, I'm going to demand that they sprinkle my ashes in Jake Tavel's laundry room!"

Another fit of laughter attacks us and when it passes, I notice that I feel lighter and buoyant. Like a balloon full of helium. The thought makes me happy. I'm smiling as I stretch the pretty salt crystal lamp to the back end of our fort. *Finally,* I crawl beneath the propped-up blankets and plop down into the cozy nest of pillows and sheets.

It's heaven. I pass Blake the last bottle of water. As she gulps it down, I glance sidelong at her. "Just promise me you're not a bed wetter."

She stops drinking and her silence somehow seems loud. I throw a pillow at her and she breaks up giggling. *"Okay! Fine! I'm not* going to *pee* on you! I'm already coming down. I can walk my big girl self to the bathroom now. How are you doing?"

Gazing at the beautiful pink lamp I lazily smile. "I think this high is just getting started, truth be told."

A knock sounds and we both ignore it. A second later Caden's voice booms through the door. *"Alex?" Oh YEAH! That's what I was supposed to do!* I may be high, but the thought of Caden seeing me this way has be instantly mortified.

Blake finally answers for me. "Accounted for." I pull a pillow over my head and try to hide. But I can still hear Aron's sound voice next.

"Alex? You're in there?" The locked doorknob jingles. *Shoot.*

"Yes..." Busted. "I'm here."

Jades voice comes through next. *"Can you come out?"*

"Or we can come in!" Caden suggests and suddenly the idea of my friends all piled into my super fort with me, sounds like the world's greatest plan.

"Yes! COME IN!" I shout at the door. Entirely forgetting about my embarrassment.

Jade's voice sounds exasperated. *"It's locked."*

I look at Blake. "Can you get up?" She shakes her head no. "Me nei-ther." The door which can't be more than six feet away might as well be a football field away. I decide honesty is best. "Um... Well, I need one of you to unlock it. From your side. Like Blake did."

"Who is Blake?" Gabriel and Caden shout from the other side.

Not a second later the door bursts open, almost coming off its hinges and Caden is the first one in. "I'm Blake." She raises her manicured hand and slowly adjusts herself to peer at him. The emotions that clash over Caden's face as he takes in our massive fort then Blake, then me, is priceless.

I give a pretty little wave. "Welcome to Chateau A'lake," I say with grandeur and smile at the rest of my friends crowding in.

Blake laughs from beside me. " I totally get it! Like Alex and Blake put together!"

Aron pushes past Caden, (who might actually be in shock) and kicks off his shoes before jumping in. And I could not possibly be more thrilled. *"Yes!"* I vault up and tackle him with a bear hug. "I'm so glad you're here!"

Blake manages to sit up and pull him into her arms. "Me too! *What took you so long?"* Aron shakes his head in bemusement at me then looks at Blake with obvious interest. "I *don't know,* but I'm so sorry to have kept you waiting!" Blake giggles at that and rests her head on his shoulder like a long-lost friend. And he seems pretty happy to be her headrest.

As Caden finally crawls in beside me I ask Aron, "Where's Deb and Tara?"

"They had to get home, unfortunately."

"And you didn't take them?"

"I didn't pick them up either. They were afraid I would scare their parents."

"That's fair." I chuckle.

"Hiiiiii," Jade lands between me and Aron and gives me the world's best hug. "I missed you! I got all my yeses first! And I didn't even get to gloat because you weren't there and gloating isn't the same without you."

Aron huffs. "You managed to do it just fine without her!"

My hand goes up and I observe it moving through the air, making my words seem more important. "It is... A disaster!" The brevity of my response and the waving hand, has me and Blake cackling. Gabriel snickers at me as he somehow squeezes himself between Jade and Aron. I scoot back into Caden to make more room and everyone settles in.

Aron speaks up. "Well, I didn't see this coming. ...Nice digs Alex."

Gabriel contentedly sighs. "My wish game triumphs." Like he's responsible for my epic fort.

Jade chuckles. "Perhaps. But I win your wish." I smile at their banter. Absurdly happy as Caden pulls out the pins in my hair and begins to play with it.

Blake yawns. "I'm going to die here."

Aron responds with mock horror. "But I've only just found you!"

Caden's breath tickles my ear as he whispers. "What did you take?"

I'm too blissed out to be embarrassed. "For my second *yes*, I ate weed with a side of cookie."

Blake and I laugh at my brilliant joke and Caden chuckles. "You ate a weed cookie?"

"Yes, but I should have just had a quarter. Instead, I ate the whole stupid thing before anyone warned me."

"Next time save some for me!" Jade complains.

Inspiration hits me. "Did I get my wish yet?"

"No." Caden's tickling my ear again and his presence is making my whole body hot.

I sit up. "Can we stay here?"

Gabriel sounds confused. "What? Like for the night?"

"I want to die here," Blake says again, much to everyone's amusement. Especially mine.

I let out a breath. "Noooo, just like. For *now.*"

Jade snorts in a very un-Jade like fashion. "What do you mean by, *now?*"

I flop back into Caden and lay on my side, facing Jade. "I never knew what "*NOW*" meant. I never had the chance to be *in* it. To be present. You know? I was too busy fighting and surviving. Foster care is a *bitch*. And the worst kind of people take advantage of the system or are stuck within it."

This is the first time I have ever talked about my past with any of them. But within the safe and warm confines of this fort, I feel utterly at ease. And I want more than anything to let them in. To be brave enough to show them all of me. Because the only people that fully recognize me, are dead or on the other side of the country, and I don't want to be alone anymore.

When no one speaks, I go on. "And anyway, when every day is about just making it to the next one, even the spots of sunshine are not as bright. Like, I never got to be a kid. No Christmases, no birthdays, no trick-or-treating, no tooth fairy. And no one to hold my hand and tell me it was all going to be okay when it really wasn't. But... Since meeting you guys... I have learned what it means to think about other things besides survival. Like singing at a coffee shop, dressing for a football game, impressing a date for my first ever school dance..." I squeeze Caden's hand. "-Or building the world's best fort!"

"For the record, I fully approve of this fort." Aron states.

Blake cuts in, "I'm..."

Several of us finish her sentence with her. "-Going to die here."

I wait for the laughter to die down before going on. "You guys have helped me to find the innocence I never thought I could have. I thought the idea of youth was lost to me a long time ago. That magic and mystery and spontaneity just weren't in the cards for me. And to *feel it* now... To feel something as pure as innocence after *everything* I have been through, it's the most incredible and unexpected gift I have ever experienced. And so... I have gotten to enjoy things like building my first ever fort. Which by the way? Is totally epic! And being here in the presence of '*now*' with my favorite people in the whole world? So yeah, my wish is to be here with you all right *now*. Because there is nowhere more important or more meaningful than this. ...And I *swear!* The magic cookie might have helped give me the courage to tell you all this? It is still one hundred percent of how I feel."

No one says anything for a beat. And then Caden snuggles into me. Squeezing me closer. Jade turns to me and holds my hand. I'm surprised to see her cheeks are wet. She meets my eyes wordlessly and I see so much love there that it steals my breath. My eyes instantly wet with happiness and belonging.

I see Gabriel's arm come around her and then Aron's arm comes over Gabriel and rests on Jade's shoulder.

Gabriel tries to sound mad but fails. "No mate. Not gonna happen."

We all break up the moment with laughter and Aron sighs. *"Your* loss."

Blake chimes in. "You can snuggle me. I love a good snuggle puddle."

I lose time as we stay like that. Talking, sharing stories, and laughing. Blake has a point. I could die happy here too. But then my escalating high gets too intense and I sit up.

Caden rests his hand on my back. "You okay?"

I can't respond to him. "Aron, I meant to ask you..." I have to stop and pull up my knees to rest my heavy head. "How do you cure being too high? I know what to do about opiates and uppers but have zero experience with this."

Aron sounds surprised. "You have had opiates and uppers and you don't know how to deal with weed?"

I laugh and momentarily feel better. "No, I was too busy taking care of Vic who did enough for both of us. But she never had any trouble with weed so this is new..." I trail off as another wave hits me and my heart stutters in my chest. Paranoia swamps me and I wonder if I can have a heart attack from weed. "I can't breath!" I whisper. Suddenly panicked.

Aron finally gets the gravity of my question. I hear him move to a sitting position and feel Caden do the same. Aron's voice sounds more alert. "We need to feed you. How does an early breakfast sound?" At that exact moment, Gabriel chokes on a particularly funny snore and we bust up laughing as Jade unceremoniously pushes him awake.

"Ready to eat?" At least she asks him sweetly.

He smiles up at her like she's the frosting to his Oreo. "*Always.*"

"My man," I chime in and crawl out of our cocoon. "Oh noooo."

"What is it?" Caden's beside me in a second and helping me to stand.

I look up at him with utter seriousness. "It's cold," I say in a little voice.

A smile warms his face and he takes off his jacket and helps me into it while everyone else gets up. As the divine warmth and smell of him insulate me, I moan happily and lean against him with a level of trust that is altogether foreign to me. "You're dreamy." He whispers in my hair as he walks us out of the room.

CHAPTER 24

" "Wait... Did I lose the bet?" Caden's laughter greets my horrified question and I have my answer. I beat everyone to the bathroom and now we're ahead of everyone. The house is dark and quiet shadow of the vibrant affair it was only hours ago. "What time is it?" I ask with a serious yawn as we step outside into the gloomy beginnings of dawn.

Caden is holding my heels in one hand and a half-empty bottle of water in his other. "No Idea. Chateau A'lake was a complete time warp."

We stop on the lawn. The wet, cold grass feeling perfect against my aching feet. Caden looks down into my eyes and smiles at me so sweetly it makes my heart hurt. "How does bacon, eggs and, French toast sound?"

My mouth drops open in a gasp. The. Perfect. Guy. "How did you *know!*"

He laughs at my shock. "A lucky guess."

I run my hands up his back and down again. Pondering from a distance that on a normal day I would never be so brave. "Are you cold?" He steps into me, wrapping his arms around me and he squeezes. Making me feel the kind of tenderness I desperately yearned for growing up. The kind of touch I told myself I didn't need. That I could do without, but here it is. And I'm no longer a lonely desperate child, but a girl on the cusp of falling in love with this boy.

His chin is a reassuring weight atop my head as he whispers. "No."

I pull back and meet his eyes, unable to contain it any longer. "Are you going to kiss me now?"

He lets out a soft husky laugh. "Do you want me to kiss you, Alex?"

Desire so strong it's sobering merges with clarity. That hyper-awareness flooding throughout my body so that I can feel each blade of grass poking my feet, the humidity in the air. The smell of him, of the night, and a hundred other things. I can even *see* better. Even through the darkness, his eyes are more yellow now and bright as they hold mine.

His large, calloused hand comes up to cup my cheek but suddenly, in a blur, he's gone and I'm hitting the ground. *Hard.* The breath rushes out of me as a light flashes past. It happened so fast that I'm stunned for a moment. But then the chilling sounds reach me and again, those lights flashing by my closed lids. I gasp and stumble up. Trying to see past the curtain of my hair. Momentarily blinded by it, I freeze again at the sound of Ash's wrathful voice.

"You would take advantage of her when she's *that far gone?* Is *that* where she has been all this time? You had her *holed up* somewhere with *you?!*"

Desperate to see, to understand, I fight my tangled dress and hair and manage to sit up. I want to stand but the palpable electricity in the air has me dizzy and nauseous. *Or maybe that was my fall?* I shake my head, trying to clear the image before me. Caden and Ash are moving too fast to trace and the flashes of light are so blinding I can't see where they are coming from or where they are going.

I focus all of my concentration on seeing them clearly and their movements finally begin to slow down enough that I can just make out their blurred forms. Caden sends a brutal kick into Ash's stomach that has him flying back. He recovers too fast and white light launches from Ash's hands to Caden's chest. But before I can replace what I saw with a plausible reality, Caden is hurtling a white-blue light back at him.

As they continue to fight like they are in some kind of video game, my brain checks out; just gives up at the impossible scene before me. They are speaking to each other in a foreign tongue that is soon drowned out by the ringing in my ears. My detachment completes itself as one of them busts a move that defies gravity. *Nope. Nu-uh.*

I numbly untangle myself and stand up. Dusting off my torn dress, *because... Fuck this,* I eye-ball my heels not too far from where the two of them are facing off, and casually walk over and pluck them from the grass. Some part of my consciousness understands that they are moving at fast forward and what I am able to decipher before me, has only taken up seconds of real-time. *Does that mean I'm moving at fast forward too or am I having a psychotic break?* With my back turned to them, I head to the street, when Ash's voice stops me.

"What are you doing?"

I take a deep breath and then another. As I finally turn back to them, I tell myself that I'm ready. That I am prepared for whatever. But as their glowing eyes reach mine? Glowing eyes that I have been telling myself for weeks and weeks now was a play of light, a trick of my imagination. I just feel totally and completely pissed. Shaking my head at the incomprehensible scene I square my shoulders. "I'm leaving you two to your, your... X-Men fireworks *jerk-off*! And I'm getting the fuck back to reality is what I'm doing!" I turn right back around but now it's Caden's voice that stops me.

"What do you mean... X-Men fireworks *jerk-off*?"

Some of my anger crumbles at his voice. An ice-cold tear escapes and it feels like the acid of betrayal as it slides down my cheek. *"Oh*, I don't know. Two stupid fools speaking in tongues like a couple of possessed idiots ring any bells? No? Nothing? How about the whole laser tag game without any laser guns part? No? Or the moving at the speed of light thing? Preternatural glowing eyes?" I finally turn back to face them but it's only Caden I see. My voice reaching an uncontrollable pitch. "Oh no! Wait! Let's not forget the reverse cooking of your barbecued hand!?" More confused tears are slipping out and I can actually *feel* the massive panic attack about to explode.

Taking a deep breath, I place my hands on my hips. My voice sounds loud even to me. "You know, I don't know if you *noticed?* But I *fell!* And that would be just fine! But when you two ninja, Jedi numb skulls started going at it? You *ruined* the most perfect dress I have *ever* even seen. Let alone worn! And I don't even OWN THIS! It's on loan! Probably worth more than I can make in a year! But does *anyone here care? No!* Because you're too busy jizzing hocus-fucking-pocus at each other!" I realize I'm screaming and abruptly stop. Breathing hard and gulping in air. They look as shocked as I should feel.

Pissed, I wipe away the useless tears. Caden slowly approaches me with his hands up.

"NO! You both stay the hell away from me. Don't..." I take another deep breath. It's freezing out and my teeth are beginning to chatter but I'm sweating. "Don't you come..." I bend over, trying to gulp in air that is too thin to breathe. The sound of heels come running towards me. At the sight of Jade's glittering heels and the feel of her hand on my back, ugly heaping sobs overtake me. "I can't... Can't breathe!" I look up just in time to catch Jades' livid expression.

"What did you do?" She hisses at the two of them.

I try, *try* to straighten. "They... They..." But my throat keeps locking before I can get anything out and I'm forced to lean over and take another breath. Dizziness making it harder to stay on my feet. Jade pulls me into a hug, and I expel a gust of air on an exhausted sob. "They ruined my dress!" I finally blubber out and dissolve into a wreak.

From my periphery I see Caden take another step closer to me and I stumble back from Jade and him, further ripping my now tattered dress. "I said stay away from me!" I scream, looking wildly between him and Ash, throwing my shaking hands out in a pathetic barrier between us.

But Caden takes another step closer, a wounded look on his face. "Alex I.."

Aron is suddenly between him and I. "I think you better respect what she's asking for." He looks over his shoulder at me. Taking in my torn dirty dress and my bloody knees. He looks back at Caden and Ash, his face hardening in a way that makes him look different, older. "I don't know what happened here... But you *both* need to leave. *Now.*" His foreboding voice seems to reverberate and though I'm grateful for the support, I'm past my limit for weird.

Taking another heaving breath, I grab Jade's hand. "Please take me home?" My wobbly voice is small and completely unrecognizable.

She nods at me and looks to Aron. "You have this covered?"

She's already pulling me down the sidewalk before a response can be heard. The trip home with Benson is a blur. Jade and I sneak into my room as the sun is coming up and she helps me to undress and leaves me in the shower. I stand under the spray, unmoving as impossible recollections torment me. Mocking my sense of reality and my understanding of everything I know to be real and possible. I squeeze my eyes shut and wrap my arms around myself. As if that will keep me together while my mind feels like it's fracturing apart. I let my jelly legs bend until I'm sitting on the floor. I put my head between my knees and continue to focus on breathing as a fresh wave of tears mix with the water, blood and dirt.

I don't remember the trip back to bed or Jade tucking me in. But when I wake up, she is asleep beside me. Her arm around my waist. Her body spooning mine. I feel utterly empty. Like all the crying and all the laughter released something massive. I gently remove her arm and scoot up to a sitting position.

I try to see last night exactly as it happened, playing it all over again in my head. Running through every plausible explanation. I was high, but not *that* high and I know what I saw. Shaking my head, I let it fall back to the wooden headboard, hitting it harder than I mean to.

Jade's voice sounds clear like she's been up for hours. "How are you feeling?"

"Better... I'm really sorry about the dress."

She just shakes her head and scoots up to lean against the headboard with me. "Not an issue. ...What happened last night?"

I shake my head again and look up at the ceiling. These are the moments when friendship is tested. Do I tell her the truth and risk sounding totally nuts? Do I let it go and try to forget the whole thing? But I *know* I can't do that. And I know I'm not going to lie to her either. I blow out a breath.

"I don't know..." My eyes land on the suit jacket hanging on my door. "One minute I'm having the best night of my life, and the next? I'm seeing things that I can't rationally explain."

Jade sits up a little straighter. "Tell me."

I look over at her for a moment. "Can we both agree that a weed cookie doesn't cause massive, completely realistic hallucinations?" She nods. "*Okay*, well I didn't drink last night other than our last toast before the party. I just had that stupid cookie but there was this one moment..." My chest suddenly feels tight and cold sweat breaks out across my skin.

Jade grips my hand. Taking a deep breath, I push on. "There was one moment where nothing made any sense. Caden and I went outside and one minute he's leaning in to kiss me and the next... He's just... *Gone*. That's when I fell and... The dress. It happened so fast. Ash was there. He was yelling at Caden because I think he thought Caden had somehow taken advantage of me. And then..." I take another slow breath. "And then they were fighting, but you know when you press fast forward to skip over commercials and stuff? How you can hardly see anything it's all moving so fast?" Jade's hand spasms around mine and I glance over at her.

"Go on." She prompts.

"It's absolutely *insane*. I know that *okay?* But I can't change what I saw. Ash and Caden were moving like someone had pressed fast forward on them." My chest starts to heave at the impossible memory. I turn towards Jade and swallow. "I swear to god I saw them throwing light, and moving in ways that aren't possible. And all I can think is that, that either the world is not exactly what I thought it was... What *anyone* thinks it is... Or far more likely, that I'm losing my mind. There was a girl in my group home that had schizophrenia. With her, it was mostly just voices, but what if..."

I can't bring myself to finish. It's like all the tears I never let myself shed as a kid were all stored up and now I'm drowning in them. Moving here has made me soft, and apparently crazy too. Jade says nothing and I feel my heart sink. Nodding my head, I speak out loud the last thing I can remember thinking before I finally passed out last night. "I *knew* this was all too good to be true. Good things don't happen to me."

Jade curses and slams her fists into the bed. But she doesn't say *anything* to me. Not that I'm not crazy, not that there is a reasonable explanation, not even that she supports me. She just breaths through her nose in agitated puffs reminding me of a dragon. Honestly, what is there to say? She launches off of the bed, startling the hell out of me, and starts pacing across my room. She finally stops on her fifth lap.

"You saw them." She tells me.

"Um... Yes..."

She shakes her head. "But how did you see them if they were moving so fast?"

"I don't know..." I close my eyes and will myself to remember it all with more clarity. My eyes pop open as I remember. "I focused in on them until it almost looked like they were moving at a normal speed again. Just like, a really fast Jedi fight scene."

Jade shakes her head again. "Do you remember anything else?"

"Ummm, even as I was seeing it, I hardly believed it. I kind of checked out on the whole thing when it got too crazy. But..." I bury my head in my hands completely embarrassed as I share the rest. "Their eyes... They were glowing. And they were speaking in another language I have never heard before."

Jade freezes on that detail and looks at me with wide eyes. "Could you understand them?"

I look back up at her, making a face. "What? *No*..." I can't understand her strange line of questioning, but I know she will eventually come around to explaining it, so I try to be patient. One thing is definitely clear. She has some idea about everything I have just told her. I listen as she paces and tries to puzzle it out.

"You saw them and you heard them, but you didn't understand them." She shakes her head. "This is highly unusual."

I scoff. "*That's* the understatement of the year. So what do you think? ...Am I crazy?"

She finally looks at me and stops in her pacing to take my hands in hers. "*No*. You are the least crazy person I know next to my Dad. Speaking of whom, I need to talk with him about all of this."

Panic colors my voice. "*Your dad?!* But he's going to think I'm nutso and tell you not to hang out with me anymore! *You can't!*"

Jade shakes her head at me and smiles reassuringly. "There is a *lot* you don't know about my dad. Let's just say he's more open-minded than *anyone* you have ever met. I promise you that. Will you trust me enough to trust him?"

"*God* Jade... I *do* trust you... But I *can't* risk losing you! I... I need you! *Okay?* You're like my family now..." More tears start streaming down and her eyes glitter back at me, full of unshed tears. Jade is no baby. She's all strength and I don't think I can survive whatever is going on right now. Not without her.

"I promise you... You will *never* lose me. No matter what happens. You're my family now too. I didn't realize how lonely I was or how amazing having a sister could be. But I know now! And there is not a force in this world that could take me away from you."

We hug each other fiercely and our pact is sealed. I take a deep breath. "If you say I'm not crazy... Then I'm *not* crazy." I let the breath out as relief washes through me. "And if you think your dad can somehow help make sense of everything I saw, then you should talk to him."

CHAPTER 25

Jade left an hour ago and I'm ignoring my phone. It went dead at some point last night and I haven't bothered to fix it. Dill is out of town for a mini tour and I'm roaming the house listlessly, now surrounded by books. I haven't spent much time in the library wing. It's pretty overwhelming. The mural domed ceilings and the looming rows of red oak bookshelves lined up like soldiers. The complex tiled floors and insane giant spiral staircase in the back? It all has the effect of transporting me to another era.

Gazing up at all the geometric constellations that are far too complex for a house like this, I wonder who designed it all and why. Mere seconds of looking at the shapes have me feeling untethered and I quickly look away. I like having my feet firmly on the ground and my mind focused on what is; not what was, or could be.

I startle as the doorbell rings and listen to Ugly scamper to the door. He gives a low *woof* to alert me. Just in case the reverberating *dong* that is loud enough to hear from the towers, isn't enough. My steps are light as I move to the bay windows and peek through the side to the entrance. I can only see part of his shoe and jacket, but that's all I need to know. Caden is here. Dashing away from the window with my heart thundering in my chest I end up toppling over. Hoping he didn't hear me, I crab walk outside of the windows viewing range like a true coward. This is not one of my better moments.

Pushing myself back into a bookshelf and focusing on the smell of all the books, I will my breathing to slow. That cold sweat that breaks out every time I think about last night, beads over my lip and I distractedly wipe it away. Then go utterly still as I hear him call my name.

"Alex I *know* you're in there. Can we please talk? I want to apologize and... Talk. ...*Please.*"

I hug my knees and rest my head there, feeling sick. It's weird missing someone and wanting them as far away from me as humanly possible. *Human. Is he even human? Oh God, and all of those stupid movies, shows, and books I loved where the girl finds out her crush is supernatural, and she just adjusts. As if! And they go on like it's no BFD. What complete and total crap!* I'm shit-myself-terrified. This scenario is not cute, not romantic, and especially not okay! But still, in the back of my mind I keep thinking there has to be a rational explanation for all of this. *There HAS to be!* But just the thought, even the *possibility,* that up is not exactly *up?* And down is not exactly *down?* Nope. No thank you. Even the hint that there could be more outside of the very safe and comfortable confines of my reality has me wanting to take the blue chill pill.

My life is messed up enough. Irregular enough, that I don't want to know, don't need to know about any abracadabra bullshit. I don't want my vampire sweetheart, my werewolf boyfriend, or some leather-loving fool from the Matrix trying to unplug me. What I want, what I need: is normal. I finally just had it within my grasp. And I'm not letting it go without a fight.

"Alex?"

My mental tirade freezes in shock. *He's in the manor? Was the front door unlocked? No... I specifically locked both locks! How the hell did he get in here? Where the hell is Ugly?* I hug myself tighter and try to stop the trembling. He's just outside of the library. If he walks in even a little bit, he will see me. *Can he hear my pounding heart? My breathing?*

Ugly, the son of a whore, trots up to me, and happily sits down right in front of me like a damn flashing beckon. *Stupid, stupid dog!* I don't know why I'm so scared. Some sort of delayed reaction or PTSD? I have no idea. But I feel like that girl in the horror movie that loses brain cells the more scared she gets. I eye the spiral staircase and consider being the idiot who runs up them. The resulting little fear fart that bubbles out as my stomach lurches is a definite *hell no.*

"Alex... Please... Don't be scared of me. Never of me, I will never hurt you." *I seriously want to throw up. If he takes one more step I will see him and this Persian runner will be over.* "I'm going to stay right here okay? I'm not leaving this doorway. If you want to come out, you can." *Not gonna happen.* "I just... I needed to see you. And tell you in person how sorry I am about last night." He pauses and waits. Like he expects me to actually respond to him.

All at once I am undeniably and completely devastated. The realization that everything has changed between Caden and I crystalizes as I hear the desolate tone in his voice. He knows it too. I cannot explain what happened last night, y*et*. But no matter what the reality? Something is terribly wrong with Caden and Ash. And the teenage boys I thought they were? Could not be farther from whatever they actually are.

I am not crazy. And I wasn't hallucinating. Something undefinable is at play here, and I want nothing to do with it or the lying bags of knobs who never told me the truth. There were signs, of course, if I had cared to look, or pay attention. I know I sensed an otherness around the both of them. The way their presence arrested me like no one else I had ever met for starters. Caden's healing. But he's the worst of all. At least Ash kind of tried to warn me. Caden just acted like I was seeing things and gas lit me like a psycho. I'm not even surprised anymore at the tears that run down my face. But this time? It's not just fear, but betrayal that has them dripping from my chin.

"Don't cry Alex. *Please don't cry...*"

No. *No no no....* There is no way for him to know I'm crying! At this point I'm over it. I feel sick and cornered in my own home and he has no right to be here. Torturing me with his beautiful voice and his terrifying presence. I don't want to hear anything he has to say. I speak in a low urgent tone to Ugly and hope like hell he understands. "*Ugly!* Make. Him. *Leave!*"

Relief floods through me as Ugly's entire demeanor changes from happy idiot to a growling, snarling predator. His head lowers and ears flatten while all his hair stands out, as he stands between Caden and I.

"Alex..."

At the sound of his voice, Ugly barks in challenge and edges closer to Caden. Foam and drool now dripping on the floor.

And Caden sounds destroyed. "I'll go okay? I'm leaving." His steps recede. "But I want you to know..." He has to speak up to be heard over Ugly. "I want you to know that I genuinely care about you. Way more than I ever thought I could." *What the hell is that supposed to mean?* Ugly inches forward and snaps. I can actually hear the wet clacking of his teeth. He's hardly recognizable from the sweet dog I have known these past months. Caden tries to placate him, but it's a lost cause. "Take as much time as you need. But... I'm here for you, okay? *Always* Alexa. And I'll wait for you. As long as it takes!'"

Ugly is over it too, because he suddenly launches himself at the door and they are both gone. A whole lot of vicious barking ensues and I half get up, wondering if my dog is going to murder Caden. Before I can decide on what to do, the commotion ends and Ugly is trotting back inside. He comes up to me and sniffs at me to make sure I'm okay. Then does his leaning against me thing until I finally give in and hug him. I let the tremors rack through my body and breath in his fur until I'm finally calm enough to wipe away my snot.

"Thanks. But don't you ever allow anyone into this house that's not Dill, Jade, or Aron." Ugly whimpers in apology. Lowering his head in contrition, I rub his ears. "It's okay. Just don't do it again. And... That was pretty awesome. You were really scary." I feel awkward talking to him like he's a human but half the time he seems to understand me better than most humans anyway.

I mean to get up. But I know the moment I do, the reality of never seeing Caden again will somehow be more real. Like if I stay, then time can be frozen for a bit. But when I move again, time will move with me. It's irrational but in the list of impossible things that have happened in the last twenty-four hours, this one seems to be the most harmless. I stay on the cool mosaic floor and welcome the numbness that creeps over me.

I wake up to being jostled. I sense Aron's presence before I crack my lids. Confirming it's him, I let them close again and wrap my arms around his neck. I let him carry me like the scared little kid I feel like. He gently lays me down in my bed and though I haven't opened my eyes, silent tears seep out. I need a plumber for my eyeballs. The leaky fuckers need fixing. Covers are pulled up around me and I curl into a ball and let Aron rub my back the way Jade sometimes does.

His quiet, tender voice almost doesn't sound like him. "You can cry Alex. It's just us."

And so I do. I hear him leave the room. When he comes back, he lays on top of the sheets and turns on his side to wrap himself around me and I see tissues in his hand by my face. I grab them wad them under my stupid dripping eyes. Too tired to do anything more. Every time I hear Caden's voice tell me he's sorry and he would never hurt me, a fresh flood comes. It's not so much what he said, it's the way he said it. And that he had to say it because he lied to me, and still he gave me no explanation. I hate him. But I already miss him.

Aron finger brushes my messy hair behind my ear and his voice sounds more gravely than usual. "Do you want to talk about it?"

I do blow my nose then. "He lied to me." I'm surprised of all the things I could have said, that's what my heart landed on first. And I guess the truth is that beyond all of the weirdness is that he betrayed me.

I hear Aron's sigh before he speaks. "Sometimes people have to lie to protect those they love... Sometimes it's not a choice."

Something about the way he says it makes me turn around and look at him. He scoots back a little to make room for me. And I'm shocked to see his eyes are red. "Aron?" He shakes his head and rolls on his back. Starring at my ceiling as I have done countless nights. When he finally speaks, his voice is steady.

"I talked with Jade. She spoke with her dad. She tried to reach you but you're not answering your phone." His mouth softens with the barest hint of a smile and he gives me a light pinch. Another tear leaks from his eye. Anxiety fills my stomach with lead. Something is wrong.

"What is it?" I ask, trying to sound brave.

He lets out another massive sigh. "Why did you come here. To Green Mont?"

His question takes me aback, but I sense that the truth is somehow important to him, so I give it to him. Trusting that it's safe with him. "I dreamed about it. Over and over again."

I watch his eyes squeeze shut and he nods. Shifting on the bed to face me. "I understand that. But what made you finally come?"

This question is harder to answer. Because by telling him, I risk putting him in the middle of something he doesn't deserve to get caught up in. "Something... Bad happened. I was defending a friend." I can't tell him anymore. He would be obligated to report me, and incriminated if he doesn't.

When I don't say anything else, he seems to consider his next words carefully. "So, you felt you didn't have any choice but to leave and this place just happened to be in your mind?"

The way he says it makes it sound like I was pushed here. But that's not even possible. Even if the universe did tamper in the lives of mortals, who am I to deserve such attention? I'm no one. Nothing Aron can say would sway me from a lifetimes worth of evidence that has proven it to be true.

"What are you trying to say?"

He scoots up, looking flustered. "Jade should be here for this."

"Why do I get the feeling that everyone seems to know something I don't? Even you and Jade! You're both asking me these seemingly unrelated questions as if it's *all connected* somehow. And it's honestly start-ing to get on my nerves! If you know something, as my friends, you have to tell me."

"Did you give me a straight answer to my last question?"

Thrown off, I stutter, "Not exactly... But I told you as much as I can."

He shakes his head at me in frustration. "*Why?*"

"I'm *protecting you!*"

"Maybe, just maybe, others are trying to protect you too."

"So there *is* something you guys are not telling me?"

The possibility has my heart leaping into my throat. Aron's silence is all the answer I need. The betrayal I wasn't coping with before magnifies tenfold. "Not telling me is not the same thing Aron! Because my life, before you guys? Was mine! And you don't have the right to know about it. You get to know about it because you're important to me. But this? What's happening now? It happened to me. And it concerns and directly affects me! As my best friends, it should have been a forgone conclusion that you would tell me every thought and theory you have, if not what you know! Because you obviously do know something! And you won't tell me?" I bite my trembling lips. *How many people do I need to lose in a single month?*

"Alex *stop*. You have no idea what you're even talking about!"

I sit all the way up. "And whose fault is that? Why don't I know any-thing Aron? You don't think I feel like the world's biggest fool right now? Because I actually thought that I belonged? That I could *trust* you guys when it's clear you never trusted me? You're being a total ass! You know that? Just tell me! ...*Please!*"

Aron slides off of the bed and stands. "I should go. I... I can't do this right now."

"*What?* You're not actually *leaving...*" Disbelief colors my voice.

"I'm sorry Alex."

"Aron! *Please!*" I don't even know what I'm asking him for anymore. To tell me the truth? Not to abandon me when I need him the most? Not to break my fucking heart more than it already is? But the boy I have spent almost every single day with since the beginning of school, turns his back on me for no apparent reason and walks out on me. "*Aron!*"

The silence that comes back at me is so much louder than my scream.

∞

I put the leash on Ugly now more for show and reassurance for others, than any real necessity. For some reason the beast ignores everyone else but me. Dill seems to be honestly oblivious of Ugly's serious training and I still haven't shown him what Ugly can really do. But the slobbering fool has kept all of my secrets so I'm happy enough to keep his. Especially given that lately, he seems to be the only one I can trust around here.

In the wake of everything that happened, I skipped Ugly's walk yesterday and he took it like a champ. Now he's fairly losing his shit as we get ready and I'm feeling pretty guilty. There's an unusual heat wave in effect for October and as we step outside, it's like walking into an oven. Thank god for sunscreen.

Pulling on my shades I look at Ugly. "Only for you." He gives a happy *woof*, like I'm the world's best invention, and we set out. I'm already sweating by block two and grumbling at myself for not taking a hat. At least the dog park will be pretty empty given the weather. I picture the little bench right in the shade that would be bliss in comparison to this misery.

I have learned a lot about etiquette at dog parks since my first debacle with Ugly. It turns out I was a real dick on my first day there. I can't help but smile at the memory though. I'm pretty sure that's one of Ugly's top days too.

Nearing the park, I feel something is wrong before I see anything. Instinct has my legs speeding up and, there it is. A man I don't recognize is talking to Maddie by a van. *A literal, grey fucking van!* My blood runs cold and I have to stop myself from screaming her name. If he grabs her now, I will never reach them in time. Ugly is whining and I look at him. There is no way that I can get to them in time but Ugly might be able to.

Forcing down my panic, I take just a second to assess the situation. Sparing no more time I kneel before him, looking him straight in his eyes as I unclip his leash. *"Protect Maddie."* And I pray that he understands. I pray that he will make it to her in time because he's the only chance she's got right now. He takes off like a shot. No warning *woof*, hardly any sound at all is made as he blurs straight for them.

I am running as fast as I can behind him and it's like his paws hardly touch the ground. This is the fastest I have ever seen a four-legged creature move and yet I don't know if it will be enough. Looking at the man, I see the moment he spots us. I falter and horror washes over me.

He yanks Maddie up and the sound of her alarm almost brings me to my knees. And suddenly I'm back at the group home. Two men have Shells in their grasp. Vic is trying to fight one off. I move to attack the other, when he pulls out a knife and holds it to Shells' throat, freezing me in my tracks.

As the knife presses into her delicate flesh I go deaf and everything slows down. Suddenly I have all the time in the world to work this out. *Save Shells.* That's all I can think of. *Save. Shells.*

I reach for the knife. It's dripping blood onto my hand.

Noise rushes back along with the rest of the room. Shells is sobbing in Vic's arms and the man that held her is crumpled on the floor, covered in blood. The other man is watching me with an inexplicable smile on his angular face. I jerk the knife up to threaten him and blood flings over his face. His strange smile now a gruesome display.

"Get back or I'll gut you like your dead friend!" I'm praying he's not dead. Praying, I'm not a murderer. But this monster doesn't need to know that. I take another step closer to him but suddenly he's gone. Just vanished into thin air. Jerking back to Shells and Vic I whisper, "*Where is he!*" But they just shake their heads, eyeing the bloody weapon in my hand. I drop it. And we all look over at the unmoving body then, and I dare to ask, "Is he... Dead?"

A little girl's cry has me crashing back to reality and I blink just in time to see Ugly latch onto the man's arm. *Save. Maddie.* For once, I am grateful when everything goes into hyper focus. The sound of keys hitting concrete registers. I reach for the keys with no thought of my vicinity from them. Only the awareness that I require them, and my fingers close around the warm metal.

Maddie is wailing and I turn around to see her in the grass next to the man struggling with Ugly who is wrestling him back into the park. The sound of barking and snarling a roar as I grab Maddie away from the man and without any thought, run her to her house. I don't remember the trip to her front door. I just know she smells like rain and wet grass and the living, as I bang on the front door with my boot.

It feels like I have been beating it forever before it finally opens and I'm shoving Maddie into the arms of her very confused mother. *"Someone just tried to take her! Call the police!"* Is all I get out before I'm running back. My stupid legs are too slow. I hear my dog yelp and the terrible silence that follows has jet fuel carrying my body to a scene I am sure to spend the rest of my life trying to erase.

As soon as I see him over my unmoving dog, I launch onto his back and wrap my arm around his neck squeezing with everything I'm worth. Pain shoots through my leg as something foreign is imbedded into it. But I numb it out as I feel him start to pull free. H*ell no!* Biting the closest thing I can find, his neck, I rip at it like a feral cat. His grip changes and he starts screaming.

He flings us to the ground and I grunt with the impact. My leg is on fire! My hold loosens just enough for him to pull free and something is yanked from my leg. Screaming erupts and as if from a distance, I realize it's me. I watch his arm raise and I come back into my body the moment the knife plunges into my stomach. As pain like I have never known paralyzes me, one thought breaks through. Ugly isn't fighting him anymore. He's not defending me.

Dread and fear for my dog overrides everything. Even through the agony, I know that something is seriously wrong with Ugly. The man is struggling to get back up, but my attention is no longer on him. I need my dog. *Where is he?* Completely disoriented, I put my hand over my stomach and do my best to stop the bleeding, as I strain to find Ugly.

But then something sends the man rocketing from my body. I finally spot Ugly to the left of me and with no more pressure on my legs I try to move to him with little success. A thump and a scream sound in the background but I only vaguely register it. Attempting to move again I try to drag myself but the pain is overwhelming. *He's so close!*

"Ugly?" I want to yell his name, but my shaky voice comes out thready and quiet.

My panic at his silence sends a spurt of strength into my flagging muscles. I let go of my bleeding stomach. My only conscious imperative is to reach my dog. With both arms, I heave myself a little closer. I'm so tired and my body is too heavy but somehow, I make it the rest of the way.

Searing pain cripples me, but then I see all the blood matting Ugly's fur and the bloody grass around him. *Oh no.* There is so much of it, too much of it! I wrap myself around him, no longer feeling anything but his shaking body and his panting chest that's working too hard.

He lets out a quiet whimper that breaks my heart. "Shhhhh. *It's okay. ...you're okay. I've got you."* My hand finds his cheek and I put my mouth close to his ear. Neither of us have much longer. And I need him to know he's not alone before I bleed out, or he does. Stroking his face, I wish so much that I could look into his warm brown eyes one more time. But I'm on the wrong side of him and I'm too weak to move. So I settle for telling him the most important fact. Words I should have said one hundred times a day to this perfect, incredible breast. "Ugly... I love you."

CHAPTER 26

Pale green eyes the color of bleached sea glass, loom over mine. His chiseled, angular face looking more like a ghastly apparition, than a mortal man. *Where is Alexa Walker?* His thin lips move, but no sound breaches his silent mouth. Not even the whisper of air. Instead, his chilling melodic voice reverberates through my skull as if a loudspeaker is lodged somewhere deep in my brain.

Paralyzing fear and confusion make it impossible to answer, let alone focus on the question. As his dull lifeless eyes squint in aggravation, I strain to remember what he just asked. *Alex... Something about Alex?*

Yesssss... Where. Is. She? His deep halting voice is like rocks grinding together with unnatural inflections in all the wrong places.

Unconsciously, my mind calls up a barrage of memories. Two men suddenly in our room. The following scuffle that ensued. Alex bursting in. The man holding Shells one second and dead on the floor in the next. Alex standing over him holding his bloody knife we never saw her take or use. The man that went after me gone before we ever saw him leave. Shells and I pooling our money and urging Alex to run. Moving to get rid of the body only to find it was gone too. No trace of blood or knife or any sign they were ever in our room at all.

Horrible realization crashes into me. "*You're* the one! The one that ghosted!"

Gooood. keep going. Where is she?

Unbidden, more memories surge up. Watching her climb out of our window. Missing her. Finally a phone call. Deciding not to tell her about the unexplainable missing body. Wanting her to have the fresh start that I can't. Wishing I could know where she is. Knowing it's for the best that she doesn't say.

Clever, clever, cleverrrrr. The violation and horror of having my mind invaded, has me gasping as bile surges up my throat. My teeth are violently chattering as my body convulses in trembles. It's so, so cold.

Yessss, death alwaaaysss is. I look at my arm and see the needle I never felt entering. *Where is Shelly Morgan?* The image in my mind of Shells back at our group home is far more upsetting than the knowledge of my coming death. I kind of expected to die young. But I never expected to betray the only people I love. The incredible high that washes over me sweeps away the thoughts and ends my suffering. The last thing I see before I drift into the warm beautiful sun, is a crow.

∞

I bolt upright, panting as sweat and tears merge together in rivers down my face. After months of dreaming about Vic's death I finally see it all in order. Every horrible gruesome detail. Until now, all the jagged and misshapen pieces of each nightmare were like shards of a broken mirror; they always left me bleeding, but never offered any clarity. Now, with the shards put together, it all makes a horrifying kind of sense.

I can't grasp how I know it. But deep down in my marrow I am certain that just like the dreams that lead me to Green Mont, my subconscious is revealing something crucial. It's more than my imagination. More than fears and memories warped into nighttime torment. No. This was real. Vic didn't overdose. She was murdered. And someone, *something* is after me.

Sudden agony radiates through my stomach and wrenches a cry from me that sounds more animal than human. And all at once I'm blinking against light, feeling all the pain in my body and hearing the incessant beeping of monitors and arguing. The sensory overload momentarily stunning me.

"Alex!" I recognize the voice, but everything is too much. Throwing my hands over my face, I let out a pathetic groan. Gentle hands catch me and I fall back into blackness.

∞

"Please wake up. *Please.* Just come back. You *have* to fight Alex." *Whose voice is that?* "I was wrong... So completely wrong. But you scared me more than *anything*." *Ash?* "I didn't know how to act... How to *be*. You were just this incredible light in a sea of darkness. But I knew you were not for me. I knew it was dangerous to even think it, but I felt pulled to you from the moment I first met you. When I found you in that ice cream shop." *Definitely Ash but...* "I had never seen anything like you before. You just felt *different*. And the more I tried to figure it out, figure you out, the more different I learned you are. But still... Even so... You're *my mirror* Alex. It's your differences that entice the parts in me I thought would always go unanswered. The parts of myself that I had given up on to survive. I thought I was protecting you by distancing. But

I get it now, okay? I get it! So you can come back to me. I'm *so, so sorry Alex*. I never wanted to hurt you. I wish I could have explained my family to you, my responsibilities, and my order in the scheme of things. It's so much bigger than you think. But despite my family, my beliefs, the very *laws* that govern my existence, I *should* have told you! I thought staying away from you was the only way to keep you safe! But now, if I could have saved you all of this suffering by keeping you close? By opening my world to you? Honestly Alex, there isn't a law that I would not have broken, to save you from this. I failed in the *only* pursuit that ever really mattered. *You*. Alex. If you just come back I will find a way to make it all up to you. I will tell you *everything*. I will be anything that you need me to be. Screw everyone else. Because this world? My world? It can't go on without you in it. It just *can't!* I *need* you..."

"*Ashar*, you are required."

∞

"-was so pissed when she found out. I wish you could have seen it. You would have gagged. But it's more challenging than I ever realized to be a peacekeeper without you. It was never really my style to interfere in the lives of mortals before you came swaggering in. I mostly kept to myself. But I do it now because I know that's what you would want. What you would do if you were here. How you made it seem so effortless... I can't begin to fathom. Your presence alone balanced the scales of everyone around you. And now everything is just... *Wrong*. So I'm officially calling it. Your beauty rest is *over* Alex. And it's time to join the land of the living. There are answers waiting for you on this side. And there is me and Aron and *Dill*. The poor guy has been worried sick. And you would *never* believe it, but you have two hunks losing their fine behinds over you. And Aron too actually. I don't know what went down between you and him, but he hasn't spoken a word since you... Since we... Well, since we found you. But can you even *imagine* it? A universe where Aron doesn't talk your ear off every day? It seems like it would be great, right? But in reality... It's just... Not. He's basically camped himself outside of your door. And I'm... I'm worried about him. But he won't talk to me. The other two are not far off. Of course, Caden has not been admitted in. So, he spends days at a time pacing outside the facilities gates. Occupationally with his *friends*. But mostly alone. I give him updates on the regular to keep him from storming in and instigating a war. But I don't imagine he will suffer the distance and uncertainty much longer. Honestly I don't know that I can either" -sigh- "So wake up. You're the strongest person I know. Get your shit together and... Just wake up, *okay?"*

∞

Pressure on my hand tells me I'm not alone. Aron's voice drifts to me from somewhere far away. "Please, please, please... *Come on! Wake the hell up already!* ...Sorry... Just... *Please.*"

It's not the first time we have had this one-way chat. And I want to reach him. To hold his hand. But lethargy weighs me down. And down...

....

A girl is screaming. A man is stabbing me. A dog is crying. Bloody grass. A dog. His wet fur against my face. And above the cloying coppery taste and smell of blood there is something else, something familiar. Someone important to me. And my heart is *breaking*. My dog is dying in my arms. *My dog. UGLY!*

I'm falling, tumbling to cold, hard ground. The familiar sounds of beeping in the background greets me. "Ugly!" My arm burns as I tug to find him. To reach him. Blinding light blasts me as I try to see him. *Crap! My arm!* Blinking to see what the burning is about, I struggle to focus on an IV connected to my arm. Blearily I look around me. Squinting against the irritating light. Blinking more to get things sharp enough to make sense. A door bangs open and I look up in time to see Aron burst in.

"Alex..." His voice cracks and the cockiest most confident guy I have ever met, crumbles to the floor before me. He just shakes his head and I hear him mumble, "Thank God." Before he breaks down entirely into shuddering, heaving sobs I shake my spinning head to clear it. *Is this real? Another dream? No. The floor is ice cold. The-.*

Ash comes in next, taking in Aron's crumpled form and my empty bed with abject horror written on his face. I feel more than see when he finds me. Mere seconds pass before I am in his arms. Scooped up and being cradled like a child. By the way everyone is acting you would think I died.

"No... Ash stop."

He freezes. "You can see me?"

Aron's cries have gone quiet as well and it's him I look at. His softly glowing eyes that transfix my own. Somehow, I know it's emotion that has their glow moving like something between water and fire; flickering like a candle and swaying like the ocean. Their depths just as fathomless. Their color undefinable but familiar. I'm too mesmerized to speak. But some last piece, some lost part of that broken mirror clicks back into place and I am made whole again within Aron's miraculous stare.

Waves of profound glittering warmth come over me, through me. Obliterating my suffering, my loneliness, my very sense of self. I am at once a newborn and as endless as time. Love unlike anything I have ever experienced shatters my heart at its presence. Reverence and awe fill me until all the holes, all the hollow places I hide are exposed and overflowing in light. Understanding that I am not apart from creation but *of it* sets my restless tired soul at peace. Such incredible peace.

And through all the light and all the love, I see her. A tiny black dot at first. As she comes closer, she takes in all the light until it is she that shines against darkness. Her flowing, fluttering form moves as if in water. A starburst of strands that expand and wave as she draws ever nearer. I am not so far gone that I don't recognize the miracle of her perfection. My chest is the only physical part of my body I can feel. Its ache and burn as I try to breathe through the impossible.

Are you God? Is this death? The response is so immediate and true, I know this knowledge has been within me all along. That beautiful glimmering light is now waiting before me. And I *know*. With undiluted love and total acceptance, I approach the light. I reach my hands out and as she comes into them the ancient grace of her; the love of her overwhelms me. With a sob, I embrace her. Because she is me.

Aron breaths out and falls back on his ass. "*I knew it!* I knew you were too weird and too, too, too... There was a reason you found us! I knew it!" He's shaking his head now and grinning like a lunatic. He has dark circles under his eyes and sharper angles to his face. He's lost weight.

The only thing I am able to get out as I come back into my body is, "*Your eyes...*" I'm trembling in Ash's arms. Too weak to stand and too dizzy to try. Still, I am unable to look away from Aron's stunning, familiar eyes. This is why I came to Green Mont. This is my destiny. But my feelings are too great for this moment. Too big to voice. And Aron is still smiling like a loon. So I look at Ash and settle on basic imperatives that can be managed. "Um... Can you turn down the lights? It's too bright in here." He inhales sharply upon seeing my face and his body goes rigid around mine.

"*His* eyes?" Aron asks incredulously. "Alex... The lights aren't on. It's pitch black in here."

Exhaustion makes it hard to even smile at his stupid joke. Ash must feel my fatigue because he effortlessly lifts me up. "I've got you." He murmurs into my hair. I wait for him to set me on the bed, but he pauses and lightly squeezes me to his chest instead. "I've got you."

Jade's voice fills me with such relief that I want to cry. "No... You don't. Put her down." Ash hesitates for a moment, then very slowly, very gently, puts me down. But I'm lost in Jades unblinking gaze. The deepest, darkest, full on obsidian eyes glitter back at me. She has a white arching sliver through each eye where her irises should be, and they are framed by tiny little pricks of light. Like moons in dazzling night skies.

I should be terrified but now, after everything, I can't be bothered. Eyes full of galaxies or not, she's *my* Jade and I need her. Reaching out to her is instinct and holding her is right. I want to tell her, tell all of them, what just happened. And to ask Aron or Ash if they could see it. But first...

"Please tell me... *Ugly*... Is he?"

"He's alive." She quickly assures me. I go slack in her arms then. Unable to stop the emotional onslaught that hits me. Aron comes to my other side and holds me up with Jade. Ash finds my hand and holds on. His own contacting over mine with my every violent intake of my breath. What I have been given. Finding them. Ugly. Dill. Maddie... Me. It's more than a second chance. It's divine intervention and a purpose beyond anything I could have imagined for myself.

Ash's voice reaches me through the torrent of processing. "It's okay Alex... I know this is a lot. But you're safe here. I am going to make sure that you are. You don't have to worry."

I calm down enough to even my breathing. "It's not that... It's just..." I look up at him then. Seeing him for the first time. His eyes, the undulating aqua marine and greens of the ocean with rays of bright light cutting through, are what have me smiling. Smiling so big and bright my face hurts. I let out a shaky breath and feel my world right itself. "It's that I know I'm where I'm finally meant to be."

Jade and Aron let me go then and I get to see how my words have transformed them, Ash included. Because some of my unbridled joy is now reflected back at me. "So not to bring up the elephant in the room... But can someone please tell me now what's up with your freaky eyes?" I try to sound casual but fail miserably.

Aron starts laughing again and Ash breaks into the largest smile I have ever seen grace his face. Jade's smile paired with her dark eyes is something I will have to get used to. I allow myself to look closer and chills race over my skin.

"Beautiful." I breath it out without thinking. Too stunned to feel self-conscious. It's like looking through windows into the night sky. My

voice comes out shakier than I want. "You *can't* tell me that's contact lenses, so don't even *try*. Is someone finally going to tell me what the hell is going on?"

"We are." Aron's smile is gone but he squeezes my free hand. I realize then that Ash hasn't let go of my other. Focusing back on Aron I catch a pained look flit over his face, but it's gone in the next second. I finally process the drawn and exhausted cast to him.

"You look as shitty as I feel." He gives me back the cocksure smile I want to see.

"At least I don't look like I have come back from the dead."

My face finally cracks. "At least I *did* come back." The whole room goes silent. "*What?* Too soon?"

The devastation reflected back at me has me quick to change the subject. "*So?* Your eyes?"

Jade leans back. "We have a *lot* to discuss. And you deserve to hear it from someone who can answer all of your questions. How are you feeling now?"

"*Tired.*" I admit on a sigh. "Where's Ugly and Dill?" As soon as I think of them, I'm home sick. I want Dill's reassuring presence and world-famous hug even more then I want answers. But I need to see Ugly. After everything that happened, I need to see him alive and well with my own eyes. Maddie too.

Jade nods. "You are in an extremely exclusive recovery center. One which does not permit outsiders. As an unofficial club member, you do not have visitor privileges." The moons in Jade's eyes glance over at Aron for just a moment and I catch his clenched jaw. "We *did* advocate for him, but we couldn't get him in. Your physician explained to him that due to the severity of your wounds and a compromised immune system, you are being quarantined. And that it would be best to allow you to heal more before risking any exposure or cross infection. Dill signed a release so you would have the best care possible. He was *not* happy about not visiting but as you were unconscious anyway and he just wanted you to get better, he didn't put up too much of a fight. He gets a phone call twice a day with updates. One from your physician and one from me."

"Wait, but you're here. Why do you guys get to be here if I am in quarantine?"

"My father is kind of a partial owner here. And we are all members. But Dill doesn't actually know we are in here with you."

"So I'm not actually quarantined? You have a doctor that lied to him?"

"Yes. To get you the best treatment and chances of recovery, there are no lengths my family would not have gone."

I try to track everything she is saying but my eyes are growing heavy. "You can't bullshit the Pickle. Not for long anyway." At the strained looks they exchange, years of reading people kicks in. "How long have I been here?" I blink my eyes to hold off the lethargy that's trying to claim me. Jade smooths my hair from my face and my eyes involuntarily close. Too heavy to open again, I give in.

Her soft voice is the last thing I hear before my familiar friend darkness comes to claim me. "You have been here just over a month."

∞

I wake up with a little more energy and my eyes are finally able to focus. It's daylight now. By the light coming through the window, I'm guessing it's mid-morning. Aron is in a chair at the foot of my bed. His head is supported by arms that graze my calves. He's dead asleep. I remember his voice through the fog. He sounded so desolate as he begged and begged for me to come back. He looks serene now. And I wonder if it really happened, or if it was all a dream.

That thought has me remembering my horrible vision of Vic. That's what I'm calling it now; A vision. Practical, logical me having visions and my friends having alien eyes. What has the world come to? I need to tell them about everything as soon as possible. But first I want the truth from them. I have this crazy niggling suspicion that everything is connected.

The stone walls around me and the high ceilings with all the frilly plaster work, leave me wondering if there are any castles I don't know about in Green Mont. There are several vases of flowers and a painting of a forlorn beauty, warming my room. I take a deep breath and am relieved to find my stomach doesn't hurt anymore with my barest movement.

"You're awake." I look back to see Aron's stormy desert eyes have the same light and warmth as the window just behind him. Slightly dazzled, I remember the arrogant but normal looking boy I met my first day in Drama.

"What happened to your eyes?"

"This must be quite a shock. Though you should prepare yourself. There's a smidge more shock ahead of you."

"I have had enough surprises to last a lifetime. I'm officially at limit."

Aron leans back in his chair and loudly cracks his back. "On the contrary. You're taking everything quite well. I have seen lesser men piss themselves at the sight of Jade's eyes."

I want to ask him more questions, but Jade had alluded to someone that would give me all the answers, and I'm ready.

"I want out of this bed. Can you help me?"

Ash's voice draws my attention to the doorframe he takes up. "There are two nurses behind me with clothing and food at your say."

"Thank you." I say a bit awkwardly. It's nice that he's here. And everything I remember him saying was nice as well I guess. But I had to learn really fast in foster care, how to let people you can't depend on, go. He ghosted through one of the hardest points of my life. So, hell yes I let him go. And I was moving on too. Just because he's ping-ponged back into my life now when he's good and ready doesn't mean I'm willing.

Aron takes my hand and I carefully scoot up so I'm not craning my neck to see him. He looks annoyed with being interrupted and I don't blame him. I wonder how long Ash was spying on us. "I'll just be outside. But we should talk. *Soon.*" Aron gently squeezes before letting go and leaving.

I nod, a bit perplexed by the look on his face. "Sure..."

CHAPTER 27

I grit my teeth as my wheelchair hits yet another bump in the large cobblestone hallway. It's not that the bumpy ride bothers me so much. It's that I don't want to be wheeled out in the first place! I can't remember ever having felt so physically weak in all of my life. My rebellious mind, which only feels sharper than ever, makes the loss of independence, even more frustrating.

While no one has expressly stated the meeting I'm about to have is important, I have picked up enough *tells* from everyone around me to understand it obviously is. The grim mood of my friends as they escort me is a silent and tense exclamation point to my suspicion. They are acting more like security as they escort me along the dramatic arched hallway.

"We're just seeing your dad and some of his colleagues?" I ask again.

The moons in Jade's eyes shift over to me for a second. "In a matter of speaking, we're almost there." Her vague response does nothing to calm my nerves. "Just, be respectful in front of my dad's... *Friends*." The word falls flat on her lips. "If there is something informal you want to say to him, do so in private, with me after we get this is over with." With a start, I realize the most calm and collected person I have ever met in my life may actually be more nervous than me. *Oh shit.*

"Remind me why we can't be informal now?"

"Because, this is an introduction first and foremost. You're being introduced to other *club members*, so everyone can see first-hand that you are trustworthy. Then, you can finally get the answers to your questions. Think of it like an interview."

"*Okay...* Well that's new." I fume as the tight anxious ball in my stomach clenches.

"I didn't want you to be worried." She defends. I get it, but if it looks like an ambush and smells like an ambush... But I decide to grouse at her later. Maybe when she's not grinding her teeth down to nubs.

We come to a stop in a marble foyer with a massive ornate arched ceilings and wide columns. I strain to see Aron behind me, and he immediately comes to my side as Jade gives the doors a brisk knock. Some lowkey meeting this turned out to be. I quickly rub my sweaty palms over my legs. These are without a doubt the largest set of doors I have ever seen. *Intimidating much?*

"Where the hell are we?"

"*Oh right! You don't know!*" Aron looks a little too thrilled to be the one delivering the news. "We're in Switzerland!"

"*What?!*" My shriek resonates just as the heavy doors open before us. Ash heavily sighs behind me, before resolutely pushing me forward. Aron's eyes glitter with mirth as I glare at him and mentally put his name above Jade's on my shit list. "You're number one." I hiss at him under my breath. He looks elated by the thought and flashes that conceited grin I know and love, and hate.

"*Naturally!*" He whispers.

I finally look away from him to the large study before me. A massive wood desk sits front and center. Behind it is the largest man I have ever seen, like *ever*. Even sitting, he's taller than the elderly monk standing to his right. *There's a monk here?* The grey woman standing at his left is only a bit taller. Their shrewd eyes assess me, and I unguardedly assess them right back. At least this kind of meeting I'm familiar with. Good thing I'm not here to be adopted.

The elegant woman is mesmerizing. With her presence alone, she challenges my every notion of age. Glossy light silver hair that's shaved at the bottom and longer at the top, is parted on the side and tucked behind her ear. She's wearing little to no makeup and yet her skin looks dewy with vitality and beauty, even as it's creased with lines. A straight nose, sharp jaw, high cheekbones and silver eyes, make a striking combination. She meets my gaze head-on with neither warmth nor recrimination. Her perfectly schooled features and sharp eyes tell me her seniority has done nothing but hone her into the dangerous beauty that stands before me now.

Soft laughter has my eyes darting over to the diminutive monk. His smiling pale grey eyes are familiar somehow. He looks incredibly exotic in this fancy room with his orange robing and shaved head. At first glance he's the friendliest of the three. And yet, my instincts tell me he's the one to watch out for. There is an implicit steel behind his gaze and in his posture that belies his apparent good nature.

A slight shifting next to him has me back to the herculean man ruling the desk. His fancy suit jacket seems an afterthought to the loose, half buttoned white shirt beneath it. He looks a little older than Dill and yet, beneath the necklaces and tattoos, is hard, defined muscle. He has thick white curling hair around his ears, and a white waving beard to match.

His piercing blue ringed eyes that go to ice in the center, are the most intimidating to meet. He seems to have little to no irises and paired with his hair, it's a startling contrast against tanned leathery skin. His masculine face is chiseled as if cut from stone. But the lines there speak of laughter and humor. The uneven bend to his nose, of trouble.

I sense a possible kinship there that's as apparent to me as the monk's duality and the woman's cunning. All of these impressions are gained within seconds and I wonder what they must think of me. I'm wearing the white spa robe they left in my hospital room over my pajamas and a pair of flip flops. I'm not at all concerned with my lack of dress in this formal setting. *Not at all.*

Ash's strong voice is almost a relief against the silence, commanding as he addresses the room. "Members of the council, I present Alexa Walker." *Council?*

I want to see Ash's face at the unexpected formality in his voice, but rather then ungraciously twisting in my seat, I find Jade instead. She is now standing by her father and the pleading look she sends me to *behave*, is clear as day and that seals the deal. Now I know a lot more is riding on this meeting than a simple introduction.

The monk with the familiar eyes, gives a formal bow. "You are welcome here, Alexa Walker. Please... Join us." He gracefully gestures to the seating area on the right, before a large balcony. Ash starts to roll me forward and I swiftly stop his momentum. I look to Aron, who immediately helps me to stand.

I slowly make my own way to the sofas with as much dignity as I can. Though the slapping of my flip flops against the stone doesn't help. No one else here has glowing eyes. I wonder if they can see my friend's true eyes or if they see only normal eyes like I did before. It's an exhausting trip but all the pain and dizziness is forgotten as the view from the windows reaches my vantage. I can't help the gasp that escapes as the vista literally steals my breath.

I don't notice that I've stopped until Jade smoothly takes my hand and escorts me past the sofas to the view. I hear the council settle in the seating behind me and quickly forget them. The vista before me is like nothing I have ever seen. My hand aches to reach the knob that is only inches away, and pull the doors open to give this stuffy place a breath of fresh air.

We are high atop a mountain, situated on a cliff face. A pure blue sky broken up by large fluffy clouds above. And green, green peaks and valleys dotted with wildflowers, trees and tiers of well-maintained farmland below. At the very base is a colorful village lining a sparkling blue lake, nestled between another mountain.

I whirl around, immediately catching Aron's eyes. "We're in freakin Switzerland!" Nothing could stop the awe and excitement I'm suddenly feeling at my first trip outside of the country. Being an occasional dumbass sometimes pays off though, like right now as the tension in the room finally breaks.

I just barely hear Jade's father behind me, cryptically whisper. *"Behold. The great threat."*

I turn around to ask him what he means when I spot a new face. He's standing by the bar to the right of the sofas and he is *gorgeous*. So pretty that he shouldn't even be real, level of gorgeous. Then he opens his mouth. A harsh, Australian accent with more bass than his twenty something age implies, comes out punchy and loud.

"Stone the crows... I waited yonks to take a slash for this Zack? You Tall Poppies are off the planet if you think this zonked bluey is more than a tacker!"

What the hell kind of language is that? I recognize some of the words but I do *not* recognize his meaning. The only thing I am sure of, is that he just called me Zack. "It's Alex."

The full weight of his crystalline gaze now rests on me, but his glower turns to confusion. Maybe he doesn't actually speak English? His voice pops like a canon. *"What?"*

Why is he yelling? "My name... It's not *Zack.* It's *Alex."*

He shakes his head in seeming disbelief and laughs derisively. *"Bonzer."*

Hunky Santa clears his throat from a leather chair by the sofas, and I'm relieved when pretty boy goes quiet. That is, until I notice how intimidatingly beautiful he is again. *Ugh.* Tearing my gaze away from him, I gingerly perch next to Jade. I feel more than see Ash's watchful eyes on me from across the room. Everything he said at my bedside floods back to me. I have to scramble to push him out of my thoughts as my cheeks flame up.

I lean heavily on my knees. This is the most activity I have had in *weeks* and I'm feeling it. Aron moves to sit at my other side and I relax a bit, knowing my friends surround me. Even Ash is a comforting presence here. The monk and silver beauty are seated across from me and Jade's dad stands behind them. Smiling reassuringly.

For some reason I'm reminded of a mouse trap. The cheese distracting the mouse, before it's suddenly trapped. I know Jade's dad but *still.* *Everyone* in this room has such a presence about them, that I can't help but feel small. Then my mind makes the connection without my being aware it was working out a puzzle.

I look back at Jade's father and then the monk. *Yep.* The similarities between them now obvious. And he has Jade's grey eyes! Or, he did. Until her eyes became, I look at her, whatever they are now. The queasiness I have been feeling all day intensifies and I don't know if it's the nerves or the tiny fact that I have had no time to process the physical changes in my friends. Let alone the ramifications it has on my comprehension of reality.

Being in this room now, I instinctively understand the limits of my imagination are going to be tested. No one has started speaking yet, so I take the opportunity to address the most familiar of the strange adults assembled here. Jade's dad. "Are you two related?" I look between him and the monk.

Instead of her dad responding, the monk commands all the attention. He smiles at me and gives the slightest of nods. "Observant for one so young."

Pretty boy scoffs from the bar. "Carn! Bluey is an Airy Fairy!"

Making a face I look at Jade. I'm dying to ask her if he has Tourette syndrome or something that has him spewing out these nonsensical combinations of words.

But the monk speaks first. "Is this true Alexa Walker? Are you an *Airy Fairy?*"

I have no clue what this *Airy Fairy* business is about, but as soon as I have access to Google I will have it sorted. For now, everyone is waiting on me to answer the silly question like it might contain the secrets to life. I don't blame them however, this old monk could fart and it would seem important.

Choked and muffled laughter sound around the room and Jade squeezes my leg. *What?* Ignoring the weird face she's giving me, I do my best to answer the monk with a straight face.

"No... I am *not* an Airy Fairy sir." My eyes slide over to pretty boy and I see him scowling at me. *There's always one.* I shrug.

The monk nods and makes a deep grunting noise. "Tell me, what have you learned since entering this room?"

I want to protest that it's my turn to ask a question. Or more like the hundred that are currently hounding me. Even more than that, I want to get rid of this feeling of being an insect under a microscope. The opportunity to turn things around a bit, is too good to pass up.

"This is his office." I gesture to hunky Santa and then address him. "An office like this means that you run things here. Your whole look is the opposite of the snazzy suit jacket you pulled over it. That tells me when you're not in meetings, you're casual, and you prefer it that way. So you're respectful of your fellow council members enough to make yourself uncomfortable for them. And that would indicate a strong working relationship between you all. Also, that you value your position even if it doesn't exactly suit you. No pun intended." I smirk at his unchanging face and shift my focus onto the monk. "Even though this is his domain, everyone defers to you. You were introduced as a part of the council so it's not your position that outranks them. If I go off of what my eyes tell me, you are the eldest member of the council present? So maybe it's in deference to your experience that leadership falls to you? Until you leave, and then he goes back to running things here." I gesture back to hunky Santa and at the monk's nod, I continue, feeling a modicum more confident. "You all have your own very specific aesthetic." I look at the silver beauty. "You remind me a little of Miranda Priestly from The Devil Wears Prada. Have you seen it?" She gives nothing away but for a slight softening around her lips. "You should see it, it's a great movie but you're like, *way* more hot." Pretty boy sounds like he's choking now. "*Anyway,* you're definitely a city dweller but definitely not from my coast, so I am betting on New York. Your outfit oozes luxury and designer." *Thank you Jade.* "I see you're not afraid of color or of standing out. Which looks like confidence, a bit of playfulness and creativity, attention to detail and passion. But there is also something a little military in the perfection of your look. Your shoes are either new or polished." I can smell the polish. Dill uses it on his boots before gigs. "Polished... Your pants are pressed. Your hair looks effortless, but it took care, and your accessories, precise. I think rules and order are important to you and likely what you excel at. Unlike him," My eyes dart back to Santa, "you enjoy dressing the part. But like him, this council and this work is important to you." Now I'm back to the Monk. You're from Southeast Asia." I look over to Jade's dad, remembering she told me he is Taiwanese. "Most likely Taiwan. And like I said, you are an honored and respected member of the council. You can be nice but... I sense you can be... Not so nice, too. You have been testing me from the moment I walked in here and you're not asking me a million questions because like me, you find information between the lines." I risk a glance at pretty boy. "You're the newest member to the council. Not because you're the youngest necessarily. But because you don't show the reverence for your peers or this... *Meeting,* that you would show to someone you had known or worked with for a long time." I look at his casual attire with significance. "You don't seem to value this position and it makes me wonder if your place on this council was not earned in the usual way. Maybe it was inherited or something like that?" He cocks a beautifully arched brow at me. "You're obviously not big on authority or formality. You don't take yourself or anyone around you too seriously and you're here out of obligation. You're from Australia. *Everyone* I'm just meeting here is from a different continent. So I bet there are more members of the council which cover the rest of the globe? This is a global organization." I look around me at the beautiful room and remember the castle-like features on the long trip here. "That has serious funding. Add that to the hierarchy you've got going? And that implies in the very least a de-mand you have to meet... Numbers. You represent more, a lot more..." *But more of what exactly? People?* I get goosebumps as I work it all out in front of them and begin to realize the scope of things. "This location is isolated. The lack of transparency, that fact that no one has introduced themselves. You are a secretive organization. *Not,* a *club."* I eye Jade at this last remark and she has the decency to look embarrassed. I feel to-tally crazy saying it out loud but looking into her eyes, it's undeniable. With my heart beginning to race, I sit a little straighter and allow myself to really look at everyone. "None of you are exactly human. Your eyes might not be glowing, but *still*. You're just... Not. I'm guessing those you represent are not either? Which makes me think you're a separate operat-ing... Government... From any that I'm familiar with."

I fully expect pretty boy to make some rude remark or joke at the ab-surdity of my read. But no one says a thing and the monk continues to smile at me. The simple nod he gives has icy pinpricks rushing over my body. My heart picks up its pace and I am pretty sure everyone can hear it. At this point it's actually *all* I can hear. This is exactly what I didn't want to know. If it's not just Caden and Ash, if it's my friends too, then I guess I don't just want to know. I have to know.

CHAPTER 28

The creaking of the leather chair has my eyes moving over to Santa, who is sitting kind of like Dill does in his leather chair. I suddenly miss him with a ferocity that hurts my heart. *I want my dad.* The title pops into my head and somehow, for one completely shocking second, the epiphany of his place in my life manages to outrank life on earth not being exactly what I thought it was. But a heartbeat later my shock has passed, and I adjust to the thought like it's been my truth all along. It's a hell of a time for a personal insight but the joy that fills my chest at recognizing him as my dad is a comforting security that grounds me.

My brain must be on overdrive because a far greater realization suddenly hits me than a whole secret civilization amongst humans. I shoot up to my feet.

"My court date!" *I missed my guardianship proceedings!* Jade rises with me and puts her hand on my shoulder. But before she can say anything the monk addresses me.

"It has been managed Alexa."

Desperately, I look to Jade. *What does he mean?* I ask with my eyes, but she only shakes her head at me and I know she wants to talk with me later about it. No, this is way too important to just pass over. I don't care if it's rude, I don't care who these people are. That court date is for Dill's guardianship!

I questioningly look to the monk. "What do you *mean?* Like the court date has been rescheduled? Or *cancelled?*" I hate that I sound alarmed, but I can't hide my feelings regarding this matter. *If I missed it...*

Santa must take pity on me because he finally joins the conversation. "Rescheduled..." With no grace, I flop back into the sofa. "...Indefinitely." His deep, smooth voice and lyrical accent have my back snapping straight. "What does that mean?" *Why do they never give any straight answers?*

Pretty boy speaks up from behind me. "It means Rafferty's rules for the bluey. The conch council and your offsiders, nut'd it out."

If it's possible, I'm even more confused. Jade nudges me and I look over to her and finally understand, if I want any straight answers, I am going to have to *wait... Great.* Closing my eyes, I strain for calm and try to assure myself that as soon as this "meeting" is over, I will be able to get some real answers from my friends.

I won't let them dodge me any longer after putting me through this circus. At least I know Ugly is okay and so is Maddie for that matter. *Thank God.* I can live with waiting for the rest of my answers a little longer, but my focus is fraying as fatigue swamps me.

The monk captures my attention. "Why do you believe you are here?"

"At first I thought it was for my injuries... But now? I'm not sure."

"You are here, Alexa Walker, because you exhibit anomalies from that of your human brethren and that of our own."

And just like that, finally, I grasp the significance of this meeting. Jade's dad called me a threat and Jade called this an interview. I am not of them, and I am not exactly of, *humans* either. After I leave this room, if I leave this room, nothing will ever be the same. Jade catches my hand again and I try to remind myself that my friends are with me. I had been hopelessly clinging to denial but I can't anymore. Not after what happened to me in my recovery room. Not after this.

I take a deep breath and look back at the monk and steel myself. He doesn't disappoint. "You decipher speeds that are not traceable to the human eye. You see defensive techniques from our people that have been masked from human detection for over a millennia..." *The lights Nix and Caden were throwing at each other?* "You now see better in the dark than you do in sunlight." *Wait, what?* "You have drawn my very great and beloved granddaughter to you, and that is significant. As like me, she prefers her own company and mind to that of the outside world. And yet she is not the only one of our kind that have gravitated to you and seem to rotate around you like planets to a sun. You absorb information, move and heal faster than any human and now..." He inhales as if speaking so much is a great effort for him. "Now you are very clearly... in transformation. So there can be no more doubt." His eyes flick over to pretty boy as if that last part was meant for him, but I'm still stuck on this *transformation* bit. "And that, is why you are here Alexa Walker. We will keep an eye on your progress and assist in making sure it goes as smoothly as possible. While also recording your changes."

I can't remain quiet any longer. "I'm sorry... record? ...*Changes?* ...My *transformation?*"

The monk nods, as patient as ever. "You have been a great topic of... *Discussion* between our kind. To our knowledge, there has never been one like you."

I shake my head, trying to grasp what he is telling me, but even as I hear his words, I remain unable to process them. "You're telling me that

I'm *changing*... That I'm... *Not* human?" The monk makes a grunting noise that sounds an awful lot like an agreement. I look over at Jade and Aron with wide eyes, waiting for one of them to contradict him. When I get nothing back but dead air I yank my hand back and stand.

"*Bugger*, Blueys gone stunned mullet on us." He shifts his gaze to me. "Need some Tart Fuel to suss it out?"

I don't know and I don't care. I try my best not to weave through the dizziness. "I'm sorry but I'm not whatever you think I am. I'm not a threat. I'm not a, a *sun*... I'm just... *Me!* ...Maybe I seem important to you because I'm hanging around important people." I eye my wealthy, beautiful friends with significance. "But I am a nobody. I have always *been* a nobody. My parents didn't want me and every potential parent after that, didn't want me. I'm mean I'm not even the *last* choice, okay? I'm nobody's choice. There has clearly been a mistake here!"

But even as I'm saying it, I'm remembering that moment in my room. That undeniable recognition and knowing that came with acceptance. Now in the light of day, it seems so far off and impossible. I'm tired, like deep down in my bones tired. It doesn't feel like I was stabbed and saw Maddie almost get abducted and my dog died only weeks ago. It feels like it was *yesterday*. Not to mention I just witnessed the murder of my best friend, first person, via some messed up vision. That P.S. I have had to keep locked down tight in a box that I can't even emotionally touch until everyone starts making some fucking sense around here.

"I came here for answers! I came here because they told me," I gesture to the traitors behind me, "That you were going to finally give me some clarity on everything. But you're just... *You're*... Not making any sense! You're making everything more complicated and confusing. And if anything, I have *more* questions now, instead of less!"

The monk and all of his contemporaries seem completely unmoved by my outburst. Not mad, or offended, or sympathetic or... *Human.* After a short pause, the monk looks around the room. Meeting the eyes of the other council members in a way that reminds me of the silent communication I often have with Jade. All at once, my energy is gone. I drop heavily to the sofa and squint my eyes against the monster headache threatening to takeover.

The monk looks back to me. "I am Yu-Kai but you may call me Kai. I shepherd Asia. This young fire," He waves to pretty boy, "is Noa Talbot of Australia. And this..." He nods to Silver Beauty.

"Is Aprella Elizabeth Lilly." She smoothly finishes for him and her features soften enough that she doesn't look quite so severe. "And I hail from New York and *do* value order as well as my roll over the eastern half of the United States."

"I am Luca Affry." The large chair supporting Hunky Santa groans beneath his shifting weight and looks more like a toy beneath him. "I represent Europe, saving Russia which is separately served." Really? *I could have sworn you were going to say the North Pole.* Noah barks out a laugh and titters sound around the room. Jade lets out an un-ladylike groan under her breath. If I didn't know any better, I would think that they could hear my thoughts.

"I am Jade's dad." My eyes meet his and he smiles at me warmly. "And I serve my daughter and wife and rep the west half of the United States." I feel like my eyes are about to bug out of my head. But whatever. S'all good.

Kai grunts and pulls my attention back to him. "Now... what answers will bring the clarity which you seek?"

I lean forward. Instinctively knowing I have to choose my questions wisely. I begin with the hardest but most obvious question. "What are you?"

"We are descendants of the sons of heaven."

I lean back and try, and fail, to once more digest his answer. My effort to ask only important questions is completely derailed. *"Wait...* You're telling me... You're... Angels?" I look around the room waiting for someone to react. But nothing. I get *nothing.*

Kai finally responds. "We are the seven factions of Nephilim. Scions of the sons of God and the daughters of mortals."

My hands are clenched so tightly together, that my nails bite into my skin. *That's real. The pain is real...* I look to my friends, trying to see them objectively. My eyes tell me what my mind tries to reject.

For some reason, I look at Noah next. His flawless beauty and long waving blonde hair. His beautiful eyes are normal enough but it's there... This subtle, ethereal, glow to him. Looking around the room I now see that they all have it. I look at Ash last. My breath explodes out of me as his eyes glow back at me. I have to fight back my sudden panic.

Jade shifts next to me and I note her looking to Noah. "She will take the tart fuel now and so will I." After a beat of silence, a glass is pushed into my hands. For once, Noah says nothing and resumes his post back near the bar.

Jade breaks the silence, "Drink." I automatically take her direction and put the glass to my lips, pulling deep. Coughing and hacking immediately ensue. I wasn't expecting hard liquor. But it's good. The burn coursing down my throat brings back some sense of reality. As soon as my throat is clear, I take a more cautious sip. Setting the cup down only when I see that my hand is shaking.

I dig my fingers into my temples, and I try to alleviate the pressure of a building migraine. Taking slower breaths and deepening them. *I can do this. I can handle this. After everything... I can handle this.* With my eyes still closed I force out my next question. "So, you think I'm... Like... Transforming into what exactly?"

The monk draws my attention back with his solemn words. "You are wholly unknown to us. You display more characteristics of Nephilim as your transition progresses... and yet, your origins are human."

"I *am* human." I protest. Shifting I try to gather my wits and my courage. "Is having visions a part of being... Nephilim?" I had meant to speak to my people about this first, but since they are into ambushing me, I am not so sure whose people they actually are. I'm ready to sort this out now. I feel Jade stiffen beside me and Aron's eyes swing over to me.

For the first time, Kai's face changes and I can see his interest before he resumes his serene expression. "You are having... *Visions?*"

"I thought it was dreams at first. Dreams that lead me to Green Mont and then... Now... It's different. I know they are not just dreams anymore."

Kai nods for me to continue. But I look past him to Ash and even though he's a bag of knobs, I know I'm safe. I remain in his gaze as I relive that terrible nightmare and tell them everything that happened to me, to Vic, in my vision.

Kai is particularly interested in the killer. "You say he telepathically communicated? That he never spoke aloud?"

"Yes. But his lips moved even though nothing came out of them." He nods then looks to his group. It might just be my imagination, but the serene old monk seems shaken.

Kai finally meets my eyes again. "Is there anything else you can tell us? Any other detail?"

"A crow... The last thing I saw... Was a crow."

Luca leans forward onto his knees and meets Kai's gaze. "Naberius?"

Kai grunts in what I can only assume is confirmation, then addresses me. "The presence of your... *Friends* outside have made it clear to all of us that you are known to the other side as well. But to be hunted by a Marquis of Hell..."

Immediately discarding the totally dramatic Marquis of Hell bit, I latch onto the *friends outside* part. "You mean *Caden?*" The sudden knowledge that he's actually here and I wasn't dreaming when Jade told me he waited outside, hits me like a ton of bricks. His smell, his eyes, his touch: it all attaches to my senses so deeply that for a moment it's as if he's in the room with me. And knowing he's been waiting for me out there for *how long? Weeks?* In Switzer-fucking-land? I understand now why he couldn't tell me about all of this. And my desperation to see his familiar face and be in his comforting embrace has me near desperate to be outside.

Jade turns to me and looks completely confused. "How do you know that it's Caden?"

I give her my first little smile since we've been in here in finally knowing something she doesn't. "You told me..."

She shakes her head. "No, I... Wait. You *heard* me? When you were unconscious? You could *hear* me?"

I want to have this talk with her. With Aron and Ash too. But I need to settle what Kai just said. "Yes. I heard you." I say shortly, looking back to him. "What do you mean about the other side? And being hunted?" Noah finally seems interested because he comes over to stand behind the sofa with Jade's dad.

Kai speaks up. "What you think of as *Hell*... and all of its subjects, is what we refer to as the other side."

Gross. I'm sweating now. A girl can only wrap her mind around so much in a sitting. I force myself to ask the rest of my questions while I still can. "What would Caden and his friends have to do with the other side?" But I'm dreading the answer.

Kai grunts and I'm beginning to hate the sound. *A grunt is not an answer!* "Your friends are of the other side." He says simply.

I'm about to interrupt him again when he holds up a hand. He wants me to think Caden's from Hell? *Hell. No.*

"We do not know their intentions in following you. Nor their rank, or their purpose. However, *Naberius* is another matter. He is what you might think of as royalty. The fact that one such as him would be after you is vital to understanding your significance and roll."

Aron speaks up for the first time and the sound of his anger breaks through the fog of my confusion. "Pardon your grace, but her *significance?*"

Kai's eyes cool as they reach Aron and he stares him down until Aron looks away. *Wow.* I need time and space to digest this whole new world.

But the main points are jumping out at me and my stomach is twisting in knots at all the implications.

"This Naberius guy, he's after my friend. Shells. Can you check on her? And protect her?" I think fast, wanting to incentivize him. "She has information on where I am. If I'm so important, someone needs to protect her." I'm *praying* she left the community home and went after her mom before the Marquess could get to her. I know she wouldn't have told anyone else where she was going and in theory, that would buy some time.

I'm surprised when it's Noah that inclines his head and moves to the desk only to come back with a pen and a sticky notes pad. He hands it to me and without having to be asked, I scrawl down her information as well as the address I memorized for her mom's place. I'm gratified when he leaves the room. I feel a fraction better knowing I have real life angel people, er... Nephilim? Checking up on her.

But I refuse to believe Caden, Gabriel or Luke would have *anything* to do with Hell or being evil. "I need my phone. And I need someone to show me how to get outside."

Kai's next words send chills racing down my spine. "I'm afraid that is not possible. For your protection, you must remain within these walls."

"Am I a prisoner here?"

The silver beauty, Aprella or Elizabeth or *whoever* she is, moves to the edge of the sofa and leans towards me. She gestures to her eye and hands me a heavy gold compact. I close my trembling hand around it and look back at her as she speaks.

"We have all traveled a long way to be here and to meet you. You are one of a kind Alexa Walker, and your transition makes you exceedingly vulnerable, even before we knew you were being hunted by a great force. But if you will not accept reasonable terms of security for your own sake, then accept them for your friends. You are changing and you cannot be exposed to humankind in this state, without exposing us, and putting them at risk."

She looks back into my eyes with significance then nods to the compact. I'm gripping it so hard now, my knuckles are white. My stomach drops as I slowly stand and move over to the window without another word. No one offers to help or follows me. My hands are shaking so bad I fumble in my attempts to open the priceless-looking compact. I take a deep breath and force my sweaty fingers to slow down. It pops open with an audible click. I carefully lift it to my face, adding my other hand to lessen the shaking, and peer into the mirror.

My world shatters and so does the mirror, now forgotten at my feet.

ACKNOWLEDGEMENTS

First off, thank you so much to my readers! You guys are amazing to embrace a new author and show up for me the way you have! The amount of support and encouragement so many of you have given me at the beginning of this journey has been everything to me! YOU are the reason the world will know the brave young Alexa and her crazy casa!

And now I get to do what I have been waiting for since I began writing this book! I get to thank the incredible woman that changed everything for me when she asked me to send her that first raw, and messy chapter. Elizabeth Tenhouten; When all of this began it was an idea. But there you were, every single day... Not asking, but demanding another chapter.

Because you were tireless, because you believed in me, because you pushed me, I did so too. Alexa Walker and her extraordinary world came into being because of you. I will never forget my amazement when you said you would die if you didn't get another chapter. Me, who had never completed a novel in my life, completed Finding Innocence in two months, for you. There is no amount of thanks I can give for forcing out that untapped potential in me. But thank you anyway!

To Mom and Dad. I called and you answered. You proofread and saw the things I couldn't. And though you were a major part of completing Alexa's world, you have been every part of completing mine! And that is what I want to truly acknowledge.

The two incredible humans who adopted and changed the lives of four kids. You guys are heroes and angels. And if there are words that exist for what you mean to me? This humble writer cannot find them.

Mom, you once told me you had originally set out to adopt a baby girl but when you met me, and you just knew. -For what you saw in me when I saw nothing. For patiently unpacking my little suitcase every time I re-packed it in that first tumultuous year. For standing up to teachers that didn't understand me. For hand-made costumes, endless nights of homework, and home-cooked meals after a full-time job. Thank you.

Dad, how am I supposed to keep this short? For your endless support. For all the times you went to bat for me. For moving me to NY even when you were scared for me. For helping me through occasions I just couldn't cut it alone. For doing the same with my three other siblings! Your kindness and giving and belief in me has me striving to be worthy of all you have given and your sacrifices in doing so. You are my hero. And I thank you.

To my partner Alex, for whom I have named my main character after. Thank you for the hours and hours you put into helping me record my audio book! Thank you for providing your original music for the trailer of Finding Innocence. And most of all, thank you for being the main character in my life! -For all of your support and encouragement, THANK YOU!

Tereza Harazimova, I wanted a unicorn of P.R., management, and social media and you gave me so much more! You made this book launch happen and for your enthusiasm, your faith, your work ethic, and creative thinking, I could not have gotten here without you! Thank you for going above and beyond so my book could too!

My proofreader Mary Dunbar. Your feedback was invaluable and Alexa's story is so much better for having your critiques! I know I gave you a mountain of work and you crushed it with feedback, ideas, and edits! Thank you so very much!

It takes a village and without you all, my cute crazy whims would be full-blown bat-shit. To my sister Victoria, so much of you is in my favorite character's love! My soul sister Shevaun Kastl, to the laughter, the tears, and the many many years to come! Our friendship is the stuff that books are made of. Thank you for inspiring the kind of friendship I want to write about. My brother Geoff and Chris, you guys make me feel safe in this world. Stephen Bodi, my chosen family, my absolute rock in the storm, my ride or die, I love you! Scott Lotzenhiser, from the first grade you have been a thorn in my side. And one of the best friends a girl could ever ask for! Thank you for always being there for me! Bryan Wright. You were the most idyllic parts of my childhood and my life is better for knowing you're still in it! Aunt June, thank you for your unconditional love and your persistence in being a support system in my life!! I treasure you more than you know!! Lauren Fitzimmons! For your confidence, your humor, your wit, your constancy, and your talent... To me, you embody the beauty and wisdom that is 'woman.' Why do you think Alex has red hair? Thank you my dear friend for being with me through thick and thin! A.J. Eaton, you are a pro and a rockstar and amid your own serious project, you took the time to assist a new author with her book trailer! And speaking of serious professionals, Julie Eason... A total stranger asked you for tips and tricks in the biz and not a day later you are talking my ears off with the most crucial knit and grit of launching my first book! You are a queen and a gem of a woman and you better believe your insight made a difference!

I know I should stop but I cannot. Dawn Jean Allen, Lorenzo Diaz, Kaley Victoria Rose, Kianna Good, Angelo & Justin Beans, Minoe Mercedes, Tommy Cappel, Charles Beckwith, Mark Fitzsimmons, Julia Wiltz, Shann Treadwell, Michelle Lloyd, you are here because of the amazing and important individual you are in my life. Thank you!

ABOUT THE AUTHOR

Karen Keith began traveling as soon as she was old enough to leave home. From sprawling cities to isolated pockets of the globe where she relied on her wits and resourcefulness to communicate. Forging friendships in unlikely places and collecting stories became a way of life.

Her first job at a counter selling makeup was the last job she ever accepted working for someone else. She dove into the world of entrepreneurship that was as diverse as her adventures; Makeup art, styling, editing, and art directing for top fashion publications, TV, and Film. She went on to launch her own company with the sole purpose of visually developing new talent. And later she opened her first jewelry store in Miami, exclusively featuring her brand. From there she built her own manufacturing house from the ground up and designing jewelry turned into design fashion collections for herself and others.

Keith didn't own a TV for most of her life. It was journaling and books she couldn't live without. Writing had always been a creative pleasure for her. But one week of intense restlessness, led to a few chapters, and from that point, everything changed. Keith quotes, "I didn't begin my first novel 'Finding Innocence,' with the ambition of a new career. But when I discovered writing a great story is the same high as reading one, there was no going back."

FOLLOW US

INSTAGRAM: @karenkeith.co

FACEBOOK: @AuthorKarenKeith

TIK TOK: @alex___walker

Join our VIP club at www.karenkeith.co

You heard it first!

- Be the first to know about forthcoming book launches, touring, latest works and promotions!

You saw it first!

-   Now you can have advanced access to digital media such as book cover art, book trailers, character inspirations, photos and sneak peak chapters from latest book launches!

You get it first!

-   Giveaways and excerpts from upcoming releases! Exclusive Invite to VIP face book group.

Printed in Great Britain
by Amazon

49895941R00215